From *The Devil and the Dark Island:*

The editor and the archaeologist . . .

Zach thought about Castle Mac an Rìgh's long-ago inhabitants. Then he thought about the Viking invasion, and his imagination began to run rampant. He mumbled, "Big, blond, hairy men, driven away from the castle, wandering around, looking for something to loot and conquer."

He glanced down at Anna, lying beside him. "One of them stumbles on this clearing and spots this tree, and under it lies snoozing a shepherd girl who didn't take refuge in the castle. She sleeps on, unaware of her danger, as the huge Viking sneaks up on her, bent on ravishment."

Anna opened one eye, and peered up at him.

"He tosses down his shield and helmet and creeps closer, unbuckling his armored breastplate. Then he throws himself down upon her."

Zach threw himself on top of Anna, who grunted in surprise. "What are you about?" she gasped.

"Ravishment. Rapine. Or kisses, at least."

"Get off," she said, pushing at him half-heartedly.

"'I vant you,' the Norseman growls in his indecipherable Scandinavian lingo, yanks the maiden into his arms, and takes her mouth in a fierce Viking kiss." Zach pulled her close, and planted a fierce Viking-style kiss on her surprised lips.

Anna wrested her mouth from his, and got into the game. "She struggles . . . "

"But her strength is no match for that of mighty Sven, terror of the seas, conqueror of the innocent and helpless."

"Helpless? No way." She seized his hair, yanked his head up, and brought her mouth against his in a long hot kiss. Then she said, "What do you think of that, barbarian invader boy?"

The White Rose of Scotland (2004)

"The haunting sequel to the love story, *Westering Home, The White Rose of Scotland* continues the ongoing romantic relationship between Jean and Darroch (and) mixes the feel of Scottish day-to-day life in its interplay of hopes, triumphs and setbacks. A wonderful and highly enjoyable yarn, recommended with as much enthusiasm as *Westering Home.*"
–Midwest Book Review.

"Sympathetically drawn characters meet and fall in love in a small Scottish island. Even if you aren't a fan of love stories, you'll love the backdrop. You can almost see the heather and smell the peat. You'll be sad to put the book down."
–Writers Notes Magazine.

" . . . plenty of rich tapestry in terms of character development, beautiful setting, and plot to keep me engrossed and entertained! And the islanders' activities and cultural mores remind me so much of the tiny rural communities where my parents grew up . . . Your characters came alive for me . . . "
–Judy, Colorado clothing designer.

" . . . an interesting, exciting love story, continuing the characters and themes of *Westering Home* . . . captures the beauty of this country and its people . . . characters are interesting and realistic."
–Judith, Eagan publisher.

"A wonderful glimpse into Scottish life, Scottish love, and Scottish lore."
– Doug, St. Louis banker.

The White Rose of Scotland was named a Notable Book 2004 by *Writers' Notes* magazine.

Magic Carpet Ride (2005)

Four stars from RT!
" . . . a beautiful, sexy love story . . . The third installment of McClellan's Scottish Island Novels features characters who exude an openness and warmth that will have readers eagerly awaiting the next novel."
–Romantic Times Book Club.

"Every character in the novel is a person I'd like to know! I feel as though I am there and don't want to leave—such a beauty of an island."
–Evie, Massachusetts bookstore employee.

The Devil and
the Dark Island

a Scottish Island Novel

Audrey McClellan

Beaver's Pond Press, Inc.
Edina, Minnesota

ISBN 10: 1-59298-132-1
ISBN 13: 978-1-59298-132-8

Library of Congress Catalog Number: 2005910719

Cover art by Carla McClellan.
Eilean Dubh map by Jane Gordon.
Book design by Mori Studio.
Illustrations by Don Ladig.

All musical compositions in this book are composed by and copyright to Sherry Wohlers Ladig and used by permission. Lyrics to "Peigi's Dandling Song" by Audrey McClellan. "Eilean Dubh" and "The Emigrant's Lament" lyrics are by McClellan/Ladig.

Scottish country dances: "The De'il's Awa' wi' the Islander" devised by and copyright to Lara Friedman-Shedlov, and used by permission. "Donald and Helen and Rosie's Wedding" devised by Audrey McClellan.

Printed in the United States of America

First Printing: April 2006

08 07 06 05 04   6 5 4 3 2 1

Beaver's Pond Press, Inc.

7104 Ohms Lane, Suite 216
Edina, MN 55439
(952) 829-8818
www.beaverspondpress.com

to order, visit www.BookHouseFulfillment.com or call
1-800-901-3480. Reseller discounts available.

Contents

Things that matter most must never be at the mercy of things that matter least.

Goethe

VERY free-form! The HAUNTED TUNE

Dotted bars indicate free tempo; not strict.

Prologue

*Eilean Dubh, the Dark Island, has a rich legacy of legend and folklore.
Popular belief has it that the hills called Beanntan MhicChriathar are the lair
of what the Islanders call The People, for they dare not speak the name of
"faery" aloud. Each flower, animal and fish has its own guardian sprite that
is never to be offended, lest bad luck result. So reluctant are the inhabitants
of the Island to speak about matters of the Unseen World that it is impossible to deduce whether or not they believe in those incorporeal beings that
the superstitious of Modern Society call "ghosts." But the Island is of such
antiquity that it is most likely that a belief in ghosts does, indeed, exist, and
that events have occurred which support such a belief.*

Robertson's Relics and Anomalies of Scotland, 1923

Bonnie Prince Jamie was taking a walk. This in itself was not strange,
for like all the inhabitants of tiny Scottish island Eilean Dubh, Jamie
MacDonald enjoyed walking.

Usually work on his croft and with his prized flock of Jacob's Sheep kept
him too busy to indulge, but this stroll was special. It was intended to get
him away from his cottage, *Taigh Rois*, and especially from his wife Màiri,
with her endless list of chores that must be done at once, if not sooner. There
were times when a new fiddle tune got itself into his head and he had to slip
away and walk along the coastline or on a path into the Island's interior, so
that the tune could present itself.

Today was one of those times.

It was a remarkably beautiful day in a spring of remarkably beautiful
days. The hard winter of heavy snow and biting cold had mellowed into a
sunny spring of early wildflowers and warm breezes from the sea. Eilean
Dubh and the *Eilean Dubhannaich* basked in the glorious weather. A
halcyon time, and no one expected it to last.

The day's bright sunshine made Jamie's golden hair glow like a halo around his handsome face. The Islanders called him Bonnie Prince Jamie, and few women were immune to his charms. The occasional car passing him on the road honked the horn in a friendly way, but if it was driven by a young woman, the honk was accompanied by an unvoiced wolf whistle. Any other demonstration of approval would mark the driver as a gusher, a designation dreaded by the reserved Scots of Eilean Dubh. Besides, Jamie was a notoriously faithful husband and mooning over him would be a complete waste of time, so practical Island maidens were content to admire him from afar.

The Islanders considered Jamie the world's best traditional fiddler. That was not gushing; their opinion was shared by a large percentage of the British folk world, who'd been wowed several years ago by his performances with *Tradisean*, the Scottish music group made up of Jamie, Màiri and fellow Islanders Jean and Darroch Mac an Rìgh.

Jamie didn't have his fiddle with him on today's venture, though he was working on a tune. It would be ridiculous to go out for a walk carrying a fiddle case, and even more ridiculous if he took out the fiddle and played as he walked. The Islanders already thought him rather odd, for he was a Skyeman, and it was a popular belief on Eilean Dubh that the inhabitants of other Hebridean islands were all a bit daft. Not as daft as Lowlanders, and not nearly as daft as the English, but still, a wee bittie strange in the head. Especially the people of Skye, who'd allowed a bridge to be built connecting their island to the mainland, so that visitors could come and go even on the Sabbath, when decent, God-fearing people kept themselves strictly at home, as they did on Eilean Dubh.

Minus fiddle, Jamie contented himself with humming as he walked along and worked out his new tune. Today he'd decided to go north along the coastline, because he felt that the tune would be improved by exposure to the sea on his right. He had to walk on the right side anyway, to keep as far away as possible from the ancient burial place, *Cladh a' Chnuic*, Cemetery Hill.

Jamie never went near *Cladh a' Chnuic*. He had the Sight, as some Highland Scots do, meaning that he sometimes got a glimpse of future happenings. What was worse, in Jamie's viewpoint, anyway, was that he had what he had dubbed the Hearing.

He heard Things sometimes, and the worst place on the Island for hearing Things was Cemetery Hill. Ancient voices spoke and moaned and babies wept in long despairing wails, and sometimes, most unnerving of all, someone laughed. It all made for an upsetting confabulation of sounds, and he avoided the place, even worming his way out of going up there for burials.

Today *Cladh a' Chnuic* had been quiet, or he had been far enough away from it, and he had worked on his tune undisturbed by the dead or the living.

As he neared the scenic outlook that was halfway between Eilean Dubh's two towns, Ros Mór and Airgead, his new tune abruptly coalesced in his mind. So that's how it goes, he thought, dumpety-dumpety-dum-dum-dum. Pleased, he stopped at the outlook, stared out over the sea, and whistled the tune a couple of times, then hummed it, imagining nonsense words that would fix it in his mind.

He turned, happy and ready to go home, and crossed the road. He would walk on the opposite side on his return journey, since Cemetery Hill had been quiet today, and that way he could enjoy the lush fields of green grass and pearly gray rocks, and the sparkling burns trickling down the low mountains called *Beanntan MhicChriathar*.

He stopped to admire a particularly colorful patch of wildflowers set well back from the verge, and abruptly felt that prickling presentiment in the back of his neck that meant something weird was about to happen. Why me? he thought crossly. Why is it always me? And what's it to be now, boggles? Leprechauns, freshly escaped from Ireland? Or perhaps fairies? He hadn't run into any of them recently, so they were due for an appearance. If it was the People, he hoped they were friendly; he'd had a couple of encounters with mischievous sprites that he'd not enjoyed at all. He stared at the flowers, hoping for the best.

Slowly, softly, a mist was rising around the wildflower patch.

A Dhia, thought Jamie, and froze in his tracks.

The mist thickened, and to his horror it began to separate into wisps that resembled human forms. The wisps formed a circle that revolved above the flowers. Then all bowed, as in the center of the circle another shape appeared, taller than the rest, and more solid. Its ghostly arms lifted and ghostly hands raised a long narrow shape to a ghostly mouth.

And then the music started.

A wistful tune, a haunting tune, a strange tune played on a primitive flute.

The wisps began to move in time with the music. They lifted transparent arms trailing mist toward the bright blue sky, and undulated, gently at first, then more vigorously. The music picked up speed, became shrill and urgent, and the dancers grew wilder in their movements. The ghostly ballet became a desperate dance begging the intervention of some undreamed-of entity, and the forms threw themselves frantically in and out of the circle with arms stretched upward in entreaty.

Jamie, cold with fear, became aware of something odd happening to his feet. He glanced down. His left foot was suspended in mid-air, on its way to taking a step forward. He was being pulled into the circle of dancers.

Fear was replaced by anger. In his forty-plus years he'd endured the Sight, put up with the Hearing, heard the pitter-patter of fairy feet, and on one memorable dark and grim night had felt the icy breath of the Great Gray Man on the back of his neck as he crossed the pasture on his way home. Damned if he was going to be dragged into dancing with a bunch of weird wispy things. "Enough is enough," he snapped angrily, not caring who or what heard him. "Will you let me be, for the love of God!"

He clenched his teeth, doubled his hands into fists and ground his right foot firmly into the earth, bracing himself against the ghostly suction. With an effort akin to yanking his leg out of quicksand, he tugged his left foot back under him, planted himself firmly on both feet and folded his arms across his chest, glaring his defiance.

As if in answer, the strange new tune grew louder and more compelling, setting itself in his mind and refusing to be dislodged. It was a good tune, Jamie realized dementedly, but he was more than willing to give it up if only he could get away. Sweating and cursing under his breath, he fought back, holding himself rigid against the music's lure, terrified that at any minute he would be able to hear—and understand—what the ghostly voices were begging for, and knowing that his sanity would not survive that.

Then, as if the music knew that it had tormented its listener to the point of no return, it changed, slowing to the measured pace of a requiem. The dancers stopped, and bowed so low that their heads swept the ground. The mist drew together into a single patch, and began slowly to disappear, like water running down a hole. The tune continued for one more repetition, then stopped.

Jamie's legs folded, and he found himself sitting on the ground, drenched with sweat, wondering what had just happened to him. He'd never seen ghosts before, though he knew in his heart they existed. The existence of ghosts was no harder to believe in than other things he'd experienced with the Unknown World.

Today, he had no doubt in his mind that he had seen ghosts.

He scrambled unsteadily to his feet, staring at the wildflower patch.

What is this place? he thought.

PART I

Welcome to Eilean Dubh

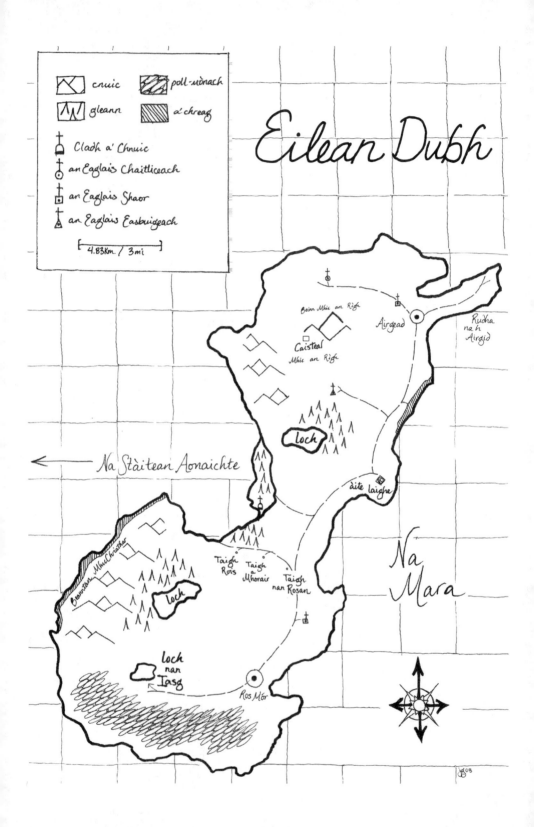

One

Speak kindly to strangers, but do not give trust until it is earned.

Eilean Dubh proverb

*J*ean Mac an Rìgh was running at full speed across the crowded pier in hot pursuit of her three-year-old daughter Rosie, who'd twisted her hand out of her mother's and taken off, headed for the gangplank of the enormous Caledonian-MacBrayne ferry that had just docked in Airgead harbor.

"Bàta, bàta!" Boat! Boat! Rosie shouted as she darted in and out of the legs of disembarking passengers. She'd once gone to Oban with parents Jean and Darroch on the Cal-Mac ferry *Princess of the Islands*, and she had adored ships ever since. Now she was firmly determined to get on board this one; perhaps it would take her to that town she remembered so well for its delightful ice cream shop near the pier.

Her mother, panting in pursuit, realized in horror that Rosie was veering dangerously close to the pier's edge. Below it was the cerulean blue of the ocean, fathoms deep. The Airgead harbor was the deepest on the Island, and falling over the edge would mean a plunge straight down into water still icy cold despite the warming effects of spring. Rosie could not swim, nor could her mother.

The *Eilean Dubhannaich* and the ferry passengers suddenly became aware of the little girl's flight and the mother's pursuit, and turned as one towards Rosie, just as an agile figure swung down from the gangplank and threw himself in front of the child, arms wide.

She screeched to a stop. "Who you?" she demanded.

Her rescuer, a tall lanky young man with a mop of dark curly hair, smiled. "I'm Zach. What's your name?"

Rosie, suddenly overcome with shyness, put her thumb in her mouth and regarded him owlishly. She'd never been told not to talk to strangers, because there were no strangers on Eilean Dubh, but she was uneasily aware that she didn't know this man.

Jean had finally resorted to her elbows to get the gaping inhabitants of the pier out of her way and arrived to throw herself down by her wayward daughter. "Oh, thank you," she gasped to Zach. "I was afraid she was going over the edge."

"She's a speedy little kid. Glad I was in the right place at the right time."

Her heart still pounding, Jean gathered Rosie in her arms, and admonished, "What a naughty thing to do, running away from Mama. You know better than that."

Rosie pulled her thumb from her mouth with an audible pop, and said, "Not runned away. Go on *bàta.*"

"You almost ended up in the drink instead of on the *bàta,*" said Jean.

Darroch Mac an Rìgh had belatedly become aware of his wife's absence from his side and of his daughter's escapade, tipped off by the behavior of the crowd, who were now chattering in excited Gaelic about Rosie's near escape from a watery grave. The Laird's daughter was the Island's pride and joy, and danger to her terrified everyone.

Darroch spotted Jean with Rosie clasped in her arms, the tall curly-haired stranger standing over them. The crowd parted in obedient waves as he strode toward them. "What's amiss, Jean?" he said.

Jean drew a deep breath. "Your daughter . . . "

It must be bad, Darroch thought; it always was when Rosie became "your daughter" instead of "our daughter."

" . . . Almost ran off the pier into the sea."

"*A Dhia,*" Darroch said, shocked.

Rosie, catching sight of her father, and aware that she was still in her mother's bad graces, cried, "*A Dhadaidh!*" and held out her arms to him.

"And this wonderful man caught her just before she ran off the edge." Jean got to her feet.

"What? We're very indebted to you, Mr. . . . ?"

"Call me Zach," said the young man.

"Zach. Thank you," said Darroch, and extended his hand. It was seized and firmly shaken. A good strong grip, thought Darroch, impressed. "I'm Darroch Mac an Rìgh, and this is my wife Jean."

"Nice to meet you," said Zach, looking over Darroch's shoulder. "Sorry, got a bus to catch," and he was off at a run toward Murdoch the Taxi's mini-bus, the doors of which were about to close.

Darroch would have offered the young stranger a ride anywhere, but he had disappeared too fast. Left with his errant daughter in his arms, he whispered firmly in her ear about the wickedness of running away and frightening her mama. The little girl nodded, chastened.

Then he turned to his wife, and found her in conversation with another stranger, this one nattily dressed and smiling with assurance. An odd little prickle of misgiving ran down Darroch's spine. He disregarded it; he did not believe in the Sight.

The stranger had said to Jean, "You sound like an American, ma'am."

"I am."

"Are you a tourist like me?" he asked, giving her an ingratiating smile.

"Oh, no, I live here."

"Is that right? Maybe you can tell me how to get to my hotel."

"Which hotel is it?"

"It's called the Rose, and it's in Ros Mór, which I think is miles away from here. Can I get a cab?"

Darroch, watching Murdoch the Taxi stow Zach's rucksack in the luggage compartment of his mini-bus, said, "You take the bus, which is about to leave."

"Thanks," said the stranger, and, grabbing his bag, he ran for the bus, shouting over his shoulder, "See you later."

Darroch thought no more about him, and turned to look up the gangplank for the expected visitors, Jean's family from her previous marriage: Rod, her son, her daughter-in-law Lucy, and their son, Andrew Russell. Rod was coming to Eilean Dubh to manage the first branch of Abbott & Son, the very successful software development company founded in Milwaukee by Jean's ex-husband, Russ.

Lucy was the first to run down the gangplank and she threw her arms around her mother-in-law. "Hi, Jean! Hi, Darroch! Oh my goodness, look at you, Rosie. You've gotten so big."

"Big Rosie," said the little girl proudly.

"And here's big Andrew Russell," said Rod, arriving with his son in his arms.

The children scrutinized each other suspiciously. Then Andrew Russell offered a tentative smile, and Rosie nodded graciously. "Look at that," exclaimed Lucy. "I knew they'd get along. And they are exactly the same age, born on the same day. They'll have so much fun playing together."

"Wait till you see the cute house we've found for you," bubbled Jean. "It's a remodeled crofter's cottage down the main road from us, and it's got a huge yard. We had Alasdair MacQuirter fence it in, so it will be a great place for the kids to play."

"I don't know about the rest of you," Rod said, "but I'm hungry, and Andrew Russell needs a nap. It's been a long trip from the States and none of us have had much sleep or food in the last couple of days."

"Come on," said Jean. "We've got a good meal waiting for you, and then you can get settled in your cottage." The party piled into Darroch's stately old Bentley and drove home.

Jean was thrilled to have her first and second families together on the Island. She'd arrived on Eilean Dubh four years ago, a fugitive from her Milwaukee home where husband Russ had shattered their twenty-year marriage by confessing that he'd been unfaithful. Seeking time and space to sort out what to do with the rest of her life, she'd come to the Dark Island on the pretext of doing genealogical research about an ancestor. In rapid succession she'd fallen in love with the Island, with its music, and finally, with its laird, Darroch Mac an Rìgh.

Darroch was now her husband, and they were the parents of three-year-old handful Rosamond Mòrag, the Island's delight and the heiress to what Darroch, at least, considered the non-existent lairdship. His great-grandfather Alasdair had given up the title a hundred years ago, but the *Eilean Dubhannaich* persisted in their desire to consider the eldest Mac an Rìgh in each generation as their laird.

Resigned to what he called "that bloody laird business," Darroch had refused the title and accepted the responsibility, and balanced his career as a television actor with his duties as the Island's hereditary ruler. He considered himself very fortunate to be, at forty-four years of age, not only a successful actor, but a happily married family man.

He was pleased with himself for having steered Jean's ex Russ Abbott into setting up a branch of his software development firm on Eilean Dubh. It meant jobs for the Islanders, and his beloved wife now had all her children and her grandchild on the Island with her, an accomplishment that had earned him Jean's enduring gratitude.

Russ, left back in Milwaukee, was less happy to see all his first family sucked into life on Eilean Dubh, but he had a new wife, Ruth, four stepdaughters, and the running of the main office of his firm to keep him busy. And since Ruth had fallen in love with the Island on her honeymoon visit there, and Russ was enamoured of the comforts of the Rose Hotel in Ros Mór and the gourmet cooking of its co-owner, Sheilah Morrison, there was every possibility of visits by the senior Abbotts.

And that too would please Jean, for she had long ago made up her differences with ex-husband Russ, and regarded him fondly for the (mostly) happy memories of their twenty years together, and for the gift of their son Rod and their daughter Sally, who also lived on Eilean Dubh, as she was married to Jamie and Màiri MacDonald's son Ian.

Darroch thought himself an incredibly lucky man. He counted his blessings every night, with a word of thanks to the One Who Listens for the gifts of a fine lusty wife to keep his bed warm and his head on straight, a delightful young daughter, two stepchildren and their spouses, and, to his considerable bemusement, a step-grandchild.

His television acting career was doing well, despite the fact that he was nearing his mid-forties, the time when many actors sank out of sight, eclipsed by younger faces. But he'd never been a conventional leading man, where beauty and muscles compensated for meager talent. He was not handsome; he was memorable, with jet-black hair, vivid blue eyes, a long elegant nose, and a face that drew the audience's eye and kept it.

He'd become a fixture on British television screens when he was thirty and had starred in "The Magician," a beloved children's program that adults loved too. It was shown first in Britain, then in America and Australia, then all around the world. His range and versatility had taken him from there into a variety of roles, and his agent Liz had just secured him a juicy part on a popular soap. The part would be written so that he could pop in and out of the show, enabling him to spend long periods of time at home.

It was Jean's favorite soap, set in the East End of London, its Cockney-accented characters falling in and out of dreadful predicaments, and he was going to be a mysterious stranger, appearing when he was least expected, catching viewers off guard.

Darroch quite liked the idea of being a mysterious stranger. It was totally foreign to his personality, and he'd already been thinking about what he could do with the part. Like the good actor that he was, he relished the idea of a real challenge.

Eilean Dubh, which had presented him with so many challenges, appeared to be settling down. He'd spent years involved in his community's governance, worried so much about its economic prospects, fretted over its children's futures, diverted so much of his income into the Trust that he'd created to finance projects for Eilean Dubh's welfare, such as Màiri MacDonald's Gaelic Playschool.

As was true with any community, there was a limited number of people willing to govern Eilean Dubh, and capable of doing it. Everyone else was too busy, too lazy, too young, too old, too eccentric, or too downright cranky to take their turn on the Governing Council. Much of the work in the past had fallen on Darroch's broad shoulders.

Now, it appeared, others were taking up the torch and stepping forward to lead the Island in the twenty-first century. He could enjoy his family and his career, and he could relax, at last.

Two

Give me for marriage a sweet-breathed woman of whom I should never tire,
Give me a perfect child, give me a way aside from the noise of the world a
rural domestic life . . .

Walt Whitman

*O*r maybe not.

When Darroch was invited by Council Chair Barabal Mac-a-Phi to meet with her in her office at the Council's modest headquarters in Airgead, he expected no more than a brief consultation regarding some historical precedent, or a matter for the Trust.

Instead, she announced without preamble, "We need you on the Council."

Darroch groaned, dismayed. "It's never my turn again so soon. My last term ended two years ago, and I've served three altogether. Why on earth do you need me?"

"Because Mairead Mac an Aba's husband's had a stroke, and she's resigned from Council to help with his rehabilitation. Gilleasbuig Mac an t-Sagairt has decided to run for her seat, and he's that infernal nuisance and bane of civilized government, the one-issue candidate."

"What's his one issue?" asked Darroch, intrigued in spite of his dismay.

Barabal snorted. "Roads. He's gone daft over roads. He wants the one lane road leading to that shack of his in *Beanntan MhicChriathar* widened to two lanes."

"What? Utter nonsense. There's not above three cars a day on that road."

"Aye, and he's also got grandiose notions about the main road from Airgead to Ros Mór. He wants that widened, and paved with concrete.

Honest Scottish macadam is not good enough for him any more; he says modern communities have concrete roads."

"Modern communities have shopping malls, giant airports and mass transit systems. I suppose he wants those as well. We can't afford it, and that's an end to it."

Barabal shook her head. "If no one else runs he'll be elected, and his vote will be the tiebreaker on the Council. He'll stall all other business until he gets what he wants. And after he gets his way he'll stall everything just to be a royal pain in the arse. You must run, Darroch; I've no one else. I wouldn't ask you otherwise, and I know Jean will be furious with me for asking for more of your time, after you've given so much."

"Jean never gets angry about anything she perceives as being for the good of the Island, but she'll be distressed, for I'm away so much for work as it is." Darroch knew he was well and truly caught, but made a valiant last effort to avoid his fate. "Surely there's someone else you can ask. What about Sìleas Mac-a-Phi, your cousin? She's got a good head and a good heart, and the seniors are underrepresented on Council."

"I asked her, but she's eighty-three, and having a bad patch with her arthritis flaring up. Ros MacPherson is trying a new course of drugs with her, and she's wary of the side effects. It seems they make her vague and sleepy. She's very conscientious, you know; she won't take on anything that she can't give her undivided attention, and she's afraid she'd nod off at meetings."

"What about Ewan MacCorkle?" said Darroch, grasping at straws. "I know he tends to natter on a bit, and he's boring as hell, but he's sound, and very intelligent."

"Involved with some soil experiment for the Ministry of Agriculture, and says the paperwork will take three hours a night for the next two years, so he sent his regrets. I think he was pleased to be asked, though. We might keep him in mind for the future."

Darroch had a sudden inspiration. "Ian the Post's Catrìona! Brighter than the rest of us put together, and she's never served on Council."

Barabal nodded. "Aye, I thought of her too, and asked her. But she's in a delicate way."

"What?"

"She's pregnant."

"Is she just! That's brilliant."

"But it's a tricky proposition. She's had two slips in the past, both of them life-threatening, so Ros has strictly limited her activities, and Ian the Post will make sure she follows his rules to the letter. Long nap every afternoon, no lifting over ten pounds, and in bed by nine every night. Catrìona says she's going bonkers with the inactivity, but she'll do whatever Ros suggests, for they're mad to have a child."

"I'm delighted for them, and I'll be sure to give Ian my congratulations when next I see him."

"Never do that. The whole thing's a dead secret. They've been through it twice before, and endured congratulations turned into condolences, and they can't bear to have that happen again. They're keeping it quiet until she's at least three months gone, which Ros says will be over the hump as far as losing it goes."

"Right. May I tell Jean, though? It's not often I hear news like this before she does. The Playschool is gossip central."

"Jean already knows."

"What? And hasn't told me?"

Barabal regarded him with pity. "Every woman knows a man can't be trusted with a secret; they'll end up blurting it out somehow. Even you, Darroch. The Playschool staff had to know, for she can't lift any of the children, and needs to take frequent rest breaks. They've been mother-henning her to death. Catrìona says they're worse than Ian." Adroitly switching the subject, she added, "So you must run for Council. We need you."

He knew he was trapped, but offered a little more feeble resistance. "I've a role coming up with the Beeb. I'll be in London off and on for weeks."

"The secretary will e-mail you each meeting's minutes, and you can send back your comments. You can vote by e-mail, as long as Council agrees you can, and there'll be no problem there. Everyone will be delighted that you're on board."

Darroch sighed deeply, and took himself off home to tell Jean that duty to Eilean Dubh called, yet again.

Predictably, Jean supported his decision to serve on Council, though she groaned inside. Darroch's career took him to London far too often and for extended periods, and she cherished any time they could spend together and hated to give any up. "It's only a couple of evenings a month," she said, to comfort them both.

"Unless I have to serve on a committee, which will be more evenings wasted," said Darroch gloomily.

"Perhaps the committee could meet here."

"What? With Rosie in her super-social phase? She'd take over. Do I want to serve on the only committee in the world chaired by a three-year-old?"

Jean had to agree. Their cottage, apart from the two bedrooms up the iron spiral staircase, was one large room, kitchen, dining area and lounge combined. There wasn't any area where she could take Rosie so that a committee would work in peace. Although the idea of Darroch trying to participate in a meeting with a voluble, squirming Rose on his lap was amusing, it was definitely a non-starter as far as reality went.

Oh, well, she'd keep herself busy on the nights when he was gone. Eilean Dubh meetings tended to run on towards midnight, as the Islanders were a talkative, argumentative lot. If she could get Rosie to bed by nine-thirty, she'd have an hour or two to work on her writing project.

She and First Daughter Sally Abbott MacDonald had had a book published two years ago, called *Eilean Dubh: Celebration of a Small Island*. Sally had written the narrative and various *Eilean Dubhannaich* had contributed: Joe Munro, the veterinarian, his photographs, Jamie MacDonald, two original pieces of music, Anna Wallace, the newspaper editor, a piece about Island wildflowers, chef Sheilah Morrison, several of her recipes. Jean's contribution was two Eilean Dubh folk tales, told to her by Darroch.

The resulting book had been a beautiful production and a mild success, selling well in London and Edinburgh bookstores, where the idea of a gentle, beautiful Island had appealed to harassed city dwellers longing for the peace and quiet of the countryside.

Now she'd set herself to a new project: collecting and putting on paper Eilean Dubh's rich treasure of stories that had never been written down in English or in Gaelic, the Island's native language. Darroch had introduced her to them, and it seemed to Jean it would be a great loss if they died out with the older inhabitants. So she'd gotten him to tell the stories in his *miorbhuileach* actor's voice with his distinctive actor's style, and she'd taped them. She was rewriting them to add to the Library's collection, and the work was going so well that she was thinking of sending the finished manuscript to Darroch's agent Liz, to submit to publishers.

There were stories of shape shifting and baby swapping, of unrequited love and lust fulfilled and unfulfilled, of greed, cruelty, and daring. Very old stories, told by *seanachaidhean*, storytellers, around the fires at night, intended to teach lessons about right and wrong behavior, and the consequences of each.

She visited the Seniors' Residence to collect the tales that only the oldest *Eilean Dubhannaich* remembered. Most of them knew English, and spoke it in a distinctive, appealing way, and when their English failed them, Darroch translated. Jean took her notes and recordings home to *Taigh a Mhorair*, and while Rosie napped, she wrote and edited. She relished both the absorbing, difficult work and the idea that she would be making a real contribution to her Island.

Besides that, working with fairy stories took her back to when she was in third grade in Milwaukee and paid weekly visits to Hosmer Library, four blocks away, and came home with her arms full of books of fairy tales.

Her mother had despaired that she would ever read anything else. But she'd finally grown out of that phase, and moved on to dog stories and horse stories and *The Little House in the Big Woods* and Betsy-Tacy.

And now, at the age of forty-four, she was back to fairy stories. In a gentle, satisfying way, it made her think of her mother.

Three

Oh, if we draw a circle premature,
Heedless of far gain,
Greedy for quick returns of profit, sure
Bad is our bargain!

Robert Browning

*T*he special by-election was held in two weeks, for there was no point in waiting and delaying Council business, and Darroch's victory over Gilleasbuig Mac an t-Sagairt was a foregone conclusion. Most *Eilean Dubhannaich* thought that the Laird should be a permanent member of the Council, and wondered why they had to vote for him at all. Democracy was a fine thing and they were all for it, but they still wanted their Laird to play a leadership role.

The idea mystified Darroch, who despised the idea of rule by aristocrats, and it aggravated him as well. He did not want to be admired or worshipped because of his ancestors' activities; he wanted to be judged on his own merits and accomplishments. He was a modest man, and it did not occur to him that that was how he was being judged, and that he had never been found wanting.

The next meeting of the Council took place promptly the week after the election. In addition to their regular business, they had a special issue to discuss and a special guest to present the issue for their consideration. Darroch was astonished when a handsome, dark-haired man in suit and tie entered the Council Chamber. He remembered the man from the day on the pier and also remembered his presentiment, and wondered briefly if he was developing the Sight, like Jamie MacDonald possessed. Utter nonsense, of course, he told himself, and dismissed the idea from his mind as he turned to listen to Barabal introduce the speaker to the Council.

"Mr. Nicholas Borth," announced Barabal. "From America, isn't that right?"

"Not by birth, but I grew up there," he said.

"And you've a proposition to present to us, if I understand your letter correctly."

"I do, indeed. If I might just bring in my materials for show and tell . . . ?"

Barabal nodded, and Nick Borth went out the door, and returned carrying a large easel and a handful of flip charts. On his next trip out he came back carrying a projector and viewgraphs. One of the younger Council members, anxious to be helpful, rushed to assist him, and was sent out to get a folding projection screen.

Darroch groaned. He'd been off the Council for two years and had forgotten how meetings could drone on, and this one had been long enough without a presentation like the one Nick Borth was preparing. He'd been hoping to make it home in time for Rosie's bath, and an early night in bed with his darling Jean. He bade the first idea a reluctant farewell, and crossed his fingers in the hope of achieving the second.

He leaned back in his chair, and assumed an expression of polite interest as Borth strode in front of the Council members and opened his mouth.

He began, "I've been a resident on the Island for three weeks now, and I want to thank everyone for the super hospitality I've been shown. Folks couldn't have been nicer to me, and I sure do appreciate it." He paused dramatically. "I'd like to give something back to all you good people, and I've had an idea that just might do that."

Hmmmph, thought Darroch, where did you get all the fancy paraphernalia if you've just had the idea? The flip chart that Borth was now dramatically unveiling was obviously professionally prepared and not something created on Eilean Dubh; there were no facilities on the Island for producing slick, glossy flip charts.

The Council leaned forward as one to study the picture that was being unveiled. It depicted a modern building, radiant with large windows and beautifully landscaped, shown against a stunningly unrealistic blue sky with a hint of airy white clouds.

Nick Borth said, "I'm a developer of fine rental properties, and I'd like to build one just like this on a section of your beautiful coastline that is going to waste."

Going to waste? Maybe, if you didn't appreciate lush green pastures filled with wildflowers and sheep and sparkling burns. Darroch was immediately suspicious. Beside him, Barabal stirred uneasily; she was suspicious, too.

"You folks have got a beautiful Island, and I'd like to see you make use of it to bring in jobs and income for everyone. This lovely building will do just that."

"What is it?" said a Council member. "What's it for?"

"It's a condominium," said Borth.

"Well, it's very attractive, but it must cost a packet of money to build. I won't deny that we need housing, but I doubt anyone here could afford a place like that," said Murray the Meat dubiously.

"It's not for your residents. It's a timeshare, for people to buy into, to give them an opportunity to experience life here on Ellen Duv."

Got to teach him how to pronounce the Island's name first off, thought Darroch. Three weeks here, and he hasn't learned that it's pronounced "ay-lin du."

"Picture this building full of well-to-do visitors, each spending a week or two here the year round, contributing to the local economy by shopping and dining out," enthused Borth.

"Where would they come from? Why would anyone want to spend their money and their time here?" asked Barabal.

Nick Borth smiled winningly. "Why, ma'am, you're selling your Island short. Not everyone wants to go to Florida or the Costa del Sol. What used to be the hot spots for vacations have become overcrowded, polluted, full of tourists on cheap holiday packages. Lots of people would prefer to spend their time in a beautiful, peaceful place like this."

The Council members looked at each other.

The guy was good, Darroch had to give him that. As an actor, he appreciated someone who could hold an audience in the palm of his hand, and Borth was accomplishing just that.

Barabal cleared her throat. "What do you want from the Council, Mr. Borth?"

"I want to purchase a parcel of land that I understand is held by the Island government, and I want planning permission to build on it. Let me show you what I have in mind." He began to turn over flip charts one at a time, describing in detail what he planned to build, and which piece of land he wanted.

Everyone recognized the place. It was midway between Airgead and Ros Mór, just south of the scenic outlook, and it possessed what was possibly the most stunning view on the Island. High upon a cliff and framed by the mountains behind it, it looked down at the cerulean waters that ringed Eilean Dubh and the waves that crashed picturesquely against the rocks.

It was an exquisite setting, lovely in every season, whether the landscape was covered with flowers or snow. Everyone recognized that it was entirely possible that timeshare apartments in a handsome building would sell quickly to the affluent few who were bored with other parts of the world.

Darroch said, "Mr. Borth, granted that you can produce an excellent building in this location, but we have no services to support the sort of customers who might buy into this property. What would visitors do for entertainment? We have no fine restaurants, no leisure facilities, no golf, yachting or skiing."

"You don't have them now. The rental accommodations will create a demand for these amenities, and by filling that demand, your people will have work now and work in the future. You will be making an investment which I guarantee will pay dividends for the Island's economy."

He smiled at the puzzled faces around him. "Just think of your Island as a mecca for those with money to spend. Imagine new shops filled with imaginative creations by your local artists, restaurants that are the equal of any in London, skiing and hunting facilities that will lure sportsmen from around the world. Work for your fishermen, your crofters, your housewives. Sales opportunities for your business people."

There was dead silence while everyone imagined a shower of jobs and money falling upon their Island, where both had always been in short supply. Visions of pound notes danced before their dazzled eyes.

Nick Borth was clever enough to know when to back away from a customer. He turned to pack up his equipment. "Thank you for your attention tonight. I'll give you time to think about my proposition, and I hope you'll consider it carefully. If you approve, we can work out the financial details later. I assure you I'll make you a very attractive offer for the property."

He gave them a broad smile, and walked out with his easel and flip charts, the young Council member following laden with the rest of Borth's equipment.

The Council members immediately broke into excited chatter. "Did you ever hear the like!" "Imagine boatloads of rich tourists. Our shopkeepers would be ecstatic!" "We'd coin money," said one man sagely, but another countered, "It'd cost us a lot. We'd have to smarten up the place to impress rich tourists, if we want them to visit here more than once. For starters, they wouldn't want to drive around on our bumpy old roads, getting rocks through their windshields and dings in their fancy motorcars." Gilleasbuig Mac an t-Sagairt would be delighted to hear that, Darroch thought. Perhaps he'd get his road improvements after all, and without the bother of being on the Council. He himself was frankly baffled by Borth's proposal. On the surface, it seemed like a good idea. Anything that put money in Eilean Dubh pockets was *miorbhuileach*, because the Islanders were always short of cash. Fishing and crofting weren't the most lucrative or dependable types of employment.

But how will it affect our environment, he thought, and suddenly realized he'd spoken his doubt aloud. The others looked at him dubiously.

"We've been building houses on Eilean Dubh for a thousand years, and the environment hasn't been harmed at all," said Murray the Meat.

"What's he going to do for water?" said Isabel Ross, the librarian from Airgead.

"MacQuirter's Burn runs right through that piece of land. He can tap into that for his water supply."

"Won't that harm the environment?" asked Darroch.

"Damned if I know," said Murray the Meat. "Have to get one of those smart university scientists from Edinburgh to tell us."

There was a concerted murmur of distaste at the idea of getting a Lowlander in to tell the *Eilean Dubhannaich* anything.

The young Council member came back in, and began to hand out thick packets. "Mr. Borth has had these proposals prepared. There's a copy for everyone. He says they'll answer all our questions."

"I suggest we go home and read the proposals; we're done with our business tonight," said Barabal. "I'll entertain a motion to adjourn."

"So moved," said someone, and "Seconded," said someone else, and the meeting was ended. Darroch tucked the fat packet of papers under his arm, said goodnight, and went home at last to Jean.

He couldn't find anything wrong with the proposal, on the surface at least. Neither could anyone else, although Anna Wallace, the editor of *The Island Star*, had a number of choice words to say about selling off prime

Island property to an outsider who wasn't even planning on living on Eilean Dubh himself.

Everyone respected Anna's opinion, though they thought she was a bit of a hothead, prone to exaggerated worries and quite daft when it came to protecting those patches of weeds that she insisted were wildflowers. The Council decided to approve Borth's request with one change: they would lease him the plot of land, not sell it to him.

Nick Borth was not pleased by the offer, but accepted it after the Council upped the number of years in the lease to twenty, with an option to renew.

Quite a bit of interest was generated among the Islanders in the proposal, and Borth had had a busy week building up support. The crowd at the Council meeting when the project was approved was considerably larger than the handful that usually attended, and there was enthusiastic applause when Nick and Barabal, representing the Council, shook hands on the deal.

Both Barabal and Darroch had doubts, but they agreed to remain neutral, and let the proposition pass. They did not feel that they could stand in the way of progress, and after all, it was just one small piece of property that was going to be leased, and one medium-sized condominium that was to be built, and one small batch of rich tourists that was going to be lured to Eilean Dubh. How much trouble could that cause?

At *Taigh a Mhorair*, later, Darroch was telling Jean and friends Jamie and Màiri MacDonald about Nick Borth and his plans. "I suppose that will put Eilean Dubh right into the twenty-first century," he said, "if we become a magnet for rich tourists."

"There will be no road signs in English," announced Màiri, who was the queen of the Island's Gaelic Playschool, and her native language's most passionate supporter. "After all our work at keeping our language alive, we'll not be catering to the whims of rich tourists. If they want to come here, they can take the time to learn what signs in the Gaelic mean."

"There aren't that many signs," Darroch pointed out. "The speed limit's the same in any language, and so are the names of our towns."

Undeterred, Màiri continued, "And there will be no special efforts to speak English for them."

Jean said, "Well, the shopkeepers speak English to me. Even though I try to get them to talk with me in the Gaelic we almost always reach a place where my Gaelic breaks down and it's easier for all of us to go on in English."

Màiri sniffed. "You are different," she said, considering the subject closed.

Jamie spoke for the first time. "Where did you say this piece of land is? Is it that bit across from the scenic outlook?"

"Yes."

Jamie shivered, remembering his experience with the misty wisps and the haunted tune. "It's not the most welcoming place to build on the Island," he said, but refused to amplify or explain his comment. It was none of his affair if fancy new timeshares came complete with dancing wisps or Great Gray Men or fairies, or any other members of the Unknown World.

Four

Cherish the storyteller as much as you cherish the story.

Eilean Dubh proverb

It was Sunday afternoon, and the traditional peace of the Sabbath had descended upon Eilean Dubh, except in Jean and Darroch's cottage, *Taigh a Mhorair*.

Rosamond Mòrag Mac an Rìgh, three years old, was at the age where she was too old for a nap and too young to go without one. Owly, irritable, and hyperactive, she had been driving her devoted parents crazy for the past hour. Everything had failed: lap sitting, cuddling, and playing dolls (something at which Darroch, with his actor's imagination and repertoire of funny voices, was particularly accomplished).

Both Jean and Darroch were growing cross with their darling, but both refused to turn on the television, Darroch because his upbringing as a Free Presbyterian made him uncomfortable with the idea of TV on the Sabbath, and Jean because she regarded it as a cop-out. Only in the most extreme of cases would she use television as a baby-minder.

She was rapidly approaching that point, however, as she remembered what pre-Rosie Sundays had been like in the early days with Darroch. Sunday afternoon had been spent in bed making love, a special time that had cemented their relationship, with the added spice of the naughtiness of sex in the daytime under the bedroom skylight.

She sighed, knowing that those days were gone, not forever, just until Rosie was old enough to take herself elsewhere on Sunday. Jamie and

Màiri's twins Ian and Eilidh were long gone from the family cottage, and the MacDonalds' Sunday afternoons together put a smile on both faces that lasted until Tuesday.

Darroch interrupted her reverie. "Let's all go upstairs for a little lie-down."

"Just what I was thinking," said Jean with a wink, "but not possible, alas."

"I meant all three of us, a little lie-down in Mama and Daddy's big bed."

"No nap," said Rosie crossly, emphasizing her displeasure by a sharp tug on her father's shirt buttons, and a determined bounce on his knees.

"No, of course not," said Darroch. "We'll all cuddle up together, and if we are very good and quiet, perhaps Mama will read us one of her fairy stories. Do you have a new one ready, Jean?"

"I do," said Jean, catching on, "and I'd love to hear what you two think of it."

"Right, then, Madam Rosie, off we go!" and Darroch slung the little girl over his shoulder before she could think of a reason to object, and marched up the iron spiral staircase. Jean grabbed a printout from the computer desk and followed.

Upstairs in the large bed, Rosie demonstrated her refusal to nap by sitting bolt upright between her parents, who reclined comfortably against the headboard.

"Is everyone ready to hear a story?" said Jean in her best motherly voice. Darroch nodded, and Rosie relented enough to sag against her father's legs. Her thumb made its way slowly into her mouth. Jean smiled at her husband over her daughter's head, and began, "It's about a wee grass fairy, and a song that she sings that makes the fairy queen angry. It's called, 'How Clan MacQuirter got its drop of fairy blood.'"

How Clan Macquirter Got Its Drop Of Fairy Blood
As told by Darroch Mac an Righ

Once there was on the Dark Island a wee grass fairy who lived in a patch of wild flag—wild iris—in the marshy lands that surrounded *Loch nan Iasg*. She was no taller than the yellow flag that she tended so diligently, and her skin was as green as the marsh grass, her hair was a tangle of yellow-green flowing like seaweed down her back, and her eyes, round as marbles, were bright emerald in color. Her wings were iridescent, shot through with glimmering streaks of peridot, turquoise, and the rich dark color of the pines on *Beinn Mhic an Righ*, the high western mountain.

She wore a forest green chemise and a many layered skirt of all imaginable shades of green, topped by a yellow laced-up vest called a kirtle. In these clothes she blended into the grasses and flowers in which she lived, and when she stood quite still neither hawk nor human could tell that she was there.

Every fairy on the Island had work to do, and the grass fairy's job was to care for the patch of wild flag. If the wind blew down the flowers, she'd plait the marshy weeds into a little sling to hold them up. If a rabbit hopped into the marsh intent upon a lunch of flag, she'd flutter around him, flapping her wings so furiously that his little bunny brain grew addled, and he'd scuttle off to find something less bewildering for his snack. If her precious flowers were attacked by insects, she'd spend hours plucking them off and throwing them into the loch to drown.

The largest sentient creatures on Eilean Dubh were her biggest challenge. She had no defense against humans, for she dared not let herself be seen. Fairy lore was full of stories about those of the People who'd let themselves be seen by humans, and who'd been captured, enslaved, even tortured. So if a human waded into the marsh intent on picking a bouquet of yellow flowers, the fairy had no recourse but to hide and watch, wringing her hands helplessly. Luckily that didn't happen very often, for the *Eilean Dubhannaich* had a distaste for getting their feet wet, unless it was to catch a fine mess of fish for dinner, or to cut the peats that kept their houses warm in winter.

So the fairy—Astarte was her name—lived happily in her marsh, tended her flowers, and every Friday night gathered with her winged colleagues in the old ruined castle of the Mac an Rìgh chiefs, which the fairy queen had appropriated for her own.

It was at one of these evenings that the fairy community heard astounding news: their queen was going to be married, and to a human!

Their reaction was that of shock and distaste, for the human in question stood before them. He was six feet tall, burly, ruddy of complexion, and crowned with a shock of flaming red hair. The fairies regarded him with horror, and wondered what on earth or in fairydom their queen was thinking, to join herself in wedlock to such a hideous creature.

But no one dared say that to Queen Oonagh, who was a tyrant, as cruel and mischievous as she was beautiful. She'd spotted Ruairidh, her human, working on the croft he shared with his wife Peigi and their baby, and her wayward heart and unbridled lust had been captivated by the muscular sweaty form, and by the loving grin and the great smacking kiss he'd given his Peigi when she brought him out a cup of tea. When Ruairidh whispered something naughty in Peigi's ear, and roared with laughter when she blushed, Queen Oonagh was smitten. No one had ever given her a loving grin or a great smacking kiss, or made her blush, for that matter, and she resolved to have that grin, those kisses and that giant form for her own.

She'd commanded an army of wild birds to sing madly in the forest, and when Ruairidh had followed the singing, wondering what was amiss with the birds, Oonagh had materialized in front of him and flung glittering fairy dust over his head. Ruairidh fell instantly, madly in love with her, and forgot all about Peigi and the bairn. Enchanted, he'd followed the Queen deep into the forest to her castle.

At the Queen's command, her fairies draped him with garlands of flowers, brought him cups of mead and plates of delicious food, and seated him in a throne just below the Queen's own gilded one, shuddering all the while at having to come so close to such an ugly beast, for fairies feared and despised humans.

"You are mine," Oonagh crooned, and Ruairidh's human brain forgot all about his human life. He was hers to command.

And that Friday night she announced her coming marriage, and every fairy in Oonagh's castle knew what that meant: presents. The greedy Queen would expect the finest gifts her fairy folk could find or create. Their minds worked furiously.

No mind worked more furiously than Astarte's. Her comrades might weave glimmering shawls and gowns of seaweed and touch them with fairy dust so that they turned into silks and satins, or change rose petals into glittering jeweled necklaces, or capture wild birds and make lovely cages of wild reeds to house them, but Astarte had no skills like these. The only thing she knew how to do was to care for her beloved flowers; she was, after all, only a little green grass fairy, no bigger than a wild flag, with no powers greater than those needed to capture and drown insects or frighten away bunnies.

Astarte fretted and worried. What present could she possibly give that would be worthy of her Queen's wedding? She would be punished if her gift were not acceptable; she might be banished from her marsh, cast out of the fairy community.

She flitted madly around Eilean Dubh looking for gift ideas, even neglecting her beloved flag in the intensity of her search, and at last, exhausted, she stopped to rest one evening on a rose bush near the door of a tiny croft house.

Inside a baby wailed, and a woman dandled it on her knee and comforted it with a song:

In your cradle dreaming deep,
Fairies come while you sleep.
Round and round your cot they fly
In the stilly bye and bye.
Chores undone when nighttime falls,
Fairies come to do them all.

While the house all quiet lies,
Safe and free from mortal eyes,
Fairies sweep and sew and spin,
Make a shirt to wrap you in.
Churn the cream and butter make,
For your breakfast when you wake.

If you crack your eye a peep,
They won't know you're not asleep.
Catch a glimpse of fairy folk,
Laughter rippling while they work.
Fairy song will tint your dreams,
Sleeping, smile till day begins.

The words of the song were nonsense, of course, for no self-respecting fairy would stoop to doing chores for a human; that sort of thing was for brownies and the occasional elf, lowly creatures who'd work for a saucer of milk and a warm place to snooze by the fireplace.

But the tune was captivating. Astarte had never heard anything like it. A *miorbhuileach* idea came to her. She would learn the song, and at the wedding she would sing it and play it on her little harp (changing the words, of course, to ones more appropriate to the People), and that would be her gift to the Queen and her human.

She returned to the little croft house night after night, hoping that the goodwife would sing the song again. And she did, for it was the only song that would comfort her wailing bairn so recently bereft of his father, who had disappeared into the forest one day and never returned.

The night of Queen Oonagh's wedding came, and the festivities in the fairy castle were magnificent. Choruses of wild birds sang, bard fairies told jokes and stories, fairy musicians played beautiful music on harps, flutes, and fiddles. Platters of exquisite food and golden chalices of fruity wines were passed, and all the fairies sang, danced, drank, gossiped and gobbled until their heads grew muddled, and the most muddled of all flew in great dozy circles around the top of the castle.

Then it was time for the gift giving, and after that would come the ceremony that would unite Queen Oonagh and Ruairidh forever, for once a human married a fairy he was forever lost to the world of men and women.

The Queen sat on her gilded throne, her human just below her on his, his belly full and his head spinning with wine. She waited, her eyes glittering with avarice, for she expected the finest gifts to be bestowed upon her. As each fairy, trembling with fear, approached the throne and presented his or her offering, the Queen leaned forward and inspected the present. If she nodded, and gave her cruel smile, the fairy tripped away, relieved, but if she frowned, the hapless gift-giver shrank, and crawled backwards from the throne, then scuttled into the mass of his compatriots, hoping to disappear from the Queen's mind as well as from her sight.

The little grass fairy was the last to approach her terrifying monarch. Offering her deepest curtsy, she knelt with her tiny harp and began to play and sing the mortal woman's song, with new fairy words.

In your cradle, dreaming deep,
Fairy child, fast asleep . . .

The effect on the company was marvelous, for they'd never heard such a beautiful tune, never having paid attention to the music of mortals. Even the Queen sat up and took notice.

The effect on Ruairidh was the most marvelous of all. He gasped, and stared at the little grass fairy. Then he rose to his feet and roared in his terrifyingly loud human voice, "My Peigi, my wife, my bairn! My wife Peigi sings that song to our bairn!"

Astarte froze. The company of fairies stilled.

Ruairidh shook his head free of enchantment and wine, and gazed wildly around at the gathering of the People, strange, wee, winged figures whose drink-muddled gazes were fastened on him. At last his eyes fell on Queen Oonagh, and relieved by the song of her spell, saw her as she truly was: horribly ugly, cruel black eyes glittering with greed and malice, nose sharply hooked, body fat with dissipation. He howled with fear, and bolted from the throne through the quivering mass of fairies, scattering them as he went.

The shocked Queen took a moment to gather her wits, and that was all that Ruairidh needed. His feet given wings by his terror, he rushed through the door of the fairy castle and dashed into the forest. "After him," howled Queen Oonagh, but the fairies, thrown into disarray and trampled by the huge human feet, their minds addled by wine, were slow to obey, and Ruairidh made his escape.

The little grass fairy, quivering at the foot of the throne, knew what was going to happen. Before the Queen could give her next command, which would surely be for her destruction, Astarte fanned her wings furiously, rose in the air and flew off through the airy ceiling of the fairy castle into the night.

"She has ruined my wedding, and set my human free from my enchantment! Catch her so that I may torture and kill her," shouted the Queen. The fairies, not knowing which culprit to pursue, jostled and pushed each other in all directions, and flew in aimless dozy circles while the Queen roared her anger.

Into the cool night air a terrified grass fairy flew madly away, flapping her wings as hard as she could, knowing that dreadful punishment would befall her if she was caught. She flew till dawn, and when the sun rose she knew she was safe, for fairies would not come out willingly in the daylight hours. Exhausted, she collapsed in the shade near the door of a crofter's cottage, and wondered what to do. None of her comrades would dare aid her, and she must find a place to hide. She could not return to her beloved flag patch, for that would be the first place searched. Reaching deep into her mind, she came up with a power she'd always had and never used, that of shape-shifting.

She would change herself into a form no fairy would recognize as the hapless Astarte. A bunny, perhaps? No, for she would be captured and eaten by a hungry fox. A flower? No, for hands would pick her and carry her away. A bird? No, for she could not sing their songs, and they would cast her out of their company and an eagle would gobble her up.

At last she came up with the perfect solution; she would change herself into human form, and seek refuge with the only creatures that fairies avoided.

She drew in a long breath, and thought hard, and whispered the rusty spell that came from so deep in her memory, and at last she began to change, growing bigger and bigger so fast that her clothes could barely keep up with her, and the little yellow kirtle strained at its lacings and threatened to pop.

She stared down at her body in amazement. Though she had become only the size of a small child, she looked enormous to herself, huge hands, long legs, giant feet, and she did not dare to think of what her face and hair might look like.

The hardest part of her transformation was the loss of her wings. They were the last of her fairy shape to go, and they disappeared with an audible snap and a painful twinge between the shoulder blades. Astarte mourned, for she could fly no more, and would be dependent on those long legs and those grotesque feet for transportation.

But she was still green. She did not think that humans would welcome as one of their own a creature with green skin. She screwed up her face in concentration, clenched her fists and willed herself to change so intently that unfamiliar human sweat ran down her face. At last the green of her skin began to disappear, and a rosy pink took its place. The last thing to change was her clothing; her lovely green and yellow fairy raiment turned into dingy rags of brown and gray.

I've done it, she thought in triumph, just as the door of the crofter's cottage opened, and a woman stepped out.

Oighrig—that was the crofter woman's name—stopped in her tracks and stared at the child lying beneath the bushes near her door. "Whoever might ye be?" she demanded, her hands on her hips.

Astarte opened her mouth, praying that sound would come out, and uttered her first human words. Her voice sounded rusty to her, like a squeaking door or the brushing of reeds against each other in her marsh. "I'm hungry," she whispered.

The kindly crofter woman's heart melted. She had never been able to have a child, and she coveted one as much as Queen Oonagh had coveted rich presents. She crooned, "Ach, ye puir wee thing. Come away inside now, and I'll give ye some porridge and a bit of bread and milk."

Astarte had no idea whether or not she'd be able to eat human food, but the smell of the fresh-baked bread made her mouth water and the taste of the oatmeal porridge was more divine than any fairy meals she'd ever eaten. She gobbled everything set before her and her round green eyes begged for more. She'd never dreamed that human food could taste so delicious.

When the fairy was replete, Oighrig sat herself down at the table, and stared at her guest. "Now, child, ye must tell me. Who are ye?"

Astarte never knew where the words came from—perhaps some story she'd overheard at a human's campfire—and she said, "I've run away from my cruel stepmother, who would sell me at the market to a horrible old man with lustful eyes."

Oighrig gasped. "Yer father would not stop her?"

Astarte lowered her gaze to the table and said, "He's dead."

"So ye've no one to look after ye?"

"No one at all."

And that was enough. When Oighrig's man, Uilleam, came home that night, Oighrig said, "I've taken in this child, who has no family."

Uilleam grunted. He'd been cutting peats all day, and was exhausted. "Can she work?" he asked hopefully. Another pair of hands would be most helpful on the croft.

Oighrig had not thought of that, and she gazed at her foundling. "Have ye any gift for work, child?"

Astarte thought hard, and at last said, "I'm very good at caring for flowers."

Uilleam and Oighrig looked at each other. Flowers, indeed, on a croft that depended on hard labor for its inhabitants to survive. Then Oighrig brightened. "If she's good with flowers, she'll be good with vegetables as well."

Uilleam grunted again, and dug into his supper. If truth were told, he'd dearly missed having children, and he knew his wife mourned for the bairns she'd carried and lost. If this little creature would make her happy, he'd keep her, whether or not she was good with vegetables. She could be taught, after all. "What's her name?"

Both humans stared at the fairy. Astarte thought furiously. What human names did she know? She thought of the woman whose song she'd stolen, and whose husband she'd freed. What was her name? "Peigi," she said at last.

"Peigi," said Oighrig. "A good name." Uilleam nodded.

Introduced to the vegetable patch and its potatoes, leeks and turnips, Peigi set to work eagerly, and soon found that growing vegetables was no different from growing wild flag. Pick the bugs off and drown them in a pail of water; build a fence of reeds to keep the rabbits away. Make a snare and catch a bunny, and her new parents would feast happily that night. As the years passed, she became well known in her tiny community, Ros Mór, as the best gardener of all the women, and the one to whom everyone came when they needed advice on raising their crops.

And she was safe from the fairies and the revenge of their evil Queen. She grew, the darling of her adoptive parents, and when she was seventeen in human years and very pretty, she caught the eye of handsome young Angus MacQuirter, who fell madly in love with her. She led him a merry dance before she agreed to marry him. Their tiny cottage had the finest garden and the most beautiful flag bordering it in all of Eilean Dubh, for as good as she had become with vegetables, she'd not lost her skill with flowers.

And no one knew that at night sometimes Peigi—once Astarte—slipped out of her cottage and drifted down to the marsh that edged *Loch nan Iasg*. There she sang and danced in the moonlight, and lamented the loss of her wings. But when she cradled her first child in her arms, and sang to her the fateful song that had cost her the wings, she knew it had all been worth it.

And ever after, however diluted, all MacQuirters have had a drop of fairy blood.

"She fell asleep ten minutes ago," said Darroch. He slid off the bed and gathered his daughter carefully in his arms. He carried her into the little bedroom next door and deposited her in her own bed, and pulled a blanket over her.

"I hope that's not a criticism of my story," said Jean as he came out.

"More likely the product of being three years old, and still needing a nap. *Carpe diem*, Jean; let's go downstairs. I'm in the mood for a cuddle on the fur rug in front of the fireplace, just like in the old days."

"Oh, lovely," said Jean, and scampered after him down the iron spiral staircase.

Rosie would be out for an hour and a half, with any luck. Plenty of time for lovemaking, and a chance afterwards for a discussion of something she'd been pondering for days.

They undressed each other slowly, and when they were naked they lay down together on the fur rug. With Jean's whisky-colored hair draped over his arm, her body soft and yielding in his arms, her green eyes half closed in pleasure, Darroch began the pleasant preliminaries to lovemaking. He kissed her breast, and when she moaned and arched up to him, he sighed happily. "This is the longest I've ever been married to anyone, and I want you more every day. Is that normal?"

"Love-crazed and sex-mad at forty-three . . . almost . . . forty-four years old," Jean said, and whimpered as his hand slipped down between her legs. "Who cares whether it's normal or not, it's *miorbhuileach*."

"You have the most beautiful body, more beautiful than any fairy. Did I ever tell you the Island story about the fairy who took a crofter named Mac an Rìgh for her lover?" Darroch whispered, doing something with his long fingers that made her gasp. "Like that, do you? How about this?" and he slipped two fingers inside her.

Jean caught her breath in wonder. "Is that part of the story?"

"Aye. He made love to her on the hay bales, and they set the barn on fire."

Burning with a fire all her own, Jean pulled him on top of her. "I love these old Eilean Dubh legends. Let's act it out, and see if we can ignite the fur rug," she whispered. He chuckled and kissed her, and she said, "I can smell smoke already."

Afterwards, they lay side by side looking up at the beams that criss-crossed the ceiling above the thick whitewashed cottage walls. Jean stirred reluctantly. Time to talk, while the wee troublemaker still slept. "Lovie, I've been thinking about something."

"You're always thinking about something, *mo chridhe*. You've the busiest mind of any woman I've ever known. If it's true that mental exercise stimulates the growth of brain cells, you'll be finding a cure for the common cold and the secret of world peace by the time you're fifty." He stretched lazily, and put a hand on her belly, thinking about an encore, as all good actors do.

"This is important, so don't distract me." She sat up.

"Maybe you'd better put your blouse on, so you don't distract me," he said.

"Be serious," she said, and before he could protest that he was being very serious about the distraction factor of her bare breasts, she blurted, "I've been thinking that I'd like to have another baby."

Darroch froze in shock, and stared up at her. "What?"

"You heard me."

"So I did, but didn't quite believe what I heard. Tell me again."

"Okay, listen up. I want to have another baby, if it's all right with you. I have several reasons."

She always had reasons, and he always enjoyed listening to her carefully thought out arguments, even though he was reeling with shock right now. "I'm all ears. Fire away."

"Well . . . in the first place, I think it would be too bad for Rosie to grow up without a sibling. You're an only child and I'm an only child, and we both know what that's like. Lonely, and the focus of both parents' attention all the time. It's nice, but it's a lot of pressure."

Darroch thought about being the Laird's heir, and how his upbringing had been carefully monitored not only by his parents but by Free Presbyterian Minister Donald and the entire population of Eilean Dubh. He had realized, uneasily, that Rosie was being subjected to the same kind of loving, intense scrutiny. "Agreed. Go on."

"That's it, really. Except . . ." she blurted, "I'd like to give you a son."

He was touched to his soul, but had to protest that one. "*Mo chridhe*, you know that's not necessary. I am perfectly happy with our daughter. Delighted, in fact, because I never expected to have even one child, and I could not love our daughter more if she were a boy. Girls are grand."

"Of course, but I have this vision, sort of, of a son to carry on the Mac an Rìgh name. One who looks just like you, with beautiful blue eyes. Every man wants a son."

"Rosie could carry on our name. She could keep her name even after she marries," he said, but he was weakening. A son; think of the wonder of it. A sturdy little lad to play football with and teach to fish and teach how not to be swayed by the pressure of being the Laird. He could do all those things with Rosie, but still . . . "There's no guarantee another child would be a boy."

"Of course not, and another girl would be *miorbhuileach*. Company for Rosie, like the sister I always wanted. But the odds are fifty-fifty that it would be a boy."

"Aye." He got up. "Let's have a whisky and talk this through."

"Whisky, in the middle of the afternoon?"

"Aye, whisky for all important discussions." He went to the sideboard and poured them both a dram, then came back and sat down by her side, draping an arm over her. "First of all, there's the question of your health."

"What do you mean?"

"Not to be too blunt about it, Jean, but you are almost forty-four. Isn't that a bit long in the tooth to be having babies?"

"Yes," she admitted.

"I'll not risk your health," he said firmly.

"I have thought about that; I had to. I've had a long talk with Ros MacPherson."

"You talked to Ros before you sprang this on me?"

"Well, I had to, didn't I," she said reasonably. "What was the point of getting you excited about the idea if it wasn't going to be possible, or advisable?"

"Right. What did Ros say?"

She took a deep breath. "He said that it had certain risks, for both me and a baby. But he said that I'd had three children, carried them all without serious problems, and birthed them easily. So the odds are pretty good."

He wasn't sure that "pretty good" was good enough; he'd have to think about that one. He tried another tack. "But the work . . . have you thought about all the work of having two small children?" Rosie already demanded more labor and attention than he would have ever thought possible, in his pre-baby innocence.

"I've been there. Rod and Sally were eighteen months apart, and there were times when I thought I'd go mad if I had to change another dirty diaper or clean more spit-up off my clothes or walk the floor with another colicky baby." First Daughter Sally had been an angel child, but much troubled with colic until she was three months old. "But I survived, and both kids turned out fine. Besides, it was different in Milwaukee." She searched for words to explain just how Eilean Dubh was different from her home town. "I was alone; my mother and Daddy had moved to New York when he changed jobs, and Russ wasn't a lot of help. Not like you, darling, you've pitched right in with baby care and housework. We've done it together, and that makes all the difference in the world.

"And we're like one big extended family here on Eilean Dubh. I feel as though I have sisters and brothers always around to give advice, share worries, and help each other out. I'm not explaining that very well, but it's different here. Children are loved and valued and part of everyone's family, and everyone's involved in their upbringing." There was that word "family" again, but it was true; that's how it was on Eilean Dubh.

"It takes a village to raise a child," Darroch mused.

"Exactly. So it's not like I'm going into this as a solo venture; I have you, and an Island full of relatives."

He said, "Màiri will be delighted. Another recruit for her Gaelic Playschool."

"And Jamie; he loves children, and he's crazy about Rosie."

"And Minister Donald; another wee Mac an Rìgh to tell about Eilean Dubh history and try to bring up as a good Presbyterian despite his father's failings."

"And Sally, who'll be thrilled to have a baby to practice on before she starts having her own."

Darroch tightened his arm around her. "I see you've thought this all out. What's a poor hapless man to do against such overwhelming female logic?"

"So you're interested in the concept?"

"I'm interested in the conception. When do we start?"

"Ros says I should be off the Pill for three months before we start trying for a baby, to let my system get back to normal. I can stop taking it tonight, but we'll have to use something to prevent my getting pregnant for a couple of months."

"And that means . . . ?" He groaned. "Don't tell me; I've already figured it out."

"Condoms aren't so bad."

"They are if you have to buy them at the Ros Mór chemist under the scrutiny of Flòraidh, Peigi and the whole raft of girl assistants, all eyes wide and curious as cats about what I'm up to, and wondering if I'm secretly sparking someone other than my loving wife."

"Oh, poor you, but you're absolutely right. Have to make a trip to Inverness to stock up, I guess, away from prying eyes."

"And jabbering mouths. Gossip is the bane of this Island. Do you suppose I could have one more bareback ride right now, before I have to don the rubber overcoat?"

"I think that's a perfectly *miorbhuileach* idea," said Jean, grinning, and she stretched out on the fur rug, and held her arms out to him. There was another angle to this baby business they'd have to talk about, but it could wait.

PART II

Enter the Cornishman

Five

A good sword and a trusty hand!
A merry heart and true!
King James's men shall understand
What Cornish lads can do!
And have they fixed the where and when?
And shall Trelawney die?
Here's twenty thousand Cornish men
Will know the reason why!
And shall Trelawney live?
And shall Trelawney die?
Here's twenty thousand Cornish men
Will know the reason why!

Unofficial national anthem of Cornwall

*T*he square in the center of Ros Mór was lined with charming old shop fronts painted in pastel colors, pink, peach, green, yellow, and even one lilac, but there was nothing remotely pretty or charming about the gaunt old two-story granite building on a narrow street just off the square. The building's upper story housed an apartment; the lower floor was the home of Eilean Dubh's newspaper, *The Island Star*.

The only light on in the building this dark and stormy May afternoon was a lamp on the editor's desk in the newspaper office. The editor herself sat there, hunched over her computer, trying to figure out how to fill a gap the size of Inverness in the front page before the paper went to press the next morning.

The simple truth was that nothing much had happened on Eilean Dubh all week. Anna Wallace, *The Star's* editor and only reporter, had covered the Rosary Society's tea at Our Lady of the Island Catholic Church. She'd written a feature story on the High School Dramatic Society's upcoming production of "Brigadoon."

The disappearance of Somhairle Mac-a-Phi's best sheepdog Ruffy while on duty in *Beanntan MhicChriathar*, the high western mountains, had received five inches below the fold, with a 30-point headline proclaiming the generous reward offered.

The grand opening of Abbott & Son's software company was not until next week, and Anna had already written articles in past issues hailing the Island's newest business and its American owner, Russ Abbott from Milwaukee, and his son, Rod, the manager. The only thing left to write about in that context was Russ's previous relationship of husband to the Laird's present wife, and that was a subject best ignored. Everyone on the Island knew about it, anyway, and it was stale news even to the most devoted gossips.

So she had a gaping hole in the front page of tomorrow's edition, and nothing to fill it. She sat and wracked her brain, wondering if she should make a story up and see if anyone noticed that it was fantasy. Journalistic ethics, learned at the University of Glasgow, ruled that possibility out, but she enjoyed toying with the idea.

The bell on the front door jangled and a man came into the office. Anna looked up, startled. She hadn't expected any visitors. It was past five-thirty, the time when all of Ros Mór's shops closed. Depressed by the grayness of the day, shopkeepers and shoppers alike had hurried home for supper and cheerful peat fires in their fireplaces. The month of May had reverted to type after a brief April heat wave, temperatures were back to normal, and the Island was in a patch of dark, cloudy days that threatened and usually produced thunderstorms.

It wasn't frightening, on peaceful, crime-free, Eilean Dubh, to have a stranger enter a building where she worked alone, but it was unusual. May was not tourist season, and visitors to the Island were rare at this time of year.

"Hullo there," said the stranger.

English, she thought. The ever-busy Island gossip network had proclaimed the arrival on an Englishman on the Cal-Mac ferry three weeks ago. She'd made a mental note to track him down, find out why he was here, and write it up for the paper, but had gotten distracted by the condominium controversy. Perhaps there was a story here to fill up that front page gap. She looked up at him with interest. "Hi."

"Sorry to disturb you, but I'm looking for a bit of help."

"What can I do?"

"I need a place to stay."

Prickles of unease ran down her spine. The stranger was tall, lanky, and vaguely disreputable. A knit cap was pulled down over a mop of coffee-with-a-touch-of-cream colored hair, which escaped to curl wildly over his forehead and ears. He wore a shabby wool sweater that had a hole in the sleeve, a knitted scarf wrapped around his neck several times, and elderly jeans with one patched knee.

A tramp, Anna thought in alarm, and remembered that her purse, in the desk drawer, was stuffed with the housekeeping money she'd withdrawn from her savings earlier that day, in preparation for grocery shopping tomorrow after she'd put this week's issue to bed.

She began in her firmest tone of voice, "If you're looking for a handout . . . "

"A handout? I said I was looking for a place to stay." He said, in a deliberately simple tone, "Perhaps you've misunderstood. I'm looking for a B and B."

There was a certain arrogance to his tone that made Anna bristle. "This is not the Tourist Information Center," she growled. "This is a newspaper office."

"I know that. The TI is closed. The sign says it's only open on Fridays until June."

"Deirdre spends the winter making jewelry for the summer trade. She doesn't keep the office open because we don't get tourists until June."

"I'm happy that Deirdre has meaningful work to keep her busy, but what do you expect people who arrive before the season to do about accommodations?"

"We expect them to stay at one of our two hotels that are open year-round. The Rose Hotel is only four blocks from here, and it's very pleasant. If you'll excuse me, I have work to do." Thoughts of pumping this unpleasant newcomer for a story evaporated. She inclined her gaze down towards the desk in a clear gesture of dismissal.

He stared at her bowed head. "I'm already staying at the Rose. I've been there two weeks and I can't afford to stay there much longer."

"I'm sorry," Anna said in exasperation. "What precisely do you expect me to do about your problem? If it's money you want, you're out of luck, because I haven't any."

The stranger's eyes widened. Really, thought Anna, they were the most delicious shade of brown. Deep, velvety brown, like melting milk chocolate. She stared into those eyes until she felt a little dizzy.

"Do you mind if I sit down?" he asked abruptly.

Yes, I do, she was about to say, but he had already sunk into a chair.

"I thought," he said patiently, "that since this is a newspaper, someone here would know about what accommodations are available on Eilean Dubh. Newspaper people are supposed to know what's going on in a community, aren't they?"

She couldn't deny that. Not only was she supposed to know, she did. Very little occurred on Eilean Dubh that the editor of *The Island Star* didn't know, including the names of all the owners of the local B and Bs, because they advertised in the newspaper. Feeling a little silly, Anna snapped, "If you'd just said that straightaway, we wouldn't be having this ridiculous conversation."

He shrugged, unconcerned by her annoyance.

Anna glared at him. Perhaps there *was* a story here, she thought viciously. *World's Rudest Englishman Visits Island.* That ought to fill up six inches on the front page, and every Islander would get a good chuckle out of it. The English were not popular on Eilean Dubh.

Then he smiled, and she got the full benefit of the brown eyes, and blinked in surprise.

"Sorry, I think we've gotten off to a bad start." He rose from his chair and extended his hand. "My name is Zachariah Trelawney, and I'm frustrated. I have got to find a cheaper place to stay for three months or I'll use up all my grant money at the Rose. It's a lovely hotel, but it costs a packet."

"Anna Wallace." She shook his hand, which was surprisingly warm, considering the cool dampness of the day. "What sort of a grant?" she asked, her newspaperwoman's instincts fastening on the most interesting thing he'd said.

His face closed. "That's none of your business."

Furious, she opened her mouth on an angry retort, but he forestalled her. "Look, can you help me, or shall I go out and wander the streets again?"

"I don't care," Anna began. If you have to sleep under a bridge, she was about to add, when he smiled again. It was a nice smile, intimate and disarming, and it quite defused her anger. "All right." She spread her arms out in an appeasing gesture. "So you're looking for a B and B." She said slyly, "How long are you planning to stay?"

His eyes narrowed.

"Yes, I know; it's none of my business, but perhaps it would make a difference in whom I recommend. Not all our B and B people take long-term guests, especially at this time of year when they're busy with other things. What are you looking for?"

He relaxed into the chair with a weary sigh. "I'd like a place that's clean and comfortable that can provide an evening dinner. Nothing fancy, just a place where I can hang out at the end of the day. I'm going to be here for three months."

Astonished, she blurted, "Three months? Whatever could you possibly find to do on Eilean Dubh for that long?"

"Research."

"What kind of research?"

"That's . . . "

"None of my business. I know." She leaned back in her chair and gave him her sweetest smile. "It's my job to be nosy. You might make a good story for *The Star*."

"No! I don't want any publicity for my project."

"Hmm." She picked up a pencil, drew a piece of paper in front of her, and pretended to write. "Mysterious English tourist, name of Zachariah Trelawney, plans to stay on the Island for three months. He refuses to say why, but is probably up to no good. Sounds like a front page story to me. Care to provide more details, or shall I make something up?"

"No!"

"Perhaps I should ring the constable's office; see if he knows anything about you. Do you have a police record?"

"Now just a moment . . . "

Anna reached for the phone.

He glared, then gave up. "Damn it, I never was any good at keeping secrets. If I tell you why I'm here, will you promise not to say or write anything about it?"

"Depends on what it is." She put the pencil down and leaned back in her chair, pleased with herself for having penetrated his reserve. "If it's skullduggery, it's my duty to tell the coppers."

"Silly female. I'm perfectly legit. I have a research grant from the Scottish Antiquities Trust and I'm looking into the possibility of prehistoric settlements on Eilean Dubh."

Anna stared at him, disappointed, seeing her big story slipping away. "Why does that have to be kept secret?"

Sighing, he said, "Because if everyone knows about it, my work will be seriously compromised. People will get excited. They'll start digging holes everywhere and bringing me decayed chicken bones, old bottles, pieces of metal and stone they've found. Some people will even plant things and pretend to dig them up. And most important, if anyone knows of possible sites, they'll start digging in them, hoping to find something valuable. Maybe squirrel away a few bits and bobs to sell privately."

He smiled wryly, looking at her puzzled face. "Everybody hopes to find the next Sutton Hoo."

Anna thought about Sutton Hoo, the richest treasure trove ever found in Britain. It was the burial ship of a very early Anglo-Saxon king, containing objects of solid gold, jewelry, coins and silver utensils, found in Suffolk, England, in the late 1930s. Such a discovery on Eilean Dubh would turn more than a few heads. She nodded slowly. "All right. I understand."

"You'll keep this between the two of us?"

"On one condition. If and when you find anything, I get the story first. Not the London *Times*, or the *Daily Sun*, or the Edinburgh or Glasgow papers. *The Island Star* gets to break the story."

"Hmmm . . ."

"That means if you strike pay dirt on Friday, you'll have to wait till Monday to announce it, because I only publish twice a week."

He grinned. "Done. Eilean Dubh's own Lois Lane gets the scoop." He stood and held out his hand again. "Shake on it?"

"Right." They exchanged a conspiratorial smile over their clasped hands.

"Now can you suggest a place to stay?" he said patiently.

"*Ceart math.* Let me give Mrs. Cailean the Crab a ring. She has a couple of very nice en suite rooms she rents in the season, and she's a grand cook. She'd probably be glad of a chance to earn some extra money." Anna dialed, then covered the mouthpiece of the phone and whispered, "Better get your cover story ready." She grinned at his look of surprise.

"Cover story?"

"Marsaili *Mhic an Aba*—that's Mrs. Cailean—is one of the biggest gossips on the Island . . . oh, *feasgar math, a Mharsaili. Ciamar a tha?*" She continued the conversation in rapid Gaelic, then hung up the phone. "Done. She'll take you. One twenty-five the week with breakfast every day, dinner five nights, packed lunches thrown in if you want them on four days, but not on Fridays because that's when she has her lady friends over for luncheon and a bit of a natter. She'll be too busy fixing fancy nosh for them to worry about you. You can take your things over there tomorrow."

"Brilliant," he said, relieved. "Thanks."

"What are you going to tell her? She's already asked me why you are here."

"Oh, damn. I hadn't counted on how nosy the locals would be. I thought I could just slip in unnoticed and go about my work with no one paying any attention to me."

"You're not in Kansas anymore, Toto, you're on Eilean Dubh now. Everybody knows everybody's business, and what they don't know, they make up. Best to have a story ready in advance."

"I should have anticipated that. I'm from a small town myself, and I suppose an island is like a small town." He smiled suddenly. "Tell you what. Why don't I take you to dinner at the Rose and you can help me concoct something believable?"

When she hesitated, he coaxed, "I'll tell you all about my project. It'll give you useful background for that future big story."

"I've got another story to write, a big hole to fill in tomorrow's edition."

"I'll help you think up something for that."

She had a sudden inspiration. "Based on your cover story . . . "

He chuckled. "*Stranger Arrives on Island, Intrepid Editor Gets All the Dirt.*"

"Except that it can't be a lie."

"Ah, journalistic integrity. A half truth or two, an insinuation, perhaps?"

"Perhaps." Anna smiled.

"Right, let's go. We'll find something in my disreputable background to spin a tale about, over dinner."

"But not the Rose. I haven't the time for one of Sheilah's gourmet two hour dinners and I'd be too nervous to enjoy it."

He turned to look at her. "Do I make you nervous?"

"Not at all. My deadline for tomorrow's paper is my worry. We'll go to Uilleam MacShennach's pizza joint. Fast and deadly."

"MacShennach . . . sounds authentically Italian."

"Best pizza in the Western Isles. Up the MacShennachs!" She switched off the desk light. "But we'll go Dutch. Can't have you spending all your research money on dinners out."

"It'll be my treat, and my money's paying for it, not money from the grant."

Anna pulled her sweater from the back of her chair and turned to the shelf where she kept her muffler and hat. As she wrapped the scarf around her neck, she watched Zach Trelawney, who had wandered over to the table where her front page paste-up was waiting further attention. He bent over to examine it closely.

Something rang a familiar chord in her mind. She looked down at herself: ratty sweater, wooly muffler. Then she looked at him. Ratty sweater, wooly muffler. At least I'm wearing a skirt, not patched jeans, she thought, and noting his knit cap jammed over his curly hair, put hers hastily back on the hook and let her own curly hair go free.

Zach said, "You get lots of hot stories here? Who's stolen Mrs. MacWhatsit's special crumpet recipe? Fergus MacSomebody's favorite sheep is sick, not expected to recover? That sort of thing."

He was close to the truth. Irritated, Anna said, "And nosy Englishman visits Island, annoys editor and she savages him in print."

He smiled at her. "Ah, the power of the press. But I'm not an Englishman. I'm Cornish."

"Are you now." She regarded him with new interest. "A fellow Celt. The Islanders will like that. English people aren't the flavor of the month around here."

"They're not in Cornwall, either. Arrogant bastards, swanning around, buying up all the best properties for vacation homes."

"We've got one of those here. Only he's building a condominium to rent to rich tourists, not vacation homes."

"How did you let a guy like that get a foothold here?"

She shrugged. "Don't look at me. I wrote a fiery editorial against it, but in the long run there was no valid reason to stop him. People sniffed the possibility of new jobs, and tourists bring in money."

"Greased a few palms, did he?"

She shook her head. "I don't think so. Even if anyone on the Council had been tempted, Barabal Mac-a-Phi and the Laird would have put a stop to such shenanigans."

He stopped in his tracks and regarded her incredulously. "A laird? This place is under the thumb of an anachronism like that?"

Anna, like any *Eilean Dubhannach*, would always rise to Darroch Mac an Rìgh's defense, in any situation. "We're not under anyone's thumb, and the Laird's not that sort of a person, anyway. He doesn't try to rule us; he doesn't want to be the boss. He's more like our conscience, our moral backbone." She'd never quite thought of Darroch like that, but once it came out of her mouth she realized it was true. "Everyone here respects the Laird."

Zach Trelawney shrugged. "Whatever. I'm an anarchist, myself. The less government, the better."

Anna said, "An anarchistic archaeologist. That will make a great headline for my story about you, and send half my readers to their English pronunciation dictionaries." She gave him a conspiratorial grin, and the two of them went out into the cool Ros Mòr night, in search of pizza.

Six

Full jolly knight he seemed, and faire did sitt,
As one for knightly giusts and fierce encounters fitt.

Edmund Spenser

In MacShennach's, as they waited for their pizza, Anna pulled out her ever-present notebook and pencil, and began to doodle. Sometimes drawing funny little pictures helped inspire her brain into action, and she was still thinking of the hole on the front page.

Zach offered, "How about a bitingly critical restaurant review? On tonight's pizza, maybe."

"Are you joking? That's one thing I can't do, criticize the local eateries. It's bad for business."

"Protecting your advertisers? What about journalistic integrity?"

She shook her head. "This is a small island, and we all stick together. A local paper's duty is to promote local enterprises, not run cheap exposés."

"But what if the pizza's really terrible? Don't you have a duty to warn prospective customers?"

"I do it by finding something to praise, then hint that the rest of the menu could be improved. Praise the tiramisu, suggest that they find a new supplier for the sausage."

"What's wrong with our sausage?" said an aggrieved voice at Anna's elbow, as the waitress set a steaming pizza in front of them. "Murray the Meat makes it fresh every day to our special recipe."

Before Anna could open her mouth, Zach said in buttery tones, "Oh, we were just talking about my cousin's restaurant in Penzance. Anna was giving me ideas about how I could tell him, tactfully, that his sausage is off." He smiled sweetly up at the waitress. "This looks wonderful."

"The sauce is an old MacShennach family recipe."

At Zach's astonished look, Anna added quickly, "Mrs. MacShennach *as sine* was born in Genoa, Italy."

"Grandma was born in Sicily," corrected the waitress, "where the Mafia come from. Nobody crosses her, or criticizes her pizza. Enjoy your suppers."

"You see what I mean," whispered Anna, as the waitress stomped away. "Thanks for getting me out of that one. My remark would have been all over the Island in an hour. *Editor Rips Local Pizzeria.* I'd never have been able to come to MacShennach's again. I'd have to go up north to Airgead to Mòrag's Little Venice, and people would accuse me of being a traitor to my town."

"I should have known better, to think you could take sides on an issue as important as eating out," said Zach. "My home town in Cornwall is just like this place. If you've got two people together, you've got a discussion. If you've got three people, you've got a debate. If you've got four, you've got a war."

"And five is a riot." Anna's mouth quirked up.

He returned her grin, and they started on their pizza.

PART III

If She Be False

Seven

For Fate with jealous eye does see
Two perfect loves; nor lets them close;
Their union would her ruin be,
And her tyrannic power depose.

Andrew Marvell

*N*ick Borth wasted no time in getting started on his condominium project. Within a week he was busy with a surveyor from Edinburgh, marking out the boundaries of his parcel of land. Construction equipment arrived on the Cal-Mac ferry, and Islanders were hired to operate it. Excavation would begin any day.

Borth kept a low profile, preoccupied with his work, but on Friday night he turned up for the *cèilidh* at the Citizens' Hall. He'd learned that nearly everyone important attended these every-other-week events, and he wanted to ingratiate himself with the locals by participating in their activities. And perhaps stir up a little trouble, because that was the kind of man he was.

He arrived late, and most of the entertainment was over. The Island musicians were noodling around, amusing themselves while others filled plates with sandwiches and sat down with cups of tea, eager for the unscripted music *seiseanan* that often erupted later in the evenings. Jamie MacDonald and his dear friend Jean Mac an Rìgh were playing together, and what had begun as fooling about was developing into a vigorous duet between Jamie's fiddle and Jean's mandolin.

Darroch stood towards the back of the room, leaning against a wall, enjoying the music. The talent displayed by his wife and his best friend never failed to astonish him, and tonight they were really on, and sparks were flying.

"Hi," said a voice behind him.

Darroch recognized the voice, but did not turn around. Something about Nick Borth set his teeth on edge. He was still uneasy about the condominium project and he wasn't anxious to encourage conversation, especially not when he was listening to Jamie and Jean. Over his shoulder he said, "Good evening."

"Amazing music. Wonderful couple, aren't they."

"They are." *If you think it's amazing, why don't you shut up and listen?* Darroch thought, annoyed.

"It's really cute, the way they look at each other; you can tell they're very much in love."

"Can you?" Darroch, surprised, inclined his head back a fraction towards Nick, then turned his attention to the two musicians. Their eyes were locked together, and their smiles were just for each other. A flicker of something unpleasant crossed his mind.

"Of course, that fiddle player is so good looking that any woman would swoon at his feet. She's a lucky girl to have a guy like that so crazy about her."

Darroch was silent, considering the implications of the other man's remarks.

"Are they married?" asked Nick Borth.

"They are." Darroch turned, giving the other man a cool look from top to toe and back again that ended with a steely stare directly into his eyes. "Jean is my wife, and Jamie is married to Màiri Ross MacDonald, who runs the Playschool. That's her over at the tea table."

"Ooops. Say, I didn't mean to suggest . . . "

Didn't you? thought Darroch. "Not a problem," he said pleasantly, and turned back to listen to the music, hoping Nick would take the hint.

But he persisted, driving the knife in a little deeper. "You're pretty tolerant, to let the two of them get so cozy. I imagine they spend a lot of time together rehearsing, to be as good as they are."

Darroch thought of Jean and Jamie's Wednesday afternoons, begun when she'd first come to the Island, when they'd gotten together in a spare room at the Rose Hotel to make music. Now they met at *Taigh Rois*, and their Wednesdays were sacred; neither Màiri nor Darroch intruded on their *seiseanan*.

Taigh Rois, with a cozy fire in the fireplace, and a bedroom nearby. Familiar as he was with their cottage, he'd never seen Jamie and Màiri's bedroom, though he'd fantasized about it enough, in those early days of the MacDonalds' marriage, when he was still hopelessly in love with Màiri. He and Màiri had been lovers as teenagers, many years ago, until his acting career had tied him to London, and she had refused to leave her beloved Island to go with him. But the last vestige of that attachment had faded when Jean came upon the scene.

"Intimate," Nick Borth crooned.

Darroch missed whatever else he'd said, with the word "intimate" resounding in his brain. He barely heard the other man say, "See you later," so preoccupied was he with Nick's earlier remarks.

He remembered another time, several months ago. He'd walked down to Ros Mór for some grocery item or other, and upon reaching the top of his hill, his cottage the second down the lane, he'd come upon a terrifying sight. Jamie's truck was parked askew, as though its brakes had been applied suddenly. Jean sat on the ground, cradling a limp Rosie in her arms. Jamie was slumped near them, head on his knees, the picture of despair.

He began to run, stumbling and moaning in his terrified flight. When he reached Jean's side, she looked up at him. "She managed to open the garden gate, and ran out into the road in front of the truck." Then, registering his expression, she said, "Rosie's all right, darling, don't worry; she's just frightened. Jamie saw her and braked in time. His quickness saved her life."

Relief took the bones out of his legs, and Darroch slumped down beside his wife and child. Jean said, "Take her, lovie. I've got to go to Jamie."

Holding his whimpering daughter, Darroch watched his wife walk to his best friend, kneel beside him and take him in her arms. When Jamie finally raised his head, he rested it against Jean's breast. She tightened her arms around him and whispered in his ear. At last the two stood up and stumbled toward him, Jean's arms firmly around Jamie.

The two of them had a special bond, he realized, and thought how *miorbhuileach* that was: his wife and his best friend, linked in love.

Watching them now, he thought, was it the love of friendship, or something else?

He'd played the role of Othello once, at his acting academy, and had the devil of a time trying to play it convincingly, for he'd not been able to accept that a man could be seduced into believing his wife unfaithful on the meager evidence of that sly scheming rat Iago. "If she be false, heaven mocks itself!

I'll not believe 't," Othello says. But he had believed it, and tragedy was the result. Darroch had a glimmer of understanding of the character now.

For several long minutes, doubt, suspicion and jealousy warred with logic in his mind.

Logic won. He knew that Jean adored Jamie; she'd said so often enough. And Jamie felt the same way about her. But there'd never been a hint of anything sexual between them. Even the flirtatious banter they sometimes exchanged was just a kind of larking about, having fun with each other.

And Nick Borth surely knew that Jean was Darroch's wife, unless the man was totally oblivious to Island society. Why would he pretend that he didn't know? What was he up to, to try to sow the seeds of suspicion in Darroch's mind?

He doesn't know us, Darroch thought. He doesn't know it would never work. Our trust in each other is absolute. Trust might be swayed for a moment, for we're only human, but it will win out in the end.

Rather to his alarm, he noticed that Nick Borth had slunk over to Màiri, who was supervising the set-up of the tea table, and he was attempting to engage her in a whispered conversation, to her visible annoyance.

Darroch pushed himself away from the wall and was about to head over to rescue Màiri, when a rumble of approving murmurs broke out, signifying the end of Jamie and Jean's impromptu collaboration. Jamie said something, and everyone laughed; then Jean riposted, and they laughed again. Intimate, thought Darroch, and was tempted, briefly, to let suspicion take control. Then he shook his head to clear out the cobwebs, and went to Jean's side.

If he still had doubts about his wife's affections, they were dispelled by the way her face lit up when she saw him. "Hello, dar . . . Darroch!" she caroled, quickly changing "darling" into his name, so as not to appear a gusher. "Did you hear us just now?"

"Aye. Fine, as always."

"Oh, it's all Jamie. I just follow wherever he leads," she said happily, putting her mandolin into its case, and rising to give her hand to her husband, ready to dance.

Later that night, draped across Darroch's lap on the sofa in front of a glowing peat fire, Jean relaxed and let the familiar feeling of contentment envelop her. She'd been happy in her first marriage, even ecstatic at times, like after the birth of her two children, and during shared family events, like camping trips and the kids' graduations from high school. But she'd never experienced anything like the happiness she felt with Darroch, her soul mate, in their little cottage, with their darling daughter soundly snoozing upstairs.

Soon, she knew, the two of them would go up the iron spiral staircase to their big bed under the skylight, and they'd make love, and fall asleep in each other's arms. Any minute now Darroch would begin the preliminaries, with his hands starting their familiar path over her willing body. Eager to begin, she lifted her head to smile at him, and put her hands up behind his head to draw him down for a kiss.

Her fingers slipped into an unfamiliar flow of black hair around his neck, and she giggled. "My goodness, your hair is getting long; you're like a pop star from the seventies. When does Eric the Scissors get back from Glasgow?"

"Another couple of weeks. His wife's father is recovering well from his operation, but they're staying on to help Meghan's mother for a while longer," Darroch said, and wondered how Jean had known where Eric the Scissors had gone. He was surprised that the women's well-developed gossip network was interested in the whereabouts of the Island's only barber. "How did you know about that?"

Jean said, "Jamie's hair. It's been falling in his eyes and getting caught in the fiddle strings when he dips his head the way he does when he plays. And once it got caught on the chin rest and pulled, and it made him swear."

That unpleasant feeling of suspicion was back in Darroch's mind. So she'd been noticing Jamie's appearance, had she, and in great detail, or so it appeared. "Look to your wife; observe her well," Iago had said.

Jean chuckled. "It's been driving him nuts. Màiri's threatened to take the scissors to it herself, if Eric doesn't come home soon." She smiled up at her husband. "I like it, myself. You look like barbarians, Jamie especially. He looks like a wild Viking."

"Hmmph," said Darroch.

"I could lend both of you scrunchies, if you'd like."

"What's a scrunchy?"

"Oh, you know, those elasticized fabric things that women wear to tie their hair back. You could both have pony tails. The Laird and Bonnie Prince Jamie, both with pony tails." The thought gave her a mad outbreak of giggles.

He could not help laughing with her. "Not barbarians, warmed-over hippies."

"Umm, far out, peace and love, baby. Especially love." She tugged on his hair until his head came down and his mouth joined hers in a kiss. A few minutes later Jean gave a sigh of satisfaction. "Oh, wow, man, like I love you. Let's go upstairs and I'll show you how much I love you."

An offer he couldn't refuse. He looked down into Jean's honest eyes, her face turned up to his, glowing with devotion, and he thought himself all kinds of a fool for letting even the hint of a doubt into his mind.

Then she put out her tongue, and licked her upper lip in a parody of a sexy come-on that made him chuckle. "Right, then, you hot little tart," he growled and pulled her off his lap and onto her feet, and gave her a little smack on her bottom. "Upstairs, clothes off and into bed, and we'll see what you've got on offer."

She gave him a teasing grin. "Right ye are, yer Lairdship," she said. She tugged her forelock and scampered up the iron spiral staircase, swaying her hips provocatively as she went.

Reassured, Darroch bent to smoor the fire before he followed her. "*Tapadh leat,*" he said aloud to the One Who Listens. Thanks for keeping me from making a fool of myself. "Away at once with love or jealousy!" He was a truer man than Othello, and a smarter one.

Nick Borth had more up his sleeve than trying to rouse Darroch's jealousy. Darroch knew it, and became suspicious when he and Jean realized that they had not seen much of the senior MacDonalds lately. The friendly drop-in visits had ceased. Màiri seemed to be avoiding both of them, which Jean noticed especially at the Playschool, and Jamie was walking around with a morose expression, talking to no one. Something was definitely wrong.

Darroch talked it over with Jean, and decided to extend a formal invitation to dinner at *Taigh a Mhorair,* an invitation that could not be refused without giving serious offense.

Dinner was quiet; Jean and Darroch had found it hard to keep a conversation going. After they finished eating and the table was cleared, he got up, got the bottle of Laphroaig and four glasses, and poured them all a dram.

Then he said, "All right, out with it. What's amiss with you two?"

Jamie took a deep breath, gazed down at the table and then up again, and said aloud what had been eating at his soul for a week. "My wife believes that I am in love with another woman."

Jean gasped, and looked at Màiri, but Darroch nodded and said, "And that woman would be Jean?"

Hearing her name, Jean glanced at him, and then realized what he had said. Her mouth dropped open in shock. Speechless, she stared from one of them to the other.

Jamie said stiffly, "I'm not at liberty to say."

"But I am," said Darroch. "Your wife believes that you are in love with my wife. Is that right?"

Jamie's mouth tightened to a thin line and he was silent.

Darroch turned. *"A Mhàiri?"*

Màiri's face was red with suppressed emotion. She growled, "I can't help what I think."

"So he got to you, too," said Darroch. "But surely you don't believe him."

She said, "I don't know what to believe," and burst into tears.

"Now just a ding-dang minute," said Jean, recovering her voice. "Are you talking about what I think you're talking about? That Jamie, the world's most faithful and besotted husband, is in love with another woman, and that woman is me?" She shook her head. "If that isn't the silliest thing I've heard since . . . well, I don't know when."

"Not only silly, but malicious as well," Darroch said thoughtfully. "I don't understand what he hopes to gain by this."

"Who?" said Jean, baffled.

Darroch looked at the MacDonalds. "You know this is ridiculous. Kiss and make up, and let's try to figure out what's going on."

Jamie folded his arms across his chest and glared. "Make up? I'm waiting for an apology. Twenty-three years I've devoted to this daft cow, man and boy, been her committed slave, and she has the colossal nerve to accuse me of something like that."

The other two turned to look at Màiri. "Well?" said Darroch.

Màiri said stubbornly, "All he had to do was tell me it wasn't true."

Jamie, on the brink of exploding, snapped, "I've told you I loved you every night of our marriage; you've never fallen asleep without hearing it whispered in your ear. If you take it into your head to stop believing me now, I'm not responsible for the consequences. And you haven't spoken to me for three days, so how could I tell you? And you haven't slept in the same bed with me for three nights, so how could I tell you? You owe me an apology, and make it good, woman, else I might not accept it."

He turned to Darroch, seeking an ally. "She's put me through hell."

"Tell me, Jamie," Màiri whispered.

Exasperated, Jamie looked at Jean and Darroch and rolled his eyes. Then he rose from his chair and stood scowling down at his wife from the full majesty of his six feet of height, his Skye blue eyes fierce. "So you want witnesses, do you," he growled. "All right, hush yer whist and listen up. I love you, Màiri Ross MacDonald, wife of my heart for twenty-three years, wife of my heart for the rest of my life. I've loved you and none other ever since the first time I saw you, running across the courtyard in the rain at Sabhal Mòr Ostaig. I've devoted my life to showing you how much I love you."

He took a deep breath, and said defiantly, "I love Jean, too. And Darroch, much as it embarrasses me to say that about another man. My love for my friends doesn't in any way interfere with my love for you, you silly *cailleach*."

"Oh, Jamie," Màiri cried. "That's the sweetest thing you've ever said to me." She leaped from her chair and flung herself into his arms.

Jamie staggered backwards, then wrapped his arms around her and looked at Darroch for support. "Women," he said, shaking his head. "Is there anything between their ears but air?"

"I've been so miserable," sobbed his wife, from the comfort of his arms.

"You've only yourself to blame for that," said Jamie sternly, and tightened his grasp on her.

"No," said Darroch. "I think we've someone else to blame."

Jean said plaintively, "Would someone mind telling me what the hell is going on?"

"It seems we have our newest incomer to thank for trying to break up our marriages," said Darroch.

Jamie growled, "Are you talking about that slimy Borth character?"

"Aye. He tried to make me believe that you and Jean were up to no good," said Darroch.

"What?" squeaked Jean.

"Aye, he was on at me the other night at the *cèilidh*, nattering in my ear about how well the pair of you played together, and how much time you must have to spend with each other to play that well, and about how intimate you seemed, and making 'intimate' sound like the dirtiest word in the English language. And after he'd finished with me, I saw him head for you, Màiri. I'm sorry; I should have stopped him."

"I'll stop him," snapped Jamie. "He'll wish he'd never heard of Eilean Dubh by the time I'm through with him."

"Understandable reaction," said Darroch thoughtfully, "but maybe not the wisest. We need to figure out what his angle is."

"Darroch, you never believed it, did you?" gasped Jean, and received a rueful smile in exchange. "Why would anyone say such a thing? Why would he try to destroy two marriages?"

Darroch shook his head.

"Unless he's trying to create a scandal. You know how people here react to that." Struck by a sudden thought, Jean said, "Perhaps he thought that you and Màiri would end up in each other's arms for consolation, if you both thought that Jamie and I were up to no good. Blackening your name, Darroch, undermining your position on the Island. The Laird, caught up in a nasty scandal."

"And dragging the woman responsible for the education of the Island's preschoolers into an unsavory situation as well. Nasty, indeed." Darroch nodded.

"Some of the most respected people on the Island, brought down by scandal," Jamie said. "The Islanders would talk of nothing else, think of nothing else. But why?"

"Because he's a low, evil, vicious toad," snarled Màiri, and vented her feelings in a stream of furious Gaelic that made both Jamie and Darroch wince.

"Unless he's just a mischief-maker who enjoys making people unhappy, it seems to me that he's up to something and using us for cover," said Jean.

"A distraction," agreed Darroch. "But what does he want to distract attention from?"

"I'll beat the truth out of him," said Jamie fiercely.

"Tempting, but probably not the best way. If he knows we've twigged his game, we may never get at the truth of this."

"And he'll try something else," added Jean.

"Aye," said Darroch. "To get what he wants, whatever that is."

"Some people just like to cause trouble," said Jean. "Maybe that's all there is to it. At any rate, we've foiled this attempt, and we'll be on guard for the next. How about a fresh cup of tea, and we'll talk about it?"

Jamie said, "*Tapadh leat, a Shìne*, but it's time for us to go home. Now that my wife's got me back, I'd like to remind her of what she almost lost."

Màiri blushed, and was still red by the time they had gotten their coats and were on their way out of the door, Jamie with a firm hand between his wife's shoulder blades.

"How did you know what was wrong with them?" asked Jean, after the MacDonalds had left.

"Màiri always tells me exactly what's on her mind, loudly and firmly, and when she went all quiet I realized her problem had to have something to do with her relationship with Jamie. That's the only thing she's never discussed with me. When I put that together with Nick Borth's whispering poison in my ear about you, and remembered that I'd seen him talking to her at the *cèilidh*, I had a pretty shrewd idea of what was going on."

"What did he say about me?" Jean demanded.

"It was what he didn't say that caused the problem."

"You mean you believed that Jamie and I . . . "

"Not believed. But it gave me a few minutes pause for thought; the Othello thing, you know. After all, Jamie is damned near irresistible." Darroch turned a little pink himself, remembering his unjust suspicions.

"Not to me, he's not, not as a lover. He's one of my best friends, but it's you I love."

"I never thought that Màiri would fall for it, though, or I would have spoken to her sooner."

"Well, she's very much in love with Jamie, and sometimes love can make you insecure," said Jean.

"You're very much in love with me, and you're not insecure," said Darroch, with a grin.

"That's because I know that you're very much in love with me," said Jean, answering his grin with a saucy one of her own.

But it gave her pause for thought, the next day, wondering what love was all about. She knew how she felt about Darroch—hopelessly in love and intending to remain that way for the rest of her life—and she loved Màiri as the sister she'd never had. But how to define her feelings for Jamie?

She was pretty sure they weren't sexual. Lust had never been a part of their relationship, despite Jamie's incredible beauty and his intense personal magnetism, and his reputation as a lover. She knew from Darroch's occasional unguarded comments that Jamie had had quite an amorous career on his home island of Skye when he was a youngster, before he'd realized that he had the power to break women's hearts with just a smile of encouragement, a wink and a nod. He'd drawn back from that power, too tender to be a heartbreaker, and had grown up to become a devoted husband to Màiri Ross. He'd fallen in love with her the instant when he'd first seen her when they were both students at Sabhal Mór Ostaig, the Gaelic college on the Isle of Skye, and he'd pursued her until she agreed to marry him.

And judging by Màiri's confidences when she and Jean were enjoying personal conversations in the way that women do, he was quite an accomplished lover. "No complaints at all," Màiri had said, with her cat-like smile of satisfaction.

But despite Jamie's loving, flirtatious manner with Jean, she was sure there was no lust involved on his side, either. There was no way he'd ever desire another woman, or even contemplate infidelity.

So what exactly was the nature of her relationship with Jamie? She'd never felt for any other man the way she felt about him, never in her past life in Milwaukee had she met anyone who commanded such deep affection from her. It wasn't just brotherly affection, it wasn't romantic, and it certainly wasn't sex—it made her intensely uncomfortable to think of herself and Jamie in a sexual context.

Their relationship had begun with a shared love of music, and she admired him intensely for his prowess as a fiddler and tune-maker. It had grown from that to a deep friendship, intertwined with their mutual love for Eilean Dubh and their respective mates.

Darroch had told her quite frankly how much he'd loved Màiri, before their devolving interests had caused them to part with broken hearts. Now she was his sister and a best friend, and that was enough for both of them.

So it must be friendship, between her and Jamie, though that seemed a pallid word for such intense emotions.

Funny old thing, love, Jean thought. Its definition would make an interesting conversation with Free Presbyterian Minister Donald, though he'd probably turn it around to a theological approach to the subject. She didn't suppose he'd have any other views except Biblically based.

PART IV

Minister Donald's Time of Roses

Eight

in time of roses (who amaze
our here and now with paradise)
forgetting if, remember yes

in time of all sweet things beyond
whatever mind may comprehend . . .

e. e. cummings

Jean would have been surprised to learn that Minister Donald was having his own wrestling match with that old devil, love.

It had started out as quite a normal Sunday. Donald rose early to put the finishing touches on his sermon, which was Biblically-based as always. This one was on greed, inspired by a viewing of several Island women having a wrestling match in the Co-Op over a shipment of sleeveless, scoop-necked blouses from a London supplier, scored through the perspicacity of Barabal Mac-a-Phi during the April heat wave. Their arrival had caused a near riot at the store as the female inhabitants of Eilean Dubh had rushed in to take advantage of an opportunity to purchase garments promising relief from the heat.

The infant summer had begun to be called *samhradh air leth teth*, a scorcher, to the considerable bemusement of the Milwaukeeans resident there, who had laboriously translated the Centigrade temperatures used in Britain into the Fahrenheit equivalent of the low eighties, which wasn't hot at all to their way of thinking. But the *Eilean Dubhannaich* sweated and complained and slowed the pace of their activities to a leisurely crawl. There were shocking reports of men removing their shirts to work bare-chested at their daily crofting and fishing tasks.

None of the men would dare appear in kirk that way, but Donald wasn't so sure about the women. He had prepared a scolding sermon, in case any female *Eilean Dubhannach* was so lost to propriety that she'd wear her risqué new blouse to kirk on Sunday morning, and show her bare arms and throat in the Lord's house. None of the women did, of course. Their sense of what was appropriate was every bit as keen as Minister Donald's. But he kept the sermon in reserve, just in case.

Since that event Donald had thought quite a bit about greed and its implications in a close-knit society like Eilean Dubh, and had at last linked it to the appropriate Biblical references, principally Matthew 6:31-34, about excessive attention to the material, and that bit in Philippians 3:18-19, about minds being set on earthly things. It had given him grist for a deeply thoughtful sermon and a much-needed reminder for his congregation.

He always reviewed his sermons early on Sunday morning, not that he ever needed to re-type them on his ancient Smith Corona, but because he might find a better word to use here and there, or a thought that needed tweaking.

Then, satisfied with his work, he breakfasted sparingly on oatmeal and toast that he prepared himself, as Raonaid Ross, his housekeeper, did not work on the Sabbath, of course. Preparing meals for the Minister on that day was neither necessary nor an act of mercy, the only work permitted to Wee Frees on the Sabbath. Next he dressed in his black Sunday suit, into its fifth and final wearing before going to the dry cleaner in Airgead, and his best white shirt, washed and pressed the Friday before by Mrs. Ross and hung in the closet, awaiting Sunday.

Dressed for the service and armed with his sermon, he tucked the Word of God, his Bible, respectfully under his arm, and made his way from the old gray stone Manse across the garden to the matching old gray stone kirk that was his (and the Lord's, of course) dominion.

After the opening Psalm, lined out by precentor Angus Morrison and repeated line-by-line by the congregation, Minister Donald assumed his place at the pulpit and prepared to give his hapless listeners the benefit of his week of thought.

He gazed solemnly out at the assembled worshippers, let his eyes roam to every face, and was suddenly struck to the heart by the arrow of love. It rendered him totally unable to speak.

The expectant faces turned up towards him included the woman who had haunted his dreams since their first, brief meeting at the wedding of Eilidh MacDonald and Joe Munro: Helen Munro, Joe's mother.

A small, brown-haired woman, she sat demurely between Joe and Eilidh in the pew below him. Eilidh, as usual, was squirming impatiently; she was not a believer, and attendance at kirk was something she often found an excuse to avoid. But today in deference to her mother-in-law's visit, she sat by her husband Joe, a devout man who'd once thought of becoming a man of the cloth himself, but had decided instead to become a veterinarian and minister to animals instead of people. He was now junior partner to Mr. Cunningham, head of the veterinary practice on Eilean Dubh.

Donald had never thought to see Helen Munro again, but there she sat, a vision in a neat dark suit with a tiny flowered hat perched upon her head. She had not visited Eilean Dubh since the wedding, but her image remained burned in his brain, next to the image of his late beloved wife Elizabeth, who'd died tragically of breast cancer ten years ago. He'd never expected to be attracted to another woman, but there was something in Helen Munro's hazel eyes and warm smile that had called to him.

It called to him now, loudly and clearly. After a long silence, during which the congregation stirred uneasily and wondered if something in their collective appearance had upset their Minister, Donald pulled himself together, cleared his throat, and began to preach. His words flowed as fluently as always, but his brain was on autopilot.

He finished, and returned to his straight-backed chair by the pulpit, and surreptitiously pulled out his clean white handkerchief and mopped his brow.

The congregation murmured in appreciation. They loved it when their Minister threw himself whole-heartedly into a sermon, and this one had made him sweat. Good show, they all thought, well done, Minister.

When the service ended with a final lining-out of a Psalm, Donald rose and marched down the aisle of the kirk, looking neither to left nor right, though he wanted with all his heart to gaze upon Helen Munro. Instead, he stationed himself by the door, ready as always to do his duty and greet each member of his flock.

Today the flock were aggravatingly slow at emptying the building and going about their business. Every one of them seemed to have something to relay to him, some long involved tale which he heard not at all, so preoccupied was he with anticipating the appearance of a small brown-haired woman in a discreetly flowered hat. He nodded and murmured, and tried not to fidget, and restrained himself with difficulty from roaring at the speakers to "Get on with it, and move along."

Even Darroch Mac an Rìgh, who as an actor was usually so alert to the behavior of a crowd and should have noticed the one gathering behind him and been brief in his comments, was preoccupied and deliberate as he stopped to speak to his Minister. "I'd like a word with you, Donald, when you've a moment," he said. "Perhaps I might stop by later this afternoon?"

"Aye, of course," said Donald, without the slightest idea of what he'd agreed to, and wishing that Darroch would take himself off. He had just spotted the flowered hat behind the plump figure of Beathag the Bread.

"Around four, then?" said Darroch, thinking with pleasure about the opportunity to discuss Nick Borth with Minister Donald.

"Hmmph," said Donald, and turned to Beathag, prepared to give her the bum's rush, and hoping devoutly that she was not intending to share a confidence with him as everyone else had this morning. What was wrong with people today, to be so chatty? Had they no homes to go to?

Puzzled, Darroch moved away, aware at last that he had not had his Minister's full attention, as he usually had. Beathag too was surprised when Donald's glance lighted on her briefly, he gave an abstracted nod, and turned past her to greet the Munros.

Ah, thought Darroch, Donald will be wanting to ask Joe's opinion on the sermon. Ah, thought Beathag, it's that flibbertigibbert Eilidh MacDonald; the Minister will be intending to say a few pointed words about the fact that she hasn't been in kirk for weeks.

Both were wrong, for Donald found himself dumbstruck for the second time that day. He had allowed himself to look into the hazel eyes beneath the flowered hat, eyes turned up to him with such a sweet expression that his knees grew weak.

"You remember my mother, I'm sure, Minister," said Joe Munro.

Remember her? As if her face had not haunted his dreams for weeks, as if her voice had not murmured into his ears for even longer. They'd exchanged only a few sentences at the wedding, but the conversation and the eyes had stayed locked in Donald's memory.

"I'm Helen," the lady said.

"Of course you are. And I'm Donald. Welcome back to Eilean Dubh. We've been waiting for your return."

Helen smiled, and Eilidh and Joe exchanged puzzled glances. Waiting for her return? What had caused this unexpected outbreak of gallantry?

"We spoke of marriage," said Donald tenderly.

Eilidh and Joe stared in astonishment.

"Indeed we did," murmured Helen. "Imagine you remembering."

"How could I forget?" Donald murmured in his turn. "We spoke of our beloved first mates, and how much we missed them."

First mates? thought Eilidh. They talked about sailors? How odd.

Joe, more perspicacious than his beloved, realized that something important was being communicated between the other two. He took his wife's arm and moved her firmly along, so that his mother and his minister could continue their reunion. "Fine sermon, Minister," he said and pulled Eilidh with him.

The Minister, aware that other parishioners awaited his attention, seized his opportunity. "You'll come to tea today? Joe and Eilidh, too, of course," he offered recklessly, quite ignoring the effect that unexpected visitors for tea would have upon Mrs. Ross, his haughty housekeeper. She was not due to return to her duties until tomorrow morning, and she'd be apoplectic at the knowledge that her employer had entertained visitors for tea without her fine hand on the cooking and cleaning. She would not say so outright, from respect for the Minister's exalted position, but there would be "hmmphing" and only slightly-muted snorts of outrage, and mumbling about the dusting not having been done before company, and a long thin nose in the air for the next several days.

There would be no problem with entertaining guests, even female ones, Donald thought; surely he could whip up a cup of tea, and there were always goodies in the pantry left for his consumption on Sunday afternoon. And though it was the Sabbath, there was no proscription against having visitors. They would probably talk about today's sermon, his usual topic of discussion with Joe Munro, and one that was most appropriate for the Lord's Day.

Helen Munro said, "We'd love to come. I'll bring some tea cakes, if I might. I baked yesterday afternoon."

"*Miorbhuileach,*" said Donald, quite dazed. "I'll look forward to it. Around four?" he added hastily, aware that the junior Munros were turning away, taking Helen with them.

She gave him her sweet smile as she turned to follow her son and daughter-in-law. "I'll—that is, we'll—look forward to it too."

Darroch Mac an Rìgh, informed later by Joe that the Minister was entertaining guests for tea, wisely decided to postpone his visit to the Manse.

As was his usual practice with everything, Donald prepared carefully for his guests. After much searching, he discovered tablecloths in the sideboard in the dining room, and selected the one he thought the nicest, a fine old cream colored lace, thereby earning more disapproval from Mrs. Ross the next day, for the tablecloth was an antique and had to be carefully hand washed, spread over lavender bushes to dry, and pressed before it was stored away. "The daft mannie," she mumbled to herself. "Why could he not have taken one of yon modern ones that need only a tumble in the washer?"

Next he located a teapot and cups. These were not hard to find, for Mrs. Ross kept them handy on the sideboard for unexpected guests. Tomorrow she would complain bitterly to herself that he had not used the best tea set instead of the everyday one, which had a microscopic chip on one cup that only she could see, but it was there just the same.

Tea, milk, sugar. The sandwich fixings were in the fridge, and the cakes were in the pantry, all set aside for his own tea, no trouble at all to find. He made the sandwiches, gammon and cress, remembering at the last minute that Mrs. Ross always removed the crusts when company came. Face screwed up in concentration, tongue between his lips, he sawed carefully at the sandwiches with a table knife, and was pleased at his efforts, despite the slightly ragged and dented edges.

The table was set, the food was prepared, the teapot sat ready and waiting. Donald mopped his brow with his handkerchief for the second time that day, feeling a new appreciation for women's work, and went to dress for company. After much deliberation he chose a white shirt, black corduroy trousers, a tie, and a dark green cardigan, not noticing that the sweater he chose had a carefully mended patch on one elbow. Fortunately, Mrs. Ross would not be aware, tomorrow, of what garments he had selected, or he most certainly would have gotten a scolding. A patched sweater worn in the presence of guests would have been too much for her to hold her tongue about, Minister or no Minister.

Ready at last, and too nervous to sit down, Donald went out into his cherished garden, and walked distractedly among his flowers to calm himself.

The Munros arrived so quietly that he did not hear them come. They had walked up, of course. Joe, adhering to the Wee Free rule about what could be done on the Sabbath—is it necessary? is it an act of mercy?— eschewed the use of a car on the Sabbath except for medical and veterinary emergencies. As they approached the front door, Helen suddenly veered away, attracted by the mass of color just visible around the side of the house. She adored gardens, and could not resist a wee keek at this one.

Donald did not hear her come, and jumped visibly when her voice caroled cheerfully, "Good afternoon. What a lovely garden!" And there she came, a vision in a flowered dress and a different tiny, charming hat perched on her brown curls, tripping down the stone walkway, in her wake Joe and an uneasy Eilidh, who'd not been able to think of an excuse for staying home.

"Do you like flowers?" was all he could think of to say, and berated himself mentally for not coming up with something more original.

"Oh, yes. I grow some myself at home. Roses! My favorite."

His roses were the Minister's pride and joy, and he relaxed a bit as Helen wandered among the beds of his prized hybrid teas, murmuring her pleasure.

At last she stopped before a gorgeous five-foot-tall bush alight with giant blooms of shocking golden-yellow edged with carmine. "Oh, my," she breathed. "What is this one? It looks like Peace, but the colors are so much more intense."

"'Even Solomon, in all his glory, was not arrayed like one of these,'" said Donald, sharing the Biblical quotation that came often into his mind in his garden. "It's Love and Peace, a descendent of the original Peace. Doesn't it have a grand scent?"

Helen bent to a choice bloom and inhaled deeply. "Muckle bonnie, as they'd say in Tyneside where I was born."

"You're a Geordie, then," said the Minister.

"Aye, I am, transplanted to the Borders by my husband when I was a lass of eighteen, but once a Geordie, always a Geordie." She lifted her face from the flower, and smiled at Donald.

His knees trembled. Helen in her flowered dress, framed by his garden of roses, seemed the most beautiful creature he'd seen since his beloved wife had died. Only one thing was needed to make the picture complete. He strode away to his garden shed, fetched the pair of secateurs that he kept hanging by the door, and headed back to Love and Peace. He selected the largest, finest bloom, clipped it and removed the thorns, then presented it to Helen. He wanted to say something significant to her, but thought only of, "'Consider the lilies.'"

"'They toil not, neither do they spin.'" She took the rose, smiled her thanks, and said, "I've often wanted to be a lily, especially when I was left alone with three children to raise so many years ago. But it wasn't in the Lord's plan. I've been toiling and spinning ever since, and it's been good for me. Builds character, you know, all that toiling and spinning."

"Yes," said Donald, looking at her thoughtfully.

"But my dear Joe was at my side the whole time, helping in every way that he could. What a good boy he is!"

Joe, approaching, heard her comment, and blushed.

"He's still a good boy, no, a good man," burbled Eilidh, coming up to her mother-in-law, and giving her a hug. "You did a fine job with him, Helen dear."

The three turned to look at Joe, who was quite red by now. Donald took pity on a fellow male and said, "Shall we go in to tea?" and offered Helen his arm in his old-fashioned gentlemanly way.

"Lovely," murmured Helen, and took the arm offered her, and the four went into the gray stone house.

Afterwards Donald could not remember the details of that tea, though he tried mightily, because he thought such an important event should be enshrined in his memory forever. They'd talked about his sermon, and about Eilean Dubh, and even Eilidh, normally awkward in the presence of the awe-inspiring Minister, forgot her shyness and chatted happily along with the others. Laughter rang through the old house, normally so quiet and restrained. It was a Sabbath quite unlike any the Minister could remember, and it was all down to the presence of sunny Helen Munro.

On his knees before bedtime that evening, Donald thanked his God for the wondrous day, and prayed for many more to come. As he fell asleep he remembered that he had asked Helen, trembling, how long she was planning on staying on the Island, and heard her reply. "As long as I'm wanted," she'd said brightly.

And that, thought the Minister, would be for a very long, long time.

Nine

Strive first for the kingdom of God and his righteousness . . .
do not worry about tomorrow,
for tomorrow will bring worries of its own.
Today's trouble is enough for today.

Matthew 6:33-34

It wasn't until a week or more had passed that Darroch got his chance to visit the Minister and share his thoughts about Nick Borth, and he left the Manse a bit perturbed. Donald had agreed that it was a very bad sign that Nick was trying to sow dissension in two marriages, and offered to preach a sermon about the evils of gossip.

But Darroch thought that the Minister had been a bit distracted, and wondered why. When he shared his concerns with Jean, later, at home, she laughed. "Don't you know why? Donald is courting Joe Munro's mother. He won't have much else on his mind, for the gossip is that he is really smitten with her. He's been driving her around the Island, showing her all the sights, and they have dinner together every night. He's even been to the MacShennachs' pizzeria, and Màili MacShennach said it was a real treat, watching him in his first encounter with a pizza, stabbing away at it with his fork and knife. He's not much of a gadabout, you know, and apparently the only Italian food he's ever eaten has been spaghetti from a can."

"Raonaid Ross is feeding Donald canned food?" said Darroch. "I'm shocked, for she's well known for her pride in her cooking."

"No. Sundays when she's not there he's been known to open the odd can or two."

"It doesn't matter, for his thoughts are lofty, far above the material. He doesn't care what he eats," said Darroch.

"Now there you're wrong, lovie, for Eilidh had him over for supper the other night, and she says he raved about her vegetable quiche."

Darroch silently pondered the idea of the Minister raving about any-thing, particularly vegetarian food. And smitten by a woman! Helen Munro was nice enough, and attractive in her quiet way, but Donald had seemed the epitome of the confirmed bachelor, after his beloved wife had died ten years ago. He'd never looked at another woman since then.

Ah, thought Darroch, looking at his darling Jean as she cleared away the teacups, love comes to us all, and a damned fine thing it is, too.

The Minister had taken kindly to Darroch's suggestion of a sermon reminding his congregation about the evils of gossip, and the following Sunday he shared the results with his listeners. They all nodded their heads and murmured in approval. In the kirk yard after the service, a knot of women gathered to discuss the sermon.

"The Minister has the right of it, as always," said Barabal Mac-a-Phi, nodding her head. "For folk here talk far too much about the doings of others."

"Aye, that's true," agreed Màili MacShennach. "It's jabber-jabber, and never mind whose reputation is savaged, and whether the stories are true or not."

"Really, Mother," said Dìorbhail MacShennach, a tall, long-limbed teenager. "Weren't you just gabbing last week about the Minister and Mrs. Munro? Isn't that gossip?" She grinned and slipped away before her mother could reply.

"That lass of yours is free with her opinions," said Beathag the Bread. "You should have a word with her about talking disrespectfully to her mother."

"Ach, Beathag, you don't understand teenagers. You have to let them speak their mind once in a while; you don't want them to grow up all sly and quiet, thinking things they don't dare talk about. You want to know what's going on in their heads. And Dìorbhail's a good lass, for all she lets her tongue run away with her now and then. She just doesn't understand," said Màili MacShennach comfortably. "It's not gossiping to talk about the Minister. It's only right and proper that we take an interest in his well-being."

"That's so," said Beathag. "The dear man's such an innocent; he needs someone to look after his welfare. I'm sure he'd be the first to agree that someone should tell him if he's about to put a foot wrong, and risk getting his heart broken."

"You certainly don't think that he'd put a foot wrong with Helen Munro, do you?" said Barabal. "She seems a fine woman, and not a heart-breaker at all."

"Ah, but will she stay the course? Is she just trifling with his affections, and planning on going back home when she's tired of the Island?"

"What else could she do?" said Màili dubiously. "You don't think he means to ask her to stay, and she means to do it?"

"Why shouldn't she? He's a fine catch, a respectable man and a Minister to boot, and her a widow for ten years or more."

"Hmmph," said Màili. "All these incomers! The Island is getting quite overrun with them."

"And that would be . . ." Barabal began to count on her fingers. "Darroch's Jean and her former husband Russ who's brought us new jobs, and her son Rod who's here to manage the company, and her daughter Sally, who's made Ian *Mòr* MacDonald a fine wife, and that young Cornishman that Anna Wallace is so taken with . . . Which of those incomers would you send back home?"

"What about that Nick Borth?" demanded Beathag the Bread. "You're not saying he's a good addition to our Island."

Màili said slowly, "But his development is employing our workers, and it will bring in tourists, which will put money in all our pockets." And he's on the brink of making us a big offer for our restaurant, which will put even more money in our pockets, she thought, but did not say.

Beathag shook her head. "I can't help but think there's something a wee bit fishy about him, that's all."

And so do I, thought Barabal, but I can't quite put my finger on it.

"Mo-*ther!*" said young Dìorbhail MacShennach, coming up behind the group. "Are you *still* gossiping? It's time to go home for supper."

Interest in the Minister's courtship of Helen Munro was spiraling out of control among the *Eilean Dubhannaich*, and Raonaid Ross, Minister Donald's housekeeper, suddenly found herself in the position of being one of the Island's most popular women. Tall, thin and dour, a fisherman's widow, she had always been an accepted member of the community, but never a popular one. She was a fixture: a person whom everyone respected and greeted when they encountered her in the Co-Op, or in the kirkyard after Sabbath services, but not one whom you'd stop for a long cozy natter.

The reason for this was that she had very little to say, and no chit-chat at all.

But everything had suddenly changed. Now she was being buttonholed by nearly every woman she encountered. *"Feasgar math, a Raonaid!* And how are you keeping?" she would be greeted cheerily, and once she had responded in her polite, distant fashion, she would find that the greeter had stopped, blocking her escape, and she would be expected to carry on a conversation. Raonaid found it very difficult.

And mystifying, until she realized that whoever had accosted her had one object in mind, that of gathering the latest details on Minister Donald's romance with Helen Munro. The third, or perhaps fourth question, after the usual pleasantries about the weather (and how *did* one respond to the remark, "Isn't it fine weather we're having?" The weather was the weather, and what could one say but, "Yes, the rain's stopped," or "It is indeed a fine day") would always be, "And how is the dear Minister these days?"

Once she'd tumbled on the reason for her sudden popularity, she was a bit resentful, at first. No one had ever bothered to ask her opinion on the weather until now, when all the women—and some of the men—were consumed with curiosity about the Minister and the incomer woman.

Her conversational skills were a bit rusty, but then they'd never been much to boast about. Her late husband Màrtainn hadn't been much of a talker himself, and their conversations had always been brief and to the point. "Will you be wanting sardines or salmon sandwiches for your lunch today?" Or, "I've a bit of beef for your dinner. Would you like roasted potatoes with that?" And he'd reply, "Aye, that'll be fine. Whatever you care to cook is grand with me."

Gradually over the period of their twenty-year marriage, until Màrtainn had been drowned in a fishing boat accident years ago, those conversational niceties had slipped into disuse as well. She knew what he wanted for sandwiches and for his dinner as well, and there had been little need to ask. Neither had been one to gab, and in fact Màrtainn had been known to boast to his mates, when they were complaining about how much their wives talked, jabber-jabber-jabber all the time, that his wife was as silent as the grave. The other men had looked at him and sighed in envy.

So learning how to conduct a casual conversation had come hard to her. It was even harder when she realized that she would be expected to come up with some interesting gem about the Minister. What on earth could one say about a man whose thoughts were mostly theological, and seldom shared with his housekeeper? (To her relief, for she wasn't much for theology. She went to kirk, absorbed the sermon, and tried to live according to the Bible's teachings, and surely that was enough for any God-fearing woman.)

When confronted with the question, "And how is the dear Minister?" she'd merely grunted in reply at first, only to find that reply discouraged only the faintest of hearts. She would be stared at encouragingly until she finally managed to blurt out something to the effect that the Minister seemed to be coming down with a bit of a cold, even if he wasn't, or that he had a lovely rose in bloom that was giving him pleasure, or that he'd enjoyed the roast beef dinner she'd fixed last Saturday night. The last type of remark caused her no end of embarrassment, for she'd been brought up to believe that it was un-Christian to boast.

The question after the one about the Minister's health was the one she was coming to dread the most, for her conversational partner would invariably bring Mrs. Helen into the conversation. The timid gossip would venture something like, "That Helen Munro is a lovely person, isn't she," while the bolder would strike out with, "Is the dear Minister still walking out with that Mrs. Helen?"

And how did one respond to that, when she'd been brought up to believe that it was un-Christian to gossip?

It was a puzzle, for Raonaid knew that whatever she said would be received with the eagerness of a cat receiving a dish of cream, and would be all over the Island within hours.

Without her quite realizing it, she began to take a wee bit of pleasure in being an important source of information. It was wicked, and she felt a wee bit of guilt as well, but it was also flattering to be greeted with interest, and she was ever so slowly becoming addicted to it.

So she started to take careful note of the Minister's activities, and especially those with Mrs. Helen, so that she would have something to say. She tried to keep her remarks innocent and as gossip-free as possible, but it was becoming harder and harder to keep her mouth from rattling on, when she was stared at with such eager interest.

This interest in the Minister's romance began to make her aware that her position as housekeeper might be in jeopardy if Donald and Mrs. Helen followed through to what appeared to be a more and more obvious result, and it sent a cold chill down her spine when she first realized this. She was over seventy, with a touch of arthritis, and had often thought it would be pleasant to retire to her little cottage with her cats and her fireplace and do only for herself, and not for a man whose thoughts were so lofty that he never noticed whether the mantelpiece was dusted or that his meal was delicious. She'd never thought seriously of retiring, though; her excuse was that the Minister needed her efforts, and it was her duty to care for him so that he could care for Eilean Dubh's spiritual needs.

To retire on her own was one thing, however. To be forced into it because another woman had usurped her position was quite another.

She grew a little resentful of the incomer, and had to bite her tongue often to keep from saying something sharp about her to the gossipmongers. Gossip was wicked, so she'd been taught; and spiteful gossip was the Devil's own language.

Ten

My heart is sair—I darena tell—
My heart is sair for Somebody;
I could wake a winter night
For the sake o' Somebody.

Robert Burns

Helen Munro was astonished, at her age, to find herself the object of a man's interest. And such a man; the highly respected Minister of the Free Presbyterian Kirk, and he was muckle bonnie, too, tall, imposing, craggy-featured, with such piercing gray eyes that she had to suppress a shiver every time he looked at her in that particular way.

He'd looked at her that way the first time they'd met, at Eilidh and Joe's wedding, and she'd been shivery then, too, to think that she'd attracted his interest, and not knowing why. She'd thought about him often after she'd gone back home, and had devoured any references to him that appeared in Joe's letters. Joe had a great deal of respectful affection for the Minister; they got together every week and discussed his sermons. Joe had written that the discussions stretched his mind, and that Minister Donald was a very intelligent man who cared deeply about the welfare of his Island and the souls for which he was responsible.

Gradually Donald had faded into her memory as a flattering interlude, and she'd not thought much about seeing him again when Joe invited her to Eilean Dubh for an extended stay that summer. She'd just retired from her job as office manager with the insurance company in her town, and was at loose ends. She'd always been active in her church, and she planned on keeping busy with the Ladies' Guild after retirement. But somehow flower arranging for the altar, taking meals to invalids, and helping out in the church library had not been as fulfilling as she'd expected, after she'd left a job that had required a great deal of mental energy, especially after the office had acquired computers and she'd been expected to learn how to operate them and trouble-shoot them too. She'd done that with great success, and enjoyed feeling her mind stretching in the process.

She was, in fact, bored, after six weeks of retirement, and the opportunity to spend some time on beautiful Eilean Dubh had been very appealing. Taking nature walks in the clean fresh Island air would help settle her mind into leisure mode, and she relished the idea of having two people to cook for instead of lonely meals for herself, as had been her situation for so many years since the children had all gone their separate ways. Eilidh had received a commission to compose a piece of music for her orchestra in Edinburgh, a great honor at her age, and a project which made her very nervous. Joe had written that she would enjoy having someone to help with meal preparation, for, as he'd said, "Supper time always seems to roll around just when she's deepest in concentration on her work, and the notes get all mixed up in her mind if she has to stop and cook."

Helen was not so sure that her daughter-in-law would like another woman in her kitchen, and was very reassured when she arrived to find that Eilidh welcomed her with open arms and a clean apron. Lately Eilidh had had several kitchen disasters when she'd been concentrating on treble clefs instead of on frying trout, and she was delighted to turn over the supper preparation to her mother-in-law while she finished her composition. "I'm so glad to see you, Helen dear!" she'd exclaimed. "Poor Joe's had more than his share of charcoal for his meals lately, Old Dog isn't getting his walkies, and I'm weeks behind in my work. You're a lifesaver."

Cooking suppers left Helen plenty of time for reading and nature walks with Old Dog, and she settled in happily, delighted to be of use to someone once more. Being a devout woman, she expected to go to church every Sunday, and was a bit dismayed to be told that the service was entirely in the Gaelic, which she didn't speak. "Oh, well, I'll just enjoy the stained glass windows and the organ music and the choir, and read the English translation afterwards that Joe gets of the sermons," she said cheerfully. She was a bit taken aback to learn that there was neither stained glass windows nor organ nor choir, just a severely plain building with a severely plain interior. And there were no hymns. Instead the entire congregation sang Psalms after the precentor lined them out, as was the practice of the Free Presbyterians.

Still, it was a church service, and she felt at home when she first settled herself into the hard wooden pews of the old gray building. She would think lofty thoughts, she told herself and be revived by the atmosphere, even if she didn't understand what was going on.

Then she looked up at the pulpit that first Sunday and saw Donald and he saw her, and a spark flashed between them and the cold kirk grew warm for both of them.

It was a very strange sensation to feel in church, Helen thought uneasily. She knew she was turning pink, and ducked her head so suddenly that the flowered hat slid forward. She berated herself mentally for being so silly, settled her hat back in place and sat up straight, hands folded, in an attitude of the perfect listener.

She and Donald took care that their glances did not meet again until after the service was over, and they met at the door of the kirk. Then they exchanged a smile of perfect understanding, and he invited her, and Eilidh and Joe, of course, to tea. That was the day their relationship truly began.

A warm and gregarious woman, Helen made friends easily, and the first friend she made was Jean Mac an Rìgh. Jean had dropped into Joe and Eilidh's cottage one afternoon to return a cup of sugar she'd borrowed, and found that though Eilidh was distracted by counterpoint, Helen was quite available for a chat and a cuppa. She and Jean found at once that they had things in common, for both were incomers to the quirky world of Eilean Dubh, and they spent a comfortable two hours comparing notes about the differences among America, the Borders country of Scotland, and a tiny little island.

And there was Rosie helping to form a bond. Helen was one of those people whom children instantly recognize as kindred spirits and to whom they gravitate for mysterious reasons all their own. Rosie stared, and edged closer, and soon was pressed up against Helen's legs, her thumb in her mouth, her hand absently fingering Helen's skirt. Helen picked her up and placed her on her lap, never losing a beat in the conversation.

Amused, Jean said, "Rosie, this is Helen. Say, 'hello, Helen.'"

Rosie said, "Hel hel."

Both women chuckled. "Hello, Helen," said Jean again.

Rosie looked obstinate, and said, "Hel. Not 'hello.' Hel hel." She repeated it twice more, in a little carol, then put her thumb in her mouth and sagged back against the older woman. "Hel," she said, and closed her eyes.

And try as Jean might, she could not get the little girl to say any more. Eventually she opened her eyes and looked at her mother, then up at Helen, and watched them placidly while they talked. When it was time to go home, she said, "Hel coming with Mama and Rosie?"

"No, lovie, Helen lives here with Eilidh and Joe."

"Rosie come see Hel tomorrow."

"I have a better idea. Let's ask Helen to come visit us."

"I'd love to. I'll see you then, Rosie."

The little girl observed the two women carefully. Then she said, sounding uncannily like her American mother, "Okay," and skipped out the door.

The friendship thus begun among Rosie, Jean, and Helen grew and strengthened as the days went on. "She's a terrific woman," Jean observed to Darroch. "If Donald has his wits about him, he'll snap her up, marry her, and keep her here on the Island."

Darroch looked dubious. It was a fine idea, but he didn't think it was as simple as Jean made it sound. Donald was hardly the "snapping-up" type; he was thoughtful and deliberate in every action he took and by the time he'd made his mind up, Helen likely would have gotten bored with Eilean Dubh and tripped back to the Borders. It was too bad, but he couldn't think of any way to speed up the process.

For her part, Helen knew she was growing very attached to Minister Donald. She hadn't liked a man so much since her husband had died, and had never expected to, and she found her respect for him growing with every conversation they had. Serious, intense, and thoughtful, high-principled and devout, Donald was the sort of man she could admire and look up to for the rest of her days. And still, she could make a little joke, and get a chuckle and a rusty smile out of him, and it made her heart expand with happiness whenever that happened.

And she thought he was fond of her. He was not a person to trifle with another's affections, and she owed him the same respect. If she could not envision herself living on Eilean Dubh, in the Minister's house and in his bed for the rest of her life, it was her duty to decide that at once and retreat, before things got any more serious between them.

The trouble with that was that she could all too easily see herself in the role of the Minister's wife. She and Donald got along like the proverbial house on fire; they made each other laugh, and it was astonishing how similar their thought patterns were. They'd even begun completing each other's sentences, something that astonished both of them the first time it happened. Mutual affection was burning brightly between them, and needed only a few more puffs of wind to fan it into the blaze of love.

Eilean Dubh was beautiful, its people were, for the most part, agreeable, and there would be plenty of work here for an active, vigorous, minister's wife. There hadn't been one in the Ros Mór area for ten years, not since Donald's first wife had died, and the work had been piling up. There was no Young People's Guild, no Bible Study group, no Fellowship Teas. The women of Ros Mór had tried to fill in, but they were all too busy with their own lives to provide the kind of lay leadership that a minister's wife could.

And Donald needed help in organizing his schedule, so that he wasn't run off his feet with his parishioners' needs, and had time for inner contemplation so necessary to keep his soul afloat. Yes, there was work here for Helen to do, and she relished the idea of becoming a busy, useful member of the community. She had quite fallen in love with Eilean Dubh and the quiet pace of life suited her down to the ground. She wanted so much to be a part of it.

She lay awake nights thinking about it all. Oh, Helen, she thought, it's a slippery slope you're on, getting interested in a man and an Island, and not knowing whether or not either one of them wants you. In the end it came down to one question. Did she love Donald, and did he love her? And if he did, would he ever get around to telling her that?

What would she say if he did tell her?

Late one night she played devil's advocate, and thought about going home, and was swept with such a wave of pain and longing she knew her answer. She loved this difficult, complicated, endearing man, and was beginning to love his quirky little Island.

Did he love her? She hoped desperately that he did, and that he would pluck up the courage, soon, to tell her so.

Eleven

Ye powers that smile on virtuous love,
O, sweetly smile on Somebody!
Frae ilka danger keep him free,
And send me safe my Somebody.

Robert Burns

*U*naware of the tumult in his housekeeper's breast, the tumult in his beloved's mind, and keenly aware of the tumult in his own heart and soul, Minister Donald was approaching the sticking point as far as courage was concerned.

He had never expected to fall in love again. He had loved his wife Elizabeth dearly and deeply, and suffered with her in her struggle with breast cancer. They'd come to Edinburgh every Monday and left for home every Friday for weeks while she was receiving treatment, traveling back and forth on Murdoch the Chopper's helicopter, a nauseating, exhausting trip that Elizabeth had endured bravely, as she'd endured everything else connected with her illness. Then in Edinburgh she'd taken a sudden turn for the worst, and it was obvious that her time was short. Donald had bowed to the inevitable, and planned to take her back to Eilean Dubh so that she could die at home surrounded by her friends and family, but before that could happen she slipped away quietly one night.

Instead of a wife, he escorted a coffin home. He was desolate, but oddly enough, Elizabeth's illness and death did not shake his faith. He did not rage against God, or demand to know why his gentle, kind-hearted wife had had to suffer while murderers and thieves lived and prospered. He accepted it all. Elizabeth had borne her cross, and her death was his cross to bear for the rest of his life.

Now he'd been granted a reprieve from the loneliness he'd endured for ten years. He loved Helen and he hoped, he thought, he prayed that she loved him too, and would be willing to spend their remaining days together on his beloved Island.

Suddenly time became important, and he was impatient to move on to the next, joyous phase. He was, after all, over sixty years old, and Helen Munro was close to that, and time was marching on. He was perfectly clear in his own mind that he loved Helen and wanted to marry her. He just couldn't figure out how to ask her.

At last, in desperation, he invited over for a confidential chat and a bit of advice the one man on the Island he considered his closest friend, someone he could trust without reservation not to snicker behind his hand at an old man's love affair or blab all the details: Darroch Mac an Rìgh. He'd given Darroch wise counsel any number of times, and now it was time for the favor to be returned.

Darroch had no idea what to expect from this meeting; he thought maybe the Minister wanted to talk about renovating the old gray stone kirk, or setting up a youth program for Island teenagers. He settled back in his chair, and looked at the Minister expectantly.

"*A Dharroch* . . . I'm wondering how you proposed to Mrs. Jean," said Donald.

Darroch quivered with shock, and blushed bright red. He had popped the question to Jean after a particularly spirited and delicious bout of love-making, and he certainly couldn't share that with his Minister, even with the juiciest details expurgated. He inhaled deeply, and parried the question. "May I ask why you are inquiring?"

The Minister wondered at the impact of what he'd considered a purely innocent question. Knowing Darroch's flare for the dramatic, he'd expected an answer involving going down on one knee, or a romantic setting like a windswept meadow full of flowers. Obviously that had not been the case. "My question is not asked out of idle curiosity," he said stiffly.

Darroch had recovered his composure. "Of course not. But regardless of how I proposed, I wouldn't recommend it to anyone, for Jean refused me. As you may remember, she insisted on being handfast instead of married for longer than I care to think about, and it was only her pregnancy that made her agree to marry me."

"Hmmm." The Minister did remember; Jean and Darroch's handfasting had been a major sensation and had only just skirted the edge of scandal. He'd never understood what that had been about, but clearly it wasn't an example he intended to follow. Might as well come out with it, he thought, and said, "I am wishing to ask for Helen Munro's hand in marriage, and am a wee bit uncertain as to how to go about it. I'm out of practice in sweet-talking a lady."

"I see." About time, thought Darroch, for the Island had had the pair of them engaged for a month now, and was beginning to gossip about the delay in an announcement. "I'm delighted to hear it, *a Mhinistear*, for she's a grand woman, and will fit right into our Island. How to ask her? Let me think for a moment."

The Minister waited nervously. If it was to be a windswept meadow, he was sure he could find a nice flowery spot, but if proposing meant getting down on one knee, he was not at all sure he could handle it. Even if he managed the getting down, the getting up would require a boost from a convenient hard surface, and would make him look like a ridiculous old man.

"A romantic setting is important," announced Darroch.

So it was to be a meadow, after all. The Minister nodded in resignation. Perhaps if he did some exercises, practiced the getting up and the getting down, he could pull it off just once. It was not as if it was something he was going to make a practice of doing.

"What about your rose garden?" said Darroch, struck by a sudden flash of brilliance.

The garden! It was liberally spotted with stone benches with which to help himself down and up, and it would soften Helen to be around the roses that she loved. He breathed a sigh of relief. "That's a grand idea. But what am I to say?"

"*Gabh mo leisgeul, a Mhinistear*, but what are your feelings for Mrs. Helen? That is, do you love her, and do you think she loves you?"

"I'm sure that I love her, and I have every reason to believe that she has affection for me as well."

"Then that's all you need to say. 'I love you, Helen, and I would be honored if you'd marry me.' That should do the trick."

"But am I not to advise her of my financial situation, and assure her that I can take care of her if we wed?"

"It's not a business merger, *a charaid*, and I'm sure Helen is not concerned about being taken care of, for she's been a widow and managed on her own for many years. It's my guess that it's love and companionship she's looking for, and you might sweeten the offer by pledging to love her faithfully until eternity, something like that."

The Minister looked indignant, and said, "Of course I'll be faithful. Anything else would be outrageous, and I'm not that kind of man."

"It's just a bit of poetry, *a Dhòmhnall*. Women like that sort of thing. But if it makes you uncomfortable, I suggest you stick to the tried and true: I love you. Please marry me. Six little words, that's all it takes."

"So I take her out into the rose garden, and that's all I say?"

"Spot on, *a Mhinistear*."

Donald was relieved that the matter could be handled that simply. He rose. "I'm indebted to you, *a Dharroch*. Might I offer you a whisky, to celebrate this important occasion?"

I certainly need one after that conversation, sprang to Darroch's lips but he stifled it just in time, and said only, "Glad to be of help. A whisky would be most welcome."

Donald turned and looked at his friend suddenly. "I hope you don't think I'm a foolish old man, wanting to marry at my time of life."

"I do not, for I was a newlywed myself at the advanced age of forty, and I can recommend marriage as the most delightful of states for any man of any age. *Slàinte mhath*," he said, clinking his glass with Donald's, "and the best of British luck to you."

Twelve

Duncan Gray cam here to woo,
Ha, ha, the wooing o't,
On blythe Yule night when we were fou,
Ha, ha, the wooing o't.
Maggie coost her head fu' high,
Look'd asklent and unco skeigh,
Gart poor Duncan stand abeigh;
Ha, ha, the wooing o't.

Robert Burns

*P*roposing in the garden required a sunny day and an invitation to tea. Unfortunately, after a month of unusually warm and lovely weather, Eilean Dubh skies grew cloudy, and rain threatened and usually occurred, every afternoon. The Minister listened to the BBC weather report in the morning, anxiously wondering as to whether or not today was to be the Big Day. It required advance planning, and he could not invite Helen over for tea each afternoon; it would seem most peculiar.

It would also be presuming on Raonaid's good humor, which seemed somehow to be eclipsed these days. She was going around with a face like doom, gloomier even than usual, and it was in the back of his mind to sit her down for a little chat and ask if something was bothering her. It was his Christian duty to inquire if she had a trouble with which he could help.

He was uneasily aware that he was not the easiest person to look after, and he knew that he had been preoccupied and distant lately. Had he offended her in some way? If so, it was his responsibility to put it right. Had he trespassed against one of her unwritten rules of housekeeping? He'd made sure that his dirty underwear and socks were tucked neatly in the clothes hamper, and that he was on time for meals, rather than sitting in his study worrying over a sermon, so that she had to call him repeatedly to come to supper. He knew from long experience that these were things that upset her, and he was being especially careful about her feelings, for he knew that his marrying Helen would seriously disrupt Raonaid's running of the household. She was a proud woman, and would not take kindly to having a mistress to supplant her authority.

But regardless of Raonaid's emotional state, he had to get Helen into the rose garden so that he could propose, and the only way to do that was to ask her over for tea. So he listened to the forecast, and went outside to check the sky to confirm that just as the radio said, there was indeed a threat of afternoon showers.

At last one morning dawned unusually bright and the sky was free of clouds. The BBC weather forecaster announced cheerily that it would be fine and sunny throughout Scotland. Donald took courage, and set his plans in motion. He called Helen, received her assent to a visit, and braved Raonaid's gloom to announce that there would be a guest for tea that afternoon.

She looked at him glumly, muttered something cross about having to postpone her plans to turn out the spare bedroom and to organize closets, and stomped back into the kitchen to make her preparations for the meal. She was perfectly aware of what he was up to, and figured that her days as housekeeper were numbered. She underscored her displeasure by making sure that the tea would be a special event, with the best dishes and the elegant second best lace cloth on the table, and by baking the Minister's favorite scones and her renowned tea cakes. Let him see what he'll be missing if he brings that woman in to replace me, she thought crankily.

Helen arrived. Attentive to nuance as always, she took note of the dishes and the lace tablecloth, and commented on how attractive everything looked and how delicious the food was. Raonaid growled acknowledgement of the compliments, and retreated into the kitchen, nose in the air.

Now was the time, Donald thought, taking a deep breath, and praying for courage to carry out his mission. "Would you care for a stroll in the garden, Helen dear?" he asked.

She noted the endearment, and hope sprang alive in her breast. Her legs were a little trembly, and the hand she placed on Donald's arm shook. He led her to the stone bench that was hidden from sight of the house and the road, and they sat down.

He was struck dumb. He was a self-assured and confident man, but a humble one as well, and it suddenly occurred to him that he was not worthy of this lovely woman, and that he was presuming too far on her good nature to ask her to share his simple life on this simple little Island. What if she said no? The thought gave him a sudden attack of nerves.

The time of silence stretched onward. Helen was on the brink of deciding that she had made a mistake. The Minister did not love her, and he was not going to ask her to marry him. She'd got it all wrong, and soon she'd be going back to her little Border town to spend the rest of her life alone and miserably lonely. Gloom threatened.

But she was a woman who was by nature cheerful and upbeat, and she preferred the devil she knew to the one hidden by doubt. She would give him a little encouragement, and if that did not work, she would have her answer. "This is a lovely garden, Donald," she said bravely. "To my mind, it shows the goodness of its maker."

Theologically attuned as always, the Minister thought her reference was a religious one. "You mean the Lord, I assume."

"No, I mean you," she said, surprised. "The Lord provided the sun and the rain and the good soil, but it's the work of the gardener that makes the flowers."

"Ah." Much struck by her comment, he mused briefly on the idea that it would make a good sermon; the Lord provides, but it is up to His people to make proper use of what is provided. What would be the relevant Biblical quotations? Then he came back to *miorbhuileach* reality. She thought he was a good man, and said so. That was most encouraging. He opened his mouth to speak.

But Helen was not done. She forged bravely onward. If nothing was to come of her relationship with Donald, at least she could tell him, discreetly, how she felt about him; that would afford her some satisfaction, anyway, in the long lonely future. "Joe said wonderful things about you in his letters to me, and now that I've gotten to know you, I am in full agreement with his opinion of you."

"Do you really think so?" said the Minister, his self-doubt slipping away.

"I'm not in the habit of telling falsehoods," she said primly, and looked away at a fine blossom on the Love and Peace rose bush.

"I would like to say that your sentiment is reciprocated," blurted Donald. "It's my observation that you are one of the finest women I've ever met."

"Oh," she began, overwhelmed, but the Minister was not through. His tongue now assumed the character of a runaway horse, and he said, gaining strength as he spoke, "In fact, my dear, dearest Helen, I find that I am deeply in love with you."

Helen stared at him, eyes wide. Things were taking a sudden, dramatic, delightful turn.

"And . . ." Donald suddenly remembered Darroch's suggestions about the importance of romance. He gathered his strength, and slipped to the ground on one knee in front of his beloved, not even noticing that the knee landed on a particularly sharp piece of rock. "I would like to ask for the honor of your hand in marriage."

"My goodness," Helen said. "It's like a dream come true."

"Is it? Does that mean . . . might I hope . . . will you . . . "

"Yes, I will." Helen bent forward, took his face between her hands, and kissed him.

An un-forecast, totally unexpected rain began, and was totally unnoticed by the lovers, who kissed with an enthusiasm born of years of kiss-deprivation. Donald sprang from his knees, quite forgetting that it was impossible for him to do so, and drew his beloved to her feet and enfolded her in his arms. Between kisses, he murmured, "I was so afraid to ask you."

"I was so afraid you wouldn't," she whispered.

He drew back and looked at her. "Were you, truly? Does it mean so much to you, to marry me?"

"It means the world," she said simply. "There's nothing more important to me than to spend the rest of my life with you."

"Even if it means spending that life on this wee Island?"

"I love this Island," she replied. "I know I'll be happy here."

Delighted, he kissed her again, and they stood together in the rain, getting soaked, and not noticing it at all.

Eventually they pulled themselves together and went into the house, scattering raindrops and muddy footprints all over. The Minister was all for calling Raonaid in and telling her the good news, but was dissuaded by Helen who felt uneasily that the situation called for more discretion, and that Raonaid would be too upset by the muddy mess to listen calmly. Best make themselves least in sight, until the housekeeper had mopped up and cooled down. "I want to tell Joe and Eilidh first."

"Of course, I quite forgot. I should ask Joe for his permission to marry you."

"Permission . . .?"

"He's your closest male relative," explained Donald. "That's the proper way to do things."

Helen was struck by a fit of giggles at the idea of her son being asked for permission to marry his mother, and laughed all the way to Eilidh and Joe's cottage.

Joe had just gotten home, roused Eilidh out of her absorption in arpeggios, and now both stood in the kitchen looking around distractedly, wondering why Helen was not bustling about with the supper. "Did she say she was going out?" asked Joe.

"I can't remember," admitted Eilidh, who'd been wrestling all afternoon with a passage in her composition that she simply could not get to come out right.

"She must have gone for a walk and lost track of the time," said Joe. Then he realized that Old Dog was standing next to him. Helen would not have taken a walk without the dog. He and Eilidh stared at each other, baffled. Then Joe went to the refrigerator and opened it. "She'll turn up. Let's surprise her by having supper well under way when she gets home."

They were setting the table when Helen and Donald walked in, and one look at their faces told the story. Eilidh blurted, "Oh, he's asked you! Oh, Helen dear, how *miorbhuileach!*" and she flew to throw her arms around her mother-in-law.

"How on earth did you know?" exclaimed Helen, who had thought, foolishly, that her personal affairs and the state of her heart were known only to herself. Despite the temptation, she'd not even confided in Jean, even though the two of them were developing a close friendship, based partly on the fact that Rosie had fallen quite in love with gentle Helen, and she'd wanted desperately to share her feelings and worries.

"Oh, everyone knows," bubbled Eilidh. "We've all been waiting for the announcement."

"That's Eilean Dubh, Mother," said Joe. "Everybody knows everybody else's business. You'd best get used to it." He smiled at the surprised look on the Minister's face.

Helen smiled, and squeezed her betrothed's arm. "I'll have a lot of things to get used to, and I'm going to love every minute of it."

Next day Raonaid was told the news by the Minister, and she immediately tendered her resignation, to Donald's surprise. He'd thought that everything would continue as before.

She offered her congratulations, and said firmly that she would go, despite his protestations to the contrary. "There can't be two women running a house," she said, to his bafflement.

Helen was not baffled by the statement, and took her courage in both hands to smooth what she knew were injured feelings on the part of the housekeeper. She knocked on the kitchen door one afternoon. "May I come in, Mrs. Ross?"

"Of course, Mrs. Munro," snapped Raonaid. "It's not my place to deny you entrance to any of the rooms, for it will soon be your house."

Not getting off to a good start, Helen thought. "I wanted to talk to you about that."

"Certainly," said Raonaid, stiffly polite. "Will you take a cup of tea?"

"That would be most welcome," said Helen, seating herself at the table.

When the tea was in front of them, the two women sat staring at each other.

"Well," began Helen. "You've heard our news."

"Congratulations," said Raonaid coolly. "I hope you'll be very happy."

"Thank you." She decided that there was no need to equivocate, and plunged boldly forward. "Donald tells me that you've resigned your position as housekeeper."

"I have."

"And quite right," said Helen, to Raonaid's surprise, for she'd expected at least a token request that she stay on, which she would refuse, of course. "For there can be only one woman in charge of a house. Donald has told me what a help you've been to him all these years. He's said that he thought you often might have preferred to retire but that you stayed on out of loyalty to him. He's very grateful for that, and says he'd never have been able to manage without you in these years since his wife died."

"He's quite welcome. It was my duty." Raonaid put her long thin nose in the air.

Helen plunged right in, though the other woman's attitude was daunting, to say the least. "I'm wondering if I might be the one now to receive your help."

"Of course." Raonaid nodded grimly. Now there would be requests for the Minister's favorite recipes, information on the meals he preferred, and other gems of housewifely advice to smooth the usurper's way. She'd provide it, of course; it was her Christian duty, but she wasn't going to make it easy for Helen.

"I have never been a minister's wife before, but I know it involves much more than keeping house for one man. I was very active in my church's Ladies' Guild back home, and a close friend of Reverend Tom's wife, and I am aware that I will be expected to minister, in my own way, to Donald's parishioners. It's in that context that I would appreciate help."

Raonaid stared at her in surprise.

"I have Donald's permission to ask you if you would accept employment as my personal assistant."

"What?"

"Your duties would include assisting me in entertaining, for I intend to invite all of the women of the parish to tea, not all at once of course, so that I can get to know them and get their ideas on how I can be of help to our kirk. I don't mean that you would just help with the cooking, although I know how accomplished you are in that way."

"What exactly do you mean?"

"You see, Raonaid—may I call you that?—you know everyone here. You'd know, for example, that Mrs. X can't stand Mrs. Y, and that the two of them should not be invited at the same time. So you'd help me plan the guest lists for each meal so that I don't make any blunders. For setting up committees, you'd know who's skilled at what, and who can be depended upon, and who can't."

A faint hope was growing in Raonaid's breast. Personal assistant, Helen Munro had said. That would be an important contribution to the kirk, and would be free of such disagreeable tasks as mending socks and folding underwear. And besides, she liked the modern, smart sound of the title.

"And there's lots more. I'll want to begin visits to folks in the hospital and to the homebound at the Seniors' Residence. That's work I can take off Donald's shoulders, and you can help me schedule those and tell me about the people I'll be meeting. And do we need a new mothers' support group? A Bible study class? A club for teenagers?

"You understand so much more about the needs of Eilean Dubh than I do, and you can help point me in the ways I can be most useful to my new home, as well as to my new husband."

"I don't know what to say," murmured Raonaid, while her heart beat a happy tattoo in her breast. She was not old and useless; she would have a new purpose in life.

"I hope you'll say yes," said Helen frankly. "For I'm in desperate need of someone to guide me, and both Donald and I think you're just the person to do it." She added, "Of course it won't be full time, for you've earned your retirement, and I know you'll be looking forward to some leisure."

Useful work during the day, and her cats and the telly at night, with no worries about tempting a man's finicky appetite at the next meal or doing his laundry. Raonaid sighed happily.

"Do say yes," urged Helen.

"I'm overwhelmed, Mrs. Munro."

"Please call me Helen."

"Helen. And if I might just have a moment to think about it?" said Raonaid, although her mind was made up already.

"Of course."

Raonaid smiled her rare smile. "Will you just take another cup of tea, Helen, and may I tempt you with another bit of shortbread?"

"Thank you. It's delicious. I've never had any luck with making short-bread. Mine always crumbles and falls apart."

"Ah, well, there's a secret to that, you see. I'll be delighted to show you, if you like, some one of these days when we're working together."

Helen, feeling she'd conquered Mount Everest, raised her cup. "I'll drink to that, Raonaid. To a long and useful association for the benefit of the people of Eilean Dubh, for our kirk and our minister. And to learning how to make shortbread."

"Amen to all of that," said Raonaid.

Thirteen

Love rules the court, the camp, the grove,
And men below, and saints above;
For love is heaven, and heaven is love.

Sir Walter Scott

The wedding was arranged quickly, for at their age, Donald said, it was best to move along smartly, so they could enjoy together the time they had left on earth. This seemed a rather gloomy way to look at it, Helen thought, and told him so, earning a smile of acknowledgement from him. Helen's outlook was cheerful and sunny, and her optimism was beginning to rub off on him.

Summoned to Eilean Dubh for the wedding were Joe's sisters Laura and Betty, Laura's husband Bob and Betty's partner Marilyn (which the Minister, in his innocence, thought meant that they were in business together, and no one disabused him of that notion; there would be plenty of time for that later). Invitations to a select group of *Eilean Dubhannaich* were sent out. Donald knew that everyone would be pining to come and watch him plight his troth, and he had no intention of his wedding becoming a source of public entertainment. At his age, and Helen's, they were entitled to a bit of dignity and privacy.

The officiating minister would of course be Tormod, from the Airgead Free Presbyterian parish. Donald and he had their theological differences, Tormod being fond of fire and brimstone in his sermons, and Donald preferring an earthier, though no less firm, approach. To Donald's annoyance, Tormod thought the idea of a man his age marrying was quite amusing, and joked that he should have the couple in for the pre-marital interview to which he subjected all his young couples. Donald put his foot down on that idea quite firmly, so firmly that he almost caused offense to his pompous opposite number, and it was left to Helen to smooth things over.

She gave Tormod one of her sweetest smiles, murmured that it was so kind of him to offer, but that she thought that it wasn't necessary for him to waste his valuable time in counseling a man and woman who'd been previously married and happily so. "I may have forgotten a thing or two about how to be a wife," she said, "but I'm sure it will all come back to me. And if it doesn't, I'll be sure to give you a shout."

Tormod was mollified, and couldn't help responding with a smile. Donald was struck with admiration at her tact, for Tormod was apt to be prickly and irritable. Such tact, Donald thought, was a valuable asset for a minister's wife; he'd chosen wisely.

Eilidh was matron of honor for her mother-in-law, and Darroch was asked to stand up for Donald. Joe Munro, of course, would escort his mother down the aisle. "Are you nervous, Helen dear?" Eilidh asked her, as the little party gathered at the entrance to the church.

"Oh, I'm scared to flinders," Helen replied, "and it's only the fact that I love the man that gives me the courage to go through with it."

Donald, waiting nervously at the altar, echoed her sentiment. "*Misneach*"—courage—whispered Darroch in his ear, with a chuckle of amusement, remembering that the same word had been whispered to him several years ago when he and Jean had taken their vows. Marriage takes courage, he thought, even if you loved the woman as much as he loved his Jean.

The small party began to walk down the aisle. Rosie, in a pretty flowered dress, was seated by her mother, and when everyone turned to see the bride, she turned, too, wondering what everyone was looking at. She pulled herself to her feet in the pew, and to her delight, she caught sight of her dear friend Helen coming towards her. She shouted in excitement, "Hel!"

The congregation froze in shock. Whoever could have uttered such a word in the Lord's house?

Rosie caroled happily, "Oh, Hel, Hel, Hel!"

Helen was overcome by giggles, and clutched Joe's arm to steady herself.

The congregation wiggled, rustled, and stared, and finally recognized the small culprit who was the source of the words. They chuckled and bit their lips to keep from laughing aloud.

Mortified, Jean tried to shush her daughter. "No, Mama! It's my Hel," the little girl cried. She twisted away from her mother's grasping hands, slid off the pew, and ran to catch up with the bride. She slid her hand into Helen's, and marched proudly down the aisle with her.

The members of the wedding party looked in confusion at each other and at the small addition to their group. Dreadfully embarrassed, Darroch said, "I'm sorry, Donald. I'll take her to her mother."

"No, let me speak to her." Donald knelt and whispered in the child's ear, "Rosie, *m'eudail,* I know you love Helen, and so do I. Will you be a good girl, now, and go back to Mama so that I can marry the lady I love so much, so that she'll stay with us on our Island?"

"Hel stay here?"

"Yes, child, if you'll be very quiet and let us get married. Can you do that?"

Rosie thought carefully, then said, "Okay."

"Good lass. Now go to Mama, and be as quiet as a wee mousie."

Rosie nodded. She turned and walked sedately back to her mother, climbed up on the pew and sat with her hands folded in her lap, the picture of propriety.

"Well done, Donald," said Darroch quietly.

Minister Donald smiled, and looked at his beloved, whose eyes were full of laughter and admiration. With great dignity, he said to Tormod, "You may proceed, *a Mhinistear.*"

And the marriage ceremony continued to its conclusion.

The congregation all but hugged themselves in satisfaction. Not only were they the elect chosen to be present at their Minister's wedding; they'd been witness to the charming intervention of the Laird's daughter in the ceremony. A grand story, and one that would pass into Island legend, about the little girl who'd shouted, "Hel!" in the kirk.

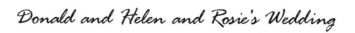

Donald and Helen and Rosie's Wedding

8 X 32 Jig for three couples in longwise set

Devised by Audrey McClellan with the assistance of Bonny McIntyre.

Tune: "Donald and Helen and Rosie's Wedding," by Sherry Ladig.

1-4   1C turn RH and dance down set to 3W; 2C step up

5-8   1C and 3W dance RHA

9-16   1W followed by 1M followed by 3W chase around 3M, across
        the set and behind 2W to top of set to end between 2C: 1W fac-
        ing 2M, 1M facing 2W, and 3W out of set at top facing down.

17-24   1C and 2C dance reel of 4 across the set while 3W (The
        "Rosie") dances setting steps of her choice (such as pas de
        basque coupée, or pas de basque turning over RS, then pas de
        basque turning over LS).

25-28   LHA 1W, 3W, 1M

29-32   1W followed by 3W chase behind 2W and turn by RH, 1W
        finishing in 2nd place, while 1M casts behind 2M, turn 2M by
        LH, turn 3M by RH to finish in 2nd place.

It was a morning wedding, with a luncheon to follow, and after that Donald and his bride escaped by Murdoch the Chopper's helicopter to Inverness. There they picked up a rental car, and drove off to a charming little Highland hotel for their honeymoon.

Both Donald and Helen were apprehensive about the wedding night. They'd exchanged only kisses prior to their marriage, and the idea of making love loomed both delightfully and terrifyingly in their minds.

Helen had sought advice from Jean, who'd been at a loss to know what to tell her, and had finally said, "Just let nature take its course, I guess. It'll get easier when you know each other better."

"I'm so glad you didn't tell me to lie back and think of England!" blurted Helen.

"What? Oh, that old Victorian nonsense. Um, you, um, enjoyed, um, sex with your first husband, didn't you? If you don't mind my asking, that is."

"Oh, yes. But that was years ago, I thought maybe things were different today. I mean, maybe there's some fancy new stuff we're supposed to do."

"Some things never change, Helen," Jean assured her.

Donald, also nervous, had turned once again to Darroch for counsel, and was able to articulate his fears a little more boldly. "I understand that it is my duty to satisfy my wife," he said, "even though I'm not quite sure what that means."

Darroch, acutely uncomfortable at being Donald's confidant—he was the Minister, after all—wished that Jamie, renowned for his romantic prowess, had been chosen instead. Jamie never minded talking about sex. "You've been married before, Donald. Did you and Elizabeth make each other happy when you made love?"

"Yes, I think so," said Donald dubiously. "She always came willingly into my arms, and whispered to me afterwards that she loved me."

'Why are you worried, then?"

"It's been over ten years since I have lain with a woman, and I have forgotten how to initiate marital relations."

"Ah. It's the getting started that worries you."

"That is my dilemma, aye."

Darroch considered carefully. "I recommend a good dinner, with a bottle of wine to loosen both of you up, and afterwards, sit yourselves down in front of a fire in the fireplace."

"And then?"

"Well, you know. Kisses, and a bit of love talk and more kisses, and let your hands do what they want to . . . " He stopped, not wanting to go into further detail.

"What sort of love talk?" demanded Donald.

"Tell her you love her, *a Dhòmhnall*," said Darroch patiently. "Tell her all the things that you love about her. How happy you are that she's chosen to spend her life with you. How beautiful her eyes are, and how sweet it is to hear her laugh."

"Aye, aye, it's coming back to me now. Go on."

"A woman likes to know that her man wants her," said Darroch. "Kiss her, and cuddle her, and say sweet things to her, and when the time is right, take her hand and lead her into the bedroom."

"How will I know when the time is right?"

"It's easy enough to know when the time is right for you, as you're a man. With women, it's a bit trickier. Maybe I should get you a book."

But Donald had been remembering his beloved first wife, and the little sighs of yielding and how soft her body became against his. *"Tapadh leat gu dearbh, a charaid,"* he said. "I think I can handle it from here."

Fourteen

Welcome, Fortune, welcome again,
The day and hour I may weel bliss,
Thou has exilit all my pain,
Whilk to my heart great pleasure is.

For I may say, that few men may,
Seeing of pain I am drest,
I have obtainit all my pay –
The love of her that I love best.

Anonymous

*E*ven with Darroch's counsel, Donald was nervous when he and Helen were alone, at last, in the cozy little suite in the cozy little hotel in a charming mountain pass just north of Inverness. They'd had the good supper and bottle of wine that Darroch had recommended, and come back upstairs a wee bit tiddly, for neither was used to drinking very much. "Shall we go to bed, Helen dear?" said Donald. "It's been a long day, and you must be tired."

Helen plucked up her courage, and said, "Yes, let's go to bed. And I'm not the least bit tired."

Donald stared at her, and she stared back. Then he bent and kissed her, gently. She moved closer. "I want to be a good wife to you, Donald. In all ways," she said. "And that means . . . " Her voice broke, and she could not continue. What had Jean advised her to do? Should she be coy, or bold? Take the initiative, or wait demurely for her bridegroom to act?

Donald had no trouble in remembering Darroch's advice. Talk to her sweetly, cuddle her, and when she seems ready, take her by the hand and lead her to bed. Putting his arms around her and drawing her close, he said, "My dear wife, I love you, and I want to hold you in my arms, and make love with you."

"Oh, Donald! Is it really that simple?"

"Aye, *mo fhlùr,* I think it is." He took her hand and turned toward the bedroom.

"Wait . . . I need to put on my fancy nightgown. I bought it just for you."

Donald whispered, "That was very thoughtful, but I don't think you'll be needing it tonight."

Helen smiled in relief. He smiled back. Hand in hand, they walked into the bedroom, and began their life together.

PART V

Anna and Zach Search for the Past

Fifteen

The exact date of Man's first settlement on Eilean Dubh is not known, but Legend on the Island tells of those who were there in the past. It is said that their dead were buried in mounds. There are many of these mounds on Eilean Dubh, and they are strictly avoided by the Islanders, for fear of disturbing the spirits. Certain areas now covered by beautiful wildflowers are also considered haunted, and no Islander will go near them, or talk about them in other than hushed voices. Such is the innocence of the Eilean Dubhannaich.

Robertson's Relics and Anomalies.

*A*nna Wallace possessed that essential attribute of all newspaper people, an insatiable curiosity. Her interest was intensely piqued by Zachariah Trelawney's archaeological quest. She reasoned that if she was going to be the one to break the big story about Eilean Dubh's prehistoric past, she'd better know what she was writing about. So she went up to the Library at Airgead, and Isabel Ross supplied her with books about the theory and practice of archaeology, and about great digs of the past, like King Tut's tomb and the Viking settlement at L'Anse aux Meadows in Newfoundland.

Her reading turned out to be quite fascinating, though some of the technical bits were beyond her. Asked one question, Zach proved delighted to explain at great length anything she didn't understand, and took to hanging around the newspaper office to talk to her when he wasn't out snooping in Island pastures and fields. When she got busy with writing and layout and shooed him away, he began to turn up at the end of her work day, usually with a picnic that he'd cajoled Mrs. Cailean the Crab into preparing in lieu of his usual supper, and he and Anna dined together in the newspaper office.

On Fridays they went out to MacShennach's for pizza, alternating who paid. After dinner, if it was the right Friday, they went to the *cèilidh*, and Zach fell in love with the Island's beautiful traditional music, mourning frequently that he'd not continued the piano lessons he'd had as a child. He developed an especial fascination with Jean and Darroch Mac an Rìgh and the gorgeous tunes they performed with Jamie and Màiri MacDonald.

Anna found Zach's attention flattering, his conversation intelligent and enlightening, and his chocolate-colored eyes quite mesmerizing. She began to realize that she was more interested in the archaeologist than in archaeology, and she had a strong feeling that her interest was returned. Zach had taken to looking at her in a manner that was half affectionate, half sexy, and Anna was enjoying it very much.

When he invited her to accompany him on his rambles around the Island, she accepted eagerly. She was used to rambling around, because she was always hunting for more patches of wildflowers to preserve, and she could kill two birds with one stone, discovering flowers at the same time as she was discovering the archaeologist. If they actually found a prehistoric site that would be a bonus, as well as a front page story for *The Island Star.*

It was a daunting task. Wildflowers were easy to spot; prehistoric sites were not. As far as Anna could figure out, any bump or ripple in the earth was a potential site, ripe for a dig, but it had to be verified by careful snooping around the base of the mound, looking for what Zach called "flakes." Those were pieces of stone split off from a larger piece of rock by a process called knapping, used by early people to create tools. The ones with edges on them were called scrapers, and were used to scrape the fat off animal skins before they were dried and tanned.

Zach showed her an example, a flake that he carried with him at all times for luck, and it looked to her like an ordinary piece of rock until he taught her to look carefully at the tiny sharpened edge that indicated human intervention.

Even though she could recognize now what they were searching for, it seemed to her that their search had a needle-in-the-haystack quality, as flakes could masquerade as ordinary pieces of stone, and came in all sizes. The smallest ones were called "micro-flakes," which Anna thought would be impossible for an amateur eye like hers to spot.

But she persevered, as much for the pleasure of Zach's company as out of intellectual curiosity.

They worked their way down the coastline first, because it was easier walking than in the interior pastures and peat bogs, and because Zach said that early settlements were more likely to be found near the ocean, where food could easily be obtained by fishing. In the fourth week of their search,

Anna and Zach arrived at a dry wall that clearly delineated the border of a property.

"We have to ask permission to walk this land," Anna said.

"Who owns it?"

"Fearchar MacShennach. He's Barabal Mac-a-Phi's grandfather."

"What's he like?"

"I don't know him very well. He stays close to home; he doesn't get out much because of his arthritis. But I've heard Barabal talk about him. Crotchety, impossible to please, and a terrible gossip. Keeps an eye on everything, pumps Barabal and her mother Elspeth for information on what's happening on the Island. He'll know about you, because he's very interested in strangers."

Zach grinned. "Sounds like just my cup of tea. Want to bet I win him over in five minutes?"

Anna stared at him. "Loser buys the pizza."

"Define losing."

"He tells you to get the hell off his land."

"You're on." He slapped the hand she extended, and they walked to the cottage.

No one came to answer their knock. Anna sighed, "He knows we're here; he doesn't miss a thing that happens around his cottage. He wants to keep us waiting just to get us off balance."

Zach said, "I'm perfectly calm and incredibly balanced," and knocked again.

At last the door opened. A grim-faced old man, leaning on a cane, stared out at them. "What's amiss that you come hammering at my door? Such a stramash. Is the world coming to an end?"

Anna said, "*Feasgar math, agus ciamar a tha, a Fhearchar. Is mise* Anna Wallace."

"I ken right well who you are, young Anna; you're the lassie that's always on about the wee wildflowers, and you put out the newspaper. Who's this mannie?"

"This is Zachariah Trelawney."

The old man considered Zach shrewdly. "Ah, the Englishman."

Zach said patiently, "I'm not English, sir. I'm Cornish. From Cornwall."

"That's part of England, isn't it, laddie?"

"Depends on who you talk to, sir."

"Well, you're talking to me, and if you say you're a Cornishman and not English, that's what I'll call you. Now what do you want? I'm a busy man; I don't have time to waste jabbering at the door."

"We'd like to ask permission to walk your property, *a Fhearchar*," said Anna.

"Is that right? You'd better come in, then." He held the door open and made shooing motions with his free arm. "Come along, come along, time's a-wasting. Wait till you get to my age; you won't be so wasteful with your minutes."

Ushered in, and ordered to be seated, Anna and Zach skirted the piles of magazines and newspapers on either side of the saggy old couch, and sat themselves down on it gingerly. Zach could not keep his gaze from wandering all over the room. There were photographs and knickknacks everywhere, shabby rag rugs covered the wood floor, and decrepit curtains, flung wide open, framed the windows. An enormous old Bible, its leather covering cracked and peeling, stood on a tall stand near the fireplace, which held a dying fire of peats and coal.

The clutter was intense, but everything was scrupulously clean.

"I suppose you'll be wanting a cup of tea," growled Fearchar.

Zach, anxious to be on his way, opened his mouth to decline and received a sharp elbow in his ribs from Anna, who said, "That would be a great courtesy, *a Fhearchar,* and we would thank you kindly for it. It's thirsty work, all the walking we've done."

When the old man had shuffled into the kitchen, Anna hissed at Zach, "We're in it for the long haul, so rest easy if you want permission to walk his land. We'll not get out of here until he's tired of us."

Zach fidgeted and muttered impatiently under his breath.

Five minutes later Fearchar returned, carrying a tray. Nudged again by Anna's busy elbow, Zach sprang to his feet. "Let me take that for you, sir."

"*Tapadh leat,*" said Fearchar and thrust the tray at Zach, who almost dropped it in his surprise. The old man turned and put a firm hand under the rump of an enormous tabby cat curled up in an armchair that faced the couch. The cat rose, stretched, hissed at him, and dropped to the floor in a leisurely manner, showing her independence by her refusal to be hurried. Fearchar grinned horribly, baring his yellowed teeth, and eased his old bones down into the warm spot she'd left.

Zach stood with the tray in his hands, looking baffled. Anna removed a pile of magazines from the table in front of the couch. "Put it there," she said.

"Sit yourself down, Cornishman. Did your mammy not tell you it's rude to loom over people? You put me in mind of the Great Gray Man. You'll be mother, Anna?"

"Aye, *ceart math*," she said, and picked up the teapot. "What do you take in your tea, *a Fhearchar*?"

"No milk, four lumps, lassie. I like my tea as sweet as I am," he said, and winked at her in an alarming way. He took a large gulp of the scalding hot tea, swallowed, snorted with pleasure, and growled, "Out with it, then. What're you about, disturbing an old man's afternoon at his nap time?"

"We're sorry to bother you. We just want permission to tramp across your land."

"Why?" he demanded. "Looking for more wildflowers, are you? Going to take my good pasture and fence it off so my sheep don't nibble your precious blossoms?"

"You don't have sheep," said Anna patiently.

"Never mind that. I was reading the day in that newspaper rag of yours, lassie, that yon Lachlann MacQuirter was selling off some of his flock. I was thinking of making him an offer he couldn't refuse. They say he has good stock. So I might be getting back into raising sheep, and be damned to your wildflowers, because sheep have to eat." He looked at her in triumph. "What do you think of that, young Anna?"

"It's your land, *a Fhearchar*, and you've the right to do as you wish with it. I wouldn't dream of trying to tell you what to do."

"That's more than that female bossy-boots Barabal, my granddaughter, does," snorted Fearchar. "She's around here every day, trying to give me orders. 'You mustn't do this, Grandda, and you're too old to do that,'" he mimicked in a high-pitched voice.

Anna knew that this was quite untrue, just like the story of acquiring sheep was untrue, because she'd heard Barabal sigh about her dutiful thrice-a-week visits to her grandfather, how careful she had to be with what she said to him, and how resistant he was to even the most gentle suggestions. She ignored the comment, and said, "Zach's a great walker, and he's on holiday. He wants to hike our Island from north to south."

"Why would he do that?" demanded Fearchar. "Hasn't he got any honest work to do? What kind of man can spend his time in walking around an Island?" He turned to stare accusingly at Zach. "Full of money, are you?"

Cornered, Anna opened her mouth to spin some sort of tale justifying Zach's unnatural interest in hiking, when Zach took control of the conversation by blurting out what he'd promised himself not to reveal to any of the *Eilean Dubhannaich*. "I'm not just walking. I'm looking for prehistoric artifacts."

"Prehistoric what?"

"Artifacts. Debitage. Lithics. Microliths. Knapped scrapers and flakes."

Fearchar turned to Anna. "Not quite right in the head, is he?"

Anna sighed, realizing that Zach had revealed his secret mission to one of the most devoted gossips on an Island devoted to gossip. "I'm beginning to think so. But it may be an occupational hazard. He's an archaeologist."

Fearchar regarded Zach with a shrewd eye. "I saw a program on telly about your lot. You grub up bodies. What makes you think there are bodies buried on my land?"

"I don't think that at all, sir," said Zach, suddenly understanding the hole he'd dug for himself, and trying to dig his way out. "In fact, it's highly improbable. The odds against finding a body, or indeed, any bones at all, are enormous. Organic matter decays quickly and skin, flesh, leather goods, anything like that, becomes part of the earth it rests on. I'm looking for stone tools, flint fragments. And piles of clam and limpet shells. Burnt nut-shells. Anything that would indicate signs of early human habitation."

He leaned forward, suddenly intent. "I'm convinced that this Island was inhabited in the Mesolithic period, and I'm looking for evidence. I have a grant from the Scottish Antiquities Trust to finance my research."

Fearchar shook his head in exaggerated disbelief. "There's somebody foolish enough to pay you to look for piles of garbage?"

Zach leaned back in his chair. "Got it in one, sir."

Anna said, "You wouldn't know it by listening to him, but he's trying to keep his work secret, so that people don't start digging holes all over the Island, and bringing him chicken bones and funny-shaped rocks."

"Ah, I see. Well, I'll not be saying a word to anyone, especially not to that fearful gossip, my daughter Elspeth, who'd have the story spread all over the Island before you get back to Cailean's tonight."

Anna noted dispassionately that Fearchar MacShennach knew where Zach was staying, and probably knew more about what he'd been doing on the Island than Zach himself did. Oh, well, she thought, and wondered why she bothered to publish a newspaper, when the Islanders were so good about keeping themselves informed. "Will you have a wee bit more tea, *a Fhearchar?*"

"I will, lass. And since your young man doesn't want anyone telling him anything, I'll not be mentioning that great old mound on the south end of my land, and the fact that I myself found some odd-shaped bits of stone on it, oh, maybe twenty years ago. I kept them," he added. "They're over there on the mantelpiece."

Zach sprang to his feet and rushed to the fireplace. Hands trembling, he pawed impatiently through the assortment of rocks, shells and bits of petrified trees lined up and tidily dusted by Barabal's careful hands, on top of the mantelpiece. Finally he seized one piece of rock and carried it to the window for a closer look in better light.

Anna rose and came to stand by him. "What do you think, Zach?"

"I can't be sure," he said slowly. "It looks like a scraper, but it's hard to tell. I'd like to have it carbon dated, though. Would you let me borrow it, sir? I'll bring it back in a few weeks. Can you remember where you found it?"

"Bring it here."

He took the rock from Zach and said, "Oh, that one. It's not from my land; it was given me by my father. He knew I liked rocks; I had quite a collection when I was a wean. Can't remember exactly where he said he found it, but it wasn't on our property. I think he picked it up when the road was being leveled for paving years ago. Down near *Cladh a' Chnuic,* I think."

Zach's shoulders sagged; he'd hoped for a more precise location. "It may be important in proving my theory, so I'd be most grateful if I could borrow it for a bit."

Fearchar waved his hand in an expansive gesture. "Take it. Mind you bring it back, though." He rose. "Been interesting talking to you, but it's time for you to run along. An old man needs his afternoon nap."

Anna said, "It's all right if we do a bit of exploring on your land?"

"Help yourself." He was clearly tiring, and anxious to be rid of them.

"Thank you, sir," said Zach, slipping the rock into his pocket. "You may have helped make an important archaeological discovery. Or not, as the case may be."

"Cheers for the tea, *a Fhearchar*," said Anna, and the two of them went out the door, which the old man closed behind them impatiently.

"Do you really think it's something important?" she asked Zach, as they made their way back to the dry wall where they'd started their incursion into Fearchar's lands.

"Can't say," mumbled Zach. "And even if it is, we don't have much of a clue as to where he found it. Got to keep looking, so eyes to the ground, and forward march, lassie."

Anna sighed, and began to walk again. At least she'd had a chance to sit down and have a cup of tea. She'd had no idea archaeology was so tiring. It was even worse than searching for wildflower patches.

They covered the area up to and around the house, and continued on to the wall on the far end of the property. Zach showed some interest in the mound, mumbling about prehistoric burial customs, and walked around it three times, but found no artifacts.

When they finally reached the edge of Fearchar's property, Zach spun around, planted his feet wide apart on the ground, lifted his arms to the sky and tilted his head back. "I am so damned frustrated!" he roared. Then he grabbed Anna by the shoulders, yanked her close and planted a hot kiss on her mouth.

Her head was whirling by the time his lips left hers.

She needed to say something important, but she didn't want him to stop what he was doing. She gasped, "Old Fearchar will be watching us. I can just hear what he's going to tell the world. 'That wildflower lassie was snogging her Englishman boyfriend out in my pasture t'other day.'"

"I'm not an Englishman."

"You're not my boyfriend, either. Gossip always gets the story wrong." Anna moved a little closer, wiggled her hips invitingly, and said, "I thought archaeology was the only thing that excited you."

"I can't imagine where you got that idea," he said, and ran a hand down her back to her rump to press her hard against him. "Why aren't I your boyfriend?"

"Are you a candidate?" she said, and snuggled closer.

"Damned right I am." Zach lifted his head and stared towards the old man's house. "Uh-oh, he's got the binoculars out; I saw them on his windowsill. I caught a glimpse of sunlight reflecting off them just now. Smile pretty for the nice man, pet."

She sighed. "So we're to be the latest item on the Island gossip circuit."

"Hey, let's make it worth their while. Let's go back to your place for some serious snogging."

"I'm hungry."

"So am I." He nibbled her ear.

"Pizza first, and you're buying, because you didn't win him over in five minutes," she said.

"He didn't toss me off his land, though. Call it a draw, but I'll pay anyway. So it's pizza, then snogging."

"In your dreams, digger boy."

"You've been in my dreams ever since I first met you, wildflower girl. How about a dose of reality?"

"We'll see," said Anna, grinning, and took his hand. As they turned to leave she glanced back at the cottage window where the binoculars glinted, and heard in her head the old man's snort of disapproval. She aimed a cheery wave back at the windows.

When Zach walked her home after pizza, she allowed a goodnight kiss and a bit of cuddling, then sent him on his way. No reason to let him have too much too soon, she thought. Let him get really eager for what she had to offer. And judging by how pleasant she found his kisses, she might have quite a bit to offer.

Sixteen

There was a Traveler lass and her lad,
In the forest green-o,
Sang this song beneath a tree,
Where they'd not be seen-o.

"To the fairy castle let us go.
Midst the stonies row on row,
Let us laugh and play a while,
Mayhap catch a fairy's smile.

"If we hear a fairy's laugh,
Increase our joy it will by half.
Luck to lovers it will bring,
If they hear the fairies sing."

Lady Grizel Mac an Rìgh

everal weeks later, Anna and Zach had covered a tremendous amount of ground in the two months of their search. She thought he was getting discouraged, and decided to distract him by a little sightseeing expedition. She packed sandwiches and the brownies she'd made from the recipe for which Sheilah Morrison was noted, and had kindly shared for the fundraising cookbook the Ros Mór Women's Presbyterian Alliance had put together. That recipe had insured that every woman on the Island bought a copy.

"Today we're going out just for fun," Anna announced. "A little walk, and a search for wildflowers, not lithic thingies. I'm going to show you a part of Eilean Dubh you've not seen before."

"Okay," Zach said. If truth be told, he was getting tired of plodding miles over the Island, beautiful as it was, without finding a hint of prehistoric habitation, and perhaps a little free-form rambling would perk up his spirits to resume the search.

They took Anna's car into the north corner of Eilean Dubh, over a bumpy gravel road that led to the foot of the mountain, *Beinn Mhic an Rìgh*. When the road petered out into a cattle path, Anna parked the car. "The rest of the way is on foot," she said.

She led him into the dark, thick pine forest that edged the mountain, along a well-traveled path that led sometimes uphill and sometimes down, into a clearing that was bursting with wildflowers of every hue and color, growing thick and knee high.

"This is brilliant," marveled Zach. "Is this one of your flower preserves?"

"Aye. I discovered it, and named it after myself; I thought I deserved it. *Gàradh* Anna, Anna's garden, I call it. It didn't even have to be designated as a preserve, because almost no one comes here; they think it's haunted, or full of fairies, or something daft like that. The few who venture this way take the paved road over the bridge on the other side of the clearing, which leads to *Caisteal Mhic an Rìgh*."

"Which means . . . ?"

"Mac an Rìgh's castle, the ancestral home of the laird of the Mac an Rìgh clan."

"That anachronism again."

"Aye. Come on, I'll show you."

They tramped through the field of flowers and up into the trees again, following a path that led abruptly downhill into another clearing, where sat a crumbling stone ruin, overgrown with vines and more flowers. In its center was a wreck of a tower from the top of which could be seen the sea, with three pine trees standing like sentinels on its top, and inside it a giant circular staircase that led nowhere. Around the edge was a deep depression recognizable as the remains of a moat, long dry.

"The castle," Anna announced proudly. "Symbol of our Island's great past, first built as defense against the Viking invaders."

It looked like a giant pile of rocks to Zach, whose interest in history was defined by all dates thousands of years B. P., the archaeological term Before the Present. But she thought it was something special, so he shrugged his shoulders and tried to look suitably impressed. "It's, uh, amazing."

"It is," Anna announced in the authoritative tones of a tour guide, "an excellent example of a eleventh-century castle, the more remarkable because it was built without reference to similar structures on the mainland, but having many of the same features that are found in castles all over Britain and Europe. That big mound in the center is the original motte, and it would have had an enclosure on the lower ground next to it called a bailey, and it all would have been surrounded by a ditch.

"The stone tower started out as one built of wood inside the bailey where the chieftain and his family and servants lived, and wooden buildings were built all around the tower for everyone else to live in. The small river flowing down the mountain was dammed and directed into the ditch to form a moat for the defense of the castle. If the Vikings penetrated this far inland, everyone could scamper into the castle and shoot arrows down at them to drive them away."

Anna took a deep breath, and flung her arm out in a grand gesture towards the ruin. "And there you have Eilean Dubh's own historic castle."

"Hmmph," said Zach. "You sound like a travel brochure."

"I wrote the one about the castle for the Island Tourist Information. You had it almost verbatim."

"Well, it's very interesting, but there's not much left of it, is there."

"It was abandoned after several hundred years, and the seat of Mac an Rìgh operations moved closer to the seacoast, which was safe once the Vikings quit coming. Then people could concentrate on making their living from fishing. The land around the castle would have been mostly worn out from intensive farming by then.

"According to legend it then became the fairies' castle, and no one dared to go near it. But eventually the locals began sneaking in to remove the stones to use in building projects all over the Island, and they are being found even today in the most amazing places. There's a few of them in the square in Ros Mór."

By now Zach was in the mood for a closer look, so they spent an agreeable couple of hours climbing over the ruins. When they were tired and hot, and had attracted the attention of an unpleasant variety of small biting insects, they called it quits.

"I'm ready for lunch," announced Zach. "Let's go back to the wildflowers."

They settled under an ancient tree on the edge of the wildflower patch and ate their lunches, and drank the bottle of wine Zach had brought. Drowsiness overtook Anna. She took off her denim jacket, folded it into a pillow, tucked it under her head, and stretched out for a nap.

Zach propped himself up against the tree, listened to the wild birds sing, and thought about the castle and its inhabitants. Then he thought about the Vikings, and his imagination began to run rampant. He started mumbling. "Big, hairy men, blond hair blazing in the sun, driven away by the arrows of the people in the castle. Wandering around, looking for something to conquer and loot."

He glanced down at Anna, lying beside him. "One of them stumbles on this clearing and spots this tree, and underneath it there's a shepherd girl snoozing who somehow missed the whole invasion, and didn't take refuge in the castle. Her sheep have wandered off to a nearby pond, and she sleeps on, unaware of her danger as the huge Viking sneaks up on her, bent on ravishment."

Anna opened one eye, and peered up at him.

"He tosses down his shield and helmet, and his long yellow hair tumbles down upon his brawny shoulders. He creeps closer, unbuckling his armored breastplate. Then he throws himself down upon her."

Zach threw himself down on top of Anna, who grunted in surprise. "What are you about?" she gasped.

"Ravishment. Rapine. Or kisses, at least."

"Get off," she said, pushing at him half-heartedly.

"'I vant you,' the Norseman growls in his indecipherable Scandinavian lingo, yanks the maiden into his arms, and takes her mouth in a fierce Viking kiss." Zach pulled her close, and planted a fierce Viking-style kiss on her surprised lips.

Anna wrested her mouth from his, and got into the game. "She struggles . . . "

"But her strength is no match for that of Sven, the fierce warrior, terror of the seas, conqueror of the innocent and helpless." Zach bent his head and growled into her throat.

"Helpless? No way." She seized his hair and yanked his head up so that they were face to face. She wrapped an arm around his neck and raised herself up to meet him, and brought her mouth against his in a long hot kiss. Then she said, "What do you think of that, barbarian invader boy?"

"I like it, oh flower of Scotland. May I have another?"

"So now you're asking, instead of taking? What kind of a Viking are you?"

"The cautious kind, who'd prefer to keep his hair firmly rooted in his scalp." He brushed his lips against hers. "You shepherd maidens are tough cookies."

"We like to conquer, instead of being conquered."

"Okay, conquer me." He pulled away from her and lay back down.

Anna stared at him, assessing the situation. Then she thought, oh, hell, why not? The day is beautiful, the birds are singing, the grass is soft, and the guy is tempting. And the girl is willing. Definitely willing. It had been a long time.

She bent over him and showered kisses on his face, chuckling as he started to moan her name. When his hand came up to cover her breast she laughed out loud. "You're an easy conquest," she whispered.

"I'm all yours. Take me."

And she did, kissing her way down his throat, unbuttoning his shirt so that her hand could tangle in his chest hairs, tugging gently, then not so gently just so she could hear him protest, faintly, against the pain. "Shall I stop?" she whispered.

"Oh, God, no," he whimpered. "I'll try to be brave, like a true man of the North."

When her mouth began to move over his chest and her hand moved lower, he moaned aloud. "What are you doing to me, woman?"

"Call it the shepherd girl's revenge," she said, then moaned herself when he opened her blouse, found the clasp to her bra and put both hands on her naked breasts.

She went back up for another hot kiss and Zach could stand it no longer. With their mouths locked together, he rolled her over so that he was on top of her, and she felt him hard against her belly.

"You know where this is going," he muttered.

"To ravishment, I hope."

"Damned right."

His lips were on her breast and his hand was sliding her skirt up to her waist and Anna realized that caution was a thing of the past. She wanted him inside her; it had been too long since she had had intimate relations with a man. "Come on," she muttered.

"I don't have a condom."

"I don't care." And she didn't; reckless desire had her in its grasp and would not let her go until it was appeased.

He yanked himself away to rip off his clothes, then the rest of hers, and came down on top of her again.

When he entered her she felt a wild rush of pleasure, and thrust herself against him to take him deeper. She yelled and wrapped her legs around his hips, imprisoning him until he took her where they both wanted to go.

She was alive, she was burning up with passion, she was crazy with need. She swept Zach away, and he collapsed on her, exhausted.

The sun shone hot on their naked bodies, evaporating their sweat, and a faint breeze blew it away. They lay, relaxed and happy.

Zach stirred, and hardened. "Again," he demanded, and began to move in her with delicate care, intending to take her very slowly this time.

Anna laughed and undulated her hips against his, and mumbled something in the Gaelic that he thought he understood, and he forgot all about a go-slow policy, opting instead for fast and furious.

Afterwards he lifted himself up and ran a tender hand over the long lean body he'd just enjoyed. "God, you're beautiful," he said.

Anna preened and stretched herself like a satisfied cat. "Thank you, my Viking. Will you take me away with you on your longboat, and make me your slave to serve you in your icy kingdom?"

"I think I'm the slave," he muttered. "You've got me right where you want me."

"Between my legs, that's where I want you," said Anna, surprising herself with such unashamed sensuality. Making love had sent a wild surge of energy through her and she felt vibrant and alive, able to conquer the world, let alone one hapless Cornishman.

"How about doing it again tonight?"

"Condoms the next time, though. I don't mind taking the occasional chance, but if this is going to be a regular event I'd prefer to be careful. I don't want to end up like my mother."

Surprised, he sat up and looked at her. "What about your mother?"

"She let herself be swept away by a wild Gypsy man . . . up here in Scotland we call them Travelers . . . and got pregnant."

"And he wouldn't marry her?"

"Oh, no, he was all too ready to marry her; he was mad about her. They had a traditional Traveler wedding ceremony, jumping over the campfire in a ring of brightly-painted caravans, my mother decked out in flowing shawls and jangling bracelets, then a marriage in the registry office, to keep my grandfather happy. But when summer was over and the Travelers were ready to move on, she refused to go with him."

"What? Why not?"

"She wanted to stay here on Eilean Dubh. Real home girl she was, living with her father, keeping house for him while he published the newspaper. She told my father he could either give up his life as a Traveler and get a job here on the Island, or take off. He took off, but it broke his heart.

"He came back every summer while I was growing up, told me amazing stories, taught me all about his people—my people, too—and we planned that when I was sixteen I'd join him in the wandering life. I looked forward to that for years. Sitting in school, in kirk, doing my stupid chores, I'd dream about being free, traveling in my father's beautiful caravan, telling stories around the campfire."

"What happened?" said Zach, eyes wide.

"He died." Anna sat up and began to pull on her clothes. "When I was thirteen. Only three more years, and I could have gone with him. I could have been a Traveler like him. But he died. My mother died, too, within six months, of a broken heart; at least that's why she said she was dying. But I think she had cancer, and didn't want to talk about it. Some people are like that, you know, and she was pretty repressed about everything except my father.

"My grandfather raised me after she died, and my Traveler family disappeared, and never came back to Eilean Dubh again. I used to think that I'd go looking for them when I grew up."

"Why haven't you?"

She shrugged. "I don't know. I got involved in Grandda's newspaper, started writing articles and soliciting ads when I was fourteen. I realized that was the future I wanted, so I studied journalism at the U of Glasgow and got a job on a newspaper when I graduated. When Grandda had a stroke I came back to Eilean Dubh and took over *The Island Star*. I've been here ever since.

"Left a great job and a great boyfriend to come back to this weird little Island." She buttoned her blouse. "Boyfriend wanted to marry me, too, but I said only if he'd come to Eilean Dubh to live. Of course I knew he wouldn't; there's nothing for him to do here. So I left him, and broke his heart, just like my mother broke my father's."

She gave Zach a long look that made him tremble, for some reason. "Better be careful, digger boy. We Wallace women are heartbreakers."

Zach was speechless. He'd learned more about Anna in the last five minutes than he had in the last two months, he'd seen her naked and touched her body, and he'd been as intimate with her as it was possible to be with a woman.

And he still didn't have any idea of what she was all about.

Zach yanked on his shirt, muttering. Clueless wonder, he called himself. Damn women, anyway. Especially mysterious women.

She refused to let him stay the night with her, after all. "You don't have any condoms, and the chemist is closed. There's no point in being totally irresponsible."

He left, disconsolate, knowing that he'd fallen madly in love with Anna during their afternoon of exploration and passion, and dreadfully afraid that she was going to break his heart, just as she'd promised.

The condoms were an excuse, because Anna had some heavy thinking to do. Despite her careless words, she'd been very close to being in love with her Glasgow boyfriend, though not enough in love to marry him. She'd rather thought she was moving that way, though, and it had been a real wrench to leave him.

But she'd had to come home, because she had to keep *The Island Star* afloat. It was her grandfather's sole means of financial support. And besides, Eilean Dubh needed a newspaper.

Gus, the boyfriend, was a newspaperman himself. He worked on the same Glasgow paper as Anna, and he understood and supported her responsibility to her grandfather and to her paper. But there was no future on Eilean Dubh for him, so he let her go.

It was her mother's story all over again.

There was no reason to think that Zach would be any different. Once he'd found his site he'd be off, back to his university, probably to a professorial rank if the discovery was a good one.

Anna wasn't trapped on Eilean Dubh. She loved her Island and her life, her newspaper and her wildflowers, and she had no intention of ever leaving again. Even if her Traveler family were to miraculously reappear, she wouldn't have gone off with them. She was an *Eilean Dubhannach* now and forever.

But she couldn't help wishing that she had someone with whom to share her life.

Damn men, anyway. She wanted to be happy without one.

PART VI

Russ's Epiphany

Seventeen

About two-thirds of patients experience prodromal symptoms days to weeks before the event, including unstable or crescendo angina . . . shortness of breath, or fatigue. The first symptom of acute MI {myocardial infarction} is deep, substernal, visceral pain . . .

The Merck Manual

*R*uss Abbott walked into his pleasant sunroom in Milwaukee, desperate for a whisky and a quiet moment. He'd felt off-color all day, and odd for a couple of weeks. He'd been unusually tired, his stomach had been bothering him, and he'd had frequent bouts of what he thought was heartburn. Ruth had badgered him into giving up fried foods, and had begun fixing him lunches to take to work, just as his former wife Jean had done, so he wouldn't be tempted to slip out for a quick fast food meal. But the heartburn episodes had persisted, bouts of sharp, griping pains in his chest that radiated downward into his arm and up to his jaw. Stress, he'd told himself, and ignored the symptoms.

He'd quit telling Ruth about the episodes, knowing that she would insist that he see his doctor for a physical, for which he was a year and a half overdue. He'd get to it one day, he told himself, but until he'd resolved the merger question he didn't want to take time for a doctor's appointment.

The proposed merger loomed large in his mind, and occupied his spare moments. A big fish in the software development industry wanted Russ's firm, and cannily presented his plan as a merger, because he could not take over a privately held company. Russ was not fooled: it was his knowledge and expertise that the other man wanted, not a merger, and the rest of the company could go hang itself as far as he was concerned.

It was an important step for Russ, for the offer was generous and the work would be interesting, but he could not bring himself to let down his long-term employees. There would be no security for them in a merger and the company headquarters would be in California, with little need for a branch in Milwaukee. Other businessmen might consider him soft in the head to worry about his workers, but it was part of his code of ethics.

He poured himself a whisky, and thought longingly of a cigar, but his brief foray into cigar smoking had been firmly quashed by Ruth after their marriage. "Not in the house," she'd ruled, and, resistant to orders as always, he'd gone outside into the garden to smoke until he'd realized that a cigar was only pleasant if he could have it in his sunroom with his feet up and a whisky in his other hand.

He could have the whisky, anyway; she was okay with that because she knew he never overindulged; he regarded drunkenness as a sign of a weak character. He poured himself a generous measure and sank into his favorite chair to make the adjustment from work to home.

Pain gripped him, so sudden and so intense that he spilled the whisky before he could put it down. The glass fell from his hand and shattered on the floor. What's going on, he thought; he'd had a proper, Ruth-approved, salad for lunch. He shouldn't be having a heartburn attack, and it certainly should not be this painful.

That was his last coherent thought before a terrible anxiety seized him. I'm dying, he thought, as the pain spread from the center of his chest into the familiar track down his left arm and up to his jaw. He broke out into a cold sweat. His pulse raced. He felt nauseated.

Ruth, help me, he screamed, and realized that no sound was coming from his throat.

He couldn't breathe. The pain became unbearable. He felt consciousness slipping away from him. You're having a heart attack, his brain whispered, as he gasped for air. This is it, Russ; you're finished.

Stepdaughter Carol appeared at the sunroom door. "Hi, Russ. Mom says to get washed up so that we can eat dinner. There's a special on television she wants to watch at seven . . . " The words died in her throat as she took in her stepfather's pallor and the look on his face. "Russ, what's wrong? Are you in pain?"

With a tremendous effort Russ lifted his right hand and put it on his chest.

"Oh, my God," she gasped, but managed to keep from saying the dreaded words, heart attack. Never frighten a patient, the voices of her nursing school instructors whispered in her ear. It's different when it's a member of your own family, she told the voices, but gathered her courage and her professional detachment. She moved swiftly to Russ and took his pulse, then pulled a blanket from the sofa and spread it over him. "You're going to be fine," she said firmly. "I'll have help here right away."

She seized the phone and dialed 911. "Myocardial infarction," she said to the operator. "We need an ambulance immediately," and gave the address of the Abbott home. She hung up the phone and went to kneel by Russ to whisper in his ear, "Everything will be okay."

She meant it, too. She was not going to let this guy who meant so much to her mother slip away. When her youngest sister, Jennie, the ninth-grader, came to the door, Carol said, "Jen, get Mom, right away. Then go stand by the front door and be ready to let the firefighters and the ambulance crew in. Have Liz and Annie go down to the street and watch for them so they know which house to come to. Hurry, honey."

Jen, eyes wide with fear, swallowed her questions and obeyed. She was not quite old enough to remember her father's fatal heart attack, but her sisters had whispered the details to her one dark night of confidences, and she'd never forgotten them.

Ruth appeared. "What is it?" she whispered, the memory of her first husband Walter's last minutes suddenly fresh in her mind as she took in Russ's pale face and agonized expression.

Carol sprang to her feet and went to her mother, her arms going around the other woman. "I think it's a heart attack," she whispered in Ruth's ear. "Stay calm, and help keep him calm. I've called 911."

It can't happen to me again, said Ruth's mind. He's too young. But Walter had been young, too. She swayed on her feet, then lifted her chin defiantly and went to kneel by her husband. "I'm here, darling," she said in a surprisingly firm voice. "You're going to be fine."

The pain was crushing his chest. He could feel his rib cage compressing. Any minute now it would shatter, sending pieces of rib ripping into his lungs, shredding them. I'm going to die, he thought, and his hand drifted down to cover hers, on the arm of the chair. I love you, he said with his eyes. I don't want to leave you. Help me.

"I love you, Russ. I won't let you go," said Ruth, her voice steady and reassuring.

Carol came and sank down on Russ's other side. She gripped his hand. "We'll get you through this, Russ," she said. "Hang in there."

A strong woman on either side of him, his hands held firmly in their grasp, two voices telling him he was going to make it. A dim hope flickered in his mind, making the pain almost bearable.

The firefighters, carrying their medical bags, arrived first. They held a quick, whispered consultation with Carol, and then moved to Russ. "Easy now, sir, you're going to be okay," said the firefighter, as she took Russ's pulse. "Are you on any medication?"

Ruth answered for him. "No."

"Has he had an episode like this before?"

"No."

Russ, realizing what had been happening to him the last several weeks, tried to speak, but was too short of breath to form words.

"Sir, we're going to put an oxygen mask on you. It will help you breathe." She slipped the mask on as another firefighter opened Russ's shirt. "This is a heart monitor we're attaching now. It'll tell us what's going on."

With the crew working competently around him, the crackle of their radios sounding reassuringly in his ear, his wife and eldest stepdaughter close beside him, and the other three stepdaughters watching in quiet terror from the doorway, Russ took a deep breath of the oxygen and willed himself to passivity. He was not aware of what was happening when he was placed on a stretcher and carried out to the waiting ambulance.

He woke up in a hospital bed connected to various tubes, beeping machines and wires, Ruth beside him, and Carol consulting with another nurse at the door.

"Darling! You're awake!" cried Ruth, and Carol and the nurse moved swiftly to him. "How do you feel?"

Russ's first reaction was fury, that something had happened to him over which he had had no control. He was always in control. He growled, "Where the hell am I? What's going on?"

Carol explained calmly about his heart attack and the emergency bypass surgery that had removed the clot blocking one artery and cleared a partial blockage from another, while Ruth rubbed his shoulder. "We're very lucky that this occurred at home, and Carol was there," Ruth said.

Russ frowned, for he did not consider anything about a heart attack lucky, but he felt too groggy to contest the point. He allowed himself to be ministered to by the women, and restrained himself from snapping about being fussed over.

His self-restraint did not survive beyond the first day, and the hospital staff was as relieved as Russ when he was allowed to go home. Ensconced in his sunroom in his favorite chair, a blanket over his legs and a doting wife at his beck and call, he groused day and night about his inactivity, and threatened to march out into the garden and smoke a cigar, now forbidden entirely by horrified surgeon and determined wife.

At last Alice, the bright young woman at his business who had become his second in command, was summoned to report to him on a daily basis about the activities of his beloved company. This kept him pacified for a couple of weeks, and then one morning he rose from his bed and insisted that he was going to work.

Ruth, remembering his doctors' restrictions, agreed to a couple of hours a day for the first week, and only if she drove him to work and back again. And only if she could stay by him in his office.

"What are you going to do in my office?" demanded Russ impatiently.

Russ gave him her fiercest look, the one that compelled obedience from her daughters, and even from her husband. "I'll knit," she announced. She was a terrible knitter, and hated it, but it would keep her hands and mind busy while she waited out the allowed two hours. Thus an uneasy truce was forged between the two of them.

She was desperately grateful that she had not lost a second husband to a heart attack, and put up with all his impatience and bad moods, but even her monumental patience was beginning to wear thin. She sought a kindred spirit to share her worries and her phone calls to Jean became a nightly occurrence. A few weeks after Russ's surgery, her voice became desperate. "Jean, I don't know what to do. He thinks he's well, and insists on going into work. But he comes home so tired and pale I'm terrified that he's going to have another attack."

Jean said, "It was always hard to get him to relax. I'm not sure he even understands the concept."

"At least the merger is off, so he doesn't have the stress of worrying about that. His potential partner didn't want to take a chance on a man who's had a heart attack before he's forty-five. It was Russ's brains the guy wanted, not the company."

"Oh, dear, that must have been a disappointment to him."

"I don't think so," said Ruth thoughtfully. "It almost seems to have been a relief. You know, I believe he'd like to slow down, but he thinks the business needs his total attention. I wish there was someone else who could take over for him, at least for a while." She sighed.

"Rod," said Jean in sudden inspiration. "Why can't Rod do it?"

"Well, that would be ideal, of course, but Russ would have to have something to keep him busy. Wait a minute. What if they switched jobs?"

"Rod goes to Milwaukee . . . "

"And Russ comes to Eilean Dubh. The pace there is more easygoing, isn't it?"

Jean said, "Of course, and Rod has got things running so well that I think he's beginning to be a teeny bit bored. A switch would be good for him, too. I don't know what Lucy would say, though. She loves it here."

"But she might like coming back to the city for a while. She could . . . I don't know. Take a class at the University? Go to concerts and the museums?"

"The family is very important to Lucy. If she knows that a switch will help Russ, she'll do it without thinking about herself."

"We'd exchange houses and cars."

"It would be a sort of vacation for both families."

Jean sighed, "I'll miss my grandson, though. He and Rosie play together nearly every day. She'll be fussed to lose her Andwew Wussell."

"It's not like it's forever."

"No. Do you think you can talk Russ into it?"

Ruth said in a determined tone, "I'm not going to ask. I'm just going to tell him."

"Good luck to you." Ruth must have a better idea on how to handle Russ than she'd ever had, thought Jean; she'd never been able to get him to take orders, and sometimes, not even suggestions. Perhaps the heart attack had mellowed him a little. But he'd always been a high maintenance husband, and she found it hard to imagine that this would ever change.

Ruth prevailed, and the "big switch" was arranged before a month was out, almost before Russ knew what was happening. Rod, a tearful Lucy and Andrew Russell left the Island by helicopter on Friday, and the Caledonian-MacBrayne ferry brought Russ and Ruth on the following Tuesday.

"*Miorbhuileach* to see you again, Russ," said Darroch as the Eilean Dubh half of the extended family gathered on the Airgead pier. "Bit of a surprise, but a most welcome one."

"Some of us are surprised that we're here, too," replied Russ dryly, earning himself a look over her shoulder from Ruth.

Rosie, between the two men, looked from one of them to the other suspiciously, and didn't unbend until Russ said, "Hi, peanut. Remember me?"

That earned him a gracious smile. Russ relaxed, took a deep breath of cool, fragrant Eilean Dubh air, and resigned himself to his new setting.

Eighteen

A regular exercise program consistent with lifestyle,
age and cardiac status is protective and enhances general well being.

The Merck Manual

*R*uss hated exercise, especially the kind that he got in his very expensive Milwaukee health club, organized and monitored by his personal trainer, performed on equipment that was carefully timed and regulated.

There was no health club on Eilean Dubh, a fact he publicly deplored, but privately rejoiced in. That kind of exercise had been boring to him for a long time, and he was glad to have an excuse to drop it.

But his doctor had insisted that he must exercise if he was to avoid another heart attack. Diet and the absence of stress would help, but exercise was an absolute necessity.

Ruth had made him promise to follow his doctor's orders, and Russ had made it a firm rule of their new marriage to keep his promises to her. He had found, somewhat to his surprise, that he enjoyed playing by the rules where Ruth was concerned. It made him feel good about himself.

From her first exposure at a Friday night *cèilidh,* Ruth had become enamoured of Scottish country dancing, as she watched the dancers flying happily over the floor, performing elegant footwork and precise formations. She'd asked Darroch for help, and he'd taught her the pas-de-basque setting step and the traveling step in fast and slow time. She was a quick learner and soon picked them up. Then, with Jean and Jamie assisting, he'd taught her the formations that make up each dance, and she began, tentatively, to try a dance or two on Friday nights.

Partnered first by Darroch or Jamie, she soon found others gravitating to her side, eager to dance with her. Like Scottish country dancers the world around, they were always ready to encourage a beginner, and Ruth's shy, sweet smile and delighted exuberance when she caught on was very pleasing to her partners.

Russ watched her and his Eilean Dubh friends enjoying themselves and came to the conclusion that he would learn to dance, too. He knew it would please Ruth to have him as a partner, and he found, as his love for his new wife deepened, that he was more and more eager to do things that would please her. Her birthday was coming up, and it would be a fine gift if he could take her hand and lead her out onto the dance floor one Friday evening.

But he would not ask Darroch to teach him; nor was he going to try to pick it up from watching the dancers. That was not Russ's way. No, he would enroll in a class, and learn how to dance with style and proper technique, like Darroch and Jamie did, with their heads high, smiles on their faces, and their toes pointed. And he would keep it secret, so that he could surprise Ruth.

But how to find a class? He would ask Somhairle Mac-a-Phi, who was rapidly becoming his good right hand at the firm. Somhairle was bright, knew what was happening on the Island and he was discreet, as well. He'd find a Scottish country dancing class for Russ, and he'd keep his mouth shut about it.

The class Somhairle found met on Thursday afternoons at the High School. It meant time away from work, but it was only two hours, and he could make that up by coming in early or staying late. And what was the point of being the boss if he couldn't cut himself a little slack, and take a couple of hours off? None of his employees would ask where he was going, or what he was doing. They would consider such nosiness about their boss's activities quite improper.

He presented himself at the High School Thursday afternoon at 1 p.m., and found the right classroom by picking out the sound of Scottish dance music above the normal chatter and hum of the school day.

He walked into the room. The teacher was at the front, organizing her notes; the pianist was at the piano, putting her sheet music in order, and students were in chairs around the room, slipping on their ghillies, Scottish dance shoes.

All the students were children, all about nine or ten years old.

Must have the time wrong, Russ thought. He walked to the teacher and introduced himself. "I want to learn how to dance. Can you tell me when the class for adults meets?"

The teacher looked at him quizzically. "I'm afraid there is no class for adults."

"Oh." Unwilling to give up, Russ said, "Well, how about high school students? Is there a class for them? Maybe they'd let me join that one."

The teacher shook her head. "Everyone on Eilean Dubh learns to dance when they are nine years old as part of our physical education program in school. There's no need for classes for older people, because they've been dancing for years."

She observed Russ keenly as a look of deep disappointment settled on his face. She knew who he was, of course; everyone on Eilean Dubh knew him. He was the Yank who was the Laird's wife's ex-husband, who'd brought a branch of his business to Eilean Dubh and created a raft of jobs. Her niece worked for Russ, and by her account he was a good boss and a decent family man. There would be no question that he was hanging around the school because of an unnatural interest in children. She did not think it would be hard to get permission from her superior to include him in the class.

She loved Scottish country dancing with a passion that made her yearn to teach the whole world how to reel and poussette, and she could not bear to turn away someone who was eager to learn. "Would you like to join our class?"

"Huh? With these kids?"

"The basics are the same for children and adults."

"But they're so little. I'm afraid I might step on one of them."

She laughed. "It will require adjustments from all the students, but that's what Scottish country dancing is all about, learning to dance with others so that everyone derives pleasure from the activity."

Russ shrugged his shoulders. "Okay, I'll give it a whirl. But listen, I'm doing this on the sly to surprise my wife. Do you think the kids can keep a secret?"

She laughed. "Oh, Mr. Abbott, no one's better at keeping secrets than children."

So Russ became the odd man out in a class of nine-year-olds, a genial Great Gray Man, a hulking presence who was a source of awe, at first, to the children, who had no idea why a grown-up was in their class. They thought it was weird, but most things adults did were weird. Even weirder, Russ was a grown-up who knew less about dancing than they did. So they began to help him out, coaching him with looks, gestures and whispers when he faltered. When he screwed up royally one day, a little girl said kindly, "Don't feel bad, Mr. Russ. We all made mistakes when we started out."

He learned the steps and the formations, reels, ladies' chain, petronella, allemande. By the ninth week of class he was attempting a rondel, no easy feat when his fellow dancers were two feet shorter than he was and the figure involved an over-and-under motion with hands joined. He had a crick in his back for an hour after that class.

The teacher gave a historical lecture at each meeting, and Russ learned that Scottish country dancing had been in danger of dying in the nineteen-twenties, pushed aside by fast, frantic couple dances of the Jazz Age. It had been saved and given new life by Mrs. Ysobel Stewart of Fasnacloich and Miss Jean Milligan, a physical education teacher. They'd collected and reconstructed old dances, located the correct music and standardized the formations. They founded the Scottish Country Dance Society in 1923, and the organization received permission from King George VI in 1951 to add the word "Royal" to its title, in recognition of its war work. The Queen was the Society's patron, and there were over twenty-one thousand members in countries all over the world.

Like most SCD teachers, the one leading this class was kind but very firm, and she commanded respect and not a little fear from her pupils, especially Russ. The etiquette of Scottish country dancing was strict, derived from its eighteenth-century heyday. There was a proper way to do everything and little tolerance for those who did not follow the rules.

Russ learned that he should bow to his partner at the beginning and conclusion of each dance, and thank the other dancers in his set of four couples when the dance was over. He learned to give his hand to his partner to lead her into the set, and never, ever, to join a set at the top, always at the bottom. He learned never, ever, to walk away from a dance in progress, even if he was hopelessly confused and irritated.

It was an activity he'd begun to please his wife, but he developed a love, at first grudging, then whole-hearted, for the formal, elegant and precise art of Scottish country dancing. And he'd become pals with the children in his class. At the end of the series of classes, he treated the teacher and the students to ice cream, and sat happily in the midst of the giggling, slurping kids, listening to them chattering in the Gaelic. *Maybe I ought to take that up next,* he thought; *if I can learn to dance, I can learn almost anything.*

Ruth's birthday came, and everyone at the *cèilidh* sang "Happy Birthday" to her. Then the next dance was announced. Russ took a deep breath, turned to his wife, and said, "May I have this dance?"

She looked at him in astonishment. "It's 'Kendall's Hornpipe,' Russ."

"Yeah, I know. I requested it." He took her hand and led her to the floor, and a set formed below them. The music began, Russ bowed to his wife, and they were off, dancing rights-and-lefts. Ruth stole glances at him frequently, noting his brow furrowed in concentration, the tip of his tongue protruding between tightly clenched teeth, and finally, his triumphant smile as they completed their two repetitions without a mistake and stepped to the bottom of the set.

She didn't know how he'd learned to dance, but she knew why: to please her. She was touched to tears. Across the set, her lips formed the words, "You are wonderful."

Immensely pleased with himself, Russ said, "Yeah, I know."

Nineteen

Before was then, was when I was
Not the person that I am.
My lump of clay is washed in rain.
My tears are gone; my life's regained!

Gibson Batch

*D*ancing was great, but he needed daily exercise. So Russ walked, every day after lunch, going out to the road that ran by the company offices. He walked for twenty-five minutes, then turned around and walked back, for a total of fifty minutes each day, five days a week.

Every day he had four choices for his walk: directional, which consisted of north to Airgead, past open fields where sheep grazed, or south to Ros Mór past the scattered whitewashed cottages, and positional, taking the land side of the road, or the ocean side, with its stunning view down the cliffs to the waves crashing against the rocks and curling under to return to the sea.

While he walked, he could think and solve problems, something he'd never been able to do on exercise machines. He was beginning to enjoy his walks.

Occasionally a car would drive past him, and the driver would slow and give a wave or a toot of the horn. Russ was alarmed by the toots at first, until he realized that it was just a friendly Island greeting.

The *Eilean Dubhannaich* were friendly to him, which surprised Russ, who'd always heard that Brits were reserved and stuck-up. His workers had confirmed that belief, at first; they'd seemed both starchy and ill at ease around him, until one day, two weeks after his arrival, when a small delegation presented itself in his office.

Somhairle Mac-a-Phi *as òige* had been designated as spokesperson, despite his youth. His English was excellent, and he had learned self-possession and fluency from his mother Barabal. "*Gabh mo leisguil*, sir," he said to Russ. "May we have a word?"

"Sure," said Russ, and thought, here it comes. Complaints, demands, worries, like any work force the world over. Why had he thought it would be different here?

"The fact is, sir, we are wanting to ask how you would like us to address you."

"Huh?" Russ said, and stared in surprise at the delegation that had grouped itself uneasily around Somhairle.

"Should we use your Christian name, or would you prefer to be called Mr. Abbott?" Somhairle said, "You see, sir, your son insisted that we call him Rod, but we are thinking that to address you that way might seem overly familiar, since you are an older gentleman. That perhaps you prefer 'Mr. Abbott.' More respectful."

The question had caused a great deal of worried discussion among Russ's workers. They all knew that Americans liked informality, and perhaps it would cause offense if they were to use the title of "mister," and seem as though they were being unfriendly. But no one was willing to go out on the limb of using his Christian name without permission.

"Well . . . " Russ realized that the entire group was staring at him expectantly. "I don't know. What do you feel comfortable calling me?"

There was a shocked murmur. "That is not for us to decide," said Somhairle primly. "We will abide by your wishes."

"My co-workers back home always called me Russ."

The group exchanged glances. "That seems a bit cheeky," said a middle-aged woman, "since we don't know you very well."

"But you called my son by his first name."

"That was different," said the woman. "He is a young man."

"You are the boss, after all," said someone else.

"Hell, I don't know," said Russ, baffled at what would be proper Island etiquette.

"Perhaps . . . " Somhairle said tentatively, "Perhaps we could call you . . . boss."

Again there was an exchange of glances, and heads began to nod. "That would be fitting," said one. "Respectful, but informal," said the middle-aged woman.

"Would that be acceptable to you, sir?" said Somhairle.

"Sure. Why not?"

Somhairle made a brief bow. "Thank you, Boss. It is a relief to everyone to have that settled."

One by one, the group approached Russ and shook his hand solemnly. He felt as though he had passed a sort of initiation rite.

The designation of Russ's honorific was one step in his assimilation to Eilean Dubh, and his acceptance of the friendly horn toots was another. He began to think that it was unjust to call the Brits cold and stuck-up, not realizing that his acceptance on the Island had been eased by his position of ex-husband to the Laird's wife, father to Ian *Mòr* MacDonald's wife Sally, and his approval by the Laird. On the whole, he thought he was fitting in quite well.

He began his walks one day after lunch, walking a little further every day, and they took him at last as far as the site of the new tourist accommodations that were being built on the coast just north of the helicopter pad. As a businessman, he was always interested in what other businessmen were up to. He stopped to eyeball the site, and give himself a little breather before starting the trek back.

He walked up to the fence surrounding the construction site, and put his eye to a peephole.

"Afternoon," said a voice beside him. "Lovely day, isn't it."

Russ turned. "Sure is."

"Great day for a walk."

"Yeah, terrific weather." Russ thought he recognized the speaker, but could not remember where he'd seen him before.

While he was searching his memory, the other man said, "My name's Nick Borth. We met at one of those party things a couple of weeks ago," he said, and extended his hand. Unknown to Russ, Nick had been watching him from the building site's headquarters, a trailer, and had hastened outside to intercept him. He had been hoping for an opportunity to engage Russ in conversation, and perhaps entangle him in his schemes.

"Oh, yeah, Barabal introduced us at the *cèilidh*. I'm Russ Abbott." Russ recognized Nick now.

"You're an American, aren't you. What brings you to our Island?" Nick asked, although he knew very well.

"I run a computer software firm, headquarters in Milwaukee, a branch just up the road." Our Island, thought Russ. That's a bit cheeky, as people here said. Pushy, he'd call it. Even though he was an employer with a stake in Eilean Dubh and a resident, at least for the next few months, he'd never say "our Island." Such a casual assumption of ownership would be frowned on, and even resented by the likes of Jamie and Màiri MacDonald, so fiercely possessive of their Island. Even Darroch might raise his eyebrows. Got to respect the boundaries, Russ thought.

"Oh, yes, I've seen your place. Are you going to be here long?"

"Don't know. I'm recuperating from a heart attack, so my son's gone back to Milwaukee to run our main office, and I've taken over from him for a while. Pace is a little slower here. My family thought it would be better for my health."

"It's pretty much of a backwater," said Nick, with a barely concealed sneer. "Sort of sleepy."

Russ bristled, a little to his surprise, and went to the defense of Eilean Dubh. "It's laid back, but I wouldn't call it sleepy. The people I employ are sharp and hard working."

Realizing his mistake, Nick backtracked. "Oh, of course. I didn't mean that in a derogatory sense. They're good folks."

"Hmmph," said Russ noncommittally, and changed the subject. He waved his hand at the construction site. "This your operation?"

"Yes. I'm building rental accommodations for the tourist trade. Help out the people here by getting some tourist money thrown their way."

In Russ's experience, a businessman was in business to make money, not help out the locals, and was never ashamed to admit to a profit motive. He was immediately suspicious. "They're not terribly interested in tourists," he said in a neutral voice.

"They'll be very interested once the cash starts flowing in." The sneer was back, and a distinct touch of condescension. "Everybody's interested in lining their pockets."

"Maybe. What sort of accommodations are you building?"

"Strictly high-end. They're going to be time-shares. There's a big European market for classy time-shares. Germans like them especially."

"People like that aren't interested in wildflower walks and a third run movie theater, which is about all Eilean Dubh has to offer. Won't they want high-end services? Fancy restaurants, golf courses, that sort of thing?"

"I've got that covered," said Nick Borth smugly. "Got a couple of things in the works. Going to be a real expansion going on around here soon." He leaned forward confidentially. "If you're interested in investments, I could put you onto some good possibilities."

"Like what?"

Nick withdrew, having planted the subtle hint. "We could get together for lunch one day and have a chat."

Hmm, thought Russ, wondering what Nick Borth was plotting. But "let them come to you" had always been his business philosophy, and being cagey was second nature to him. "I have lunch in my office and then take a walk. Doctor says I have to get exercise every day."

"Dinner then? Name the night."

Russ shook his head. "I'm a newlywed. Wife expects me to eat dinner with her every evening."

"Bring her along."

"I'll check our calendar. I wouldn't mind having a look at your building site, though, and hearing about the properties you have for sale. Might invest in one myself, since I plan on spending a fair amount of time on the Island. Be easier than remodeling the little cottage we're renting right now." He shook his head. "Kitchen is straight out of the eighteenth century. The wife hasn't complained so far, but I'd like to get her some shiny new stuff." He knew perfectly well that Ruth loved her old-fashioned cottage; she'd said it was like playing house. She'd have no use for a modern building without atmosphere. But he was interested in getting a look at Nick Borth's operation, and feigning interest in buying one of the properties was a way to do it.

"Come on in right now," invited Nick Borth. "I'll show you the prospectus."

Russ shook his head. "Sorry, I've got to get back. I make a point of taking the same length of lunch hour as the staff gets; it's good for morale. I'll be late if I don't hurry along now."

Nick Borth raised his eyebrows, but did not pursue the subject. "See you another time, then. Give me a call and we'll set something up. Here's my card." He fished it out of a pocket.

What an operator, thought Russ. He carries his business card even in work overalls. He took the card and looked it over, then stuck it in his pocket and held out his hand. "Be seeing you."

"I'll look forward to it," said Borth. "Have a nice day."

On the walk back to work Russ pondered the encounter, and resolved to find out more. If the project was on the up-and-up, he might consider putting some money into it. He had a feeling, though, that something a little shady was going on. He never had trusted slick operators, and that was exactly what Nick Borth was. He could always spot them. He was a bit of an operator himself.

So he made an appointment to talk to Nick one afternoon. Nick welcomed him warmly, and showed him around the site of the new condominium. Afterwards they sat down in the construction trailer and Nick broke out the whisky. He had learned that much on Eilean Dubh, that serious discussions were always accompanied by whisky. Russ disappointed him by asking for a cup of tea instead.

"I don't drink in the middle of the day," Russ said. "Too hard to concentrate the rest of the afternoon, and I get sleepy." And he wanted a clear head for Nick's schemes.

Disappointed, Nick said, "I don't have any tea. How about a cup of coffee?"

"Great," said Russ. "I keep a little percolator in my own office, myself. Haven't gotten used to all this tea-drinking they do here."

To Russ's disappointment, the coffee was instant, and the creamer was from a packet. He accepted the cup, and said casually, "Quite a project you've got going here."

"You don't know the half of it. I've got big plans for this place," said Nick, leaning back in his chair.

"'Zat so?" said Russ noncommittally, forcing down a gulp of the dreadful coffee.

"Oh, yes," said Nick, assuming that the American would be on his wavelength. "There's a lot of money to be made here. I can see a real tourist paradise unfolding before my eyes."

"What do you have in mind?"

"The condos are just the beginning. That's for the people with money."

"Got a way to keep them happy, have you?"

"With a golf course, and a couple of fine restaurants. I've got an offer in for that pizza place in Ros Mór; I'm going to turn that into an up-scale bistro. Have a contact in London who's salivating at the idea of opening an exclusive little joint that will earn a couple of Michelin stars."

Okay, thought Russ. Nothing wrong with that. If the man wants to go off the deep end and start up a fancy restaurant, more power to him. The MacShennachs will make a packet from selling the pizzeria to him, and probably take the money and open up a new pizza joint. What will happen to the bistro in the winter when there are no tourists is Nick's problem. "Not a lot of profit there," he said.

Nick took a long expansive breath, and smiled. "Oh, that's not where the money is. I'm thinking a motel north of the condos, and a fun fair with expensive rides and cheap food, and maybe a campground, although those guys don't spend much money. Got to get their dough with souvenirs. We could create Eilean Dubh's own Loch Ness monster in one of those little lakes they've got here. Sightings of Nessie always bring in tourists around Inverness; Scottish Tourist Board says so. I've done all the research. We'll start the rumor, and I'll get the locals producing little stuffed Nessies for the tourists. Maybe call them *Dubh*-ees." He pronounced the word "doobies."

He exhaled luxuriously. "I've got a lot of plans for this coastline. The money will be growing on bushes, just ripe for plucking."

Russ sipped coffee to give himself time. "Sounds like you've given it a lot of thought."

"Oh, I have. You want in?"

Russ equivocated. "My capital's pretty tied up in the business right now. What did you have in mind?"

"Tell you what," said Nick. "I'll draw up a prospectus for you, and you can give it a look-see."

"Okay. For starters, though . . . what do you plan to do if this doesn't all work out the way you've planned?"

"Hey, buddy, there's always a way out of something that doesn't work out, isn't there?" Nick winked at him.

Yeah, thought Russ. Take the money and run. Leave behind bankruptcy proceedings, people out of work, buildings falling into shambles. There's always a way out, if you are short on scruples.

He shook hands on leaving with some reluctance; Nick Borth's hand was clammy, and Russ had already decided that he didn't like him well enough to touch him. Had to observe the formalities, though.

On his way back up the coast, hurrying a little so he wouldn't be late back to work, he was accosted as usual by Fearchar MacShennach, who lived in the dilapidated cottage just beyond the scenic outlook. The old man had taken a liking to Russ; he was curious about incomers, especially Americans, and as a devoted gossip he was always eager to find new stories with which to annoy his granddaughter Barabal. She came in several times a week to clean, cook and bring the home-baked goodies that he loved. Barabal detested gossip, and it irritated her no end to have to listen to Fearchar's sly hints about Eilean Dubh goings-on, and especially, wrongdoings.

The old man was hobbling at full speed from his cottage, his wispy gray hair and beard waving in the breeze, his shabby overalls fluttering about his bony legs. "Hullo, there, Yank. Thought I'd missed you today."

No such luck, thought Russ, already planning his escape strategy. He didn't have any more time today for idle chatter, but his basic decency and respect for his elders would not let him snub the old man. "Hi, there, Mr. MacShennach. How are you?"

"Arturitis is terrible, as usual. It's this damn weather."

In some surprise, Russ took note of the beautiful sunny day. "I thought it was rain that bothered folks with arthritis."

"Hmmph. It bothers me every day, rain or shine. I'm a martyr to the arturitis, that I am. Wait till you get to be my age, young man. Aches and pains, that's what the end of life is all about."

"Sorry to hear that," said Russ. How was he to escape without giving offense? Fearchar would be perfectly willing to chatter on all afternoon about his physical complaints real and imagined, and once he got started he was like a boulder rolling downhill, gathering speed as he went and crushing all sensible conversation in his wake. A phone call, that was the ticket; he'd tell the old guy that he couldn't stop to talk because he was expecting an important call.

Fearchar surprised him with a sudden change of subject. "Been down to see that other Yank's doings, have you?"

How the hell did he know that? He must have binoculars trained on the road, Russ thought, so he could keep an eye on everything that happened. "I took a look, yes."

"What's he up to, then?" demanded Fearchar.

"Building condominiums."

"Aye, I know that," said the old man impatiently. "But what's he really up to? He's a sly one, that fellow. Wouldn't trust him an inch." He leaned forward in a confidential way, and came close to losing his balance. Alarmed, Russ put out a hand to help him, but Fearchar shrugged it off. "If it's just some hoity-toity condomimiyum thing, what's he want with my land?"

Russ looked at him in surprise, then remembered his conversation with

Nick Borth. Of course, to build his cheap motel and fun fair, whatever that was, he'd need more property. It had not occurred to Russ that Borth's plans would include this lovely stretch of the coast, so wild and uninhabited, except, of course, for Fearchar's cottage. A surge of indignation went through him. A tacky development, here? It was outrageous. Russ didn't realize it, but he was beginning to think like an *Eilean Dubhannach*, with their protective love for their Island's natural beauty.

"Has he made you an offer?"

Fearchar looked at him slyly. "Maybe he has, maybe he hasn't."

"Well, I hope you aren't planning on selling to him. Nobody here is going to like what he has in mind."

"What's that, then?" said the old man, leaning close again.

Too late Russ realized that Nick Borth's plans had been told to him in confidence, one businessman to another, and even if he despised Nick, he should not reveal what had been said. "You ought to ask him that, when he comes around to make you an offer."

"Too late for that," said Fearchar, looking smug, "for he's already been around waving his Yankee greenbacks under my nose."

"You've not accepted!" Russ said in alarm.

"Ah, well, that's my little secret, isn't it, but I was wondering if I might get a wee bit of help from you in determining what a fair offer for my land might be."

"I have no idea what land is worth on Eilean Dubh."

"You're a businessman."

"Not a real estate agent, though. You need to ask somebody who knows about local property values. Why don't you ask Darroch?" he added, struck by a sudden idea. Darroch would put a stop to these shenanigans, Russ told himself; he would not allow his beloved Island to be desecrated.

The old man drew himself back. "I'll not be involving the Laird in my personal affairs."

"Think he wouldn't approve?"

Fearchar bristled. "Why wouldn't he? And why would I care if he didn't? It's my land and my business what I do with it."

Russ shrugged, not wanting to get any further involved with a situation where he could do little to help. He couldn't resist one further admonition, though. "You'd better find out what Nick Borth wants with your land before you go making deals with him. I wouldn't trust that guy any further than I could throw him."

Fearchar looked a little puzzled by the unfamiliar figure of speech, and while he was pondering it, Russ made his escape with a polite, "Got to get back to work. See you around, Mr. MacShennach." And he set off at a trot, leaving the old man looking after him in disappointment; he'd hoped for a much longer chat, and much more information.

Dubh-ees indeed, thought Russ as he jogged along, his indignation growing with every step, and what he was envisioning making him shudder. Junk souvenirs and fast food. Litter. Neon signs flashing day and night. Traffic congestion. And if it didn't work out, what would be left but skeletons of decaying buildings, unemployment, traditional businesses destroyed for a quick profit.

My business, Russ thought, and came to a sudden stop. He'll want the land that I have on a long-term, ironclad lease, mine to do with as I like. He'll want me to close up shop, and turn the land over to him for exploitation. I'll bet he's about to make me an offer he thinks I can't refuse. And if I accept, and Fearchar accepts—he's the linchpin, right in the middle of the two properties—Nick Borth will have control of the entire coastline from the cemetery all the way up to Airgead.

Shaking his head, deep in thought, he walked slowly back to his office, shocking his employees by returning ten minutes late from lunch.

The De'il's Awa' wi' the Islander

8x32 Reel for two couples in a longwise set

Devised February 2005 by Lara Friedman-Shedlov. The story of an encounter with the devil: The woman flirts with, then flees from him. Determined to ensnare her, the devil pursues the woman. He catches her, captivating her with his charm, and dashes away with her, but finally, she sees through his tricks and loses him among the stones.

1-2	1C turn LH halfway. 1W finish facing out.
3-4	1W, followed by 1M, dance down behind 2M and across the set.
5-8	1C turn LH about 1 1/4 to finish 1W facing up between 2C, her partner behind her.
16-16	1C dance shadow reel of 3 across the set with 2C, giving LS to 2M to begin. At the end of the reel, 1C turn quickly by RH halfway to finish in the middle on own sides facing down.
24-24	1C lead down the middle and up to 2nd place on own sides.
25-32	1C and 2C set and dance RH across halfway, set and dance LH across halfway.

The De'ils Awa' Wi' the Islander

Twenty

A man who is clever is an asset to himself;
a man who is clever and good is a treasure to the world.

Eilean Dubh proverb

$\mathcal{S}$everal evenings later, the Mac an Rìghs and Abbotts were dinner guests at *Taigh Rois,* and the conversation turned again to Nick Borth's machinations. Time had not made them any wiser as to what was going on with the incomer.

"We've given him everything he's asked for," said Darroch. "What else could he want?"

"One thing he wants is old Fearchar MacShennach's cottage," Màiri said. "Barabal said he'd been round to her mother, pretending to be concerned about the old man's health, and insinuating that Elspeth wasn't a good daughter if she didn't pop Fearchar into the Seniors' Residence right away. And Elspeth taking him his dinner every day, and doing his cleaning and laundry as well. Not a good daughter! She's a saint, for old Fearchar has got the crankiest disposition of anyone on the Island, and has never been known to thank her once for all she does for him."

She added, "Borth offered her money for the cottage, to try to bribe her into making the decision he wanted. And she thinks he's been sneaking around, ingratiating himself with the old man, knowing that he's the owner of the land. Fearchar has a brand new telly, one of those great big ones, and he won't say where he got it, but Barabal's sure it was a gift from Nick Borth."

"Why would he want that old place?" wondered Jamie. "Barabal says it's such a wreck it'll probably have to be burned down after Fearchar dies."

"He wants more property? He's already got a big chunk of land on lease," Darroch said. "Why does he want so much?"

Russ stirred uneasily, wrestled with his conscience regarding Borth's confidences, and loyalty to his adopted Island won. "You don't get it, do you?"

"Get what?" snapped Màiri.

"It's the coastline." Then, when they still looked baffled, he said, "Thanks to Ruth and my doctor, I've been doing a lot of walking since I got here, and it's all been up and down that stretch of coast north and south of my firm's headquarters. You guys have lived here all your lives; you don't realize just what you've got." His voice softened with affection. "It's gorgeous, the most beautiful place I've ever been, and probably the equal of anything on the Riviera or Florida or Mexico. And it's completely unspoiled. There's not even any litter. I've never seen anything bigger than a gum wrapper.

"I've been talking to that old guy, that whatshisname MacShennach. He's a nut for chitchat; he comes out and starts in on me nearly every time I go by. I used to stop, just to be polite, but that wasted my time for walking and I had to turn around and go back to work without getting in my daily three miles. So I tried waving and going on past, and damned if he doesn't come out and start hobbling along with me, and gabbing up a storm. He keeps up with me pretty good for about a mile before his knees give out and he has to turn back. He's eighty-nine, you know, so he can't walk as far as I can, and he's got a little arturitis . . . arthritis . . . in his joints."

He looked abashed, and said, "We've gotten to be kind of friendly. He's a real interesting old codger. Full of fascinating stories, and he always gives me an earful. One thing he likes to do is brag about his property. Do any of you realized how much of that coast he owns?"

The others shook their heads.

Russ said, "It stretches from the boundary of the land my business is on all the way up to the property Nick Borth has leased, and that parcel goes all the way to Cemetery Hill. If Nick could get his hands on the old man's land he'd control two-thirds of the most beautiful, undeveloped coastline in Scotland. Maybe even in the world. And he'd own outright the largest chunk, the one that's right in the middle."

"What would he do with it?" asked Jamie.

Did he have to spill everything he knew? Couldn't they put two and two together? God, they were innocents. Russ said patiently, as though talking to slightly dim-witted children, "Well, what would you do with it if you were a crooked, in-it-for-the-money, don't-give-a-damn-about-the-environment property developer?"

"Develop the hell out of it, and never mind about what he was spoiling," said Darroch, looking grim.

Russ nodded. "Now you've got it. He wants to build cheap rental properties, and everything that goes with them, to appeal to hordes of tourists. The Island would be overrun with them."

"Souvenir shops and hot dog stands," offered Jean with a shudder.

"Oh, that would be terrible," said Ruth. "It would spoil everything."

Russ said, "He wants more than the coastline; he wants to create a little empire of tourist businesses. He's already got his eyes on a couple of restaurants. He's made an offer on one of them."

"The MacShennachs' pizzeria!" gasped Màiri. "Uilleam's wife told me someone was interested in buying the place, and they were considering the offer seriously."

"He plans to turn it into an upscale restaurant," said Russ. "For his big-spending timeshare clientele."

Darroch said, "How do you know all this, Russ?"

Russ smiled. "Oh, Nick and I had a long chat the other day and he confided a few ideas to me. Not all of them, I'm sure. He's not the sort to tip his hand completely. I'm violating a confidence in telling you all this, and it goes against my ethics as a businessman, but you've got to know, since you haven't scoped it out yourselves."

He took a deep breath, and said, "I figure he wants me to close my business, throw my people out of work, and go in with him as an investor. Turn my lease over to him so he can get that property too." He looked at them. "You guys gave me that lease with no strings attached, and an option to buy. I can do just about anything I want to with the property. Bad idea, folks."

"We trust you, Russ," said Darroch gently.

"Yeah, and I'm not going to stab you, or my employees, in the back. It wouldn't be ethical. But that's not how Nick Borth thinks." He took a deep breath. "Here's what I know so far. He's building the condos, working on acquiring the restaurant to go with them, and he'd like to build a golf course. That's for the big spenders. He wants old man MacShennach's property for the cheap tourist trade, build a motel, maybe a fast food franchise or two. He wants my land either for a low-end campground or something he calls a fun fair. I don't know what that is, but I think it involves carnival rides. He said something about a casino, too, but he hasn't figured out if gambling is legal here."

The others stared at him, appalled, and Màiri sputtered, "It's outrageous. He'd ruin our Island to make himself rich."

"Very, very rich, if it all works out. Eilean Dubh would become a Scottish Disneyland, without the Mickey Mouse ears."

"It's been known to happen," Darroch mused. "A tiny, isolated place taken over as a playground for the . . . "

"Yobbos," finished Jamie. "The rich ones and the poor ones."

"But the transport . . . how would tourists get here? There's just the twice a week ferry, and the helicopter . . . "

"I imagine that he wants to buy that, too," said Russ quietly. "Develop the helicopter pad for a full scale airfield."

There was a shocked silence.

Russ said, "I sure could use a cup of tea. Or coffee, but I suppose that's unlikely."

Jean and Ruth both jumped up, and Ruth said, "Of course you can have coffee. I'll fix it, Jean. The rest of you keep on talking."

Darroch returned to his musings. "Mind you, he might be able to sell the idea of turning our Island into a fun fair. There are enough people here who could use a job who might be persuaded to support such a scheme."

"If he hires our people," said Jean. "I've heard he's replacing Islanders with workers from the mainland, from as far away as England. He claims our people don't have the needed skills. Ian the Post told Catrìona and she told me. Ian's cousin Alasdair MacQuirter was fired the other day, and a guy from Aberdeen brought in to replace him."

"Never!" said Jamie. "Alasdair's the best carpenter on the Island."

"And a smart guy. If anything rotten is going on at that building site, Alasdair would figure it out."

"Hence a good reason to fire him," said Jean.

"And anyone else who puts two and two together," said Jamie.

"What has he got to hide at the building site?" wondered Darroch.

"Well, his construction guys have to have access to his plans. Maybe there's something in them that shows what he plans for the rest of the coast," said Russ.

Màiri demanded, "What are we going to do?"

Russ said, "The way I look at it, I figure you're stuck."

"What do you mean?"

"He's already got the timeshare property. All he needs is the old guy's land, and he'll have enough coastline to do what he wants, even without my lease. You don't have any zoning laws, do you?"

Darroch said, "Never needed them. It never occurred to anyone that we would need them."

Russ shook his head sadly. "He gets old Fearchar's place, he puts his low cost stuff and the fast food joint in, starts advertising for package tours, and your quiet Eilean Dubh is toast. It'll become Tourist Town Arizona."

"Barabal would never let her mother sell Fearchar's property to Borth," said Màiri.

Darroch said, "But neither of them owns it. Fearchar does, and he's very much alive. What if he could be convinced to sell? Nick will offer him a lot of money, and it would be a real temptation to him to want to get that much security for his family. He's very stubborn, and opposition from Barabal might just get his back up. He calls her a female bossy-boots."

Russ added, "Nick has been to see the old guy several times. Brought him cigars, which he refused, and whisky, which he accepted, and sounds as though that big television he brags about came from him, too. He's pretty suspicious of outsiders, but Nick's a smooth talker. It'd be his idea to find out what the old man wanted, and get it for him to ingratiate himself."

"But he's working on Barabal's mother, too."

Russ smiled. "In case the old guy pops off before the deal's done. Nick Borth covers all the bases."

Ruth said, "Perhaps you could pass zoning laws."

Russ said, "That takes time, baby, and they have to be written right; otherwise a team of smart lawyers will demolish them. And your lawyers would have to be top notch, and would cost lots of dough."

Darroch said, "There has to be something we can do."

"You've got my word on my use of my leased property, so the key has to be old Fearchar. And I'm going to work on him, keeping him reminded of how beautiful the land is, and its historic value, and stuff like that. Listen to his stories about the past. If I could find an angle so that you could put up a historical marker on his land, something about the MacShennachs, he might not sell." Russ grinned ruefully. "Trouble is, nothing ever seems to have happened on that piece of property, at least nothing the old guy's told me so far. No Viking invasion, no ancient monastery, no great battles. Just good grazing land for sheep, and nobody puts up a marker for that. But I'm working on the problem."

Darroch said, "You're a terrific guy, Russ. We owe you a lot."

Russ shrugged. "Hey, no big deal. I like this place, and I don't want it ruined. I guess I'm starting to think of it as my Island." Then, realizing what he had said—my Island—he glanced quickly at the *Eilean Dubhannaich* to see if he'd presumed.

But they were all smiling. Jamie said, "Damned right it's your Island. Welcome aboard, Russ."

Embarrassed, Russ buried his face in his cup of coffee and tried to look casual about his acceptance into the Island clan.

PART VII

Darroch Goes Out on a Limb

Twenty-one

What use is it to build up treasure,
if it does not benefit your own?
For true wealth comes only from the family.

Eilean Dubh proverb

*T*he old man opened the door at Darroch's first knock. *"Feasgar math, a Mhic an Rìgh,"* he greeted the Laird, using the formal style of address. Like all Eilean Dubh residents, he regarded the Laird with admiration and treated him with respect.

"Feasgar math, a Fhearchar," replied Darroch.

"Will you come in and sit a while?" invited the old man.

"Tapadh leat." Darroch walked into the crowded front room and took a seat on the sofa, moving a pile of magazines from one end to the other. He had not noticed the tabby cat, which gave a startled yowl when the magazines were placed on top of her. "Oh, poor kitty," said Darroch and rubbed her back. She purred, and settled down with her head on his lap.

"She's a fearful nuisance," said Fearchar. "Will I take her away?"

"No, no, leave her. I quite like cats. This one is a fine animal."

"She'll do," said Fearchar briefly. "She keeps the rats away, at least."

Darroch repressed a shudder, although he did not really think that there were rats in the old man's home. Mice, however, were quite another thing. No doubt the cat earned her keep.

Next Darroch ventured a comment upon the weather, and Fearchar made a rejoinder, and after about five minutes of polite chat the old man said, "The Laird is a busy man, and I'm thinking he's not come here to discuss the weather with me. Although if you want a prediction, my knees are telling me to expect rain."

"Is that so?" answered Darroch absently, trying to find the words for his mission. Plunge right in, he thought. *"A Fhearchar*, I'm here to discuss this fine property of yours."

"Don't tell me you're wanting it too! Haven't I had enough discussions about it with that Yank?"

"What Yank would that be?" said Darroch cannily. "We've several Yank incomers."

"Not the one that was married to your Jean once upon a time, the one that comes by my cottage so that I'll waste my time talking to him. I mean the fellow that's building those fancy condominnies on the piece of land next to my property."

"Aye, that one. That's precisely what I've come to talk about."

"Well, talk away, *a Mhic an Rìgh*. I'm listening."

Careful, careful, thought Darroch. "Might I be so bold as to inquire if he has made you an offer on your property?"

"And why might that interest the Laird?"

"Because if he buys your land he will control a very large section of our coastline, and some of us are worried about what he might do with it."

"What's the worry?"

"There are suspicions that he is planning to develop the whole area into a fun fair to bring in hordes of tourists."

"Hmmph." Fearchar disliked strangers. *"Sasannachan?"*

"Aye, and all manner of others."

Always contrary and ready for an argument, the old man said, "To hear some folk talk, tourists are what the Island needs. They bring in gobs of money, so I understand."

"Aye, and litter, traffic, and crime."

"You can't stop progress, *a Mhic an Rìgh*," said Fearchar, an avowed enemy of progress of any kind.

"True, but we can control it, if we can control development of our coast. It's one of our few assets, that beautiful coastline."

Fearchar snorted. "Don't see why. Just rocks and water, that's all there is to it."

Realizing that the discussion was going nowhere, Darroch tried another tack. "If you're thinking about selling your property, perhaps you'd care to discuss it with the Island Trust."

"Aye, that Trust. Your doing, isn't it."

"At first, but now there's a committee that says what projects the Trust will fund, and they're interested in keeping our Island from being overrun by developers."

"You think the Trust could match the Yank's offer?"

"I won't know until I know what offer the Yank has made," said Darroch patiently.

Fearchar hesitated, as though he would not say, but a lifelong pattern of deference to the Laird asserted itself, and he named a figure that made Darroch gasp.

"That much?"

"Aye."

We're in big trouble, thought Darroch, and wished yet again that Nick Borth had been stopped before he got a foothold on the Island. *"Gabh mo leisgeul* . . . it's none of my business . . . but what would you be doing with such an enormous sum of money?"

Fearchar lifted his head and smiled proudly. "I want to send my great-grandson to university."

At last, thought Darroch, a problem he could get a handle on. "A grand idea. Young Somhairle's very bright, and top of the table in the High School. What university were you thinking of for him? Edinburgh? Glasgow?"

"Ach, no, I'd something better in mind."

"What could be better than a good Scottish school?"

The old man took a deep breath. "I will be sending him to Harvard, in the United States of America."

Darroch could not help himself; he choked on his tea. He managed at last to gasp, "Are you serious, *a Fhearchar*? Harvard?"

The old man bristled. "And why not?"

"Well, the cost, for one thing. And would he want to go so far away from home?"

"He'll go wherever I tell him. He's a good lad. And I will be able to pay the cost, once I've sold my land to yon Yank. It will be enough. I know, because I have written to them and asked what their fees are. I will have enough to send Somhairle to Harvard for four years, room and board, books and tuition, and have enough left over to keep myself in a neat little apartment in the Seniors' Residence."

Sinking fast, Darroch tried one last feint. "I understand that admission standards are very high. Perhaps Somhairle won't be able to get into Harvard."

Fearchar bristled, and Darroch knew he'd made a mistake. "Are you telling me that my grandson is not smart enough to get into a Yank university?"

"No, of course not," said Darroch, making a gallant effort to regain control of the conversation. "Somhairle's a fine lad. But it may not be just grades and brains. It may be alumni recommendations, string-pulling, entered since childhood, that sort of thing."

"We will see." Fearchar folded his arms across his chest, and looked defiantly at Darroch. "I would not like to be thinking that the Laird would want to stand in the way of an Eilean Dubh lad getting a fine Harvard education."

Darroch rose, saying sternly, "I wish nothing but the best for all our Island children, being a father myself, and I'm certain that you know that is true, *a Fhearchar*. And should Somhairle need a letter of recommendation to Harvard, I'll be pleased to write one myself. I'll bid you good day now."

The old man, somewhat abashed, went to hold the door open for the Laird, and bobbed an infinitesimal bow as Darroch went out.

Once outside, Darroch let his shoulders slump and his brow furrow as waves of worry enveloped him. The old man was determined on a course of action and had a good use for the money he'd receive from the sale of his property.

Would it be right to try to talk him out of it?

Would it, in fact, be possible?

He headed home to share the bad news with Jean.

PART VIII

Anna and Zach Hit the Jackpot

Twenty-two

Near the snow, near the sun, in the highest fields
See how these names are fêted by the waving grass,
And by the streamers of white cloud,
And whispers of wind in the listening sky;
The names of those who in their lives fought for life,
Who wore at their hearts the fire's center.
Born of the sun they traveled a short while toward the sun,
And left the vivid air signed with their honor.

Stephen Spender

*Z*ach's spirits were sagging. Anna knew that, and even making love wasn't consoling him. They were running out of places to search for prehistoric sites. They'd walked most of the interior of the Island, peered into peat bog cuttings, skirted forests, waded burns, and all that was left to search was the wee bit of coastline south of Fearchar MacShennach's property, between the helicopter pad and Ros Mòr, where Nick Borth was building his condominiums.

"I'm at my wit's end," Zach said, scuffing his feet on the road. "I've searched everywhere, and not a hint of a site. It's down to the wire, too; I'm almost out of grant money. If I don't find something soon, I'm busted."

"Don't give up hope," Anna consoled him. "We'll keep looking." She stopped in front of the fence that barred the construction site from the road. "I wonder how the work is coming on the evil condo development?" She found a peephole in the fence and peered through it. "Damn, I can't see a thing. There's a big yellow machine in the way."

"Let me look." He put his eye to the hole. "That's a bulldozer. I can't see around it, either."

Turning to leave, Anna stubbed her toe against an object on the ground and bent to pick it up. "Hmm, Eilean Dubh bloodstone. I haven't ever seen such a big piece." She turned the large flat stone around in her fingers.

"What's that you've found?"

"Piece of our native rock, pretty stuff. Rather rare these days. It was mined for jewelry beads in Victorian times until they worked the seam out. Usually found up in the mountains. I wonder what it's doing here."

Zach took the stone from her hands and stared at it in mounting wonder. "Dear God," he breathed. "It's a flake."

"You're joking."

"Anna, you angel, you're brilliant! You've found a prehistoric tool!"

"Right here in the middle of the road? That's ridiculous, after we've scoured every other inch of the Island."

Zach stared at the flake, then scanned the roadside, then lifted his eyes to the construction fence, his mind working and his heart beginning to pound. His gaze rushed along the fence to the gate, and to the trailer that had been brought in for use as the site office. Then he began to run. He screeched to a halt outside the fence in front of the trailer door, and stared through the mesh. "A split stone," he cried, and sank to his knees, gazing at a large piece of rock that had been put in place to serve as a step.

Baffled, Anna came to stand by his side.

Zach peered at the stone lovingly. "It's cracked. It must be a hearth stone," he crooned. "Look, there's the residue of charcoal, that greasy stain on the side. Oh, Anna! A knapped flake and a split stone! We've found it!"

"Found what?"

"The site. It's got to be near here; that's where the construction guys found the stone and dragged it in to use as a step. And the flake is something a worker picked up, and dropped." He jumped up and dashed to the nearest peephole in the fence. "Damn, I can't see much through this one either. But that's surely a bit of a wall. Dry stone wall for livestock? Or could it be the wall of a house?" Almost dancing now with excitement, his eyes alight with joy, he cried, "Anna, we've got to get inside that fence!"

She stared at him. "Well, I don't see how we could do that. The gate's chained shut, and the fence is too steep and high to climb. Can it wait until tomorrow?"

"No, no, it can't wait! I've got to get in there now. Don't you realize what this means? They might be tearing up my site, and they have to be stopped. If they disturb it, we'll never be able to conduct a proper dig. They'll scatter artifacts far and wide, mess up the levels, destroy the continuity."

"But the land is leased to that Nick Borth *diabhol* for the condos. How can we stop it even if it is what you've been looking for?"

"The law, Anna, it's the law. They can't dig on a designated archeological site. I've got to get in and verify it, right now, before it's damaged any further."

Anna said, "All right, steady on, don't get your knickers in a twist. Calm down and let's look for a way to get in." She moved to the fence and began to move along it methodically, following it past the gate and around the corner towards the back.

Zach started along the fence in the opposite direction. When they met again in front of the gate, both shook their heads.

"Absolutely impregnable," said Anna.

"No way in. Damn," said Zach. "It'll have to be a ladder, then."

Anna stared. "You're going to climb over that fence using a ladder?"

"Do you have a better idea?"

"No, but where will we get a ladder?"

"Cailean the Crab's got a tool shed full of builders' tat. He's sure to have a ladder. Let's go!"

When they were nearly back to the car, Anna looked over her shoulder and spotted a car slowly pulling in behind them. "Oh, hell," she said. "It's the constable, Mr. Nosy Boots MacRath himself, and he's going to want to know what we're doing here."

Zach's brain was working so rapidly he surprised even himself. "Get in the driver's seat," he ordered, "and release the latch on the bonnet."

He pulled the hood up and stuck his head under it just as the panda car's door opened. "Try it, Anna," called Zach.

"What?"

"The ignition. Hello, constable."

"Evening, sir. Having a wee bit of car trouble, are you?"

"She stalled on me. Just having a look to see . . . umm . . . " Since he knew very little about automobile motors, Zach's imagination failed him. He stuck his head back under the hood and pretended to fiddle with a wire. "Try it now, Anna," he called.

Anna turned the key in the ignition and the car started.

"There we go," said Zach, and slammed the hood shut. "Loose wire, I think. Have to take her in to the garage tomorrow."

"I'd best follow you to where you're headed, sir, in case it happens again. Wouldn't want you stranded with night coming on." The constable walked to his car.

Cursing under his breath, Zach climbed into the passenger seat. "We've got a police escort, Anna. Drive slow and easy to Cailean's."

When Anna turned into Cailean's lane, she gave a cheery wave as the constable's car sped by. "He's away home to his dinner. We won't have to worry about him for the rest of the night, unless we're too obvious about this breaking and entering lark."

Scowling, Zach said, "We're not committing a crime. We're trying to prevent one." Ignoring the private entrance to his room, he knocked on the front door.

It was opened by a small boy. "Whazzup, Zach," said Cailean the Crab's middle son Peadair, who was addicted to American hip-hop music and slang.

"Wotcher, sprout. Your dad around?" said Zach.

"Nah, him and Mum are still down at the shop. Wanna come in and play a video game till they get home and make me do my homework?"

Zach shook his head, aware of Anna and her raised eyebrows signaling in disbelief, *you play video games?* "Can't, got work to do. Your dad got a ladder?"

"Check out the tool shed," advised the boy, already beginning to shut the door and turn back towards the television set.

There was a ladder in the shed, and Zach rubbed his hands together in glee. "Just the ticket."

Anna said dubiously, "How are we going to get it in the car?"

As hard as they struggled, they could not get the ladder into the car crosswise without its end extending dangerously out across the opposite lane of the road. Finally they wedged it diagonally from passenger seat to rear seat, and Zach sat in back to hold it in place while Anna drove.

At the building site they hauled the ladder out and walked along the fence, looking for the best place to set it up. "What are you going to when you reach the top of the ladder? You can't jump down three meters without breaking an ankle, and you'd never be able to get out again," Anna said. "If you're caught in there you'll get done for entering illegally, and have to research your site from a jail cell."

"I'll perch on top and take pictures," Zach said, fishing his digital camera out of his pocket. It had traveled everywhere on the Island with him, so that he could document anything he found, and so far it had had little use.

He climbed the ladder. Steadying himself, he got his first good look at the site, and was struck dumb as the full glory of what they had discovered stretched out in front of him.

Anna, waiting impatiently below, shouted up at him, "What do you see? Is it what you'd hoped for?"

Zach turned to her, his eyes full of wonder. "Oh, yes, it's everything I'd hoped for. They've cut into a mound, the Philistine bastards, and I can see a dry stone wall, and a stone bed built into the wall. And post holes. It's a classic late Mesolithic site. Anna, there's a bunch of those mounds! I think it's a village!"

"Hurry up and take your snaps before the light goes," Anna advised, "and before some nosy parker comes along and asks what the hell you're doing up on that ladder. If anyone sees you it'll be all over the Island before morning."

Zach took pictures until the camera battery died. "We'll print them out and then we'll have the evidence. You can do that with your computer, can't you? I don't have a printer for my laptop."

"Right, but what do we do with the pictures?"

"Show them to the construction people tomorrow, of course," said Zach impatiently.

"You think Nick Borth will stop work on his prized project on your say-so and a handful of pictures? The guy's a hard-nosed tyrant accountable to no one, and we won't get any help from the crew because he's replaced our local lads with folk from the mainland who won't give a damn about archaeology. They'll be against stopping, in fact, because it'll mean an end to their paychecks."

He stared at her, realizing she was right.

"If anything," Anna mused, "it'll make Borth drive them to work faster, so they can obliterate the evidence."

"What are we going to do?"

"Get the ladder. We can't leave it here; it's a sure tip-off that somebody's interested in what's inside that fence." Together they wrestled the ladder back into the car; then Zach looked at Anna again. "What's next?"

"We need help. Get in the car."

"Anna, where are we going?"

She threw herself into the driver's seat and started the ignition. "There's only one person on the Island with enough clout to stop them right away."

"And that would be . . . Superman?" Zach said sarcastically.

"No, you berk, that would be the Laird."

Zach scowled. "The anachronism."

She scowled back at him. "The most respected man on Eilean Dubh, whose word is law. If he wants something done, it happens. Just because he doesn't assert himself very often doesn't mean he doesn't have the authority."

She sped off, shifting gears with a clash that made Zach wince, and headed for the newspaper office. When she'd hooked up the digital camera to her computer and printed out the pictures, she looked at them in awe. "These are brilliant. Even I can see it's some sort of building thing."

He crowded close to peer over her shoulder. "That's the door opening, I think, and look, that's a bed built into the wall. Typical of Mesolithic buildings. Later on the beds stuck out into the room, but these are entirely within the wall."

"This one's the clearest. I'll use it for the front page. Spread it across the whole page above the fold," Anna mused, already writing the cutline in her mind.

"You can't run the story till I say so," said Zach.

"Of course, and the sooner we get that project stopped the sooner we can announce your great discovery. Come on, we've got a visit to pay."

Hands full of the precious pictures, they piled into the car and headed for *Taigh a Mhorair.*

PART IX

The Laird to the Rescue

Twenty-three

Out spake their Captain brave and bold,
A merry wight was he:
"If London Tower were Michael's hold,
We'd set Trelawney free!
We'll cross the Tamar, land to land:
The Severn is no stay:
With 'one and all,' and hand in hand;
And who shall bid us nay?"

Unofficial Cornish national anthem

*A*t *Taigh a Mhorair*, Jean and Darroch were finishing supper. Jean was clearing the dishes from the kitchen table while Darroch fed Rosie her favorite dessert, puréed pears. It was a time of day they both enjoyed, one that made them feel very much a family. They did not expect to be interrupted and the knock on the door was a surprise.

Jean went to answer.

"Sorry to disturb you," said Anna, "but we've got some exciting news."

"I'll make a fresh pot of tea," began Jean, but Zach said, "No, no time for that."

"No time for a cuppa? It must be exciting," said Darroch, and leaned forward to wipe pears from Rosie's mouth. "You'd better sit down, then."

Anna sat obediently, but Zach could not bring himself to take a chair. He paced back and forth nervously. "Will you tell, Zach, or should I?" When he shook his head impatiently, Anna sighed and said, "Well, it's like this. Zach is an archaeologist and he's here to find the footprints of early man. And he's found them, and the site has to be preserved immediately."

"Early man . . . ," began Jean.

"And woman," said Anna.

"Hmm," said Darroch. "How many years ago was that? Prehistory was never my strong suit."

Zach threw himself into a chair. "Probably eight thousand years ago."

Both Jean and Darroch looked suitably impressed, and Darroch said, "You're an archaeologist? Who's funding your research?"

"The Scottish Antiquities Trust."

Darroch said, "And where is this site?"

Anna said, "It's Nick Borth's construction project, and work has to be stopped on it right away before the site is destroyed."

Jean and Darroch froze in shock. Then they looked at each other, and a wild hope flashed between them. Darroch said slowly, "What evidence do you have?"

"I've found . . . or rather, Anna's found . . . this." Zach pulled the piece of bloodstone from his pocket.

The older couple stared at it. "Your evidence is a piece of rock?" asked Jean.

"It's a flake. A prehistoric tool made by knapping, which means using a tool to knock bits off a core stone to make other tools. This one looks to me like a scraper."

"For preparing hides for tanning," added Anna helpfully. "We picked it up outside the construction site. And Zach climbed a ladder and looked over the fence, and he says there's a dry stone wall inside the site. Right, Zach?" She looked at him for confirmation.

Controlling his growing excitement, Darroch said, "I don't mean to be skeptical, but how do you know it's not a wall built two or three hundred years ago? Dry stone walls are common on Eilean Dubh."

Zach began to rattle off the other things he'd noted from the ladder. "They've uncovered quite a bit of the first part of the site, and I could see enough to convince me of the possibility of Mesolithic habitation. Here's pictures I took that show signs of postholes in a circle, which indicates a temporary settlement of huts, preceding the stone buildings. Mesolithic people were hunters and gatherers, and it was only at the end of the period they began erecting permanent buildings and becoming dependent on farming. So this is probably a permanent site built on top of a temporary site, which is not uncommon. If we're lucky, it will shed some light on the transition between Mesolithic and Neolithic civilizations." He paused for breath.

Darroch picked up the flake and turned it over in his long fingers. "How do you prove your theory?"

"Radiocarbon dating of the artifacts, AMS—accelerator mass spectrometry—of the smaller samples of organic matter."

"Which is done where?"

"I'll send samples to my university."

"Which will take how long?"

Zach scowled. "Too damn long. By the time I get them back, the site will be wrecked by those construction yobbos."

Anna implored, "Please, Darroch. We have to stop the work on the condos, and we have to stop it tomorrow. We've got to have your help."

Darroch said, "Anna, you need to talk to the Council."

She shook her head. "It will take too long, and once Nick Borth gets on to what we've discovered, he'll destroy the evidence so he can carry on building."

Jean said quietly, "She's right, lovie."

Darroch sighed. "What do you want me to do?"

"Go to the construction site tomorrow and tell them it's being shut down, by the authority of the Laird," said Anna.

"Who has no authority at all . . . ," he began.

"But Nick Borth doesn't know that," said Jean.

"No," said Anna, and they all looked at Darroch.

Finally he grinned. "Worth a try," he said.

"You'll do it?" demanded Zach.

"Oh, yes, I'll do it, with pleasure." said Darroch. "I've been longing to put a spanner in that particular work for quite some time now." Then he added, "I think I'll get Barabal Mac-a-Phi for reinforcements, though; she's Chair of the Council."

"And Màiri, in case someone needs to be shouted at," said Jean.

"And Ian Mór MacDonald; he's big enough to intimidate anyone."

"Jamie, with his fiddle, for a musical accompaniment?" said Jean. "Maybe he'll compose a new tune for us. 'The Mesolithic Rescue Reel.'"

"Right, then," said Darroch. "Convene the mob at what time tomorrow, Anna?"

"Eight, so that we get them before they get the bulldozers switched on."

Zach, who'd been growing increasingly desperate at the thought that he might not be able to save his beloved site, stared at the three of them, and felt tears of relief spring into his eyes. "I can't thank you enough," he said at last.

"Don't thank us, lad," said Darroch. "This might be the most fun we've had for ages."

As Anna and Zach walked out to the car, he said, "That's quite an anachronism you've got there."

Anna smiled to herself.

A stout crew, summoned by telephone the night before, assembled in front of the construction site the next morning. There were Darroch and Jean, Sally and Ian *Mór* MacDonald, Barabal, Anna and Zach, and Màiri. The women had had a consultation, and come up with a contingency plan to stop the dig in case reason failed, one they hadn't told the men about. Jean and Màiri were quite looking forward to it. Jean had often regretted that she had been born too late to be a protester, like in the sixties, and Màiri's nature was naturally confrontational.

To Màiri's annoyance, Jamie had flatly refused to come along. He had made it a strict policy to avoid the construction site since his encounter with the misty wisps. He said nothing about that encounter, of course; instead, he volunteered to baby-sit Rosie. "For you'll not be taking her along, if there might be fireworks to come," he said.

Màiri agreed, grumpily.

They had decided the night before that the confrontation with Nick Borth should take place inside the trailer, so that the workers wouldn't know what was happening and rally to their boss's assistance and the defense of their jobs. Since they couldn't all fit inside the trailer, Darroch, the Laird, Barabal, the Council Chair, Zach, the archaeologist, and Anna, the newspaper editor, had been elected as spokespersons. Ian *Mór* MacDonald posted himself outside the door to insure that there would be no interruptions.

The gates were open, and the rescuers drove their cars inside, cannily inserting them in the spaces around the earthmoving machines. The designated party advanced on the trailer, and Darroch knocked on the door. When Nick Borth opened it, Darroch said pleasantly, "Good morning, Mr. Borth. May we come in for a wee chat?"

Borth stared from one determined face to the next. "What's going on?" he demanded.

Darroch put his foot on the step and swung himself into the trailer, and Borth was forced to retreat to allow him room. "Come in," Darroch said to the others. "Perhaps you're not knowing our young friends, Mr. Borth. This is Anna Wallace, our newspaper editor, and Zachariah Trelawney. He's an archaeologist."

Both extended their hands, smiles fixed on their faces.

"It's a lovely day," offered Barabal, receiving a puzzled look from their quarry.

"Quite warm for this time of year," said Darroch, and the others murmured assent.

"Yeah, it's great," said Borth. "Say, I don't mean to be rude, but I've got a lot of work in front of me today. What can I do for you folks? Contribution to some worthy Island cause, perhaps? Shall I get out my wallet?" He gave them his best professional smile.

"Kind of you to offer," said Darroch, "but the fact is that we—that is to say—Mr. Trelawney and Ms Wallace—have made an astonishing discovery about your property here." He returned Borth's smile. "We wanted you to know about it right away."

Borth stared.

Darroch turned expectantly to Zach, who blurted, "You're digging up an immensely valuable historic site. It's Mesolithic."

Darroch sighed. He had hoped for a more tactful approach.

"So what?" snapped Borth.

"Well, you can't do it," said Zach flatly. "It's against the law. You'll have to stop."

"What the hell are you talking about?"

Darroch threw a warning glance at Zach, and said in his most reasonable voice, "We are afraid that you will have to stop your construction activities here, because we have reason to believe that it is an important archaeological site which is protected by law from unauthorized digging."

"Unauthorized digging?" shouted Borth, turning red. "I have an ironclad lease on this property and you know it, damn it, all of you. I can do anything I want here."

"Except dig it up," said Anna, smiling.

"How the hell can I build a condo if I can't dig up the ground?" Borth bellowed.

"Ah, that's the problem, you see," said Barabal. "You can't dig here until the site is authenticated. And after it is authenticated, you definitely can't dig it up. So we're saving you trouble in the future, by having you stop now."

Borth took a deep breath, and attempted to get control of his temper. "Run that by me again. You think that there's a . . . a . . ."

"Mesolithic site," offered Zach helpfully.

"Whatever. Where is your proof?"

Zach held out his hand, the scraper in the middle of his palm.

"That's a piece of rock," snapped Borth.

"Ah, but it's a special piece of rock," intervened Darroch. "Zach?"

"It's a scraper," Zach said proudly. "A Mesolithic tool, found by Ms Wallace in front of your fence."

"Now let me get this straight," snapped Borth. "You expect me to give up a multi-million pound project because you've found a piece of rock out in the road?"

"There's more," said Anna. "Your doorstep is a hearthstone."

"And we have pictures to prove that the mounds that you have uncovered with your earthmovers give clear evidence of a Mesolithic settlement," said Zach.

Borth growled, "Where did you get the pictures? You don't have access to my construction site."

Anna and Zach glanced at each other, and he said, "I climbed a ladder and looked over your fence, and I saw the evidence and took pictures of it."

"That's trespassing, and I'll have you done for it. I demand that this fellow be charged and taken to jail," Borth snarled.

Darroch said, "Umm, that's a tricky one. Was Zach trespassing when he looked over the fence? Can you trespass without setting foot on the property?"

Barabal said, "Perhaps we should call Constable MacRath and ask him."

"I don't need some hick constable to tell me my rights. I have a lease on this property and I'm going ahead with my construction work. And you're all crazy and you can all get the hell out of here."

Darroch said, "Mr. Borth, I would advise you against such an action."

"Who the hell are you to advise me?" growled Borth.

"He's the Laird," said Zach, earning himself a surprised look from Anna.

"I don't give a damn if he's the Queen, the Duke of Edinburgh and Charlie Prince of Wales all rolled up together. Get off my property," shouted Borth, even louder.

The Mesolithic rescue team exchanged glances. What should they do now? All of them knew they were on shaky legal ground, and if Borth refused to comply, they had no authority to stop him from destroying the site until Zach's university returned conclusive proof that the site was one that had the protection of law. Their bluff had failed.

"Get out," said Borth coldly, sure that he was within his rights.

Borth's construction foreman, with a cautious look at Ian *Mór*, stuck his head inside the door, and said, "Beg pardon, sir, but there's some women, uh, ladies, who are in the way of oor machines. Can ye ask them to move so we can get to work?"

Snarling, Borth pushed his way past the others and stomped out the door.

He saw Jean, Màiri and Sally, nestled comfortably on a blanket in front of the earthmoving machines. They were opening up picnic baskets.

Anna and Barabal went to join them, and settled down on the blanket.

"Isn't this fun?" said Jean. "It's like the sixties. We should have flowers to stick in their bulldozer machines."

Màiri glanced at her, not understanding the reference. Then she pulled a thermos jug out of her basket, and cups. "Tea, anyone?" she asked.

"I'll have a cuppa," said Barabal, settling down on the blanket. "It's been a thirsty morning."

"And me," said Anna.

"Did you bring sandwiches, *a Mhàiri?*" said Jean.

"Salmon, egg and cress, and two with gammon. Any takers?"

"I'll have the egg and cress, please," said Jean. "Is the cress from your garden?"

"No, it's from the Co-Op. Mine perished in the drought," said Màiri. "My garden is nearly ruined, and it will be finished off entirely if we don't get a bit of rain."

There were clucks of sympathy from the others, and they all shook their heads at the perversity of the weather. "Cailean the Crab says the heat is proof of global warming," said Barabal.

"He's right, and that's why weather is getting so much more violent all over the world," said Sally. "It's because the ocean is getting warmer."

"I don't know about the ocean, but have you noticed the cows recently? They're out into the lochs, hock deep in water, all to keep cool." Màiri handed out sandwiches.

Nick Borth advanced on them. "Ladies!" he shouted. "You've got to move. You are in the way of my machines."

Jean smiled. "That's the general idea, Mr. Borth."

He gave them a furious look, then turned to his foreman. "Get them out of here," he snapped. "Use force, if you have to."

The construction workers exchanged uneasy glances.

"I wouldn't do that if I were you," said Ian *Mór*, stepping forward to stand in front of the women, arms crossed, six foot six inches of muscle, bone and grim determination.

The construction workers took a step backwards, then stared at their boss. One of them said, "No part of my job is manhandling ladies." The others nodded agreement.

"Sit down, Ian," said Sally. "And have a cup of tea. We don't need to worry about these nice gentlemen being rude to us." She smiled at the workers, who shuffled their feet and inched away.

Nick Borth said in a deadly calm voice, "You women are all trespassing, and I'm calling the constable to remove you."

"There's five of us, and only one of him," said Sally. "Not to mention Ian *Mór,* but he'd never stand in the way of the law taking its proper course."

"Wouldn't I?" said Ian, and he grinned.

"If you're talking about Constable MacRath," said Barabal, "I believe he's quite busy today. He's giving a talk to the High School about the dangers of drugs. There'll be a question and answer period, which could take a while, for those young people are very talkative and full of questions." She sighed. "It's a shame we've only the one constable, but on the other hand it's a good sign, that we've not that much crime on Eilean Dubh to be requiring more police. Don't you think that's true, Mr. Borth?"

Flummoxed, Nick Borth said, "Yes. No! Damn it, I demand police protection, and I don't care what that dumb copper is up to, I want him here right now. You're the head of the Council, Mrs. Mac-a-Phi, and you're responsible for making sure that my rights are protected."

"What rights might those be, Mr. Borth?" she said.

"My right to exercise the terms of my lease, which give me permission to build my condos on this land."

"Ach, well, I'm thinking that a wee bit of a wait won't make that much difference to you, will it?" said Barabal comfortably. "This is a quiet Island

and we like to take things slowly and wait until the facts are in before we make our decisions. And surely, if this really is an important historic site, you wouldn't want to dig it up, would you?"

Nick Borth said, slowly and distinctly, "I don't give a Goddamned fiddley fuck in hell about your damned historic site, and be damned to anyone who gets in the way of my work."

The women looked dreadfully shocked, and Darroch and Ian *Mór* bristled. Ian snarled, "You'll not be using that kind of language in front of ladies, Borth. I don't know what it's like where you come from, but on Eilean Dubh we don't talk that way when our women are around to hear."

Sally, who'd heard Ian curse with amazing fluency when he slammed a hammer on his finger instead of on a nail, grinned, then assumed an affronted expression. "Mother," she said to Jean, "You should cover your ears before he says anything else."

"That's right," said Zach, entering the fray. "You watch your damned language, you damned incomer," conveniently forgetting that he was an incomer too.

Anna grinned at him. "My, I'd love a cup of tea, wouldn't you, Barabal? I hope you brought enough cups," she said, looking anxiously at Màiri. "Otherwise I can just be off home and grab a couple more."

"No, no," said Jean pleasantly. "There's plenty of cups. Plenty of sandwiches, too." She slanted a look up at Borth. "We're in it for the long haul, aren't we, girls."

The other women nodded in agreement, and Sally said, "Is Elizabeth Thomas bringing the sleeping bags, Màiri?"

"She is, as soon as she can collect them from her Girl Guides. Luckily they've not got an overnight camping trip planned, so they're happy to lend them to us."

Jean wriggled in an attempt to find a more comfortable place on the blanket. "Darroch, just bring some cushions and a folding chair with you when you come back tonight, won't you please? This ground is damned . . . uh . . . dratted . . . uncomfortable."

Darroch grinned down at her. "I'll do that, *mo chridhe*. Is there anything else you'll need?"

"Oh, I'm sure I'll think of a couple of other things," said Jean demurely. "It depends on how long we have to stay here." She looked at Borth again. "And that depends on Mr. Borth, of course."

"I'm calling my lawyer," Borth snarled, and stomped back to the trailer. He stopped on the step, and shouted back at them, "And that stupid constable, too. So don't get too cozy, because you're going out of here."

Jean said in a whisper, "Can he really throw us out?"

"Of course," said Darroch. "You're trespassing. But as Barabal has pointed out, there are five of you, and only one constable. He'll wreck his back if he has to drag you all out."

"Oh, there's more coming," said Jean. "Elizabeth with the sleeping bags, and Ian's Catrìona said she'd look in by and by. Isabel's organizing tonight's supper and she'll bring some of the gals from Airgead who want a piece of the action. So if it's dragging that's wanted, we can keep the constable busy."

"To say nothing of the fact that there's no place to stash us," said Sally. "I've had a look at the jail in the Council building, and it's strictly a two-holer. What's he going to do with us after he's dragged us out?"

Amused, Darroch said, "He could release you to the custody of your husbands, I suppose."

"Your husbands will decline," said Ian *Mór*. "It's my night off duty, and I'm organizing a knees-up with the lads for nosh and a spot of poker. Got to seize the opportunity for the mice to play when the cats are away."

The women looked mildly alarmed at the idea of poker, and he added, "Low stakes only, of course, Sal; you needn't look as though I'm going to bet the ranch."

Everyone laughed, and they all sat down for a bite of lunch. Two hours later, when they were all chatted out, they watched Constable MacRath's black and white panda car pull slowly into the driveway, stop, and the officer get out and take a leisurely look around. He spotted the gathering, and gave them a salute.

"Jiggers, the cops," said Jean. "We're busted."

Darroch started to get to his feet, then settled back down. "We'll let Mr. Borth have his say first, I think."

Borth had his say; they could all hear the shouts coming from the trailer, and the low measured tones of the constable replying. Several minutes later the officer emerged from the trailer, notebook in hand, and advanced to the little group on the blankets.

"Afternoon, all," he said, looking around. "Mrs. Barabal, as the Chair of the Council, and the highest ranking person here, saving yourself, of course, *a Mhic an Rìgh*," touching his hat to the Laird, who responded with an irritated nod, "may I ask you for a wee bit of information about what's going on?"

"Certainly, Constable," said Barabal. "We are engaged in crime prevention."

"Begging your pardon, ma'am, that's not the way yon mannie in the trailer tells the story. Could you be more specific?"

"I'll defer to Mr. Trelawney," she said, turning to Zach, who presented the details of the archaeological site with remarkable restraint, though he was unable to keep himself from finishing with an indignant, "And that Philistine wants to destroy eight thousand years of history!"

Constable MacRath scribbled busily in his notebook. "Eight thousand years of history. Right. And your proof of this is what, sir?"

"The proof has been sent to the University of Glasgow for analysis," said Anna quickly. "As soon as it's authenticated we'll give you a full report, in writing."

"When might I expect that, Anna lass?"

She shot a quick look at Zach. "Soon."

"Could you be more specific?"

Crossing her fingers behind her back, Anna mumbled, "A couple of days. Maybe a wee bit longer."

"Hmmm." The constable scratched his head thoughtfully, knocking his tall hat askew. "Well, we've a dilemma, I fear. Mr. Borth wants you all done for trespassing and interfering with his legal rights to continue his work. I have to admit that he's got some justification for his charges."

Barabal said sternly, "We are preventing a crime from taking place, Constable. As you requested at our last Council meeting, everyone on the Island is encouraged to take an active part in crime prevention."

"Aye, aye, that's true, ma'am. You'd be keeping Mr. Borth from incurring some very serious charges, if I understood you correctly, lad," he said, nodding at Zach.

"Very serious indeed," said Zach. "I'm not a lawyer, but one thing I do understand is the law regarding the protection of historic sites."

"So as I see it, and you'll correct me if I'm wrong, what's wanting here is the written proof that this is indeed a genuine archaeological site of considerable importance to our Island, and you're asking that work be delayed until it arrives."

"Got it in one, Constable," said Darroch.

"I'll just go and have another chat with Mr. Borth, if you'll all excuse me." The constable touched his hat yet again, and headed back to the trailer. More shouts were heard. MacRath emerged, shaking his head. He approached Barabal, and said, "Mr. Borth is not a man of great patience."

"Aye, we've figured that out already," she said. "What are you going to do?"

"Here's my take on it," said MacRath, rocking back on his heels as he proudly produced a bit of American slang, gleaned from the telly. "The weather looks to be holding fine, and I can't see that it will do Mr. Borth's business any harm if he backs off on his work for a day or two. Patience is a virtue, as Minister Donald said in his sermon Sunday, and I've encouraged Mr. Borth to practice it as his Christian duty."

The members of the group cheered.

"But," added the constable, "I'll be expecting that written proof within several days, and I must warn you that if you decide to leave the property, even at night, Mr. Borth will be fully within his rights to lock his gate, refuse you all entry, and continue with his work."

"We're prepared to stay," said Jean.

MacRath leaned down and said in a confidential tone, "He's got some right bruisers working for him, and I wouldn't put it past him to order them to try to throw you out. My advice to you is for the men to go home, and you ladies stay. There's not a man on his crew would dare manhandle females, for they know they'll see the inside of our wee jail for a good long time if they so much as touch you. I'll be down on them like an eagle on a eider duck, charge them all with GBH, and shut down Borth's whole operation so fast he won't know what's hit him."

"We expected as much, Constable, and thank you for the warning," said Jean. "We women came fully prepared to engage in civil disobedience."

"Oh, no, Mrs. Jean, never say that," said Constable MacRath, shocked. "For that's defying the law, and it would be my duty to take you all in and charge you."

"Yes, Constable," said Jean meekly.

PART X

The Sit-in

Twenty-four

If you want a job done,
get a woman to do it.

Universal proverb

The first night of what Jean was coming to think of as the "sit-in" passed uneventfully. She, Màiri, Sally and Barabal took the evening watch, and slept out under the stars in the sleeping bags borrowed from the Girl Guides. No one had any trouble falling asleep, after all four had enjoyed the beauty of the night sky and the opportunity to engage in some intimate female sharing about husbands, children and sex.

Jean was awakened once in the middle of the night by music, eerie flute music that reminded her of Native American folk tunes on compact discs she'd owned at home in Milwaukee. One of the construction workers must have left a radio on, she thought drowsily; odd that a guy like that would have a taste for New Age music.

It was definitely New Age-y. The unaccompanied flute poured out sad notes that spiraled to the highest registers, then cascaded to the lowest like a waterfall pouring down *Beinn Mhic an Righ* after a spring rain. The music gave Jean the most amazing mental pictures, circles spiraling together, then apart, then freezing into three interlocked rings. The pictures were in color, softly muted as though seen through a gauzy curtain.

I must be dreaming, thought Jean drowsily. That was odd, because she had no recollection of ever dreaming in color, and certainly not with a musical accompaniment. It was very pleasant, and a bit threatening, like the Disney movie *Fantasia*.

When she woke she had only the dimmest memory of her dream, or vision, or whatever it was, and that quickly faded in the light of day.

Morning was rather less pleasant than the previous evening had been. The women awakened to the realization that there was no way to wash their faces and hands or brush their teeth, and all started out the day feeling distinctly grubby.

"I wonder if the construction guys would let us wash up in their trailer," muttered Sally, trying with limited success to get a comb through her tangled mass of hair.

"Do you want to ask them? I don't," said Jean, with a shudder. The atmosphere emitted by the workers had been definitely unfriendly, and none of the women could blame them, for it was their jobs and paychecks that were being threatened by the sit-in.

They shared out the remaining water in the jug someone had brought last night, dividing it carefully so that each woman could do what she wanted with her share, drink or wash to her preference. "We should have arranged for our guys to come and ferry each of us home for a tidy-up," said Jean, and the other three agreed.

"Let's have them bring us a bottle of wine for bedtime," said Sally. "It'll help me get to sleep. Something kept me awake for the longest time. Odd, that I can't remember what it was . . . just a weird feeling, I guess."

Barabal glanced at her, and nodded. "I thought I heard moaning in the middle of the night."

"I heard music," said Jean.

Màiri, who'd never heard odd things in the middle of the night and had never been given to weird feelings of any kind, said, "Probably the sleeping bags disturbing your rest. Mine had a lump in it. I finally rooted around and found a pocket knife that my Girl Guide had left behind." She shook out her bag and rolled it up carefully.

Ian the Post arrived shortly afterwards, bearing a picnic basket with jugs of tea, freshly-baked rolls, and hardboiled eggs, packed by his Catrìona. He took a break from his route to share some news: the sit-in was the talk of Eilean Dubh, and everyone, of course, had an opinion about it.

"Most are behind you," said Ian the Post, "although one or two are concerned that you're keeping the construction laddies from earning an honest dollar to protect some old rubbish dump."

"Hmmm, a PR—that's public relations, Màiri—problem," said Sally. "What can we do to get our story out?"

"Anna Wallace is taking care of that," said Ian. "She's putting out a—what did she call it—a large page, or a . . . broadsheet, that was it . . . to explain what you are doing."

"Good old Anna," said Jean.

"Top of the table," said Sally, who liked football slang.

"Full marks," said Barabal approvingly. "She's a good lass, even though it is her boyfriend that got us into this stramash."

"Is he really her boyfriend?" asked Sally, and the women's ears pricked up, eager for new input on a relationship they'd all wondered about.

Ian the Post stirred uneasily. All the women were suddenly reminded of the presence of a man, and reluctantly set aside the Anna-Zach story for dissection at a later time. "I'll be getting on now," he said, getting to his feet. "My Catrìona will be joining you shortly. She sends her apologies for not coming right away, but she has a bit of trouble with the mornings. I assume you're all aware of her situation?" His ears turned pink at the tips.

"We are, and we'll take good care of her, so you've no need to worry," said Barabel. "And our men will be stopping by now and again, so if she needs to go home there'll be someone to take her."

"Oh, she'll never go home before the end of her shift, for she's determined to do her bit for the archaeology." Ian smiled proudly, and left.

"Another good lass," said Màiri approvingly.

"Womanpower," said Jean. "We just needed a cause to mobilize it."

Barabal, slipping on her imaginary Council Chair hat, said, "Perhaps we can think of a project to keep all the women involved, once this is over."

"Let's get through this one first," said Jean. She'd been postponing as long as she could her morning trip to the site's Porta-loo, an installation made ripe and smelly from two weeks worth of visits by the construction workers. Nick Borth had not been diligent in arranging to have it pumped out; that involved an expensive visit from the mainland, an expense he'd been reluctant to incur. The men had toilets in their trailer, he reasoned; if any of them were too prissy for the Porta-loo they could use the alternative. But most of the men viewed a trip to the portable facility as a test of their manhood. Inside toilets were for sissies.

Jean definitely considered herself a sissy. She emerged from the Porta-loo barely controlling the impulse to gag, and wondering if she could work up enough courage to ask the men for permission to use their inside toilet. Catching a look of dislike from one of them lounging in front of the trailer, she put aside that thought for another occasion.

That occasion arose with the arrival of Ian's Catrìona. She was in that stage of her pregnancy that involved the frequent and urgent need to urinate. She emerged from her first visit to the Porta-loo an alarming shade of green, and just as Jean noticed and darted forward to help her, she vanished again into the Porta-loo. The sounds of retching were distinctly audible.

No stranger to morning sickness, Jean felt her own stomach quiver uneasily even though she wasn't pregnant, and she rushed to get a moistened towelette that had thoughtfully been packed with the picnic basket. "Catrìona's being sick," she told the others, and hurried back to lend a supportive arm when the sufferer emerged.

"Ach, the poor lassie. Will this be too much for her, do you think?" worried Màiri.

"She must go home, if it is," said Barabal. "There's enough of us to mind the shop, and she can help by seeing to provisions."

"She won't leave," Sally said. "She told me she's absolutely determined to do her part. She loves this coastline, and was appalled to hear what Borth was planning."

The other two clucked worriedly, and fussed over Catrìona when she came back until that young woman was ready to scream with exasperation. "Have done," she said firmly. "I'm all right, and that's an end to it."

It wasn't. The distressing scene was repeated several times, and Jean finally screwed up her courage and marched over to the workers' trailer. She knocked.

A lanky young man in an undershirt and jeans came to the door, and viewed her with disdain. "Whaddya want?" he growled; at least that was what Jean thought he said. His Glasgow accent was so thick as to be almost incomprehensible.

"I'd like to talk to your foreman, please," Jean said bravely.

"Coom awn in, then, why doncha."

The trailer was filled with a thick layer of smoke. At one table sat four men playing cards and smoking, their expressions glum. Another man was slumped in a chair reading what appeared to Jean to be a particularly repulsive girly magazine, judging by the cover. Two others were sacked out on the couches, taking out their ennui in sleep. Over the entire room hung the miasma of vigorous, healthy workers who were bored out of their skulls with unaccustomed inactivity.

The foreman appeared. He was shorter than Jean, and shaped like a fireplug, with massive shoulders and several days worth of beard gracing his square face. He was wearing a faded tee shirt with "Up the Granite City" emblazoned on the front. He was one of the Aberdonians, and slightly easier to understand. "Yaz?" he said in an unfriendly tone.

"I'd like to ask a favor, if I may."

"Whazzat, then?"

"One of our women is pregnant, and using the Porta-loo makes her sick."

"Whyn't she go home, then?"

"She won't. We've asked her."

"Whaddam ah supposed to dae aboot it?"

"We want to ask your permission to let her use the toilet in the other trailer."

He turned back to the other men. "Ye hear that, lads? One of our lady guests wants to use oor facilities. Seems the Porta-loo is too much for 'er delicate sensibilities."

The others guffawed. Then an older man stood up, stretched, and said laconically, "Why not let 'er?"

The men growled, and one commented, "Why should we?"

"She's preggers, dincha 'ear? None of yez ever been around a lass like that? Pissin' and 'eavin', that's all they dae."

"Your wife, or your sisters perhaps? You'd know what it's like," said Jean.

"My wife couldnae keep anythin' doon for t'ree months," said another man.

"Mine camped out in the bog," said another. "Thought Ah'd hafta move her bed inna it."

"Ah, g'wan, Chaz. Let 'er use the one in the sleeping trailer. We don't gae in there in the daytime, anyway," said the older man.

The foreman looked Jean up and down, then turned to his comrades. "'Zat awright wi' the rest of ye lads?" No one offered an objection. "Awright. Why the hell not?"

"The other ladies, too," said the older man.

"Geez," said the foreman in disgust. "Like runnin' a nursery for wee girlies, this is. Yeah, go ahead." He bowed elaborately. "Oor facilities are at yer disposal, madam. Anything else we can dae for ye?"

"No, that's great. Thanks so much," gasped Jean, scarcely able to believe her success, and she scampered back to her friends before he could change his mind.

"Thank you, Jean," said Catrìona. "I could have managed, but thank you."

"No, you couldn't," said Màiri firmly. "I think we'd better have a look at that toilet, though. Those great clods using it for three weeks, I can imagine the state it's in. Not one of them will have thought about a tidy-up."

She disappeared into the sleeping trailer and came out grimacing. "Just as I thought," she announced. "They seem to have been using the walls for target practice. Men really can be such animals. I'm going to swamp it out, for there's cleaning supplies in the shelves next to the toilet."

"I'll help you," said Sally bravely.

They worked for an hour, and came out pale, but triumphant. "Fit for use by civilized creatures," Màiri said, with a disdainful glance at the workers lounging about in front of the recreation trailer, who'd been watching the women's efforts with interest.

One of them got to his feet and ambled back to the sleeping trailer to see what they'd been up to. He came back to his mates, looking impressed. "They cleaned the bog, lads. Ye could eat yer supper off the floor in there."

There was a rumble of manly disdain that covered up considerable relief. Most of them realized that the toilet had gotten into a revolting condition, but no one had wanted to offer to clean it; that would have been considered sissy.

A very young worker said timidly, "Ye think they'd do the one in the rekkie trailer, if we asked 'em nice? It's a tip."

Seeing approval on his subordinates' faces, Chaz the foreman mumbled, "Yeah, awright. Ah'll ask 'em. They owe us, anyway."

Jean and Barabal volunteered to do the cleaning, and were gratified to receive mumbled thanks from several of the workers.

"They're not so bad, after all," said Jean.

"That young one in the Glasgow Celtics shirt is kind of cute," added Sally. "I might just chat him up later on."

The others looked at her, scandalized, and Màiri said, "You're a married woman, Sally."

"Yes, mother-in-law. You think that big lummox of a son of yours would let me forget it? I just want to establish friendly relations with the guys over there. We're going to be working in pretty close quarters for the next few days; might as well be on good terms in case we need another favor." Sally grinned.

"And besides, he is cute," said Jean, returning the First Daughter's grin.

Relations between the two camps had definitely thawed. The third night around the women's campfire, when conversation lagged, they turned to music. Jean had had Darroch bring her guitar for just such an eventuality, and Elizabeth Thomas had brought songsheets. They sang through her entire Girl Guide repertoire, and all the Appalachian folk songs Jean and Sally could remember, and were winding down with Eilean Dubh's lovely Gaelic tunes, most of which were wistful and haunting, the perfect late night sort of music. Jean was briefly reminded of her flute dream, but forgot it again when she noticed with some alarm that their little encampment was now ringed with large hulking shapes. The faint odor of cigarette smoke drifted over them. Were the lads not music-lovers, and were they going to be evicted forcibly?

"G'wan," said a voice. "Why'd cha stop?"

"Do you like our Island music?" said Jean.

"It's bonnie," said an Aberdonian accent.

"Bit peely-wally," said a Glaswegian one. "Let's give 'em a good chune or twa from the city, lads," and he bellowed:

I belong to Glasgow, dear old Glasgow town;
But what's the matter wi' Glasgow, for it's going roun' and roun'!

An enthusiastic chorus of male voices joined in.

I'm only a common old working chap, as anyone here can see,
But when I get a couple o' drinks on a Saturday, Glasgow belongs to me!

The first voice crooned soulfully:

I've been wi' a couple o' cronies,
One or two pals o' my ain;
We went in a hotel,
And we did very well,
And then we came out once again;
Then we went into anither,
And that is the reason I'm fu';
We had six deoch-an-doruses, then sang a chorus,
Just listen, I'll sing it to you!

And they roared out the chorus again. By the time they'd finished the second verse, the women were joining in enthusiastically.

"Great song," said Sally.

"Here's a better one," said an Aberdonian, and began:

When I was a lad, a tiny wee lad, my mother said to me,
"Come see the Northern Lights, my boy, they're bright as they can be."
She called them the heavenly dancers, merry dancers in the sky,
I'll never forget that wonderful sight, they made the heavens bright.
The Northern Lights of Aberdeen are what I long to see;
The Northern Lights of Aberdeen, that's where I long to be.
I've been a wand'rer all of my life and many a sight I've seen.
God speed the day when I'm on my way to my home in Aberdeen.

The women joined in again. Then one of the men, with a sly grin just visible in the firelight, began to sing, *"Oh! Ye canny shove yer granny aff a bus!"*

Màiri, with a chuckle, leaned over to Jean and whispered, "Jamie used to sing that to me when we were at school, and he wanted to get me in a good humor." And she sang loudly, *"Ye canny shove yer granny, coz she's yer mammy's mammy . . . ."*

She and the men shouted, *"Ye canny shove yer granny aff a bus!"* And they continued describing the variety of relatives that could be shoved off the bus, finally concluding, once again, that one's mammy's mammy was not one of them.

Sally elbowed Jean. "That may not be the silliest song I've ever heard, but it's close."

After a bit, one of the men said, "Give us another one of yer Gar-lick songs, Missus. One of the quiet ones, like."

Jean obliged with a medley of lullabies. The men listened, and when she'd finished they began to drift off to bed, most murmuring their thanks for the sing-song. The women crawled into their sleeping bags, looked up at the stars, and fell asleep, feeling that they'd done a good day's work.

Relations had definitely thawed, and on the next day the women invited the workers over for supper, and were astonished at the quantity of meat pies, bridies and cranachan (all catered by Sheilah Morrison) that the men could eat. The husbands watched the workers, suspicious at first, and then they too thawed, and everyone enjoyed a fine meal. "'At's the ticket," said Chaz the foreman. "'At's good nosh, 'at is."

The husbands paid a variety of visits during the days of the sit-in. Darroch brought Rosie each time, and she made a hit with the construction workers by walking up to them boldly and staring at them with her thumb in her mouth. They amused themselves making a variety of funny faces and noises, all to get her to laugh, and chortling heartily when they succeeded. Rosie protested loudly when Darroch scooped her up to take her home, and Jean thought it was as much because she didn't want to leave her new friends as it was her reluctance to leave her mother.

The only husband who had not appeared was Jamie. At last on the fifth night he could no longer bear being separated from Màiri. He was missing her dreadfully, and that finally compelled him to overcome the primitive dread roused in him by the wildflower patch. He'd seen the misty wisps in the daytime, he thought; perhaps they did not come out at night.

He drove the old Austin into the site very slowly, and sat in it for a while. Màiri grew impatient, for she'd missed him too, and she stalked over to the car. "Are you getting out, or are you just sightseeing?" she demanded.

Jamie scowled up at her. "In a hurry to see me, are you?" he snapped. Then he got out of the car, swept her into his arms and kissed her so passionately that she staggered when he let her go. The construction workers whistled and stamped their feet in approval, and one shouted, "Gi' 'er anither ane! That's the oney way to shut a lassie's gob." The women giggled behind their hands.

Màiri glared at them all, brushed at her clothing and stomped with dignity back to the women's circle. Jamie followed, and it was a toss-up as to which one was scowling the more fiercely.

"Feasgar math," said Jamie, regaining his composure, and looking around at the women. "You've been making friends." He nodded towards the workers.

"Music soothed the savage breast, and so did cleaning their toilets," Jean said.

"Hmmph," he said, not understanding the toilet reference. The music he understood, and produced his fiddle case from under his arm, to everyone's delight. He tucked the fiddle under his chin and began to play a lively jig, reasoning that music might also soothe the misty wisps.

The Mesolithic Rescue Reel

Jean joined in and an impromptu *cèilidh* began. Jamie produced a new tune, which he announced was called "The Mesolithic Rescue Reel" in honor of the sit-in, and the bolder of the two camps approached each other, took partners and danced merrily around the campfire.

When everyone was tired of singing and dancing, silence fell briefly. Then Sally said, "Ma, tell us one of your stories." The request was enthusiastically seconded, and Jean found her briefcase and pulled out the tale she'd been editing the last two days.

"I could read you one about the selkie and the saint," she said tentatively.

"Go on, then," said Màiri.

Everyone found places to sit around the campfire, and Jean began.

How Daragh the Monk Brought the True Faith to Eilean Dubh, and Why the Eilean Dubhannaich Carry the Bloodlines of the Seals and the Picts

As told by Cairistìona MacChriathar

Once there was in the Land of Lorne in Scotland a handsome young man named Daragh, a tall, sturdy youth with eyes as blue as the bluest of lochs. He was the second son of the Lord of Lorne and a Pictish princess named Talorna. He was a hearty, vigorous, talkative youth, and his parents were pleased to have him as insurance should anything happen to their eldest son, the heir. But one day he took it into his head to become a monk in the nearby monastery of Lorne, and at last talked his parents into agreement, arguing that it was traditional for a younger son to enter the church. And why not this one, reasoned his parents at last, for there was a third son and a fourth, to support the heir.

Daragh presented himself to Abbot Camshron of Lorne and announced that he had found his vocation, and that he wished to join the order.

Abbot Camshron sighed. It had been a bumper year for novices and the monastery was bulging at the seams with eager young men, all fasting and praying at the most inappropriate times and in the most inappropriate places, assigning themselves unnecessarily severe penances, and quite disrupting the placid daily life of the order. He did not look forward to adding another candidate, and local stories had it that young Daragh was particularly bumptious. But he was the ruler's son, and could not be denied entrance without giving serious offense to the Lord of Lorne.

Then the Abbot had a brilliant idea.

"I will accept you into our order and confer upon you a most sacred task. Go you to the Dark Island that lies on the horizon, and if there be people there, convert them to the True Faith."

Young Daragh gulped. He had quite looked forward to monastic life, which under genial Abbot Camshron and his immediate predecessors had lost the rigidity of the original rules of the order, so that its members led a convivial life that featured sports, farming and large noisy banquets. In addition, the monastery housed an order of nuns, for in the early days of the Celtic Church it was common for religious houses to hold both sexes, and some forty busy, buxom, bustling young maidens shared the sprawling old building and the daily life of the monks. By all accounts that Daragh had heard, it was quite a jolly existence, full of hard work, good food, good ale, flirtation, and laughter.

But he was not to be permitted to share this life; he was to cross the unruly sea populated with monsters to an Island no one had ever visited, and where legend said even more hideous monsters lurked.

He protested, "How am I to get to the Dark Island? The sea between our lands is full of fearsome beasts, and no one who has ventured so far has ever returned."

The Abbot said smugly, "God will show you the way."

Daragh was baffled, and as always when he was in that state, he sought the counsel of his mother, the Pictish princess, who was a wise and learned woman.

"Columba of blessed memory crossed the sea upon an oak leaf," said Talorna, when told of her son's problem.

"I am not a saint, and could not possibly fit upon an oak leaf."

"God will show you the way," said the princess, and led her son to the shelter of an enormous old oak tree. "Pick me these leaves," she commanded, and as Daragh pulled leaves from the oak, Talorna plaited their stems and wove them into a wee raft.

When she had finished, she took a final, larger leaf and fashioned it into a sail, lashed it with braided blades of grass to a twig stuck in the middle of the raft, and said, "Behold your ship."

"But the ship is tiny and I am huge!" cried Daragh in dismay. "It will never hold my size and weight."

"All things are possible to true believers," said the princess. "Do you believe?"

"Of course I do," said Daragh, though he was not sure what she meant he was to believe in.

The princess rose, and extended her arms over her son. She began to chant in her Pictish language, which only she knew in the Land of Lorne.

Daragh, who was wishing that he had paid attention when his mother had tried to teach him her language, suddenly felt himself changing. He was shrinking. He grew smaller and smaller, and in the space of two minutes he was the height of a man's knee.

The princess bent, picked up her son and cradled him in her arm. She took the raft in her other hand, and carried both to the shingle beach that edged the sea. "Now you begin your journey. Go in peace, and teach whoever lives on the Dark Island about the True Faith. Remember always that God will show you the way, if you believe."

"But, Mother!" cried Daragh. "I'm only the height of a man's knee! How am I to preach to men who are three times my size? They will never listen, and will brush me aside as a monster, or kill me for being an evil spirit."

Talorna smiled. "This is the last thing that I will teach you, so listen well. This is the spell you will recite when you reach the Dark Island, and it will restore you to your full size." She began to chant, stopping before she reached the last word, for it would have changed Daragh then and there. That word she whispered in his ear.

She had to repeat the chant three times before Daragh felt that he had learned it, and three times she whispered the final word. Then she waded out into the sea, put the raft down, and put Daragh upon it. "Fare thee well, my son!" she shouted.

The outgoing tide swept the tiny raft upon its bosom, and Daragh's journey began, as the tide carried him over bounding waves, in and out of the reach of hungry fishes circling beneath the boat and bumping up against it now and then, trying for a nip at the young man's bottom.

A storm blew up and sent the raft spinning. Daragh caught the end of the grass braid and lashed himself to the mast so that he would not be washed overboard. Lightning crackled and thunder crashed, and the driving rain soaked him through and through as he clung dizzily to the mast.

At last the storm was over, and the sea calm again. In the distance Daragh saw the outline of the Dark Island coming closer and closer. Soon the waves were lapping at its shore, and a particularly large and aggressive wave cast the raft upon the beach.

Daragh scrambled to untie himself, then jumped from the raft and pulled it up the beach to the shelter of a patch of reeds. Exhausted, he flung himself to the ground. I've reached the Dark Island, he thought, and lay waiting for monsters to appear.

At last it occurred to him that he would be better off preparing for monsters if he was his own normal size. He jumped to his feet, and began the incantation his mother had taught him, finishing with a flourish on the word she'd whispered in his ear: "Shimsheenshan!"

Nothing happened.

He tried again, with the same result. He was sure about the incantation, but wondered if he had the final magic word wrong. He tried several variants.

"Sheenasherrieshan!"

"Shannasherrieshinnie!"

"Shinnashinnasherrie!"

Nothing. It was beginning to look as though he was to remain the height of a man's knee forever.

If he was, he had better find a place to hide when the monsters came. He pulled the raft further into the reeds, and using twigs and grasses, improvised a shelter and a little bed.

That done, he realized he was hungry and thirsty. He took care of the thirst by downing drops of dew that still clung to the grass. But what to eat? Baffled, he prowled through the reeds until he came to a bird's nest set low on the ground, with eggs in it the size of melons to Daragh. He grabbed one and staggered back to his lair.

There he cracked open the egg and sucked out its contents. It tasted gamy and odd, but he was too hungry to care. Then he lay down to sleep.

His dreams were many and curious, and all of mothers. First a giant mother bird appeared and accused him of murdering her baby, then his own mother reprimanded him for not paying better attention to the magic word. The last dream was the strangest. It was of a beautiful dark-haired woman with a baby in her arms, and she was singing to it.

He woke with a start, and discovered that he had slept the night through, and that it was a glorious sunny morning. He drank some dew, and chewed on a blade of grass for nourishment, made too uneasy by his dream to go back to the bird's nest.

He stretched, and tried the incantation again, hoping that his mother in his dream had shaken the magic word loose in his brain, but had no success. He made up his mind to go exploring.

Just then he heard the sound of giants' voices, and shrank back into the reeds in terror.

Three enormous fishermen were coming to the beach, carrying a boat upon their heads so that they looked like a giant six-legged beast. As Daragh watched, quaking, they lowered the boat to the water, got in, and rowed away, singing lustily. Not monsters, Daragh thought, but so huge! forgetting that he himself was only the height of a man's knee.

He sank back onto the ground, dejected. How was he supposed to convert giants to the True Faith? Like as not they'd skin him and eat him for dinner, laughing at his temerity in trying to teach them anything. In his imagination he could hear them singing, "Boil him up, boil him up, boil him up for dinner, boil the wee man for dinner."

He fell asleep in his dejection, and was wakened by a slap, slap, slap upon the sand. A large black seal was making its way along the beach, headed for his patch of reeds. Daragh scrambled up, ready to flee.

But the seal stopped a ways from him, gave itself a shake, and its fur pelt slid off, revealing a beautiful naked young woman with long glistening black hair, the image of the young mother in his dream.

Daragh stared in amazement.

The woman bent and lifted a large rock, and took something from under it. She shook it out into a long white dress, which she put on. She picked up the seal pelt and folded it, and placed it beneath the rock so that it was entirely hidden. Then she strolled away down the beach.

A selkie, thought Daragh. He'd seen the legendary seal woman, and knew where she kept her pelt. If he took it away, she'd never be able to return to the sea. He ran to the rock and burrowed in the sand beneath it to the pelt. It was unbelievably soft and luxurious, and smelled of the sea. It would make him a fine warm cover in his little lair. He tugged at it.

He could not budge it, for the weight of the stone. Ah, well, he thought, reconsidering, why should he deny the seal woman her passage home, just so that he could stay cozy in the evenings?

Besides, he had his own work to do. He straightened his shoulders and marched off through the reeds and grasses, seeking the settlement of men and women to convert to the True Faith. He would find them, then consider again how he was to regain his height.

By sunset he'd not come to the end of the marshy patch of reeds that bordered the sea, and he had to scuttle back to his lair before nightfall, clutching for his dinner an egg he'd found in another nest.

Chewing on the thick yellow yolk, he sat under his shelter, disheartened, and moping so about his own plight that he almost missed the return of the selkie, her change into a seal, and her graceful slide into the sea.

Some days passed in this fashion, with selkie and fishermen coming and going, and disheartening rambles through the reeds seeking the Islanders' village. Then one night it all changed.

The seal maiden was late in returning, and a huge pale moon was casting its cool shimmering light over the waves when she came at last. Daragh, who'd watched every night to see her, had fallen asleep, disappointed. Now he woke to the sound of great sobs that tore at his heart and soul.

The selkie sat by her rock, crying her eyes out.

Daragh crept from his lair to her side. "Why do you weep, seal woman?" he asked tenderly, for he was by now half in love with her, and he could not bear to hear her sorrow.

She jumped in terror, momentarily diverted from her woes, then laughed in surprise when she saw him. "Why, it's a little mannikin. Who are you, wee one?"

He drew himself up to his full height, still no higher than a man's knee, and announced, "I am Daragh of Lorne, and I am a monk come to the Dark Island to bring the True Faith to its people."

"Is that so? Well, as you must know, I am a selkie, and I am betrayed in love by one who refuses to marry me, though I carry his child."

"Why won't he marry you?" asked Daragh.

"He's already married," said the seal maiden sulkily.

"Oh, how wicked! So he seduced you and cast you aside?"

"Something like that," she muttered, for if truth were told, she'd done most of the seduction, having had a mind to try out an earthly lover as had some of the other seal women, and talked about it lasciviously in the women's circle at night under the water.

"What are you going to do?" Daragh asked.

"I cannot take a human baby into the sea, even in my womb. I cannot stay on land; my lover's wife will incite the other woman to stone me to death, for these humans of the Dark Island will not allow an unmarried woman who is with child to live."

Ah, thought Daragh; he'd come to this place just in time, if its people were so cruel. He'd have to teach them about kindness and forgiveness. But what to do now, to save the seal woman? "I will marry you," he announced.

"You?" she said, and exploded in laughter despite her woes.

Daragh said crossly, "Why not? I am a monk and an ordained priest come to teach these people about the True Faith, and I am a prince of Lorne. My father is the Lord of Lorne, and my mother is a Pictish princess. I am making you a very good offer."

The selkie bobbed him a little, half-mocking curtsy. "And I am a princess of the seal people, so I am your equal, and a very good match for you as well, Your Highness. But it won't work, for no one will believe that a mannikin the height of a man's knee could have put his child in my belly."

"But I am a man fully grown, and shrunk by my mother to this size so that I could sail upon an oak leaf to this Island to bring the True Faith to its people."

"Can't you un-shrink yourself?" demanded the selkie.

"I could," said Daragh, "if I could just remember my mother's magic word." And he hung his head, ashamed.

"Ah," she said sadly. "So that's an end to that. I'm going down to the sea to prepare for death." She turned and walked away.

In a few minutes he heard her wailing, long desperate cries that made the hair on the back of his neck stand up. It was an awful noise, that of a soul in torment. She might at least have stayed here with me so that I could comfort her, Daragh thought resentfully, covering his ears with his hands. He searched his brain in the hope that the magic word might magically reappear.

It didn't. He threw himself down on the ground in a temper tantrum quite unsuitable for a monk. Arms flailed, legs kicked, and he added his wail to those of the selkie.

He cried until he could cry no longer. Then he lifted his head and looked down the beach at the seal woman. She was standing, her long black hair flowing to her hips, the picture of despair, arms at her side, shoulders slumped, head bowed, thinking about death.

Then, as Daragh watched, something broke the surface of the sea, and a huge brown seal waddled out of the water and up the beach to the selkie, slap, slap, slap upon the sand. The two engaged in an animated conversation consisting of grunts, barks and whimpers. Finally the brown seal waddled back to the sea and into it.

The seal maiden sank down upon the sand.

Bursting with curiosity, Daragh ran along the beach and crouched beside her. "Who was that?" he demanded.

"My mother."

"What did you say to her?"

"I told her that I was with child by a human and so I could never return to my people, and that I could not join the humans on the Island because my lover was married. And that I must die, there being nothing left for me on land or in the sea."

"What did she say to you?"

"That mine was a sad and tragic story," she replied, and tears began to fall from her eyes once more. She wiped them away with her long black hair, and wept again.

"Now, now, no more crying," said Daragh, terrified that the heart-tearing wails might start up again. "Come back to my lair in the reeds and we'll talk."

"There's naught to talk about," she mumbled, but allowed herself to be led away by the little man, his hand grasping her skirt.

He made her as comfortable as possible, plying her with flower bells full of dew and choice stems of grass. He even risked the wrath of the mother bird and stole another one of her eggs. The selkie drank and ate, stifling sobs between each bite, and at last she lay down to sleep on the bed of grass Daragh had made for her.

He lay down as close to her as he dared and shut his eyes, but sleep eluded him for a long while. Just as his eyelids were drooping shut, he heard a slap, slap, slap, upon the sand. He sat up just in time to see the large brown seal again, this time changing into a beautiful older woman. She changed so fast that he caught only a glimpse of her nakedness, and in an instant she was clothed in a long white dress. She turned and stared at Daragh, and came straight to the point. "You are willing to marry my daughter?"

"Aye, with all my heart."

"Even though she carries another man's child?"

"Aye, for I love her."

"Even though you know she is a selkie, and may desert you after the babe is born and return to the sea?"

"Aye, for I love her with all my heart."

The seal mother stared at him. "You are not as other humans. Why are you so small?" she demanded.

"Because my mother made me small so that I could sail upon an oak leaf from the Land of Lorne to the Dark Island to bring its people the True Faith. And because I am so stupid that I forgot the last word of the magic incantation that would change me back to normal size."

"Who is your mother?"

"She is Talorna, the Pictish princess, wife to the Lord of Lorne."

"Hmmm," said the seal mother, and quick as a fairy's wink she donned her pelt and changed into a seal, and went slap, slap, slap upon the sand down to the beach and into the water.

Daragh lay back down upon his bed of grass, quite overcome.

The next morning he woke to the smell of delicious food cooking, and opened his eyes to the sight of the young selkie tending a fire over which roasted a fat rabbit that she had trapped. "Arise, husband-to-be, for I have prepared your breakfast," she said.

Daragh scrambled to his feet, his heart great with joy, though he was still only the height of a man's knee.

They dined together, the selkie gnawing on one of the rabbit's legs, and Daragh nibbling on one of its cheeks. And while they ate, the seal maiden told stories of her life beneath the sea, and Daragh told tales of the Land of Lorne.

Then they parted. The selkie went off to gather grasses to improve her bed, while Daragh smoored the fire so that no one from the Dark Island would discover their hiding place. He spent the rest of the day alternatively on his knees praying, and standing reciting his mother's incantation, hoping to remember the magic word.

The day passed, and at evening they were together again, eating the last of the rabbit at the side of the revived fire.

Presently they heard a slap, slap, slap upon the sand and up the beach came the large brown seal. As before she shed her pelt, and assumed human shape.

"Good evening, mother," said the young selkie.

"Good evening, child. Not dead yet?"

"Good evening, my lady," said Daragh. "Will you have some rabbit?"

She shook her head, saying, "On the shores of the Land of Lorne walks a woman with hair as black as the bottom of the sea, and she wrings her hands and cries out."

"It is my mother," said Daragh, trembling.

"I have seen her, I have heard her. Over and over she cries one word."

"And that word is . . . ?" whispered Daragh, scarcely daring to hope.

"That word is . . . Shimshinnee."

He sprang to his feet and shouted, "Shimshinnee! Shimshinnee! Shimshinnee!"

And he began to change.

First he was the height of a ten-year-old boy. Next a fifteen-year-old. And in the next instant he was himself, Daragh, son of the Lord of Lorne and the Pictish princess, and a proper size of man.

"Oh, my," said the young selkie, looking at him from under her lashes, and thinking what a very handsome lad he was, much handsomer than the red-haired deceiver who had gotten her with child.

"I am myself again," said Daragh, and he knelt at the feet of the seal mother. "Thank you with all my heart, my lady. Will you tell my mother that I am restored?"

"That I will, for she is sorely worried about you. And will you marry my daughter, and be a father to the child that is none of yours?"

"That I will, for I love her with all my heart, and I vow to love the child as well," and saying that, he drew the seal maiden to his breast. "Will you be mine, my . . . what is your name?"

"Selkies don't have names," she said.

"Then I christen you . . . Shimshinnee, so that I will never forget to remember." He looked at the seal mother, perplexed. "We must go to the people of the Dark Island to tell them of the True Faith, and that God will show them the way if they do but believe, but first we must be married so that Shimshinnee and the child will be safe. Who will marry us?"

"I will," said the seal mother, and Daragh did not dare to protest that their nuptials would not be of the True Faith if they were conducted by a seal. Instead, he and his bride knelt at her feet while she spoke magical seal words over them.

He rose, and said to his bride, "Come, let us go to the people of the Dark Island and tell them of the True Faith."

Shimshinnee had no idea what he was talking about, but so enamoured was she of her handsome young husband that she would have gone anywhere with him. "Gladly," she said, and gave him her hand.

"You cannot go in those rags," said the seal mother, and with a wave of her arm she produced from under the sealskin a fine furred robe for Daragh, and a beautiful golden gown for Shimshinnee, and jeweled crowns for each.

Thus arrayed, they took their leave of the seal mother, and made their way to the nearest village, where they were greeted with cries of awe, and not a little suspicion. But the people of the Dark Island were as curious as cats, and wondered who the incomers were, and so they made them welcome and prepared a feast.

After everyone had eaten, and lay back in front of the fire fat with food and drowsy with their potent homemade brew, Daragh rose to his feet, and began to preach about the True Faith. The Dark Islanders looked at each other, eyebrows raised. Then they looked at Daragh and Shimshinnee, glittering and regal in their elegant clothes, and then at themselves again, and the rags that clothed them. Perhaps if they believed in the True Faith, they too would have elegant clothes and a happy, prosperous life.

Besides, some of the things that Daragh was saying reminded them of their own beliefs. This "God" that he spoke of: was that not the same as their own One Who Listens, the mysterious force that ruled their lives? The concepts of heaven and hell were not new to them, either. In the way of primitive people everywhere, they took ideas from the invader's faith and mingled them with their own, and both they and Daragh were happy with the results.

And when they came to Daragh with their problems, he prayed with them, and after that said, "God will show you the way."

The Dark Islanders would nod in agreement, for they'd always believed that the One Who Listens would show them the way.

So Daragh and Shimshinnee settled into their new home, and presently the seal woman was delivered of her baby. To her immense relief, it did not look at all like her red-headed lover, who'd given her suspicious glances of half-recognition since she'd first appeared, and none whatsoever after he'd seen the child. The baby was a girl, plump as a seal pup, with large eyes that darkened to brown as she grew, and a faint covering of black fur upon her skin, which dropped off within a week of her birth.

After the birth of the babe, the selkie began to think of her life under the sea, and contemplated returning to her seal people. The yearning was strong. But she had grown to love Daragh and her babe, and she had made a vow to herself when he'd married her and saved her life, that she would remain with him until the end of her days. So she took her pelt from beneath its rock and presented it to him, and begged him to hide it where she could never find it, so that she would never be tempted to leave him. And this he did, and she stayed upon the Dark Island and grew old, and was revered by her people as the wisest and kindest of women.

Shimshinnee and Daragh had seven sons in their life together, all with their father's blue eyes and their mother's black hair, and each one grew to manhood and married, and founded a clan. There was, first of all, the heir, who took the name that Daragh had given himself when he'd come to the Island: Mac an Rìgh, the Son of the King, for he was the son of the Lord of Lorne and a son of the King of Heaven.

The other sons called themselves MacChriathar, Mac-a-Phi, Murdoch, MacQuirter, MacPherson, and Ross, and soon by marriage all Dark Islanders belonged to one or the other of these clans.

And that is how the True Faith came to the Dark Island, and why all Dark Islanders carry the blood of the seal people, the Pictish princess, and the Lord of Lorne.

"Crackin' good tale," said Chaz the foreman into the silence that followed the end of the story. "Rekkin it's true, do ye?"

Jean said, "Well, there really was a Daragh who came over the sea from Scotland to bring Christianity to the Dark Island. He was a saint in the early Celtic church. I can't vouch for the part about the selkie, though."

"Never mind. True or not, it's a grand story. Thanks, Missus," Chaz said. "Come on, lads, it's beddy-bye time. The ladies have got a hard day's work of sitting coming up tomorrow. We'll let 'em get to their dreams."

Chuckling, the men got up and drifted back to the construction trailer. Jamie lifted his fiddle once again and found himself, to his horror, playing the tune the misty wisps had taught him. He could not stop until he'd played it through three times. Then he found that Jean was staring at him oddly. "What's wrong?"

"Oh, nothing. It's just that . . . I've heard that tune before, but I can't place it."

"Where did you hear it?" he demanded.

"I don't know," she said, baffled. "It almost seems as though . . . don't laugh . . . it almost seems as though I heard it in a dream."

"I'm not laughing," said Jamie soberly.

Twenty-five

We shall not, we shall not be moved,
We shall not, we shall not be moved,
Just like a tree that's planted by the water,
We shall not be moved.

Textile workers' song, U.S.A.

A week passed. Constable MacRath had taken to visiting the site every day, a worried expression deepening on his face when no news was produced for him about the authentication of the site. He made a duty call on Nick Borth every visit, and subjected himself bravely to a cacophony of shouts and threats that seemed to increase in volume each time. Then, with relief, he took himself off in his panda car.

Nick was holed up in the trailer, making phone calls to his lawyers which resulted in more shouting, fueled by a bottle of whisky he kept handy in a desk drawer. Frequently he came out, stood on the doorstep, and glared at the women as though hoping to annihilate them with his stare.

The construction workers watched it all with interest, having already bidden farewell to their future paychecks. Nick owed them for two weeks work, and they were making plans to demand their money and scarper for the mainland in search of other employment. Meanwhile, they were enjoying the bounty that the canny women doing the provisioning were providing for the sit-in ladies: pies from Ian's Catrìona, brownies from Sheilah Morrison, lemon curd and bread rolls to spread it on from Isabel Ross, Helen Munro's light-as-a-feather scones, and other goodies from other female Islanders.

The sit-in crew was happy to share, both to keep the construction workers on their side, and to keep the pounds off their own inactive bodies, for the treats provided were so fattening that, as Sally said, "You might as well rub them directly on your hips as eat them." Opportunities for exercise were limited, although the women were beginning to take it in shifts to stroll up and down the road, never leaving the site unguarded for a moment in the fear that Nick Borth might dart out and shut and lock the gates, and order his bulldozers back into action. His men would have no choice but to obey.

Jean and Sally kept up the ties that had been established with the workers with occasional brief visits to pass the time of day. Observing one young worker struggle to mend a rip in his shirt, Jean volunteered to take over the project and her aid was gratefully accepted. She was good at sewing and soon found herself the recipient of other projects, socks to be darned, torn out sleeves to be reinserted, buttons to be reattached. Overwhelmed, she offered them to the others, and they were taken up with alacrity, for the women were growing bored and as Màiri said, "We can't just sit here gossiping, dredging up old scandals; there won't be an intact reputation left on the Island."

Sally, amused by the sight of three of Eilean Dubh's most vital and intelligent women sitting around the smoored campfire by day busily plying needles and thread and gossiping, dubbed them the "Sewing Circle." She declined to participate, for she was all thumbs at sewing, she said, but she made herself useful by helping the workers write letters home. If they got stuck on spelling, or finding the right word, Sally was there to assist. One of the older workers confided in great secrecy that he "wrote a bit of verse now and again," and would like her opinion on it. "Never showed it to a living soul before," he mumbled, terrified of being overheard by his mates. She read it, and told him it was very good, and gave him the name of a little magazine she knew of that bought verse from unknown writers. Delighted, he went off to get his work, and she helped him compose a letter to the magazine and select the best poems to send off with it. "Maybe I've given a hand to the next Robert Burns," she told the other women with satisfaction.

This pleasant state of affairs could not continue forever, they all knew, for Nick Borth was growing visibly more agitated each day, and his tongue-lashings of the hapless constable grew in volume each time the policeman appeared. MacRath shuddered with apprehension every time he entered the trailer, and came out with his hat under his arm, mopping his brow.

Then one glorious afternoon Anna Wallace and Zach Trelawney appeared, shouting in triumph, "It's been confirmed!" Everyone gathered around them in great excitement, including the workers, whose interest in archaeology had increased as their hopes for further work dimmed.

Zach shared around the fax he'd received from the University. The scraper flake had been carbon-dated to an age of eight thousand years; he and Anna had found an authentic Mesolithic site. The fax was passed from hand to hand, and read with great respect, for it was on the University's letterhead, and its authenticity could not be denied.

"Right, then, lads," barked the foreman. "Let's get oor back wages from yon mannie and scarper. He's stalled us long enough," and a small army of workers gathered and marched on Nick Borth's trailer, grimly determined to get what they'd earned, and be off to more lucrative employment.

"Nick Borth has got to be told that his project is finished," said Barabal.

"Better wait for reinforcements," advised Anna. "We've called Darroch, and he's gathering the men to come and help. Everybody wanted to be in on the fun."

Soon Darroch's Bentley and Jamie's little red Austin appeared and unloaded Somhairle Mac-a-Phi *as sine* and *as òige,* Barabal's husband and son, Ian *Mór,* Ian the Post and his Catrìona, and Eilidh and Joe Munro. Last to come was Russ, who'd hastened home to get Ruth to join in the glorious *dénouement.*

Everyone gathered in front of the office trailer, waiting for the construction workers to complete their business with Borth. They came out, chuckling and grinning, waving checks in the air as though to dry the ink. "Your turn now, Missus," said Chaz the foreman to Barabal. "Give 'im 'ell, for 'e's a right bastard, and wasn't goin' to pay my lads for the work they've done, until we threatened to dangle 'im over yon cliff by his ba . . . uh . . . by his ankles."

"We've got to wait for Constable MacRath to make it official," said Barabal, just as, as if on cue, the panda car pulled into the driveway.

The Constable emerged, settled his hat firmly on his head, and approached the group. "Afternoon, all. I understand you've something to show me that will clear up this spot of bother."

Zach produced the fax.

It was carefully scrutinized. Then the Constable said, "Right. Will you fill me in on chapter and verse of the law, laddie, so I don't make any mistakes? Archaeological legalities weren't covered in my police training course."

Zach coached him in the legal terms known to every archaeologist. Then the Constable approached the trailer door and was about to knock when it opened, and Nick Borth stepped out and stood staring at them, arms crossed over his chest.

How odd, thought Jean; his eyes are gray, but I never noticed before that they are red-rimmed. There's something not quite human about this guy. Jamie, quicker-thinking, put his hand over Rosie's face as she nestled in Darroch's arms; he'd heard about the evil eye and he was not taking any chances of harm to the most vulnerable among them.

"So you think you've won," said Nick at last.

"We know we have," said Barabal, "and we've written proof of it from Mr. Trelawney's university. This site has been authenticated."

"This is an official archaeological site and as such is being registered in the Sites and Monuments Record," began Constable MacRath, not to be upstaged, and determined that the formalities should be observed. "It is now under the management of the Regional Archaeologist and his or her officially-determined representatives. It is protected by the Ancient Monuments and Archaeological Areas Act passed by Her Majesty's Government in 1979 . . . "

"Shut up, you stupid copper," said Nick. "At least I won't have to listen to you bleat on any more. As for the rest of you . . . you've lost your chance to put this backwater on the map. I could have made you all rich and your Island famous."

"We don't want to be rich and famous," said Darroch, who'd been both and knew it wasn't all it was cracked up to be. "We're happy as we are. Our Island is too precious to us to sacrifice its beauty for a few coins."

"A few million coins," scoffed Nick. "You hayseeds don't know what you're throwing away."

"We know what we're keeping," said Darroch quietly.

And, happy to let the Laird have the last word, the group turned their back on Nick Borth and walked away.

Later, as they folded up their blankets, chairs and cooking equipment, Somhairle Mac-a-Phi *as sine* said thoughtfully, "Mind you, the odd bob or two from the tourists would have been a welcome treat. Our last electricity bill from Scottish Hydro was something shocking, no pun intended."

Everyone sighed. Most of them had harbored fantasies about what an influx of new money would have meant in their lives, and all had willingly sacrificed those fantasies for what they'd seen as the greater good of the community. But reality was hard.

"Maybe the price of fish will pick up," said Somhairle Mac-a-Phi *as òige* hopefully.

"More likely it won't," said Chaz the foreman, who'd come up to join them. "My Da's a fisherman, and he's never seen the price of fish go any way but doon. And the stock of fish, as well. But if it's any consolation to the lot of yez, Ah'm right chuffed not to have had a hand in ruining your coastie. Ah'm planning on bringing the family here next year for oor summer hols, for it's gae bonnie, 'n' the wifey 'n' the weans like the nature mixty-maxty. So there's a tourist shilling or twa for yez to look forward to."

He paused, glanced back surreptitiously at his fellow workers, and said in a lowered voice, "Besides, there's something dodgy about this construction site. Ah've had bad dreams the whole time Ah've been diggin' in it, and Ah cannae think you'd get much return business from tourists to a place that gives 'em nightmares. Not that Ah believe in boggles 'n' suchlike, mind."

The sit-in women stirred uneasily, except Màiri, who said, "Well, I didn't have any nightmares, but I surely am looking forward to my own bed tonight." She caught Jamie's eye. He raised his eyebrows and leered, and she blushed bright red.

A construction worker elbowed another, and said, "Ah rekkin there'll be one or twa tired lasses come the morn, fer they've all been awa' from their oon beds and their wee mannies the week." The other guffawed.

Zach shouted suddenly, "Three cheers for the ladies! They saved our dig!"

When the cheering died down, Russ said, "I'll stand all of you to the tipple of your choice at the Rose, to celebrate."

"Aw, will ye listen oop?" shouted a worker. "The Yank's buying a roon. Everybody inna the cars 'n' head for the boozer!"

"Ah'm for the next roon," yelled another worker. "Mah paycheck's burning a hole in mah pocket, and ah've no wee wifey or weans to spend it on, so it's drink up, lads."

"I wish I had a mobile phone, so I could warn Sheilah the Tartan Army's invading," whispered Darroch to Jean.

"She won't mind. We're bringing her a load of tourist business."

The sit-in women lingered to finish shaking out and rolling up their sleeping bags, and packing their cooking supplies. Jean said, "Do you know, I've enjoyed this, apart from missing Darroch and Rosie."

"And a comfy bed," added Màiri.

"And an even comfier husband," added Sally.

Anna Wallace walked over, leaving Zach staring in blissful contemplation at the archaeological site. "He's right, you know," she said. "You women saved the dig. Nick Borth would have had it completely torn up ten minutes after he'd heard our news."

"Group hug, everyone," said Sally, opening her arms. Jean came enthusiastically. The Scotswomen followed, a little stiff at first, not being used to such American free expression of emotion. But soon everyone was into the spirit, laughing, hugging, patting each other on the back.

"Up the revolution!" Jean cried. "Womanpower rules!"

"Aye, well, I don't know about that," said Màiri, detaching herself. "I do know that I'd better not find a sink full of dirty dishes at home, or there'll be another demonstration of womanpower, and another revolution."

"Amen," said someone.

Jean was uncharacteristically silent that evening, at home. She was processing the many things she'd learned from her fellow *bana-Eilean Dhuibh* during the sit-in. Ian's Catrìona had particularly given her food for thought, since she was pregnant, a state Jean was contemplating with interest and apprehension. Catrìona had spoken about her joy in having passed the point in her pregnancy when, according to Ros MacPherson, she was likely to lose the baby.

"Ian's so happy," she had said one morning. "Losing the other two devastated him, for he's desperate to have a child."

"Ian *Mór's* hot to trot into paternity, too," said Sally. "He keeps hinting, and I keep telling him not yet. I'm not sure I'm ready to be tied down. I've still got lots of ground to cover and lots of stories to write about weird British stuff." Sally wrote articles for a travel magazine about haunted houses, ghosts and other strange events that had occurred in Great Britain, and traveled the entire country doing research.

"Ach, no hurry," said Màiri comfortably. She liked the idea of a grandchild, but was not quite sure she was old enough to be a grandmother. "Don't let yourself be rushed into it. You'll know when you're ready."

"I've been ready for five years," said Catrìona softly, and the others were silent, out of respect for her losses.

Jean knew that she was ready, too, both emotionally and physically. Her period had resumed its usual clock-like accuracy, and Ros MacPherson had confirmed that she was back to normal, three months after she'd stopped taking the Pill. And it wasn't watching Catrìona knit booties that stirred her emotions; it was the certainty that what she wanted to do was the right thing to do.

She and Darroch snuggled happily into bed that evening, after Rosie was tucked in. Overstimulated by the excitement of having Mama home once again, the little girl had demanded stories and songs until Jean was quite hoarse from the telling and the singing and the repeated assurances that yes, she was home to stay, and no, she wasn't planning on going away again.

Now Jean rested comfortably in Darroch's arms, catching a relaxed breath or two before turning to her next delightful task, that of telling him that they were good to go, baby-wise. He was stroking her gently, stem to stern, and she knew where that was leading. Might as well give him the news right away. Then she heard him open the drawer of the little table on his side of the bed. "Won't need that," she said.

"And why not, Miss Sharp Ears?"

"Because . . ." How to say it in a poetic, romantic manner? Nothing came to mind, so she blurted, "We can move into full baby-production mode."

"Ah." He was silent for a moment. She heard the drawer open and close again. "Everything's shipshape and Bristol-fashion, then?"

"Righty-o." She put her hands on either side of his face and drew him down for a kiss. "Fire away, captain."

His chuckle was lost in the kiss.

When he slipped into her after a delightful period of mutually-appreciated cuddling, both experienced the perfect moment of completion they always felt during the act of intercourse, a moment that glowed like a pearl, shimmered opal-like in a myriad of colors, shining in the radiant awareness that life had found them three thousand miles apart and brought them, somehow, together in this bed.

Afterwards, Darroch rolled over so that she lay on top of him, elbows on his chest, with him still inside her. "You are the most beautiful woman in the world, and I am the luckiest man in the universe."

"I'm the luckiest woman in the universe, and the happiest."

"Husband, wife, child . . . "

"And the prospect of a fourth. Are you getting used to the idea?"

"Not only used to it, but fantasizing about it. While you were gone, Jean, and I was here in my lonely bed with nothing for company but my imagination, I had this vision of the four of us, sitting here propped up against the headboard. Me with the wee creature in my arms, swaddled in blankets, you curled up next to me with your head on my shoulder, and Rosie leaning over you, poking at the creature with her favorite thumb. 'Don't do that, Rosie,' I said, and she withdrew and snuggled up to you with her thumb where it belongs, in her mouth. Then the creature opened its eyes, and gave me a wink. 'That's telling her, *a Bhobain*,' it said."

"It. Was it a girl or a boy It?"

"Sometimes one, sometimes the other, although I admit most of the time it was wearing football kit, with Inverness Caledonian Thistle emblazoned on its wee chest."

"Could have been a girl footballer."

He shook his head. "No, I think not. Football's the one thing the lasses haven't invaded yet, though I daresay the time will come when we've co-ed sides."

"Hope I live long enough to see that day . . . I think."

"Stranger things have happened. Are you ready for another bit of baby-making?"

"I am, aye, Daddy."

He rolled her over, and she protested. "I was wanting to be on top this time."

"Next time, maybe." He began to move in her, and was getting lost in the sensation, when he heard a little voice.

"What Daddy doing to Mama?"

Jean heard it, too, and groaned. A parent's worse nightmare: being caught in the act of lovemaking by your child.

Darroch recovered first, and decided quickly that the best defense was a good offense, just like in football. He levered himself up, and demanded sternly, "What are you doing out of bed, Rosie?"

Silence.

"Rosie, how did you get out of bed?"

More silence, then, "I climbed."

"Out of your crib? What have Mama and Daddy told you about doing that?"

"Not."

"Why?"

Rosie looked at him owlishly. "Might fall."

"And?"

"Get hurted."

"And Mama would . . .?"

"Cry because Rosie was hurted."

"Daddy might cry, too. Do you want Mama and Daddy to cry?"

"No." The thumb went back into her mouth.

"Right then, Madam Rosie. Back to your room and Daddy will tuck you in, and there you are going to stay for the rest of the night."

Rosie turned obediently and walked out of the room. Darroch followed her, first grabbing his shorts and pulling them on. He remembered and understood at last Jean's reservations about going to bed naked when there was a small child in the house. Kids certainly did change your life, he thought.

PART XI

Borth's Last Stand

Twenty-six

No exorciser harm thee!
Nor no witchcraft charm thee!
Ghost unlaid forbear thee!
Nothing ill come near thee!
Quiet consummation have;
And renowned be thy grave!

William Shakespeare

Since there was considerable curiosity about the archaeological site, Zach offered to lead an expedition to it the following week and explain his theories. Alasdair MacQuirter, the carpenter who'd been fired, volunteered to come along and talk about the construction work that had been done. A large group headed by the Laird followed Zach and Anna into the site.

Everyone thought that Nick Borth was gone, as he'd not been seen lately, and it was a great surprise when he came out of the construction supply shack, holding an object in his hands. He surveyed the group. "All of you lot, get out. That's my first and only warning."

Alasdair MacQuirter said, "Mr. Borth, sir, be careful. That's dynamite you've got there."

Borth grinned. "I know it, and in a minute this entire Island will know it. I might not have my condos, but you're not going to have an archaeological site, either."

An alarmed murmur ran through the crowd, and Darroch said, "What are you about, Borth?"

"I'm going to blow up this moldy heap of rock scraps." He smiled, and looked around at them in triumph.

"What?" gasped Zach, shocked at the idea of such sacrilege. "You'd destroy a precious part of history, just because you can't make a profit on it?"

"That's right." Borth reached into his pocket and drew out a cigarette lighter. "And I've already given you warning, so get the hell out, right now, or suffer the consequences." He held the cigarette lighter up in the air and raised the stick of dynamite. "Handy, isn't it. There's always dynamite around a construction site."

Darroch said, "Get back, all of you. Nick Borth and I will talk about this quietly, just the two of us."

"No more talking, Mr. High and Mighty Laird. I have nothing more to say to any of you." He waved the stick of dynamite in the air. "This is going to speak for me."

"You'll blow yourself up along with the site, Mr. Borth," warned Alasdair.

Nick gauged the distance to the dig. "I've got lots of experience with dynamite. I know enough to keep well away. But the rest of you had better scatter, because it's all going up. Get back now, I warn you."

Jean said, "Please, Nick, think about this."

"Oh, I've thought about it. And I know just what I'm doing and I'm going to do it, right now." He moved the cigarette lighter closer to the fuse on the dynamite.

The group shrank back in terror.

Something shimmered in Jamie's mind, some ancient voice whispered in his ear, and he was compelled to speak. He stepped forward and placed himself at the center of the dig. "I don't think so."

Màiri gasped, and would have bolted to him had Darroch not wrapped a strong arm around her waist, and the other arm around Jean, preventing them from moving.

Jamie said, "Think again, Borth. You won't be allowed to get away with it."

Darroch said, "The police will have you in jail . . . "

Nick snorted. "You think I've afraid of that stupid Island copper?"

"Not the copper," said Jamie, his voice unnaturally calm. "Others will see that you pay, and keep on paying."

"I'm not afraid of you yokels," blustered Nick.

Jamie smiled. "You might get away from us, but you won't escape Them."

"What the hell are you talking about?"

Jamie turned, and waved his arm over the dig. "The Ones whose spirits remain in this site. Can't you hear Them, Borth? Listen very carefully." He turned towards the dig and stood motionless and attentive. "They're talking to you, Nick," he said over his shoulder.

Complete silence fell over the crowd as they strained to hear what Jamie was hearing. Everyone knew that he had unusual psychic abilities, but they'd never seen him demonstrate them before, and they were quivering with curiosity and apprehension to see what would happen next.

"They've been here for eight thousand years, Borth, and you can't get rid of Them with dynamite. They'll follow you wherever you go. Listen to Their voices, and imagine what it would be like to have Them with you the rest of your life. They won't be gentle with you, either. They'll whisper in your ears, day and night, and cry for Their lost Island. They'll haunt your dreams. You'll never be rid of Them."

Eilidh said, in a half whisper, "They are here. I know it."

"Who are you talking about?" gasped Borth, beginning to tremble.

Jamie smiled again, and it was if none of the crowd had ever seen him before. A change had come over him. He was as pale as death, and taller and thinner and older, and his facial features were more pronounced, the high cheekbones sharper, the nose more commanding. He intoned, "They are the spirits of the dead, Nick Borth, who will haunt you forever if you destroy Their homes."

The crowd muttered, and began to move uneasily, shuffling their feet.

Màiri froze in Darroch's grasp. Jean felt a cold chill prickling down her spine, and a restlessness in her scalp as though her hair was beginning to stand on end. Darroch felt it, too, and tightened his hold on both women.

Jamie cried in sudden agony, "Can none of you hear? Am I completely alone with Them?"

Eilidh came to stand by him, slipping her slender hand in his. "I hear, but I don't understand. What are They saying, *a Dhadaidh?*"

A look of pain came over Jamie's face. "I can't quite make it out. There's fear, and anger . . . " He shuddered, and a drop of sweat trickled from his brow and was caught on his long eyelashes. He closed his eyes impatiently and blinked it away, and remained standing with eyes closed, swaying. He cried, his voice an eerie wail, "They're begging . . . *A Dhia!* They're begging us to save Their graves! Oh, Christ, I can't stand it!"

He wrenched his fingers from Eilidh's and slammed both hands over his ears. The crowd watched in horror as tears, mingled with sweat, began to run down his face. He staggered, and it was Eilidh's arm tight around his waist that kept him from falling.

Nick Borth, though trembling, was still defiant. "Nice try, MacDonald, but I don't believe in spooks and boogeymen and things that go bump in the night." He raised his hands and the lighter once again.

Jamie straightened and color began to return to his high cheekbones. His voice was eerily calm and commanding, as though it were the voice of an ancient priest. "Look over there, Borth. Look at that patch of wildflowers, near the middle of your site."

The crowd's heads swiveled to face the wildflowers.

"Why do you think the flowers grow so abundantly there? They're nourished by the bodies of the Ones who came before. That's the burial site for Their village. That's the place to blow up. Throw your dynamite into Their graveyard, Borth, if you dare, and be damned to a lifetime of voices in your head."

Eilidh covered her father's deathly cold fingers with her own warm ones, and stood side by side with him. "Do you hear Them, Mr. Borth?" she said clearly. "There's a message now, just for you."

Borth stood, white-faced, still as a statue. He stared at the wildflower patch, then turned back towards Jamie. His mouth opened, but no sound came out. He shook his head and grabbed at his ears, as though trying to dislodge something. "Make Them stop," he begged, staring at Jamie.

Jamie smiled.

Darroch said softly, "Give it up, man. You're outnumbered." He turned to the construction worker. "Take the dynamite, Alasdair. Mr. Borth doesn't want it anymore."

The young man stepped forward and held out his hand. Nick Borth, trembling, shoulders slumped, head hanging in defeat, put the dynamite into the outstretched palm.

Darroch said, "Get out, Borth. Get off our Island. There's a Cal-Mac ferry leaving at three from Airgead. That gives you an hour and a half to get your things together and get on it. None of us will interfere with your leaving."

Nick Borth looked around at the circle of implacable *Eilean Dubhannaich* faces, then cast a glance out over the site that he had expected to be the scene of his triumph, envisioning for the last time the proud row of high-priced condominiums he'd planned to build.

Then he looked at the wildflower patch beyond the crowd. He shuddered, and stumbled forward. The circle parted to let him out and watched as he retreated through the gate.

When they heard the noise of a car starting and pulling away, the Islanders turned back to look at Jamie, and each other.

Darroch said urgently, "Go to your husband, Màiri, and help him into the construction trailer. He'll be needing to sit down. Joe, get to the telephone in the trailer and call Sheilah and Gordon at the Rose. Warn them that Nick Borth will be checking out, and tell them not to delay his departure. Tell them to forget the bill and just let him walk out of there; the Trust will pick up the tab for his stay. Tell them to let him go quietly and without hindrance."

Galvanized into action by the Laird's words, the crowd broke up. Alasdair MacQuirter carried the dynamite, gingerly, back into the construction shed and snapped shut the lock hanging on the door. Jean rushed forward to help Màiri escort Jamie into the trailer. Eilidh hurried to open the door for them, and darted inside to find a chair for her father.

Zach Trelawney turned to Anna. "That was the damnedest thing I've ever seen. Did he really hear those voices? It made my flesh creep."

Jamie stopped, suddenly, in front of Anna, and fixed her with a penetrating gaze. "Not a word of this in that paper of yours, do you hear me? There were no voices, no dynamite, no threats."

Darroch said, "Mr. Borth gracefully bowed out on his plans, once he realized the importance of Zach's discovery, and he has left our Island without fanfare."

She said, "But the story—it's the biggest story I've ever had!"

Jamie said severely, "There is no story."

Darroch nodded, watching Anna, his blue eyes intent on her face.

She gave in, abruptly. "Hell. All right, damn it. Anything for a quiet life."

Both men nodded at her and turned toward the trailer. When young Alasdair came out of the shed, Jamie said to him, "Not a word about any of this to anyone."

"Of course not, Mr. Jamie. My lips are sealed. It's naught to me, anyway."

As the others left, Zach put a comforting arm around Anna's shoulder. "You still have the story of the archaeological discovery. Exclusive rights to an interview with the supervisor of the dig. That's me, love."

She gave him a rueful grin.

In the trailer, Darroch began to ransack Borth's desk drawers. "Where is it? Damn it, I know he'll have one; he had boozer written all over him." He made a small triumphant noise when he opened a bottom drawer and pulled out a bottle of whisky.

Darroch brought the bottle to Jamie, whom the women had helped into a chair. "Get some of this inside you, man; you look like death on toast."

Shuddering and choking, Jamie drank, and a bit of color began to return to his cheeks. "Damn it," he said. "That was the worst experience I've ever had in a lifetime of bad experiences with Them." Then, realizing what he'd said, he lifted his head and glared at the four watchers. "You'll forget that," he commanded. "Nothing's happened."

Darroch chuckled. "Right. And I thought I was a good actor. You've put me to shame, Jamie, *mo charaid*." Then he looked more closely at his friend, and recoiled in shock. "It wasn't an act. You did hear something. What was it?"

Jamie looked him straight in the eye. "Never ask me that again."

Darroch stared at him, then turned away, repressing a shudder. There were, he knew, things in the world best not talked about, especially if they involved Jamie.

Jean grinned and bent down to kiss Jamie's cheek. "But you're still our hero."

Eilidh said chattily, "Daddy always has such bad times with voices. Just like up on Cemetery Hill. I don't mind them, and even Joe has gotten used to them, though he's an incomer and had never heard anything like that before. But Daddy hates to even go up there . . . " She stopped abruptly, conscious that three people were staring at her in astonishment, and that her father was glaring furiously.

"Hush yer whist, ye silly wean," snapped Jamie.

"Oh, right. Sorry, Daddy," said Eilidh, and gave them all a conspiratorial smile. She had never minded talking about her unusual spirit experiences, and had forgotten that it was anathema to her father to even mention it.

"Jamie," began Màiri, "did you really hear—"

"Drop it, *a Mhàiri*," said Darroch in the Laird's commanding voice, and she subsided, although a sidewise glance at her husband let him know that she didn't consider the matter closed.

Outside, Zach stood staring at the site. "Wonder if he's right," he murmured.

Anna said, "About what?"

"The wildflower patch. About it being fertilized with ancient bodies. Makes perfect sense."

"You're not going to dig up those wildflowers. Not until I find out if any of them are endangered species," she said firmly, staring at her lover.

"Of course not," he growled. "You can't just go tearing into what might be an ancient burial site. There's a technique called ground penetrating radar; works by using electromagnetic energy to survey a site to get some idea of what's in it. It tells us where to dig without having to tear apart the whole thing. I'll have to contact one of the firms that does it . . . " Musing, he walked forward toward the wildflower patch.

Anna sighed in resignation, and followed him.

Inside the trailer, Jamie said, "Now I know where that tune came from."

Jean understood, even if no else one did.

PART XII

Anna and Zach Seal the Deal

Twenty-seven

Shall we nevermore behold thee;
Never hear thy winning voice again,
When the Springtime comes, gentle Annie,
When the wildflowers are scattered o'er the plain?

Stephen Foster

That day Anna knew that her life was changed forever. Zach had made his great discovery, and now he would go back to his university, basking in glory, probably writing lots of learned papers for learned publications and getting advanced degrees by the armful. Oh, well, she thought, it was fun while it lasted, ignoring the pain in her heart that parting with him brought.

Zach was pacing back and forth in front of his site, imagining his dig set up and ready for action. "Damned convenient, all these trailers and the Porta-loo. We'll use Borth's office for our headquarters, and the workers' trailers for accommodations for our staff. Won't need these bulldozers, though." He shuddered, and slapped one of the huge machines disparagingly.

She listened to him rambling on, then said, "So when will you leave?"

"Oh, right away. Got to get back to my university and start setting up the dig. Recruiting workers; that's the first job. There'll be lots of students wanting to help out."

Was he even going to say good-bye, or "thanks for the help and encouragement"? Or was she just a closed chapter, now that he'd gotten what he wanted. She kicked at a stone crossly.

"Don't do that, Anna; you might be disturbing an artifact. We have to treat the site with kid gloves now."

How about treating her with kid gloves? she thought mulishly. She muttered something under her breath.

He stopped and looked at her. "What did you say?"

"I said, I suppose you're in a tearing hurry to leave."

"Oh, I am, I am, for the sooner I leave, the sooner I'll be back."

A surprising bit of hope sprang to life in her breast. "You're coming back?"

"Of course. Got to supervise the dig, haven't I." He stared at her. "Were you thinking that I'd go off and leave my site to someone else to explore?"

"I didn't know . . . "

He said patiently, "It's my site, Anna. I'm the one who's going to excavate it, bit by bit, layer by layer, year by year."

"You think it'll take years?" Astonishing how cheerful that idea made her.

"Oh, yes. A complicated dig like this one means hunkering down and taking plenty of time. Digging in the fine weather, analyzing what you've found and writing it up in the winter. You can't rush archaeology. It's like lovemaking, or relationships. And speaking of relationships . . . " He gave her a long look.

"What about relationships?"

"Well, there's ours. We've explored the first layer quite thoroughly. Now it's time to dig a little deeper."

"What do you have in mind?"

"What I have in mind is that we should get married."

She stared.

He shuffled his feet, then said crossly, "All right, I know that's not the most romantic proposal in the world, but I've got a lot on my mind." He looked at her face, wondering what her expression meant. Was she going to say no? He couldn't have that; because he was mad about her, and wanted her for his wife. Best tart it up a bit, so she'd have to consent. He dropped to his knees in the dirt of his site, and said, "I love you, dearest Anna. Please say you'll marry me."

"That's more like it," she said, while a flock of wild birds began to sing inside her brain.

"Are you going to say yes?" he asked, wishing she would hurry, for something was digging into his left knee and he couldn't help but wonder if it was a microlith.

"I'm thinking about it."

They stared at each other. Then Zach found the magic word that would do the trick. "Please."

She weakened, but warned, "I'm not leaving Eilean Dubh. If we get married, this is going to be our home."

"Of course it will be our home; where else would we be? If it'll make you happy, I'll start moving my things from Mrs. Cailean's to your apartment tonight."

"Steady on, no need to cause a scandal, digger boy. We wait until we're spliced to co-habit, on Eilean Dubh."

"Well, how soon can we get spliced?" he asked in his most reasonable voice as he got to his feet.

"I thought you were going to Edinburgh to make your arrangements."

"I am. That will take . . . say, three to four weeks . . . and then I'll be back, cap in hand, ring in hand, ready to tie the knot. That gives you time to look out a proper frock, acquire a bridesmaid or two, find the parson, book the church. Gives my mum time to pack up the family and scoot up here from Cornwall, too."

"You have a mother and a family?"

"Of course, did you think I was hatched from an egg? Three adoring brothers, two doting sisters, a gaggle of in-laws and a pack of noisy nieces and nephews. I'd better book the Rose for them. We'll need the whole place, for there's about twenty-five of us."

She goggled at him. "Twenty-five?"

"Yes, you're not getting just me, you're getting a whole family. And we're Cornish, so that means extra dividends: there's a boatload of rellies, including Cousin Jacks and Cousin Jennies who've emigrated all around the globe. If you want to go to Australia or Wisconsin someday, we'll never have to pay for accommodations. We'll just bunk in with a cousin or three."

Overwhelmed, Anna finally remembered to shut her mouth, which had been hanging open in astonishment. She'd been a loner for so many years, since her Grandda had died, that she could hardly conceive of belonging to a large family. She rather thought she'd like it.

Seeing her smile, Zach bounded up off his knees. "I take it that's a yes, then," he said, and without waiting for an answer clutched her to his breast and planted a huge kiss on her mouth.

Darroch, Jean, Jamie, Màiri, Eilidh and Joe, coming out of the office trailer, were witnesses to the kiss. For the second time in a week, cheers rippled across the archaeological site.

Twenty-eight

The best laid plans of men may go astray,
but the wise man knows this,
and always has a new plan in his pocket.

Eilean Dubh proverb

*B*ye-and-bye Darroch realized that there was someone he'd forgotten, someone who would be devastated by the collapse of Nick Borth's schemes: Fearchar MacShennach, who had schemes of his own. He resolved to visit the old man and gently console him by offering financial support for young Somhairle's college education. The Trust wouldn't run to Harvard, but it could pay for his education at a fine Scottish university; he was an excellent student with excellent grades, and if he wanted more education, he would have it.

Settled uneasily on Fearchar's saggy old couch, the tabby cat happily ensconced on his lap, Darroch began, "You'll have heard of the end of the project for building on our coastline, I suppose, *a Fhearchar.*"

"*Tha gu dearbh.* Do you think I live in a cave? I know everything that happens on this Island. That cat's taken a rare liking to you; you'd best take her home with you."

Darroch repressed a shudder at the idea of adding a crabby old tabby to his already congested household. "I think not, for she'd miss you."

"Hmmph." Adroitly, Fearchar changed the subject. "Yon Yank came a cropper with that archyology chappie, didn't he. Mind you, when the Cornishman came to ask my advice, I thought he was onto something. More between his ears than cotton, I reckon."

"Aye. You're not to worry about your grandson's education, though," Darroch said, and prepared to launch into his spiel about a scholarship to a fine Scottish university.

"Ha! What education?"

"We can't offer him Harvard, but the Trust will see that he's taken care of . . . "

"Never you mind about that, *a Mhic an Rìgh*. It's all in hand. We MacShennachs can take care of ourselves. Our young laddie has a mind of his own," Fearchar said proudly. "And he'll not be needing your blessed Trust's help, for he's set up fine for the future."

"What do you mean?"

"Our other Yank . . . the good one . . . has big plans for our lad. He's offered Somhairle a rare grand job, that of manager of his software-fixy place. He'll be reporting directly to yon Russ himself."

"Is that so?" said Darroch in surprise.

"Aye, it's so, for the Yank's as sharp as a needle and knows a bright laddie when he meets one, and our Somhairle is as bright as they come. Russ told me so himself. Of course, he thinks highly of the lad, knowing what sort of stock he comes from." Fearchar preened. "Not that I had anything to do with it, mind you. Never a word did I say to Russ about giving the lad a leg up; he figured it out for himself, and young Somhairle came to tell his old great-grandfather about it before he told his mum and da. 'Great-Grandda,' he says to me, 'I've been offered a promotion by my boss, and I'm going to accept it.' 'What about your university education?' I says to him. He says, 'My boss needs me too much for me to go jaunting off to university for years. He says he'll stand me to courses on the mainland, and I can work on my degree in business bit by bit as I can be spared from work, for more education will make me a more valuable employee.'"

"I see."

"'What about Harvard?' I says. And what do you think that young scamp said?"

"I can't imagine," said Darroch, bemused.

"He said he doesn't want to go off to the United States, because he's just persuaded his third cousin, the oldest MacShennach lass Dìorbhail, to marry him, and he's afraid if he leaves her for too long some other laddie boy will waltz in and carry her off." He chuckled hoarsely. "That lassie's a rare handful; got a mind of her own and pretty as a sunrise full of daisies. He brought her around to meet me, and I could see at once that he was right. 'Marry her quick,' I told him, 'or you'll lose her, for you don't find a lass like that one under every bush, and she's hot to get on with the business of life.'

She wants to get married and have her family, so she says, while she's young enough to keep up with a gaggle of weans."

He leaned close to Darroch, and his fierce old eye closed in a horrible wink. "Promised me a great-great-grandchild, she did. Think of that, *a Mhic an Rìgh*: a MacShennach dynasty on Eilean Dubh, with me as its pattriack. Look to your laurels, laddie, or we'll be taking over."

Darroch, tickled to the depths of his soul by the old man, said, "Oh, I shall, *a Fhearchar*, I shall. And thank you for the warning."

PART XIII

Baby On Board

Twenty-nine

Blessings on the hand of women!
Fathers, sons and daughters cry,
And the sacred song is mingled
With the worship in the sky—
Mingles where no tempest darkens,
Rainbows evermore are hurled;
For the hand that rocks the cradle
Is the hand that rules the world.

William Ross Wallace

Summer turned into fall, fall led into winter, and winter crept tentatively towards spring. Anna Wallace and Zach Trelawney were married and settled into her apartment, her spare room transformed by piles of books and papers into his office. Minister Donald and Helen Munro were married and settled into the gray stone manse, a huge old desk tucked into a corner of the kitchen for Helen and Raonaid to do their planning, scheduling and recipe exchanging.

And Jean was pregnant.

To her relief, and Darroch's, this pregnancy was progressing smoothly. She'd had only mild hormonally-fueled mood swings, and even her morning sickness was mild. She began to think she'd get through it all unscathed; her weight gain was under control and her stretch marks were minimal since she'd taken to rubbing into the skin of her belly an old traditional concoction prepared by one of the women in the Seniors' Residence. She didn't know what was in it, and didn't care, since it seemed to be working.

She and Darroch had faced their ultimate fear bravely, that a baby born to a mother in her forties might have birth defects. They'd gone into Edinburgh each month for an ultra-sound and other tests, and waited out the results, trembling, hands clasped. They'd discussed what they would do if something were wrong with the baby, keeping in mind their advanced age, and the fact that responsibility for a damaged child would fall, ultimately, on Rosie's young shoulders.

Then they'd each written on a separate piece of paper what they would do if they got bad news from the tests. They'd folded the papers and exchanged them. They'd tucked them, unread, into the top drawers of their dressers, each with a prayer to the One Who Listens that it would never be necessary to read them at all.

And the news continued to be good: the child was perfect. After each medical visit they'd celebrated at a favorite little Italian restaurant in Edinburgh, and the next day boarded the helicopter for home, hearts light.

Now they were at Ros MacPherson's office for Jean's biweekly check-up. Jean was behind a screen, being examined. A consent stream of murmuring came from behind the screen, Ros's deeper voice and Jean's soft one. Darroch flipped through a magazine, paying no attention whatsoever to its contents. These examinations made him nervous, and it was always a great relief to hear Ros say that all was well, as he always did.

Ros emerged from behind the screen, and said nothing. He sat down at his desk and made notes while Jean dressed and came to sit beside her husband. Then he turned to them, his expression so serious that both were instantly on their guard.

"Something's wrong. What is it?" said Jean, squeezing Darroch's hand nervously.

Ros regarded them intently. "The baby's in a breech position."

"I'm sorry, I don't understand. What does that mean?" said Darroch.

"The baby's bum first," replied Jean, then regretted her inelegant language. "I mean, instead of its head down, ready for birth, its position is reversed, and the bottom would come out first. Right, Ros?"

"Is that bad?" asked Darroch, still baffled.

"It makes for a more difficult delivery, with possible problems," said Ros.

Sensing an attack of physician reticence, Jean put up her head and stared at him. "You might as well tell me what the problems are, Ros. I've had three babies and I can take it."

"Right," said Ros. "Well, the worst possibility is that the baby's head, being the biggest part of its body, might get stuck in the birth canal, and that's a true medical emergency, because the cord will be pinched and the flow of oxygen cut off."

"Is it possible to turn the baby into a head first position?" Jean asked.

Ros shook his head. "Very difficult, and unlikely it would stay that way. A breech baby is quite determined to be breech."

"So what do we do?" asked Darroch, trembling with anxiety.

"A caesarian is sometimes indicated in these cases."

"Oh, no," said Jean. "Major abdominal surgery, yuck. Weeks to recover. How will I take care of two little kids after having that?"

"Well, it's early days yet. We have time to think about it. I'll consult with young Ian and get his ideas. But I want you in hospital, Jean." Then, as she started to protest, he said firmly, "I'd planned on putting you before you are due anyway, because of your propensity for rapid delivery. We'll just move that timetable up a bit. We can't have you trying to deliver a breech baby at home."

"Quite right," said Darroch, who didn't entirely understand the situation, but had no intention of going through the birth of another baby in their cottage, as had been the case with Rosie three years ago. His nerves hadn't completely recovered from that event. "When do you want her in, Ros?"

"Let me see. You've never delivered early, have you, Jean? I think perhaps a week before your due date should be sufficient."

"But that's in four weeks. Damn it," said Jean, "I can't spend all that time in the hospital; I've got too much to do. And I've never spent a night away from Rosie, except when we were on the Borth barricade, and on our Edinburgh overnights. How will she cope with Mom being gone for a whole week or more?"

"She can come to visit you and stay as long as you wish, Jean. You won't be bed-bound, and you can play with her out on the grounds and in the children's waiting room. We'll just have you here so we can keep an eye on you."

"Leave Rosie to me," said Darroch, "and to Sally and Jamie and Màiri. I've got plenty of reinforcements."

"It's for the good of the baby, Jean, as well as for your health," added Ros, and Jean had no choice but to accept the situation.

"I don't even know how to knit," Jean complained as they left the clinic. "What am I going to do for a week in a hospital?"

Thirty

If you want something done right,
do it yourself.

Universal proverb.

*J*ean was as busy as a flea on a dog's back getting her life together so that
she could go into hospital without worries about leaving husband and child
adrift for a week. Once again she washed clothes and cleaned and froze
meals, despite the fact that Darroch was a fine cook who could feed Rosie
and himself quite well. It made her feel better to leave something of herself
at home for them.

They'd had a disappointment a month or two earlier. The manuscript of
fairy tales had turned out so well that Jean sent it to Liz, Darroch's agent,
so that she could approach possible publishers. But Liz had rung up with
worrying news: the publisher of *Eilean Dubh: Celebration of a Small Island*
had declined the new book, saying that a collection of fairy tales aimed at
both children and adults would never sell, and he could not afford to take
a chance on it, the publishing business being shaky, as always. Other publishers had declined for the same reason; and besides, it did not fit their
lists, they said.

"You'd think they'd never heard of J. K. Rowling," grumbled Jean.

"Ach, well, never mind, Jean," said Darroch. "You never planned on it
being a bestseller anyway. The important thing is that it's written, and our
Eilean Dubh tales and legends will be recorded in print." Then he had a
grand idea. "We'll publish it privately, here on the Island."

Jean, who had resigned herself to nothing more than a photocopy of the stories being made for the Library, a disappointment after she'd gotten the idea of a larger audience, said, "What do you mean?"

Darroch said slowly, as the idea unfolded in his mind, "We have a first-rate printer here, Anna Wallace. She can run off copies for us."

"We'd have to send them off-Island to be bound."

"We'll finance the publication by a grant from the Trust, do it up right with first class paper and all. Everyone on the Board of the Trust will support an undertaking so important to Eilean Dubh's cultural history."

"But the design of the book . . . "

"The High School graphic arts class. We'll get some of those clever students to do the book design as a class project."

"Oh, what a good idea! And the art students can illustrate it. Remember the High School Art Fair last year? There are some wonderfully talented kids here. And I'll get Sally to edit, and the English class can copy read and proof read. We'll have a beautiful book, and it'll be all Eilean Dubh-produced."

"We'll flog it to independent book and gift stores, as well as having it for sale here on the Island, and take whatever profits there are after paying back the Trust's investment and give them to the High School."

"You are a genius, darling," said Jean, gazing at her husband admiringly.

"Aye, that was a *miorbhuileach* inspiration, wasn't it. Quite brilliant," and he grinned with satisfaction.

The idea was accepted with enthusiasm by the teachers at the High School, and the students were enthralled by the idea of being part of the production of a real book. The business students, not to be outdone by their colleagues in the art, English and graphic arts classes, came up with the notion of pre-selling the book, and soon were busy soliciting the *Eilean Dubhannaich* for orders. Sales were brisk.

Taigh a Mhorair became the center of a bustling little publishing business, with students coming and going, and copies of the manuscript in one stage or another traveling back and forth between cottage, High School, and finally, to Anna Wallace's *Island Star* printing company. Anna's building was crowded with students and adults when the first set of galley proofs was run off, and the sound of celebratory bottles of champagne and sparkling fruit juice popping filled the building as the proofs were passed from hand to hand amidst satisfied rejoicing.

None were more satisfied than Darroch and Jean, who'd demonstrated once again that Eilean Dubh could be self-sufficient and hold its own against the uncaring outside world. "Next we'll publish an edition in the Gaelic," said Darroch, and Màiri, at his elbow, cheered.

They took a chance and printed one thousand copies. They'd had pre-orders for about a third of that number from the *Eilean Dubhannaich*, and nibbles from a number of independent bookstores where the previous Eilean Dubh book had sold well.

The copies were crated up to be sent by Murdoch the Chopper's helicopter to the bindery near Inverness that Anna Wallace had discovered. Jean waved them off with relief, and settled back to enjoy—she hoped that was the right word—the last week of her pregnancy, in hospital.

Thirty-one

Rest easy while you wait for the birth of a bairn,
for there'll be no rest when it's come.

Eilean Dubh proverb

𝒟arroch lay flat on his back on the narrow hospital cot, debating. Jean was within a day or two of her delivery date, and he'd taken to spending the last few nights in hospital with her, on a cot supplied by the staff. Rosie was safely at home in her own bed, with Sally and Ian *Mór* occupying his and Jean's bedroom. Now he wanted very badly to crawl into bed with Jean. Was it worth the risk of being discovered by a night nurse making her rounds, with the embarrassment that would bring to all three parties?

Well, why the hell not? They were married, after all, and a husband's place was in bed with his wife. Besides, he knew that Jean would be more comfortable if she could lie on her side with her aching back propped against him while she slept. Pillows didn't do the job nearly as well.

And he was decently dressed; he'd made the enormous concession of buying pajamas, which he'd never before worn, feeling extremely silly as he'd pawed through the selection at the Co-Op. He'd eschewed stripes and pictures and mottoes; the pair he'd purchased was a conservative pale blue, nothing to shock visiting nurses.

He got up, crossed the room, and crawled into the high hospital bed, receiving a sleepy murmur of welcome from his wife.

With his arm wrapped securely around Jean, Darroch was at last able to relax. Relaxation brought its own train of thoughts. Life with Jean was a series of steps, he mused, each one leading to a higher plain of contentment. He thought all the way back to their first days, when they'd met and become friends, and had slowly fallen in love.

It was the slow progression of that relationship that pleased him the most, in retrospect. There'd been no sudden, irresistible stab of lust that had propelled them at once into each other's arms and into adultery, as was common in novels and movies. Instead, they'd become firm friends, bound together by music and the Island, and they'd grown into a relationship that became sweeter and more enduring every day. They'd conducted themselves honorably all the way, restraining themselves from becoming lovers until Jean's divorce had come through.

And now they were married, and she'd given him a daughter, and was on the brink of presenting him with another child. Love, companionship, wonderful sex, and a family. What more could a man ask for in a wife? It was a beautiful, old-fashioned love story, and he and Jean were hero and heroine. Always had a soft spot for those old stories, he thought.

He snuggled her closer, and cradled her breast in his hand. Nicely rounded by nature, it was even plumper and fuller now. Getting ready for baby, he thought fondly. Soon he'd have to share with a nursing infant. Might as well have a wee nibble while I still can without getting a mouthful of milk, he thought, and bent over her, unbuttoning her nightgown. He uncovered her breast, and put his mouth on her nipple and sucked gently. Ah, what delight his wife's body gave him, he thought.

Jean stirred, and murmured her pleasure.

He didn't want to wake her, so he took his mouth away.

"Don't stop," she said drowsily.

"Sorry, didn't mean to disturb you."

"That's all right. I like being disturbed that way."

He chuckled, and suckled again, and nuzzled her tenderly.

"It's hard to sleep, anyway. May as well have a little fun."

"Is the bairn restless?"

"Aye, always, nowadays. Wiggly as a worm, the wee one is. Probably be a circus acrobat when it grows up."

He slid his hand down to her expanded belly and caressed her, feeling the child move beneath his fingers. "Ah, *mo chridhe*. Have I told you lately that I love you?"

"Sounds like a song cue. Aye, you have, but I always like to hear it."
She wiggled drowsily against him, with predictable results. She giggled.
"Nice to know I can still turn you on, even though I'm as big as a barn."

"More of you to love," Darroch said, cuddling her.

The night nurse pushed open the room door. On the brink of entering to
check on her patient, she paused at the sight of another person in Jean's bed,
easily recognizable by its length and the drift of black hair on the pillow.

No need to intrude, she thought. The Laird was keeping watch over
his lady.

Darroch had gone perfectly still when the door opened. When it closed,
he whispered in Jean's ear, "That was a close one."

"Like being caught necking on the sofa by our parents," she said, giggling.

"Aye, for a moment there I was sixteen again."

Jean laughed and drifted off to sleep. He lay awake for a few minutes
longer, listening to the quiet of a hospital at night; then he too slept.

A violent storm had been brewing all afternoon, and Jean had fretted,
worrying about Rosie. "You know how upset she gets about thunder,
Darroch. Perhaps you should go home to be with her."

Darroch said, "No need to worry. She's with Sally and Ian."

Jean muttered, "Sally's afraid of thunder and lightning, too."

"Then Ian will have his hands full, but I'm sure he'll cope."

The storm moved in with a vengeance, bent on inundating Eilean
Dubh. Jean and Darroch were awakened early the next morning, Darroch
by a violent clap of thunder and flash of lightning that slashed through the
window curtains, and Jean by a sudden contraction in her nether regions.

She stiffened against the pain. Darroch felt her body go rigid in his arms.

"It's beginning, isn't it, Jean," he whispered in her ear.

"Oh, my God, yes, here we go again. And what the hell is happening
outside?" she cried as another rumble of thunder shook the skies.

"The storm's finally come," said Darroch, feeling her relax as the contraction subsided. "And it's looking like a humdinger, as you Yanks say."

"What would you Brits call it, a wee spot of bother? It's weird, it
starting just when baby's getting ready to come. Is there some old Island
prophecy about a child born in the middle of a horrendous thunderstorm?"

Darroch didn't know of any, but promptly began to make one up, just
to distract her. "Oh, yes, the story goes that the child will have a voice like

the thunder's roll, and eyes that flash like lightning, and will be a great and renowned warrior. Unless, of course, it's a girl."

"What? Girls can't be warriors? What about that Queen Boadicea who fought off the Romans?" Jean demanded.

"Hmmm, yes, I forgot about her. A woman warrior, then, renowned for her strength and courage," he said, repressing a shudder at the idea of another pugnacious female child arriving to share the nursery with small, fierce Rosie. Must be those damn Mac an Rìgh genes; his ancestors were a quarrelsome bunch. Or maybe it was the Yankee side. They'd turned out to be quite aggressive in their two hundred years of history. Scot and American: what a formidable combination.

Jean grew rigid again as another contraction began, and Darroch rubbed her belly, keeping one eye on the lighted dial of his wristwatch. Had it been five minutes since the last one, or were they closer together? He'd give her one more contraction; then he'd call for help.

When she could speak, Jean said, "I'm trying to enjoy this experience, because it's definitely going to be the last one, boy or no boy."

"You know I don't care whether or not it's a boy," began Darroch.

"No, but I do. I want you to have a son, my darling, who'll grow up to be just like you, handsome and sweet and smart and . . . Oh, you brute, you beast, what have you done to me! Oh, God, if men had to suffer like this the race would be extinct!" And she shrieked as the contraction reached its peak and agonizing pain thrust through her.

That's it, that's definitely it, I am definitely getting help right now, thought Darroch, swinging his long legs out of bed just as the door opened and the night nurse flew in, summoned by Jean's shriek.

"Is it starting, Mrs. Jean?" she cried, scurrying to the bed.

"Is what starting?" murmured Jean, sinking into the valley of relaxation between contractions.

"The baby . . . " began the nurse and the rest of her speech was drowned out by the most vicious clap of thunder so far.

"Aye, baby's coming," shouted Darroch, snapping on the lamp by the bed and blinding the three of them. He grabbed his clothes and headed for the bathroom to dress. "Go and ring Ros, right away!"

"Ach, he's right here in hospital, no need to ring him, *a Mhic an Rìgh*. He's stayed here every night since Mrs. Jean was admitted. I'll just fetch him." The nurse scurried out the door.

Ros had indeed stayed there every night, his excuse being that it allowed Ian some time off to help with Rosie's care, but in reality because he did not intend to miss the birth of the Laird's second child. He'd missed the first, but he was going to be present at this one, especially since he knew Jean would have a hard time of it, given the baby's breech presentation. He'd gone over and over the decision to avoid a caesarian if possible, wondering if it had been a mistake. He'd consulted his medical books and discussed the situation with young Ian *Mór*, whose medical training was more current than his own, and prepared his mind to take any action that might be needed to insure the safety of mother and baby.

The thunder had kept him awake, and when the nurse hammered on the door of his room, shouting, "Mr. MacPherson, oh, come away now, Mrs. Jean is in labor," he was on his feet at once, struggling into his clothes.

"The contractions are two minutes apart, Ros," reported Darroch when the doctor burst into the room, still buttoning his shirt.

"Right then, very good. Jean, how are you doing?" Without waiting for an answer he snapped, "Darroch, nurse, let's get her sitting up in bed so that gravity can help."

"Now, Jean," Ros crooned, sitting on the bed beside her. "What's up with our bairn?"

"He's knocking on the door, Ros, and it hurts like hell."

"The welcome mat is out. Let me have a wee keek at his progress." He lifted the sheet covering Jean and examined her. "Ah, you're fully dilated, *mo leadaidh*, and we should expect action very soon."

"It's already begun," grumbled Jean and her voice rose into a shout. "Damn it!"

Nurse Elasaid Morrison, the midwife, summoned by the night nurse, marched majestically into the room and took in the scene at one glance. "Gloves for Mister MacPherson, nurse, and a delivery sheet under Mrs. Jean's bottom, at once. Didn't they teach you anything in nursing school?" Turning to Darroch, she said, "*Feasgar math, a Mhic an Rìgh.* Nurse will show you to the waiting room. You'll be best off there."

"I will not," said Darroch indignantly. "It's my wife and my baby, and I'm staying."

Nurse Elasaid clicked her tongue at such modern notions as a husband being present at a delivery, but another scream from Jean distracted them all.

Darroch stared at his wife, who was flushed and sweating, her hair a tangled mass and her mouth wide open as she yelled, and thought he'd never seen a more beautiful woman in his life. He sat down and put his arm around her, offering comfort and support along with his profound admiration.

"Here comes baby," said Ros, his voice muffled by the sheet now draped over his head. "Ach, you're doing a grand job, Jean, keep it up. Slow and easy now."

Jean was too winded by the latest contraction to snarl, as she wanted to snarl, that she was keeping it up, and concentrated instead on controlling the strong urge to push that she felt. She'd rehearsed birthing scenarios with Ros, and he'd told her there would come a time she must try not to push, in case the baby's jaw got hung up as it came down the birth canal, and needed careful manipulation by the doctor to free it.

Separation of the umbilical cord from the mother's body and the loss of flow of oxygen to the baby while it was still *in utero* were the possible medical emergencies they faced.

Outside the room a small crowd of patients and staff had begun to gather as word had spread that the Laird and Mrs. Jean's baby was being born. Nurse Elasaid caught sight of them as she stood waiting to assist Ros, and snapped at the night nurse standing behind her, "Close the door, girl! Let's have some privacy for our patient."

The nurse scuttled to the door and shut it against the crowd of eager faces.

The most ferocious clap of thunder and flash of lightning of the night ripped across Eilean Dubh, and the lights went out.

Darroch and the nurses yelled in shock, but Jean and Ros hardly noticed the sudden descent into darkness, so intent were they on their labors. Ros was stretched half across the bed, head and shoulders completely covered by the sheet, working entirely by touch now, grasping and turning the small slippery body as he manipulated it down and out. "Nearly there. Hold back, Jean, *mo ghràdh, m'aingeal.*"

Torn by pain and desperate to end the struggle, Jean moaned, "I can't stand it any longer, Ros. I've got to push!"

"Give me one more second, *mo luaidh.* One more . . . Now, Jean! Push away!"

Jean pushed, a great effort that sent the baby sliding into Ros's waiting hands, just as Darroch realized, bemused, that the doctor had been addressing his wife in terms more suitable for a lover than a physician. He'd realized that Ros had a soft spot in his heart for Jean, but "my love?" "my angel?" Wasn't that pushing the envelope a bit? What is this strange power you have over men, *mo Shine*? He promptly forgot his misgivings when he heard Jean sigh in relief, and a small primitive wail like a cat mewing.

Ros took a deep breath, and announced, "'*Se gille a th'ann* . . . it's a boy! Your son, *a Mhic an Righ*."

Darroch blurted, "How can you tell? It's pitch black in here."

"The proof is in my hands," said Ros.

The night nurse came scurrying back in the room clutching two flashlights and a large battery-operated camping lantern. "I found some torches in the emergency closet," she gasped in triumph.

"Well, turn them on. What are you waiting for?" said Nurse Elasaid.

The nurse obeyed, clicking on one after the other so that everyone in the room could see the small red object lying across the palms of Ros MacPherson's hands.

They all stared in awe.

"Take the baby, Elasaid," commanded Ros, the protocol of hospital titles forgotten.

"The cord . . . "

"It snapped in the delivery. But he's breathing; I gave him the kiss of life as soon as he came out, and he's fine. Clear his nose and throat, start the Apgar." Ros shot a tender glance at Jean. "A grand job, *mo leadaidh*. We're very proud of you."

"Thanks, Ros. I couldn't have done it without you. After four babies, it's great to have a doctor on hand who actually does something."

In the glow of the flashlights and lanterns, Ros and Jean exchanged a long look of comradeship. Then he turned to take the baby back from Nurse Elasaid, and put him in his mother's arms just as the emergency generator kicked in and the lights came back on.

Everyone blinked, and the baby gave a soft cry.

Jean looked down at her child with an expression of such tenderness that Darroch's heart melted into a puddle in his chest, and he yearned to throw himself down on his knees in front of his wife in worship of the pair of them.

But being a gusher was not the Eilean Dubh way. He bent to give Jean a tender kiss on the cheek. Then he allowed himself a good long look at the child.

"Your son, Darroch," whispered Jean.

"My son," he breathed, and with trembling hands drew the blanket back so that he could take in the full wonder of his little boy's body. "Will you look at that," he said, awed, and put his index finger on the child's tiny penis and testicles. Tears gathered in his eyes and ran down his cheeks.

The child opened his eyes and stared up at his parents in newborn confusion.

The room was absolutely silent. Then Ros cleared his throat and Nurse Elasaid suppressed the undignified cooing that threatened to escape her, and said, "Give the babe to his *Dadaidh*, Mrs. Jean, and let us have a look at you."

Alone with the baby for the first time, Darroch carried him to the window so that they could look at each other in the light from the just-rising sun. The baby was long and lean, a respectable eight pounds in weight, but an inch or so beyond average length. He looked like a miniature greyhound. Darroch thought he could see hints of Jean around the nose and mouth, and was pleased. Rosie so closely resembled her father; it would be nice to see the MacChriathar side coming out in the new addition to the family.

Storm-born, he thought. *Balachan na gailleann,* the boy of the storm.

His name would be, by tradition, Alasdair Darroch Mac an Rìgh, but they would call him Gailleann.

Thirty-two

Mac an Righ baby born,
and it's a boy!

Island Star headline

*T*he Island was a-twitter with the news of the birth of a son to the Laird and Mrs. Jean. There had never been such a stramash. Hospital staff and patients fought for the phones, and one enterprising soul rang Anna Wallace, waking her from a sound sleep in husband Zach's arms. Zach demanded to know at once if she was going to publish an extra, a special edition of *The Island Star*.

"I don't do extras for babies," she said. "If I started that, where would it end?"

Zach said, "But it's the Laird's baby, his son."

She regarded him with a raised eyebrow. "So?"

"So it's special, it's important."

"Is it, now? You've changed your tune, my little anarchist. I thought the Laird was an anachronism."

He looked her firmly in the eye. "He's our anachronism, and this is our Island's baby. Publish, woman!"

In the end she decided he was right, though it gave her a chuckle to realize how quickly he'd assimilated to the Island's social structure, and she put out another broadsheet like the one she'd done about the sit-in. After all, it was her duty as a journalist to keep her constituency advised of important news, and this was certainly important, judging by the chattering of the *Eilean Dubhannaich* she encountered as she distributed the broadsheet to the shops for sale, and the way copies were snatched up.

The main topic on everyone's lips was whether or not the baby supplanted Rosie in line for the non-existent (if only in Darroch's mind) lairdship. "Rosie's the first-born," said some. "A lad takes precedence over a lass," argued others. "Who says?" demanded the more militant younger women. "This is the twenty-first century; get with it. Women are equal."

Anna had hastened off to the hospital, once she'd decided to publish the broadsheet, and used her journalist's credentials to be among the first to see the baby, and definitely the first to photograph it, just edging out Sally. The two women compared photos on their digital cameras, both cooing and ooh-ing over the new arrival.

"He's so sweet," sighed Sally.

"Makes you think about having one of your own," agreed Anna, surprising herself.

"Aye, it does," said Ian *Mór,* pushing his way between the two women so he could look at the photos. "How about it, Sally lass?"

"Don't rush me," said Sally, but her tone was not nearly as definite as it had been in the past. Her pal Catrìona had had her baby girl several months ago and was divinely happy, and Ian the Post was even more hopelessly besotted with her than ever and wild about the baby. And Darroch was gazing at Jean as though she were an angel, the Queen and the first woman president of the United States all wrapped up in one. Not that she had any complaints about her Ian's adoration, but it certainly would be nice to have a little of that madonna-worship directed at her humble self. Gave a girl something to think about, anyway, and even Anna Wallace, former confirmed spinster, was looking thoughtful.

PART XIV

Darroch is Honoured

Thirty-three

*I*an the Post brought the day's mail up to the cottage personally, and knocked on the door, rather than leaving it in the box by the gate. "It looks important," he said, when Darroch opened the door. "Such a fine envelope. I've never seen the like before."

Darroch took the envelope and turned it over several times in his long-fingered hands, assessing the return address and the weight of the paper. At last he took a knife and slit it open carefully. He read the letter, and groaned in horror and disbelief.

By command of the Queen, he was to be awarded a knighthood in the Birthday Honours List for his services to the entertainment industry. He would become Sir Darroch Mac an Rìgh.

He'd spent nearly all his adult life avoiding a title, and now a title was being thrust upon him.

The idea was preposterous, he thought. What had he done for British entertainment but have the great good luck to get the plum role of the Magician, and have that luck continue into a successful career? If he was to be honored, why not for creating and financing his Island Trust, or for serving on the Governing Council, or for his efforts to preserve the Gaelic language? All of those had required sacrifice and hard work on his part, and mental effort as well.

But to be honored for acting! That seemed too frivolous to believe.

Well, he wouldn't accept it. Other people had turned down honours, and he could as well.

Jean, coming down the stairs after having settled both Rosie and month-old Gailleann for a nap, chirped cheerfully, "What's in the mail today, lovie?"

"This," he said, tossing the royal letter down on the table. He would have preferred to keep it a secret and write a distinguished refusal so that no one would ever know, but Jean had come in just at the wrong moment.

She picked up the letter with a little sigh of appreciation for the weight and quality of the paper, and when she read it she sat down hastily. "Oh, my," she said.

"Hmmph," growled Darroch, and picked up a newspaper.

"What an honor, darling! Congratulations."

He murmured something, and pretended to read the paper.

"Aren't you thrilled?" she asked, baffled at his reaction.

"No," he snapped.

"Why not?"

"Why should I be?"

"Why shouldn't you be?"

He sighed deeply, and put the paper down, resigned. "Because I have spent my life trying to get rid of one title, and here's another one I don't want being thrust at me."

"Oh," she said, staring at him.

"I'm going to refuse it," he said.

"Oh . . . can you do that?"

"I certainly can. Others have."

"But won't you be hurting the Queen's feelings?" said Jean innocently.

"Jean, this isn't the Queen's idea. The Honours are determined by the government, and they've probably picked me because they need another Scot on the List."

"You don't know that," she said. "Remember that article in your scrapbook that said that the Queen loved *The Magician* and watched it with her grandchildren, and they all enjoyed it. Maybe she suggested your name."

"And maybe she didn't."

"I think you ought to consider this seriously."

"I have."

"You can't have," she pointed out in the voice of reason. "Ian the Post has just brought the mail."

"Jean, I don't want a title, especially not one given by a government full of Englishmen who are just looking for a bit of publicity because they've honored another actor."

She was silent for a moment, then said in a small voice, "Would I have a title, too?"

Amused in spite of himself, Darroch said "You'd be Lady Mac an Rìgh. What's an American lassie to think of that?"

"But the Islanders have already called me Lady Mac an Rìgh, remember, after our wedding."

"That's just a courtesy title, part of that bloody Laird business."

She was quiet again, for a longer period. Then she said stubbornly, "I still think you ought to consider it."

He said in his haughtiest Laird voice, "It's a matter of principle." Then he picked up the newspaper and pretended to read. An uneasy silence fell. Darroch thought he could almost hear Jean's mind working, and ignored it.

When Jamie and Màiri came over later, Jean fretted and twitched and finally blurted out, "Aren't you going to tell them?"

"Tell us what?" asked Màiri.

"Whazzup, dudes?" said Jamie, showing off a bit of slang he'd picked up from watching (when Màiri was not around) the latest American hip hop videos on ITV. He was a musician, after all, and it was his responsibility to keep up with musical trends, or so he reasoned.

Darroch growled, and tossed the letter to Màiri, sure of her support. She was as confirmed a republican as he was, and regularly denounced aristocrats and the aristocracy with the fervency of a head-hunting Jacobin.

She read it, and said, "Hmmm," and handed the letter to Jamie, who said, "Titles seem to pursue you, *a charaid*."

"He's going to turn it down," said Jean.

"Are you, indeed?" said Màiri. "Why?"

"Why?" yelped Darroch. "You know why, right enough."

"Do I?"

"Because," he said, as elaborately patient as though explaining to young Rosie why her new brother couldn't walk or talk, or in fact do anything but cry and produce smelly diapers, "I don't want another title, having spent all my adult life trying to get rid of one."

"I always did wonder why you were so adamant about refusing the title of laird," she mused.

Darroch looked at her as though she were a favorite puppy that suddenly bitten him in the ankle. "What do you mean? We talked and talked about that years ago, and I thought you understood and sympathized. I don't want an inherited title that I've done nothing to earn."

"This isn't an inherited one; it *is* one you've earned," she pointed out.

"For being an actor," he scoffed.

"No," said Jean, "for being a *good* actor. And for winning awards and playing benefits to raise money for worthy causes, and for giving your income as an actor to the Island Trust to help your people."

"The people creating the Honours List don't know about that," said Darroch crossly.

Màiri said impatiently, "Really, Darroch, how can you be so sure? With all their spies, that MI5 thing, and the Inland Revenue, the Establishment probably knows all about you, including your charitable contributions, the size of your Y-fronts, and the state of your dental work."

"And the Queen loved *The Magician*," added Jean.

At that non sequitur, Darroch said to the other two, "Jean is under the impression that the Queen herself is keen to give me a knighthood because she enjoyed my television program, and that it will hurt Her Majesty's feelings if I turn it down."

"Maybe she's right," said Jamie, entering the fray at last.

"Utter nonsense," snapped Darroch.

"I say again, Darroch, how do you know?" Màiri snapped back at him. "Why isn't it possible that you are being honored because of your performance both as an actor and as a decent human being?"

Darroch's mouth set itself in a thin stubborn line, and he refused to answer.

"The thing is," said Màiri, "a title's damned useful."

Goaded into responding by that bit of nonsense, he growled, "What for? Getting reservations at a posh London restaurant, and being bumped by an earl, who's then bumped by a duke, who's then bumped by the prince of Ruritania?"

"No," she said patiently. "For getting grants, favors and publicity. People always seem to pay more attention when a title speaks. I don't know why that is, but it's true."

It was, and Darroch knew it. He was silent for a few moments, chewing over that idea. "You seem to be saying that I should accept it."

Màiri said, "Aye," and Jamie nodded. Jean said, "Don't look at me; I'm prejudiced, because I want to be able to tell my friends back in Milwaukee that I'm Lady Mac an Rìgh. I can see the headline in the *Sentinel* now: *Home Town Girl Makes Good in Blighty*." She was only half-joking.

Darroch tried one last effort. "How can I continue to support Scottish independence if I take a title from the Crown?"

Jamie said, "Hasn't slowed Sir Sean Connery down. He's still backing the Scottish Nationalist Party to the hilt."

Darroch mumbled something about being outnumbered, and resigned himself to his fate. He went to the sideboard and got the bottle of whisky and four small glasses. Jean said, "Oh, boy! Glenmorangie, my favorite. A dram of that will have the wee bairn sleeping like a top after he nurses."

"Worked for me with the twins," said Màiri.

"So what is it, then, Darroch?" asked Jamie, accepting a glass of whisky. "A celebration, or a wake?"

"Probably a bit of both," he replied. Then, to get even with Jean for supporting the opposition, he added, "Of course this means a trip to London, a presentation at Buckingham Palace, and a tap on the shoulder with a sword from HM."

Jean's eyes grew huge. "A real sword? I thought that was just in books. You mean they don't just mail you a certificate or something?"

"No. You have to collect it in person."

"Am I invited?" she said shyly.

Darroch wasn't sure, but wasn't going to pass up an opportunity to tease her. "Oh, aye, families are always invited to watch the ceremony."

Jean clutched at her chest in the vicinity of her heart, which had begun to flutter wildly. "Oh, my God! I'm going to meet the Queen! What am I going to wear?"

Several days later, the state of Jean's wardrobe had assumed the dimensions of a major crisis. Her waistline had not yet returned to its pre-baby state, and her breasts had gone up two cup sizes from nursing. She'd assumed she would wear her kilted Mac an Rìgh tartan skirt, and was frantic when she tried it on, and found that the buckles that fastened it were too far apart to close. It could not be altered because of the pleats.

Nor could she button her frilled white blouse and her velvet jacket over her expanded breasts.

The kilted skirt outfit was the only thing she owned that was dressy enough, as it turned out that the investiture was an evening event and very formal.

"I'll take you into Inverness and you can choose something new," offered Darroch, wondering what all the hysteria was about.

"I've shopped in Inverness, and there are no stores there with evening wear!"

"Edinburgh? Glasgow? Or we can go down to London early."

"In all my life I've never been able to find a posh frock when I went looking for one; in Milwaukee the best clothes I had were those I stumbled on when I wasn't looking. Oh, why did this have to happen after I've just had a baby and my figure is ruined?"

"You still look lovely to me," said Darroch staunchly.

Jean resisted the impulse to get her broom and swat him a good one. "Let's see how lovely you think I am when I meet the Queen dressed in some old rag."

Darroch chuckled, then realized too late that she wasn't trying to be funny. "Rest easy, *m'aingeal*. I'll go for help." He dashed out of the house and ran to *Taigh Rois*. "Màiri, the wife's in hysterics; can you come and soothe her?"

"Whatever is wrong?"

"It's that foolishness about what she's to wear to the investiture."

"What? You mean that's not sorted yet? Ach, poor Jean, I'll come right away." At the door she turned and looked at Darroch, who'd slipped guiltily into a chair. "Aren't you coming?" she demanded.

"I'll just stay here and have a word with Jamie."

"He's out."

Darroch narrowed his eyes at her, and folded his arms across his chest. "I'll wait until he gets back." There was no way he was going back into that dangerous maelstrom of female emotions, not until Màiri had soothed Jean's ruffled feathers.

"Men," she said disapprovingly. "No help at all in a crisis." She left, then popped her head back in the door for a parting shot. "This is all your fault, anyway."

No, it isn't, thought Darroch crossly. I didn't want the damned title, but nobody listened to me. Feeling very put upon, he went to the sideboard and helped himself to a dram of Jamie's whisky. Extra large, in revenge.

In *Taigh a Mhorair*, Màiri, as usual, took charge. "Let's go through your wardrobe and see what we can find."

"I've already done that three times, and there's nothing, nothing at all." Jean's voice teetered perilously close to tears.

"No bits and pieces you could cobble together?"

"I don't want to meet the Queen wearing bits and pieces!"

"*Ceart math, ceart math*. Now hush a wee bittie, and let me think. Maybe I've got something you can borrow."

"Màiri, I'm five inches taller than you, and I've got a bosom like a beached whale, thanks to the bairn. You don't own anything that would fit me."

"Aye, you're right. How about Sally?"

"She's too tall, and two sizes smaller, and her idea of formal wear is a velvet mini-skirt and a tee shirt that doesn't have a smart-ass saying on it."

"Hmmm." Màiri sat silent for a moment, then got up and headed for the iron spiral staircase. "I'm going to have a wee poke through your clothes."

"Don't wake the baby! My milk's probably curdled from anxiety."

Too nervous to sit still, Jean got up and made a pot of tea, and was sitting at the kitchen table moodily drinking a cup when Màiri came downstairs triumphantly, a linen garment bag in her arms. "I've found the perfect thing!"

Jean stared. "That's my *Tradisean* dress, the one I wore on tour when I was pregnant. I can't wear maternity clothes when I'm not pregnant."

"Just because it doesn't fit like the paper on the wall doesn't mean it's maternity clothes. It's a perfectly good and perfectly beautiful silk dress with graceful flowing lines, and you looked lovely in it. Remember all those groupie-men who wanted you to come out with them?"

Jean giggled. "Remember how angry both Jamie and Darroch got when guys tried to chat us up?"

"Mad with jealousy," Màiri agreed complacently. "And a world of good it did them both, too. Now let's have this one on you, and see how it looks. It hasn't got any spots or stains, has it?"

"Oh, heavens, no, I was always very careful with it, and I had it cleaned and put in the garment bag when we finished touring."

"Right. Slip it on."

There was no full-length mirror on the first floor of the cottage, and Jean didn't want to risk waking the children by going upstairs, so she had to rely on Màiri for her reflection. "How do I look?"

"*Miorbhuileach*," pronounced the other woman. "And if my word's not good enough, I'll ring Darroch to come back home and take a look."

"He's no help; he says I look beautiful in everything I put on."

"Men really are—what do you call it—clueless, aren't they. No use at all when an honest opinion is wanted. Let me ring Sally, and get her down here."

First Daughter Sally bounded in a few minutes later. "Hi, guys, what's happening? Wow, Ma, what a super dress. That turquoise is just your color, you know?"

Màiri said, "Your mother is going to wear this to meet the Queen."

"Good choice, Ma. What sort of wrap are you going to wear with it?"

"Wrap?"

"You know, a little shawl or something. Cover up the bare arms, give it a more formal look. Like your velvet jacket you wore at your wedding. Would that work?"

"Too tight," said Jean in despair.

"You need to wear something in your tartan," decided Màiri. "There's time for Elspeth MacShennach to make a shawl, if she's got yardage left."

"Wait, I'm getting an idea. Give me a pencil and paper, quick!" cried Sally. She sketched out a little jacket, cut away in front like a tuxedo, and flaring out into a peplum in back. "Pleats around here, and a velvet shawl collar. How's that?"

"Very nice," approved Màiri. "I'll ring Elspeth."

The seamstress thought that she had enough tartan, and agreed to get working on the project right away. She was thrilled that one of her creations was to be worn in front of the Queen, and said that she would make an original pattern from Sally's sketch.

Vastly relieved, Jean went upstairs to take off the precious dress and hang it up, while the other two women helped themselves to cups of tea. When Darroch cautiously poked his head in the door an hour later, all was serene on the home front.

Serene, until Jean thought about her hair. "I haven't had my hair done since the last time I was in Milwaukee. It looks like a rat's nest!"

All three women looked dismayed. It did not really look like a rat's nest, but it was clear that it had not had a professional styling for some time. Neither Jean nor Màiri patronized Frizzy Fiona, the Island hairdresser whose specialty was Margaret Thatcher-style perms.

But this was a problem Darroch could deal with. Liz, his agent, he announced, knew all the top stylists in London, and he was sure that she could get Jean an appointment for such an important occasion.

"Get someone at the stylist's to do your makeup, too, Ma, on the big day," advised Sally. "Your usual little dab of lipstick won't cut it this time."

A cat can look at a queen, Jean thought, but only if she's got the right frock, the right hairdo, and the right shade of eyeshadow.

Thirty-four

Pussycat, pussycat, where have you been?
I've been to London to visit the Queen.

Nursery rhyme

The children were left behind in Ros Mór. Jean and Darroch figured they could do the London trip in two days, one to arrive, one for the investiture, and home on the third day, thanks to Murdoch the Chopper's helicopter and frequent flights from Inverness to London. Jean expressed multiple bottles of milk and froze them for the baby, and since her milk flow was well established, she worried only about keeping herself from leaking during the time away from the hungry mouth. She'd have to stuff multiple pads in her bra, she thought, so that she didn't dribble on her beautiful dress in front of the Queen.

They'd considered taking Rosie to the investiture, since each honoree was allowed three guests, but Jean thought carefully about it, and put her foot down. "She won't remember it anyway when she gets older, and probably won't care. And considering what happened at Donald and Helen's wedding . . . "

"Ach, that wasn't so bad," said Darroch.

"Shouting 'hell' in a church is not your idea of bad? Aye, I know everyone understood, but are the Royals likely to understand if Rosie pulls one of her tricks at the investiture?"

"What are you anticipating?"

"Heaven only knows. At the least, she'll put her hand in the Queen's and ask to be taken to the potty, and at the worst . . . the mind boggles. Maybe she'll demand a piggyback ride from one of the Gurkhas . . . or . . ."

"Pull aside a curtain, and expose MI5's secret cameras . . ."

"Or trip on the red carpet, and grab at a Chippendale table to save herself, and topple a priceless Ming vase to the floor . . . "

Both parents shuddered. Rosie would stay with Sally.

But Sally said wistfully, "I wish I could go."

And Jean and Darroch looked at each other. Of course, the First Daughter should go. She would love the ceremony, she would adore meeting the Queen, and she deserved to go, as Darroch's stepdaughter and a *bona fide* Eilean Dubh resident. But who would take care of the children?

"My bid's in for Rosie," said Jamie, who adored his almost-niece. "She can help me with my Jacob's Sheep."

"Russ and I would love to have the baby," said Ruth shyly. "If you'd trust us with him, that is." Russ said, "Sure, we'd love to have him. He's almost our grandson, after all. I mean . . . well, he's some relation to us. He's my former wife's son, so doesn't that make him almost my grandson? Or stepson, or something?"

Done. The village in action, thought Jean. Two children dispersed to the tender care of loving aunts, uncles and almost grandparents. Two parents dispatched to London, to receive whatever accolades the world would bestow upon them, and a daughter coming along to take notes on what happens.

Works for me, Jean said to herself.

PART XV

Two Yankee Girls Meet the Queen

Thirty-five

God save our gracious Queen,
Long live our noble Queen,
God save the Queen!
Send her victorious,
Happy and glorious,
Long to reign over us,
God save the Queen!

United Kingdom national anthem

*T*he three arrived in London, settled themselves in the flat, and that night had dinner on the flat's balcony, which overlooked the Thames. The next morning Jean was off to the posh hairdresser that Liz had found, and returned beautifully coiffed and made up. Sally went with her to provide reinforcements in case the hairdresser wanted to hack off the long hair Jean had been growing for three years, and she had to put up a fight to save it. The make-up artist thought Sally was a beauty, and offered to do her face, too, and she accepted.

Preening in front of the mirror, Sally said, "Wish old Ian *Mór* was here to be dazzled by all this glamour." Despite her mother's worries about the tee shirt and the miniskirt, Sally was quite smartly turned out in a blue velvet jacket and a discreetly knee-length skirt in her MacDonald tartan. Where she'd gotten this outfit, Jean had no idea.

Darroch took their picture with the digital camera loaned by Anna Wallace, who'd instructed them to take lots of snaps for *The Island Star's* front page. Sally asked for shots of her mother and herself. "For the back cover of our next book," she said.

At last they were ready, and off they went by cab to Buckingham Palace, and all, even Darroch, were impressed as they drove through the tall black iron Palace gates that afternoon. This is how royalty keeps its hold on the nation's imagination, he thought ruefully: pomp and circumstance. He had to admit it was pretty impressive, if you liked that sort of thing.

There was plenty of that sort of thing in the Palace. First they walked into the Grand Hall and up the curving marble stairs of the Grand Staircase past walls set with portraits, into the enormous Victorian Ballroom where an orchestra from the Queen's Household Division was playing in the musicians' gallery. Then Her Majesty entered, attended by two tall Gurkha Officers, and the band broke into "God Save the Queen." She was wearing a peach-colored silk evening dress ornamented with a bosom full of medals and decorations, and to Jean and Sally's delight she was wearing a tiara, its gorgeous diamonds sparkling in the lights. Flanked by members of the Queen's Body Guard of the Yeoman of the Guard in their royal red Tudor uniforms, standing at attention while the national anthem played, she was a regal, commanding figure.

"I thought she was short," whispered Sally to her mother.

"She is, compared to us enormous Yankees," Jean whispered back. "It's because she's the Queen that she looks larger than life."

"Nice dress," said Sally.

Along with the one hundred other recipients and their guests, Darroch's party had been briefed by the Gentlemen Ushers on how to behave when they were presented to the Queen. They were to wait until Her Majesty spoke before they said anything, and they were to wait for her to extend her hand before they stuck out theirs. "And don't squeeze, please. The Queen shakes thousands of hands every year, and runs the risk of injury with each one, if people get nervous and squeeze her hand too hard."

They were to address her as "Your Majesty" the first time they spoke, and call her "Ma'am" after that.

They were also instructed on the proper time to curtsy, until Jean shook her head and said, "We're American citizens. We don't curtsy." She and Sally had discussed the issue with great intensity, and both had concluded that curtsying was not the American way. "We'll bob our heads politely," said Jean, and Sally had agreed, with a little tinge of regret. "How often do I get a chance to curtsy?" she'd said.

"Why would you want to?" Darroch had growled. "People are equal."

"Some are more equal than others," Sally had replied.

The Gentleman Usher had nodded, and not pressed the curtsying issue. "Hope I can keep my knees from bending of their own accord," Sally said.

"Remember, it's the principle of the thing," said Jean. Darroch just snorted.

Then Darroch's name was announced by the Lord Chamberlain. He approached the dais, his tall lean kilted figure held as severely upright as a soldier's, and knelt on the Investiture stool to receive the Accolade. The Queen raised her father's sword, tapped him gently on each shoulder, and he was invested as Sir Darroch Mac an Rìgh.

Jean knew what emotions warred in him as he knelt to the woman who represented a tradition he did not believe in or approve of, and wondered if he had gritted his teeth the entire time.

Afterwards the Queen made the rounds of all those honored and their guests to speak to each one. She spoke first to Darroch, then turned to Jean. "Are you enjoying your stay in Scotland?" she asked.

"Well enough to stay there for four years so far, Your Majesty, and to plan on staying for the rest of my life," replied Jean.

The Queen said—and Jean swore, afterwards, that her eyes were twinkling—"It must be the magic of the Island. Or perhaps it's the Magician."

"Some of both, Ma'am," said Jean, repressing an undignified grin. Ha! She'd been right, the Queen did remember Darroch's television program. Wait till she got a chance to gloat over him about it.

"I understand you have a new baby, Lady Mac an Rìgh, a little boy. Your second, I believe?"

"It's Darroch's and my second child, Ma'am. I have two children by my previous marriage, one of whom is standing next to me."

"Four makes a nice full household, doesn't it," said the Queen, who had four children of her own. And as Sally was presented, she said, "Are you a visitor to Scotland, Mrs. MacDonald?"

"No, Your Majesty. I married an Eilean Dubh man who's become one of our Island doctors, so I'm living there, too, like my Ma . . . uh, my mother."

"It's good to hear that the population of Eilean Dubh is growing," said the Queen. "The Islands need more people," and with a gracious nod of her head she moved on to the next guest.

Darroch's agent Liz had pulled strings and gotten them a reservation for a late supper that night at a very exclusive and posh restaurant. Dressed to the teeth, the ladies exquisitely made-up and every hair in place, Darroch elegant as usual in his kilt and velvet jacket, they swanked in and ordered champagne and a ruinously expensive meal. They spent most of dinner discussing the ceremony, always coming back to the Queen, discovering something new about her appearance or her words to talk about. When Sally had sighed over the tiara for the third time, Darroch said, "Enough! Can't we talk about something else? You two have certainly had your heads turned by the royalty lark."

"I know," said Jean. "But you've got to remember we're Americans, and we've both grown up on stories of queens and princesses and handsome princes. Remember all the fairy stories I used to read you, Sal?"

"Yes, but this was the real thing, not a story. I nearly died when the Queen called you Lady Mac an Rìgh, Ma."

"I nearly died when you called me Ma in front of her."

And they were off again, giggling so madly that a distinguished older man at the next table, wearing a tuxedo and an impressive mustache, gave them a disapproving look. Then he noticed how pretty Sally was, and the look turned perilously close to a leer, until Darroch frowned at him fiercely and he turned away with regret.

All in all, it had been a full day, and they were happy to return home to the flat, and a sound sleep, and the joyous reunion the next day with family and friends on Eilean Dubh.

Jean still didn't know Darroch's true feelings about the whole investiture thing and the title, and she thought it best never to ask. She took a guilty, un-American pleasure in being Lady Mac an Rìgh, and decided to leave it at that. Let sleeping dogs lie was one of her mottoes, learned after years of marriage to two complicated men.

PART XVI

Màiri's Grand Scheme

Thirty-six

Blithe and merry, blithe and merry,
Blithe and merry we'll be a'
And make a cheerful quorum.

John Skinner

Several weeks later, Jean and Darroch were summoned to the Playschool by Màiri. When they arrived with Rosie and Gailleann, they discovered a crowd was gathering. It was not just mothers and the occasional father collecting their children; other members of the community were arriving as well.

First came Sheilah and Gordon Morrison, carrying covered trays which they put on the long tables that had been set up on the far side of the room. Sheilah began whipping off the coverings to reveal sandwiches and desserts, while Gordon went out again. He reappeared shortly carrying more trays.

"My goodness," exclaimed Jean. "What's going on? Are we having a picnic?"

"No, it's a meeting. Didn't I tell you, Jean?" said Màiri innocently.

Darroch, who was hoping for a quick getaway and a leisurely lunch at home, groaned. He disliked Island meetings, which were by tradition lengthy and contentious.

Next to appear were Eilidh and Joe Munro, accompanied by Helen and Minister Donald. Helen hurried across the hall to assist Sheilah, while the Minister stood by, looking uncomfortable. He was not accustomed to attending meetings that he was not chairing.

Minister Tormod from the Airgead Presbyterian Church arrived, followed by Father Ian MacDonald of Our Lady of the Island Catholic Church, and Father Michael Eliot, vicar of the tiny Anglican congregation, and his wife. Minister Donald came over to join them, relieved at clerical reinforcements, and the four religious formed a knot of black in one corner, while Mrs. Eliot scurried over to the food tables to lend a hand.

Marsaili and Cailean the Crab, Murray the Meat and wife Seonag, Beathag the Bread, two women from the Co-Op, and two more from *Co-Op nan Figheadairean*, the knitters' cooperative, came in. Jean nudged Darroch. "Who's minding the shops?"

Anna Wallace and Zach Trelawney arrived, talking and laughing with Sally and Ian *Mór* MacDonald, and after them Elizabeth Thomas from the High School, Isabel Ross from the Library, and Ian the Post, who'd flown through his mail route with lightning speed so that he could attend with his Catrìona and the baby.

When Ros MacPherson arrived and took up a position near the door, ready for a fast exit in case duty called, Jean said, "Wow. I hope nobody on the Island gets sick in the next hour or two."

Barabal Mac-a-Phi came in and headed for Màiri, and the two engaged in an earnest conversation.

Jamie appeared out of nowhere, and with Somhairle Mac-a-Phi, Zach and Ian, began setting up chairs in the center of the room.

When Russ and Ruth walked in, Jean stared in open astonishment.

Darroch whispered, "Close your mouth, Jean, else flies will get in."

"I can't help it, I've never seen so many important Island people together in one room before. What's going on? And can you tell if Sheilah's brought any brownies?"

But they couldn't see the food tables, because Màiri and Barabal were herding people towards them, saying, "Fill your plates, and sit yourselves down so the meeting can begin." Obediently the *Eilean Dubhannaich* formed a neat queue in front of the sandwiches.

When nearly everyone was seated with their lunches, and only a few stragglers were left at the tables, Màiri, Barabal at her side, stood up in front of the group.

Just as she opened her mouth, Jamie came in with Lady Margaret Morrison on his arm. "Look who I found outside," he said, grinning.

Lady Margaret paused, leaning on her cane, and sent a regal smile around the group. "*Feasgar math*," she said.

"*Fàilte, a Mhairead*," said Darroch, and as the highest-ranking *Eilean Dubhannach* present, he moved forward in welcome. He bent to kiss her cheek while a seat in the middle of the front row was hastily vacated for her. "*Miorbhuileach* to see you. You're looking very well, *a charaid*."

"*Tapadh leat, a Dharroch*," said Lady Margaret. "I suppose I'm meant to say 'Sir Darroch' now, aren't I?" She smiled mischievously.

"I wouldn't recommend it," said Jean, coming to stand by her husband's side. "Hi, Margaret, how are you?"

"I'm grand, thanks, and looking forward to seeing the Laird's newest bairn. *Feasgar math*, Rosie. *A Dhia beannaich mi*, how big you are getting!"

The little girl grinned and to her parents' astonishment, she bobbed a little curtsy.

Màiri moved in to regain control of the situation. "Sit here, Margaret, we're just beginning. Sheilah, will you fix Margaret a plate and a cup of tea?"

"No need to fuss, my dear. Sheilah, one lump please and a splash of milk, and a cucumber sandwich or two, if you have some. And a brownie, of course." Lady Margaret seated herself and bestowed her smile on her neighbors, who smiled back. The elderly English aristocrat, a Gaelic speaker whose grandmother was an *Eilean Dubhannach*, and who regarded herself as one as well, was a popular figure and very welcome on her infrequent visits to the Island.

Màiri said, "I declare this meeting officially open," and everyone settled expectantly into their chairs. She spoke in English, almost never heard in the Playschool, a rare concession to the non-Gaelic speakers present.

She paused and scanned her audience like an experienced mistress of ceremonies, then announced, "Eilean Dubh seems to be in the middle of a population explosion." Her gaze rested first on Jean, who grinned, then went to Ian's Catrìona and the babe in the bucket next to her. Then she looked, eyebrows raised, at Sally and Eilidh sitting together in the front row. They giggled and elbowed each other. When she looked at Anna, that young woman gave her a blank, self-possessed stare in return.

Màiri continued, "So it's time to build an addition to the Playschool, and we are here today to discuss the financing of that project."

A murmur of "Ahhh" went up from the crowd, and heads nodded in satisfaction. A promising subject, one that would require lots of debate.

"Barabal and I have come up with an idea, and we have discussed it with Russ Abbott, who has provided much valuable . . . uh . . . input, I think it's called."

Jean gawked at her ex-husband, who looked modestly pleased with himself. She knew that look well; it meant he had done something immensely clever. He certainly was digging himself in on Eilean Dubh, she thought.

"We are," said Màiri, pausing for maximum effect, "going to hold a Celtic Folk Festival. Our group *Tradisean* will invite all the friends we made on our tour of Britain to join us here for a grand celebration of Celtic music. It will run for five days next August."

Darroch stared, completely astonished. Jean whispered in his ear, "Never tell me you didn't know anything about this, you sly fox."

Recovering, he whispered back, "But I didn't. She started to talk to me about some plot she was hatching once or twice, but I was too preoccupied with you and Rosie and the baby, and then with the title foolishness, to pay much attention."

Jean said, "Do you really think anyone will remember *Tradisean*, after three years?"

"Liz told me a while back that the CD is still selling, and she wondered if we'd thought about recording another. I told her that you were expecting, and that there'd be no chance of us touring to support a new album if we made one. I thought that was the end of it . . . but . . . I wonder. Do you suppose Màiri's been in touch with Liz?"

"Nothing Màiri does would surprise me."

"Or me," said Jamie, appearing at her elbow, and overhearing. "I knew she was up to something, going around all smug-faced and sly, having long conversations with Barabal on the phone and luncheon meetings with yon Russ, but I didn't ask. I was afraid to, if you must know the truth. I'm always happier when I don't know what's going on in that redhead's mind."

Màiri, noticing that the attention of three of the key participants in her scheme had wandered, turned to them. "I thought we'd call the festival, '*Tradisean* presents A Visit to Eilean Dubh.' Russ said we should take advantage of our, um, name recognition and marketability. Isn't that what you said, Russ?"

Russ nodded. "Yep, that's what I suggested."

"Russ has a lot of experience in, um, marketing, um, things," said Màiri.

"Not folk festivals, of course," said Russ, "but the way I look at it, selling is selling, whatever the product is."

"So now we're a product?" hissed Jean to Jamie and Darroch. "I've never been a product before."

"I have," said Darroch grimly.

"To increase our, um, marketability, we need someone of national stature to be our chairperson," Màiri continued.

"I can round up a minor royal to do that, if you'd like, *a Mhàiri*," volunteered Lady Margaret, who was enjoying herself immensely. She loved plots and plotting, and it was clear to her that Màiri had come up with a good scheme.

"No need for that, *a Mhairead;* we have our own home-grown member of the nobility. I request that Sir Darroch Mac an Righ act as Festival chairperson," Màiri announced, knowing and not caring that Darroch would be infuriated by her use of his still-annoying title.

Jean heard her husband growl, and squeezed his hand reassuringly.

"And Lady Mac an Righ as co-chair, of course."

Jean looked puzzled, then understood whom she meant. "Oh, my. Me?"

"*Tha gu dearbh,* of course," said Màiri firmly. Then, seeing that Jamie was barely repressing a snicker at Darroch's discomfiture, turned her gaze on him. "We'll have a fiddlers' workshop as part of the Festival, and Jamie will be in charge of that."

"Me?" he yelped. "I don't know how to be in charge of anything except sheep."

"Don't worry," said his wife smoothly. "I'll help you."

"*A Dhia,*" he muttered. "Stuck under my woman's thumb, as usual."

"You'll do it, won't you, Jamie?" whispered Jean.

"Oh, aye," he said in resignation. "When it comes to a choice between sleeping on the couch for six months or running a fiddlers' workshop, the fiddlers have it hands down."

Pleased with herself, Màiri resumed spinning her web. "We'll have to have food, and Sheilah, I'd like you to be in charge of that. Marsaili and Gordon, will you organize the accommodations? Anna, you'll do our publicity; Isabel can help you with any research that you need for your articles. Russ will supervise our marketing, of course," and she gave him a special smile. She continued around the room, assigning responsibilities to everyone, even the four ministers, who were asked to be present, one for each day, to open the evening concerts with a prayer. She finished with, "*A Mhairead,* we'd be pleased to have you be our Honorary Chairperson."

Lady Margaret said with a gracious nod, "I'd be delighted, my dear. And of course, if you have any little bits and bobs of work you'd like me to do, just ask."

No one thought that a lady of Margaret's age would have the stamina to do much work for the Festival, but they smiled and applauded politely.

By the end of the meeting everyone who was anyone on Eilean Dubh was firmly ensnared in the Folk Festival scheme.

Picking up Gailleann in his Moses basket to take him over to Lady Margaret for her inspection, Jean said thoughtfully, "You know, I don't believe we voted on this idea of having a Folk Festival. And now all of a sudden it's a reality, and we're all involved."

"Blame it on your ex-husband and my current wife," said Jamie. "They've turned out to be quite a combination."

"Not that I think it's a bad idea," continued Jean. "But I'm just surprised, I guess, that everyone went along with it without a moment's thought or argument. I didn't argue about it because I wanted to get out of there before Gailleann woke up and needed a feed, or Rosie started one of her shenanigans."

"Well, it is a good idea, and should be rather a lot of fun if our people can figure out how to adjust themselves to a crowd of tourists," said Darroch. "But as to whether or not it will make any money, I have my doubts. The Island can only accommodate so many visitors, after all, so we can't count on a huge attendance."

"We'll make a fortune from the limited edition tee shirts alone," said Russ, walking up to them just in time to hear Darroch's comment. "The fact that it's small and exclusive will make everyone want a piece of it."

"Television rights," said Màiri, appearing next to him.

Russ nodded. "And the CD sales, of course, though we'll have to pay royalties on those to all the artists involved, unless we get them to donate their fees to the Playschool fund. Good tax write-off, so they'll probably bite."

"Posters," said Màiri. "Autographed by *Tradisean*, of beautiful Eilean Dubh scenes, the pictures taken by Joe Munro. We won't have to pay anyone for those; it'll all be profit, and we'll make them all limited editions too so we can charge a mint."

And she and Russ left the Playschool arm in arm, talking business at a rapid clip.

"Well," said Jean. "I guess that's all under control. *'Tradisean* presents A Visit to Eilean Dubh' is going to be a moneymaker. That'll be a great thing for the Island, to have an infusion of dough rolling in."

"Aye," said Darroch. "The only decision left is whether to have gold or silver plated faucets in the toilets of the Playschool addition." He turned to Jamie. "That's some wife you've got there."

"*A Dhia beannaich mi,*" said Jamie mournfully. "I suppose she's going to be too busy for sex for the next nine months. Maybe I will opt for sleeping on the sofa, after all. It would be far less painful than running a fiddlers' workshop."

Thirty-seven

Sing heaven imperial, most of hicht,
Regions of air mak armony;
All fish in flood and fowl of flicht,
Be mirthful and mak melody.

William Dunbar.

Despite Màiri's assurances that she would not be asked to do much work, "since you've the new baby, and Darroch's away to London for that soap opera stramash," Jean soon found herself deeply enmeshed in the organization of the Festival. She was, after all, co-chair, and could not let a little thing—two little things—like the children keep her from doing her share of the work.

And Màiri kept a subtle pressure on, popping her head into *Taigh a Mhorair* several times a day, saying, "Can you take a wee keek at this press release, please, Jean; I can't ask Anna because she's got this week's *Island Star* to get out," or, "This will only take a quick phone call, and I haven't time to wait on hold. If you just could ring them, Jean, *tapadh leat*," and she was gone.

The editing was no problem, except for keeping the stacks of paper out of Rosie's eager hands. They could not be left on the floor beside Jean's favorite chair, as the little girl loved to wade into a pile, shrieking with delight as sheets flew all over the room. Darroch had discovered this unhappy fact when he'd left a script by his chair and had had to spend a half an hour putting it together.

The phone calls were something else again. She planned them carefully for the baby's nap times, settling Rosie on the sofa with a batch of her favorite picture books piled around her, and waiting until the child was absorbed in a book before dialing. There was the inevitable, "He's on another line; will you hold?" And the inevitable wait. No sooner did the voice she wanted come on the phone did she look up and notice Rosie, with an almost-four-year-old's immaculate timing, get up, cross the room, and push a chair to the sink. To her mother's horror she struggled up on it, fat bottom wiggling in delight, and came to a shaky standing position, with one hand reaching for the hot water faucet.

Jean jumped up. Leaning over the sink, clutching a protesting, wiggling little girl, balancing the phone between ear and shoulder and trying to make sense of the conversation, she cursed this and all folk festivals now and forever.

It took only one more thing to make the episode complete: the wail of a hungry two-month-old baby echoing down the spiral staircase. Just as Jean was about to concede defeat and hang up on the caller, the door entered and Jamie MacDonald slipped in, with a backward glance at the outside. "Is it safe?" he gasped.

"Depends on how you define safe," said Jean, as Rosie twisted free and lunged off the kitchen chair, landing first on her feet, then toppling back on her bottom to sit down hard on a baby's rattle. It hurt, and she wailed in pain.

Jamie dashed across the room and swept her up in his arms, and, distracted, she stopped crying. Mindful of her son's yells from upstairs, Jean blurted into the phone, "Sorry, can't talk, I've got a brand new baby." The voice on the other end chuckled and said, "So have I. Twins. Take a moment if you need to. I'll hold."

Looking at Jamie tossing Rosie up in the air, hearing her squeals of delight, Jean said, "It's all right; the cavalry has arrived," and swiftly completed her business. Then she ran up the iron spiral staircase and soon returned with a now-dry but cranky and hungry baby. She flung herself down on the sofa, threw a diaper over her bosom for modesty's sake, opened her blouse and settled the baby to nurse. "How did I get myself into this fix?" she mumbled crossly. "One child wasn't enough. Oh, no, I had to have another." She stroked the baby's plump cheek lovingly.

"Ach, well, they'll look after you in your old age," said Jamie.

"Assuming I survive that long." Relaxing into the baby's contented suckling, she looked up at him. "What did you mean, safe?"

"I'm hiding from the trouble-and-strife, who's got it into her head that I know something about the making of recordings of concerts. She wants to pick my brain, she says. Sounded painful, so I decided to scarper." He put Rosie across his knees and began to give her a horsey ride, making her giggle happily.

"I recognize that idiom. She's been talking to Russ again," said Jean.

"Aye. She talks to Russ three and four times a day. I don't know how the poor man gets any software fixed."

"Oh, he's loving it. He loves being in the center of the action, keeping several balls in the air at once. Who says men can't multi-task?"

"You don't suppose that there really isn't a Celtic Folk Festival, and all this is just a cover-up for the two of them having a mad affair," Jamie said.

Jean shook her head. "Not a chance. Màiri's too smart; she's not the type he has . . . had . . . affairs with. He likes . . . liked . . . them dim."

Russ had had affairs? Sensing he'd wandered into deep waters, Jamie backed off, remembering something Darroch had said once about how he and Jean had shared the pain of adultery. Not sure what to say next, he opened and closed his mouth, with no sound coming out.

Jean read his mind, and laughed. "Don't worry, that's all in the past. Think no more about it."

Maybe, Jamie thought, but he'd keep a closer eye on Russ from now on. The buxom redheaded wife was a tempting morsel for a predator to want to gobble up. "Mind you," he said, adroitly changing the subject, "It's Somhairle Mac-a-Phi I blame for this Festival lark becoming reality. It nearly foundered on the rock of not having enough accommodations for visitors. Then he came up with the notion of using the High School for people to sleep in, on cots in the classrooms. Brilliant idea, of course, safe and warm and dry inside, and there's even lockers for them to store their bits and pieces, and a fine big cafeteria for fixing their breakfasts. The world's biggest B and B."

"Has the question of who is making the breakfasts been sorted?"

"Oh, yes, for every ladies' organization at every one of our churches has grabbed a day, and look forward to remodeling their parish halls with their share of the profits. And the Girl Guides and Boy Scouts are going to make and sell box lunches."

"What about suppers? Is the Festival providing those in the package too?"

"No, for clever-clogs-wifey says that the Island restaurants deserve to have the evening meal business."

"There aren't enough restaurants! Two pizzerias, a chippie, a couple of tearooms, and the two hotels. How are they going to feed several hundred visitors, even in shifts?"

"Here's where it gets even more clever. There will also be an evening meal offered in the cafeteria, for a price that doesn't discourage competition from the local eateries. The Scouts and Guides are doing beef stew one night, the Seniors' Residence is doing trad Eilean Dubh food another, and herself is dangling the privilege of catering in front of several other groups for the last two evenings. She thinks of everything."

"That's brilliant. Spreads the profit around to everyone. And the High School was a *miorbhuileach* idea. I suppose the evening concerts will be held in the school auditorium . . . "

"Managed by the students, who know how to operate all the stage equipment and lights. And there will be dances, two nights, in the Citizens' Hall, all manner of Celtic hoofing, Breton and Welsh and even Cornish, taught by visiting teachers."

"Sounds like it's all well in hand."

He sighed. "Yes, for she's gotten a grand response from the folk musicians, even from as far away as Brittany, all keen to come and spend their hols pickin' and singin' on our wee Island, heaven knows why. They'll be wined, dined and bedded in the Rose, paid for by the Festival, since the folkies are donating their talents."

"Cheer up, Jamie, it might be fun."

"Fun," he said gloomily. "I remember fun. I used to have it, now and again," just as the door blew open, Màiri right behind it like an avenging Valkyrie.

"There you are, Jamie! I've been looking all over for you."

"Now you've found me, I'll tell you once more I don't know anything about the recording of concerts."

"Ach, never mind that, that's all sorted. I found an expert, and he'll be donating his time. I wanted you and Jean to see the list of workshops. I've just confirmed the last one." She handed sheets of paper to both of them.

They had to admit, it looked pretty amazing. There were wildflower walks by Anna Wallace, archaeological lectures and tours of the Mesolithic dig by Zach Trelawney, hikes up *Beinn Mhic an Righ* led by Elizabeth

Thomas, folksong exchanges in the Rose's Residents' Bar on Thursday evening led by Kenneth Morrison, the collector of Eilean Dubh's songs, even lectures on Gaelic sources in the Library by Isabel Ross, for the truly devoted folkie. And of course the fiddle workshops, led by Jamie and Eilidh. There was plenty to keep people busy on the four nights and four and a half days of the Festival, and they'd get a grand tour of Eilean Dubh's wonders in the process.

Jean was listed as leading a fairy tale and legend workshop, with the assistance of Darroch Mac an Rìgh. "We should sell lots of copies of your book at that one, Jean," said Màiri. "I think we should order up a second printing."

Jean put a diaper on her shoulder and settled the baby for a good healthy burping session. She wished that Darroch were here. He'd gone off to London with a guilty feeling of relief at evading Màiri's machinations, to start his role as a mysterious stranger on the Cockney soap opera. He'd hated to leave Jean with the new bairn and a Rosie slightly resentful about the Usurper Baby and very attention-seeking as a result, but he needed the work to keep himself viable as an actor, and their budget needed the money. Ensconced in their London apartment, he studied his lines for the program, and wondered what was going on back home. He wasn't entirely sure he wanted to know.

Thirty-eight

If from life you take the best,
If in life you keep the jest,
If love you hold;
No matter how the years go by,
No matter how the birthdays fly –
You are not old.

H. S. Fritsch

B usy as she was, Jean wasn't going to skip her weekly visits to the Seniors'
Residence that gave everyone there a chance to cuddle the two Mac an Rìgh
treasure children, and Jean a chance to sniff out any fairy stories or legends
she'd missed. It was while she was having a cup of tea with Cairistìona
MacChriathar, the elderly long-lost cousin she'd discovered early in her time
on Eilean Dubh, that she got her most *miorbhuileach* idea. She was absently
fingering a crocheted doily on an end table, telling Cairistìona how much it
reminded her of the work her own mother had done.

"She didn't crochet anything this fancy, though; she just did simple patterns like the pineapple one. She liked to keep her fingers busy while she
thought, she said."

"Ach, well, I like to keep busy, too, and figuring out complicated patterns keeps my brain agile, and they say that keeps away the old-timers'
disease." The older woman sighed. "I don't know what to do with all of the
ones I've made, though; most people don't want them any more. They call
them dust-catchers."

"I love them, but I had to put mine away when Rosie started walking,
for she'd grab at a table for support, catch a doily, and pull everything,
including lamps, off onto the floor."

"Any time you want more, let me know. I've been at it for years; I started
when I quit smoking." At Jean's raised eyebrows she said, "Yes, I used to

smoke; everyone did during the War. It was practically a patriotic duty. I finally kicked the vile habit by keeping my hands busy. I've whole dresser drawers full of my work."

"May I see them? I can at least admire them here, if not in my cottage."

Cairistìona indicated the dresser in question with a nod of her head, and Jean opened the drawers and pulled out armfuls of intricately-crocheted doilies, table runners, and a couple of lacy tablecloths. "There are beautiful. Couldn't you sell them in Deirdre's gift shop?"

"She only wants to sell her jewelry, and modern tat like tee shirts with silly sayings on them." The older woman sniffed in disdain.

"Yes, but . . . " Jean went silent, an idea growing in her head. "Why couldn't we sell them to the visitors at the Festival? They'll all be wanting souvenirs of their stay."

"Deirdre's not interested."

"No, I mean . . . I think I mean . . . a crafts fair. Real Eilean Dubh handicrafts."

"A handful of crocheted bitties?" said Cairistìona dubiously.

"All kinds of things. Sweaters from the knitters co-op, *Co-Op nan Figheadairean*. And . . . a *Chairistìona*, do any of the other seniors do crafts?"

"Oh, aye. Anndra MacQuirter whittles, the sweetest little wooden animals you ever saw. Seonag makes wall hangings out of scraps of fabric, Calum makes wee houses out of matchsticks—he's built a whole village in the recreation center—and Màili sews doll clothes. And Uilleam Ross makes stained glass. He used to do it in his room, but everyone was afraid he'd set the place on fire, so we made him move his work out to the garden shed. Siùsaidh's got her wheel out there, and she throws pots. Oh, and Peigi Mac-a-Phi makes sachets out of the lavender she grows in our garden. It's all a waste of time, for everyone's given what they make away as presents for years, and nobody wants any more of them. Still, it keeps us busy, and we have produced some beautiful work."

Jean felt giddy with excitement. "A *Chairistìona!* We'll set up a whole room in the High School for everyone's crafts."

"For display, you mean?"

"No, for sale! Authentic Eilean Dubh handicrafts. They'll sell like hot-cakes."

"Hmm. I don't mind saying that I'd like to give that Deirdre one in the eye, for she's never seen any worth in my crochet work. And I wouldn't mind making the odd bob or two. I've still got one or two bad habits I'd like to support, like having a wee dram now and then, and ordering the newspapers from Edinburgh to see what's on in the wicked world."

"I have a feeling you—and the others—could make enough money to support any amount of bad habits. And you could give demonstrations while you sit at your sales tables, so it would be educational as well, keeping the traditional arts alive. It's one of the mandates of the Festival."

"Well, now, that sounds just grand. Where do we start?"

"Can you arrange for me to see samples of the other seniors' work?"

"No time like the present," Cairistìona said, reaching for her two canes, and struggling to her feet. "Let's take the grand tour. Even if this doesn't work out, everyone will be pleased that there's interest in their bits and bobs."

Desperate to share her plan, Jean burst into *Taigh Rois,* as much as she could burst into any place with a baby strapped to her chest and an over-stimulated almost-four-year-old clinging to her hand. Màiri and Russ were seated at the kitchen table having one of their frequent conferences, each engrossed in what the other had to say. "Oh, I've had the best idea!" Jean shouted.

"Cup of tea?"

"Thà gu dearbh. But listen first!" And she blurted out the details of the handicraft fair.

The other two stared at her. Both said, "Hmmm."

Russ said, "Is what they produce good stuff? Is it saleable?"

"Aye, and it's authentic. Real, home-produced souvenirs of Eilean Dubh." She bubbled, "You should see the little houses and the stained glass. And the seniors are excited about making things with a Festival tie-in, like wooden musician figures and pottery mugs with our logo on them. And Cairistìona is going to crochet little shoulder shawls perfect for chilly Festival evenings that women will die for."

"What's their inventory? Will they need supplies? Where are they going to get the front money for that?" said Russ.

"Well . . ." Jean had not thought that far ahead, but he was right; although the seniors had lots of items they'd made already, they'd need to step up production to meet what she anticipated as a huge demand.

"How are buyers going to pay for purchases?"

"Money, of course."

"No, not cash. They'll want to charge what they buy, and they'll buy more if they can charge it."

Jean deflated. Trust Russ to come up with all the business-y negatives. Of course the seniors couldn't take credit cards. That was not in the least practical. Damn, she should have kept her great idea to herself until all the kinks had been worked out. Was she going to have to disappoint her friends? They'd been so enthusiastic about the project; she'd left them making excited plans about what they'd do with their windfalls.

"If this is going to happen, it'll have to be handled like a proper business," Russ said with his customary air of authority. "We'll set the seniors up with a bank account they can draw on so they can order materials to begin production right away. And get a couple of credit cards on board, the most popular ones, so that purchases can be charged. We'll have to have tight inventory control so we know who gets paid how much and for what; that will tell us what are the best selling items to produce for the next Festival. I'll vouch for the bank account and provide seed money."

"Oh, Russ, that's great. So you really think it will work?"

The other two looked at her in surprise. "Of course it'll work," said Màiri. "Did you think it wouldn't?"

"You've got to have more faith in your ideas, Jean," said Russ, like a big brother.

"We need a catchy name for the crafts fair," said Màiri, and she and Russ were off and running.

Relieved, Jean sat back and listened to them brainstorm. It might not be exactly the same idea as hers had been when they got done, but it would still be a good one, and the three of them were going to make it work. She felt a new respect for the organizational skills of her best friend and her ex-husband.

PART XVII

The Folk Festival

Thirty-nine

The birds awake, the flowers appear,
Earth spreads a verdant couch for thee;
'Tis joy and music all we hear,
'Tis love and beauty all we see.

James Thomson

The majestic entry of the Cal-Mac ferry into Airgead harbor Monday at 1 P.M. signaled the beginning of the Folk Festival. On Friday it would depart, bearing away the several hundred Festival-goers it had delivered five days earlier.

Tuesday and Saturday were the normal arrival days for the ferry. Màiri and Russ had puzzled over this for some time. If the ferry kept to its usual schedule, they would lose a day from the Festival without a Monday arrival. And they needed to have everyone out on Friday, so that cleanup could be done on Saturday to have everything tidy again by the Sabbath.

Without controlling who arrived on the ferry, they would have no way of keeping from the Island those who had not booked, and they ran the risk of inundating the Island with casual visitors who would come in hopes of finding accommodations and tickets to Festival events.

"It will be a madhouse," said Màiri. "Every bed is spoken for and there's simply no place for drop-ins. What will we do if people come without reservations? They'll have to sleep in the streets."

"Hmm," said Russ. "Seems to me the solution is to charter the entire ferry, and not let them take anyone on board without a package ticket for accommodations and Festival events."

"What about people who come on the regular Tuesday and Saturday sailings?"

"Those sailings will have to be cancelled."

Màiri was shocked at the very idea. The Tuesday and Saturday sailings were sacred; they had been set in stone for years, and it would be a major undertaking to disrupt the schedule. "What? How do you propose we do that?"

"Contact the ferry people, of course, and ask them to make the change."

"Why would they agree?"

"Because," Russ said patiently, "We're offering them two fully-booked charter sailings to replace two scheduled stops for one week. How many people come and go on the ferry each of the two regular days?"

"About half a dozen."

"There you are," said Russ. "A guaranteed full ferry on two days, all in exchange for dropping two regular stops for one week. Let's get in touch with Cal-Mac and see what we can arrange."

In the end, it was a letter to the chairman of Cal-Mac that cut through the considerable red tape and the hemming and hawing by underlings, and got the regular ferries replaced with the charters. The letter was signed, under duress, by the newly created Sir Darroch Mac an Rìgh. Màiri insisted that the signature was what had done the trick, and even he had to admit that his title came in handy in this situation.

The Festival package offered included accommodations with breakfast every day, round trip passage to and from Eilean Dubh out of Oban, and entry to the Festival events of the purchaser's choice; opening and closing concerts, concert or dance two nights, and workshops (advance sign-up required). Lunches and evening meals were each Festival-goer's responsibility. The package was priced at £250 for B and B accommodation in the High School, £25 extra for a private home B and B, and £50 extra for the hotel in Airgead, the Rose being fully booked for the visiting *artistes*.

"The price seems a bit dear," worried Màiri.

"On the contrary, it's quite a bargain," said Russ. "I've priced out holiday packages offered by British travel agents, and you can't get a trip like this for this money anywhere. Only £50 a day per person, including entertainment, accommodation and some meals, plus transportation to and from Oban."

The customers evidently thought so, too, for tickets went rapidly, and two weeks before their deadline, Màiri and Russ announced in triumph that the Celtic Folk Festival was a sell-out, and there was even a waiting list.

Now the Festival-goers were arriving, and the long awaited event was about to begin. Sally had come up with the idea of making the Festival more user-friendly by dividing the visitors up into what she named "pods," because, she said, it sounded cozy, and would make people think of whales and darling dolphins. The pods were groups of around twenty-five people, each group with an *Eilean Dubhannach* as its leader. That way, she said, the impersonality of the Festival would be replaced by friendliness. If a visitor had a problem or question, he or she could discuss it with the pod leader, rather than trying to contact someone in an impersonal, busy Festival bureaucracy, all of whom would be scurrying around on their assigned tasks.

All the organizers had had nightmares about people milling around the Airgead pier haphazardly on arrival, with no way to organize them into their buses for transportation, but Sally's idea worked beautifully. Each pod was assigned a color, and each visitor had been contacted and asked to wear something in that color on arrival.

Every leader had a banner in his or her pod's color. Visitors found their correct group, got acquainted with their leaders and fellow Festival-goers, and were loaded on the correct buses for transport to their accommodations. Enough school buses were available so that no one had to wait more than an hour for transportation, with the buses making two trips each.

Then they had the afternoon to settle into their digs before reconvening in the High School auditorium for the opening concert. Everyone milled about in the High School parking lot, enjoying the beautiful evening, until a voice over the tannoy announced, "Willow ricket olders beefsteak ersatz. Deacon serve isa butt toboggan."

They correctly interpreted this as, "Would all ticket holders take their seats. The concert is about to begin," and filed inside.

"Here we go," said Jean, and *Tradisean* took the stage to cheers. Minister Donald gave the opening prayer, Lady Margaret and Darroch welcomed everyone, and the music began.

The opening concert was glorious, and visitors, performers and organizers all retired to their beds that night feeling that the Folk Festival was off to a grand start.

Forty

We're a' met taegither here tae sit an' tae crack,
Wi' oor glasses in oor hands, an' oor wark upon oor back;
For there's no' a trade amang them as can either mend or mak'
Gin it wasna for the wark o' the weavers.
If it wasna for the weavers, what wad they do?
They wadna hae claith made oor o' oor woo',
They wadna hae a coatie neither black nor blue,
Gin it wasna for the wark o' the weavers.

Scots folk song

It was a great relief that the opening concert had gone well, for it had dawned on *Tradisean* only three months before the Festival began that they would have to expand their repertoire. On their tour they had performed virtually the same program night after night in different cities for different audiences, and for *cèilidhean* at home, the crowd wanted the same old songs, so there was no pressure on Jean to learn new material that the others had known from childhood.

But they couldn't go out on stage four nights in a row and perform exactly the same program. They'd have to have a different one for each night.

"We'll have to double our rehearsals," decided Jamie, "and organize some new tunes. That shouldn't be too difficult, if we work hard."

Darroch said, "I've been rooting through my trunk of music, and I've come up with some things we haven't done for ages. We know them, so it's just a matter of getting Jean up to speed."

"Umm," said Jean, only half-listening. She was busy exchanging secret smiles with the baby at her breast, who rolled his eyes up at his mother as he suckled. Those eyes were getting to be a deeper blue every day, she thought happily; in a few months they'd be as blue as Darroch's.

"Here's my candidates," said Darroch, handing sheet music to Jamie and Màiri, who murmured approval of his choices. "Do you like those?

Miorbhuileach. Jean, that leaves you with . . . let me count . . . eight new songs to learn."

Rosie crowded up against Jean, making sure that the Usurper Baby wasn't up to any cute tricks that would take attention away from her. Distracted, Jean said, "Rosie, love, don't poke at Gailleann; no one pokes you when you're eating. What did you say, Darroch?"

"I said, there's just eight new songs for you to learn."

"Ummm . . . how many?"

Three pair of eyes stared at her, and Darroch said patiently, "Eight."

"Oh, right. Eight, wow. I hope they're not too hard."

"Well, there's one or two . . . maybe three at most . . . that are a bit tricky. Don't worry, your Gaelic's up to it, and we'll all help you."

"Okay." Eight seemed like rather a lot, but she had several months to work on them, so she should be able to handle it.

But she couldn't. Darroch was called away to London for some preliminary conferences about the Cockney soap opera, and Jamie had a crisis with his Jacob's Sheep, and Màiri had a crisis with an outbreak of stomach flu at the Preschool. So there was no one to practice with or to help her with pronunciation, and the cassette tape that Darroch had left with her broke.

Even worse, she had no quiet time for memorization of lyrics. With her father gone and her mother occupied with the Usurper Baby's persistent, painful, diaper rash that made him cranky, Rosie decided it was time to reassert her supremacy over the Mac an Rìgh household. She began a series of almost-four-year-old pranks that ranged from the mildly irritating to the truly dangerous and that kept Jean on her toes all the time.

She thought each day that she could work on her music while the pair napped, but she found herself so tired that she couldn't resist the temptation to get off her feet for a few moments. Then Rosie would wander in, half asleep, dragging her favorite blanket, and crawl into bed with her mother.

Jean would realize that she and Rosie didn't have much private time together now that Gailleann was here, her heart would soften and she'd gather the little girl in her arms for a cuddle. Rosie lay beside her, her long black hair spread out over the pillow, her small slender body relaxed, and stared up at her mother with those remarkable turquoise eyes that were an improbable combination of Darroch's blue and Jean's green. Her nose was long and elegant like Darroch's, and she had her mother's generous mouth.

She was exquisite, and that realization always left Jean pondering the responsibility of having a raving beauty in the family.

And then she and Rosie would fall asleep, and not wake until Gailleann did, and another afternoon's opportunity for practicing and memorizing was gone.

The tunes were no problem, but the Gaelic lyrics were. In desperation, she wrote out the words to the first four songs and pinned them up around the house: on the kitchen cabinets, on the fridge, on the medicine chest in the bathroom, and on her bedside table. That way, she figured, she could learn them little by little, four songs at a time, by osmosis, if no other way.

As soon as Darroch returned, *Tradisean* gathered at *Taigh Rois* for rehearsal, the children left at home under First Daughter Sally's supervision. The four ran through some of their familiar material. That went well, so Darroch turned to Jean. "Let's try one of the new songs," he said, looking at her expectantly.

She checked her guitar tuning and began. She warbled the first line, and was relieved to see approving smiles. Encouraged, she launched into the second line.

The other three looked puzzled, and Darroch glanced down at his sheet music.

Uh-oh, must have pronounced something wrong, she thought, and hastily began the third line of the tune. She felt quite comfortable with this one and closed her eyes in the sheer pleasure of singing. She opened them again before tackling the fourth line, and saw that the others were staring at her.

Damn. She was sure she'd had that one nailed. "What's wrong?"

The others glanced at each other uneasily. Darroch cleared his throat. "*Mo chridhe* . . . I don't think you realized . . . " He glanced down at the floor, then up at Jean. "You've just sung the first line of each of three songs."

Dumbfounded, she stared at him. "Are you sure?"

"Quite sure."

"You sang each one beautifully," said Jamie loyally.

"You need a bit more work, that's all," said Màiri.

Jean gulped down a sudden lump in her throat. She'd tried so hard and still she'd made a mess of it. "I can't do it," she blurted.

Darroch, knowing how hard it was for her to admit defeat in any quarter, since she prided herself on being a "can-do" American, said in his most reassuring tone, "Of course you can."

"She can't," said Màiri in her abrupt way. "She can't, and it's wrong of us to ask it of her. She's got too much on her plate as it is, with two small children."

Jean said, "It was different when it was just me and I had all the time in the world I needed to practice; I could work for hours if I had to. Now there's the baby, and Rosie seems to take every spare moment, and so much laundry . . . I try to practice while they nap, but I've been tired, and I keep falling asleep."

"And I've been gone, and no help at all," said Darroch.

"I've let you all down," said Jean, as tears threatened.

"Nonsense," said Màiri briskly. "It was nonsense to ask you to learn eight new songs with no help at all. I don't know what you were thinking, Darroch," she added.

He looked hurt, then realized that by blaming him she was giving Jean a chance to save face and regain her composure. "Quite right. Now let's think of what we can substitute for that material."

"It's a Celtic festival, not a Scottish Gaelic one," said Jamie, who'd been thinking hard. "I think Jean should sing her Appalachian music. It came from Scotland and Ireland, and that will show how the Old World music turned into that of the New World."

"Oh, could I?" Jean cried. "I could use songs I already know."

They all stared at Màiri, whose word was law. She nodded. "*Miorbhuileach* idea, *a Sheumas*."

"Brilliant," agreed Darroch. "I look forward to hearing your own music again, *mo ghràdh*."

Tears threatened again, this time from relief. Jean at last managed a smile, and began to search her memory for old favorite songs. There was "The Banks of Red Roses," which became "Pretty Polly" in Appalachia, and "Lord Randall," and "The Unquiet Grave." She wished she had her Child's or *The Ballad Book of John Jacob Niles*, but they were in the Abbott house in Milwaukee. She'd have to do research on the Internet. But there was plenty of material, and they could do arrangements with Darroch singing the Scottish version before she sang the Appalachian one.

Four performances in four days for the same audience, and a new problem loomed. Jean did not consider herself especially vain, but she had her share of feminine ego, and she didn't want to wear the same outfit every night. Sure, the turquoise dress was gorgeous and flattering, but it would look tired and repetitive after four nights, and what if she spilled something on it, or had an encounter with a nail backstage at the High School?

Well, there was one thing Jean could do: she could get herself back into her kilted skirt, her frilled blouse and her velvet jacket, the outfit she'd worn to be married in several years ago. It would not be easy, but she was determined that she could do it. She put herself on a rigorous program of diet and exercise. She couldn't restrict her diet too much, since a nursing mother needed calories, but she could cut out desserts and say no to glasses of wine—they weren't good for Gailleann anyway. She could increase her intake of fruit and veg to satisfy her hunger.

And she could exercise, but that presented its own set of problems. Really, it was amazing how complicated life was when you had small children, Jean thought; it had been fifteen years since she'd been in that situation, and she'd forgotten the details.

No longer could she stride down to Ros Mór and back whenever she felt like it, because she could not push the pram and hang onto Rosie at the same time. The little girl loved to dart across the road, zigzagging back and forth like a demented seagull, and coming back to her mother's side just long enough to cast a suspicious eye over the Usurper Baby, snoozing peacefully in the pram. Jean knew she couldn't rely on the kindness and caution of other drivers on the road to watch out for a small wild child.

Thinking creatively, she set herself a schedule of walking down their own lane to the sea and trudging back up the hill, pushing the pram with Rosie dancing beside, behind and in front of her. There were almost no cars on their lane and what there were, were driven very slowly, so it was safe.

Of course the lane was considerably shorter than the two-mile trek into Ros Mór, so every day, rain or shine, Jean and her ensemble of children marched up and down until her pedometer said that she'd done the required number of steps. Then all three came inside and flopped down for naps.

It worked, and Jean found to her delight that she was shrinking, and was triumphant when she fit once again into the kilted skirt ensemble. That outfit would open the Festival and the turquoise dress would close it, and what would come in between was a mystery until Sally intervened. Quizzed, Màiri had admitted that she'd begun to think about the clothes problem too. All she really had to wear was her MacDonald tartan skirt. "I suppose I could get some new tops," she said in a worried voice.

"We can do better than that, mother-in-law," announced Sally, and organized Jean and Màiri into a shopping expedition to Inverness. "We're going to let our hair down and go a little crazy and grab ourselves some flash gear."

"At our age?" said Màiri dubiously, but allowed herself to be swept along.

What they found in Inverness was jeans, two pair each, and some Sally-approved flash tops to go with them. "Jeans are what all the rock stars wear," asserted Sally.

Maybe so, but Jean and Màiri decided to dress for the second night's concert at Sally's cottage, just in case Darroch and Jamie didn't approve of them looking like rock stars. They showed up at the High School twenty minutes before they were to go on, not leaving enough time to be sent home to change. "As if I would," sniffed Màiri. "Me neither," said Jean, but she knew if Darroch disapproved of something she wore, her confidence would collapse like a clothesline in a gale, and she'd change immediately.

Jamie caught his first sight of his wife, and began to twitch. "What's that you've got on?" he demanded.

"Blue jeans. Although I don't know why they're called that, because this pair is black. Do you like them?"

"They're—ah—tight," he said, through gritted teeth.

"Aye, they are. Sally said they are supposed to fit like the paper on the wall." She twisted her head around to look at her plump rear end, the movement drawing the fabric even tighter. "I only hope I can sit down on the piano bench," she said, wiggling seductively.

Jamie shot an infuriated look at Sally, who he could see was trying not to laugh. "And what's that—thing—you're almost wearing above the jeans?"

"It's called a tube top," she replied. "The only problem with it is that it tends to slip down." She grasped the edge of the top and pulled it up higher over her breasts.

"You are not going out on the stage with your shoulders sticking out as bare as an egg," snapped Jamie, at the end of his tether. "I won't have all the men in the audience gawking at you when you're half naked."

"Of course not, *a ghaoil*," said Màiri demurely, having gotten the reaction she'd hoped for. "I've this little shoulder shawl that Cairistìona

MacChriathar crocheted and is selling in the Seniors' Craft Fair. Isn't it pretty?" She shrugged into a lacy confection through which her skin peeked temptingly. She peered at herself in the mirror, admiring the way the cerulean blue of the shoulder shawl brought out the color of her eyes, and smiled her little cat smile of satisfaction.

The glimpses of flesh were not lost on Jamie. "I'd send you home to change if we had time," he growled.

"But we haven't; we're due to go on in fifteen minutes. Don't fuss any more, *a Sheumas,* come and give me a kiss for luck." When he approached, she turned her head and presented him with her cheek. "Not on the mouth. Sally spent half an hour doing my make-up."

Darroch couldn't help feeling sorry for his friend, once he'd gotten over the shock of seeing his own wife decked out in tight jeans and a shoulder-baring, scoop-necked satin blouse in a vivid shade of fuchsia.

Jean wasn't quite as assured about her own appearance as was Màiri. "I don't know about this outfit," she said uncertainly. "Sally said we should let our hair down and go a little crazy for once, but I'm not sure I should have let her talk me into this top. Do I look all right?"

"You look lovely," Darroch said, to Jean's relief. "I quite like your new look and I agree with Sally. Let your hair down."

The hair in question was very pretty. It retained the contours of the smart styling she'd gotten for the investiture, but had grown out to a softer look, and she'd rinsed it in vinegar to bring out the shimmering whisky-colored highlights. One thing puzzled her. "My jeans are just as tight as Màiri's. How come you didn't make a fuss like Jamie did?"

"Ah, well, there's a reason for that," Darroch said, looking uncomfortable. "It's because your bottom is not quite as, ah, rounded as Màiri's, so the tightness is not as, ah, blatant."

"Aye, I'm kind of flat," said Jean wistfully. "I guess she's what you'd call voluptuous and sexy."

"I would call her that, indeed, but not to her face, and risk a slap. Or a punch, if Jamie happened to hear me say it."

Jean chuckled and put on her own Cairistìona-crocheted shoulder shawl, hers in discreet black. She took a final look in the mirror and consoled herself that even if she wasn't voluptuous, at least she'd gotten her figure back to pre-Gailleann shape.

And she didn't look bad at all, for someone who'd had four children and was pushing forty-four. Not bad at all, at all. She thought about the fitted tuxedo-style jacket covered in bronze spangles that she'd gotten to go with her jeans for tomorrow night's performance, and smiled her own smile of satisfaction, as they headed out onto the stage.

Forty-one

O, *rattlin', roarin' Willie, o, he hei'd to the fair,*
An' for to sell his fiddle an' buy some other ware,
But partin' wi' his fiddle, the saut tear blin't his e'e,
And rantin', rattlin' Willie, ye're welcome hame to me.

Scots folk song

No one on Eilean Dubh had envisioned the disruption that the Folk Festival would cause to their placid, well-ordered lives. They had anticipated a neat stream of visitors cheerfully funneling themselves to meals, workshops and concerts like trains on a well-run railway line.

Instead, people spilled over the banks and flooded into the roads between Ros Mór and Airgead, and out into the streets of both towns. They congregated on the corners trading stories, lies and jokes, their laughter rippling up to the beautiful blue sky, for the weather was, to every Islander's amazement, fair, warm and sunny.

Impromptu *seiseanan* broke out all over, inside the pubs and the hotels and out on the streets as musician met musician, each of them bursting to share their favorite songs, riffs and hot licks. No one slept; everyone jabbered, drank and made music. As a jazz musician would say, "The joint was jumping."

Festival-inspired romances blossomed. Kisses were shared in private corners and public places, to the shock of respectable *Eilean Dubhannaich.* Undying love was pledged, undying until the end of the Festival and everyone went home.

Darroch came back from a shopping trip into Ros Mór Wednesday morning with his ears ringing from the noise of the crowds. He'd walked for the exercise and had been glad of it once he'd seen how the streets were crowded with visitors and he'd imagined himself piloting the Bentley through the mob. "They're eating and drinking and gabbing away at the top of their lungs everywhere, and it's all a person can do to get from point A to point B without being trampled or crushed," he told Jean.

He'd moved with eel-like speed and dexterity on his errands in the Co-Op, aware that he was on the brink of being recognized and not wanting to become the center of an autograph-seeking crowd, since Jean was at home anxiously awaiting the milk and juice he'd been sent to get. Years of practice as a well-known actor had taught him how to avert his glance, duck his head and turn his shoulders slightly so that no one got a really good look at him for long enough to know that the Magician was amongst them.

Recounting the morning's observations, he suddenly began to chuckle. "You ken how our Màiri was so careful in arranging the nosh so that every visitor could be assured of three well-balanced meals a day? That's all gone awry, for what people want is junk food that they can eat on the fly so they don't miss any of the fun, and they've discovered the Co-Op's snack shelves.

"The Co-Op manager told me that the visitors have bought up all the crisps, biscuits, nuts and pork pies that she'd expected to last for at least a month. Even the jars of Marmite and all the sandwich bread loaves have been sold out. She's sending Murdoch the Chopper to her wholesaler in Inverness on an emergency run early tomorrow with orders to load the helicopter with everything he can find that's crispy, crunchy, fatty and salty."

He started to laugh and it was several moments before he could continue. "Here's something *miorbhuileach,* Jean. A whole gaggle of little old ladies has appeared behind card tables all around the Square, and they're selling sandwiches out of ice chests, and bottles of some strange-looking liquids that I couldn't identify. I said to one of them, 'That had better not be your lethal elderberry wine that you're selling without a license, *mo leadaidh,* or you'll have Constable MacRath down on you like a gull on a herring, and you'll be spending the rest of the week inside the four walls of our wee jail.'

"'Ach, no, *a Mhic an Rìgh,'* she cackled,"—here he did an uncanny imitation of a little old lady voice—"'That's naught but my own homemade sody pop.' So I took a swig and almost keeled over from the alcohol content.

"But I noticed the women were ducking the bottles out of sight when young people came up to their card tables, and none of the visitors have cars, so I suppose there's no harm to it as long as they don't poison anyone with their homemade fish paste sandwiches." He shuddered.

Jean was envisioning the Square full of people reeling happily around, loaded to the gills on elderberry wine. "*Caveat emptor,* lovie. Let the buyer beware."

"You're right, for they could go to a proper restaurant or tuck into one of Màiri's nutritious box lunches packed by the Guides and the Scouts." He paused for a sip of tea. "The strangest part, Jean, is that those little old ladies are the widows' corps of Eilean Dubh. They all wear ankle length rusty black dresses and their hair in buns, and most of them haven't seen the light of day in years. In fact, I spotted two whose funerals I swear I went to ages ago, and where they came from I haven't the courage to wonder about."

He leaned closer, and said in a dramatic whisper, "And auld Mistress Una Mac a' Ghobhainn, she that lurks in the wee flat up over Murray the Meat's shop, who must be ninety-nine if she's a day—she's set up her card table in the stairway leading up to her flat and she's selling raisin tarts out the doorway's window. Murray's fit to be tied but he doesn't dare say anything to her, for everyone on the Island knows she's a witch."

Jean began to laugh helplessly.

Jamie showed up at *Taigh a Mhorair* before the concert, and when Darroch shared what he'd seen that morning, he said, "That's naught compared to what happened in Ros Mór this afternoon. Someone left a gate ajar in a field near town and a fine flock of sheep got out and went walkabout in the High Street. Wall-to-wall fleece, it was."

"With all those people around? What happened?" asked Jean.

"Myself and a couple of the lads set out to round them up, and a grand time we were making of it when I got . . . distracted."

"What by?" said Darroch, wondering what could have distracted Jamie from sheep, his favorite subject.

"One or two autograph seekers," he said evasively.

In fact, there had been considerably more than one or two. Jamie had been aiding in the sheep roundup, having the time of his life walking down the High Street with arms outstretched, shouting "Ho" and "Hey there" along with two other men, friends of his who raised sheep, as he did. They managed to corral the flock in the courtyard of the Island Building Society, where the animals milled about, stamping their hooves and looking baffled, under the leadership of a cross old ram who could not make out what had happened to his fine grassy pasture.

Chatting and waiting for the arrival of Fergal Ferguson's Fergus, acknowledged to be the finest sheepdog on Eilean Dubh, Jamie and the others had been analyzing the merits of the flock in front of them, which they'd recognized as belonging to Ruairidh MacQuirter, and wasn't he just going to have a word to say to whoever had left the gate open.

Right about then, Jamie noticed the crowd that had gathered and that appeared to be growing bigger. He thought they'd been attracted by the sheep roundup, for they'd laughed and cheered and applauded and come perilously close to spooking the flock completely out of control. But they were staring at him and nudging each other. "It's him, I'm sure of it," he heard someone say, and when another shouted, "Hi, Jamie," he responded with a wave before he realized what he was doing.

That was all the crowd needed. They surged forward to surround him, elbowing out of their way the men with whom Jamie had been chatting. Those two looked at each other and grinned, and Jamie caught an exchange of remarks in the Gaelic that turned his ears pink. "Make way for the star," was the gist of those comments, and though they were not meant unkindly, he was mortified. He could handle a crowd's adulation when it occurred where it should, on a stage, but not here, not in the midst of proper men's work.

The faces surrounding him were bright and inquisitive, and most of their owners were searching their persons for pen and paper. Some were already thrusting these at Jamie.

The sheepdog Fergus arrived in the truck with his human. The dog hopped down, sized up the situation quickly, and slunk over to the flock in a business-like manner with menace in his eye for any sheep that dared to challenge him. The cross old ram, for form's sake, darted forward a few feet and looked around. Catching a threatening movement from Fergus, he scampered back into the safety of the flock, where he stood, pretending to be in charge.

Jamie had been looking forward to seeing Fergus work the sheep. It was a complicated drive with many distractions, up the road past shops and onlookers, over the hills and down the dirt road to Ruairidh MacQuirter's pasture, and any true sheep man would take pleasure in the clever dog's handling of the situation. But the crowd around him was growing, and he feared they'd interfere with Fergus's careful work with the flock. Corralling the crowd like sheep, he herded his admirers back to the sidewalk.

He signed autographs, hoping that would be the end of it. But to his alarm he saw that the crowd was growing, not diminishing, as word spread throughout the square that one of the Festival stars was loose amongst them. Even worse, his admirers had begun to talk to him. At his left elbow, a somber young man in black-rimmed glasses had begun a lengthy analysis of Jamie's improvisational techniques, a discourse so complicated that Jamie could neither follow nor understand it. On his other side was an earnest young woman discussing kindred themes in English and Scottish folk song. Two teenaged girls seemed to be under the delusion that he was married to Jean, and kept asking, "Where's the wife, Jamie? Can we get Jean out to sing a song for us?" and giggling madly.

The horror of his situation was compounded by the reaction of his fellow *Eilean Dubhannaich*. They knew it was cruel to laugh, but they simply could not resist the temptation of a good chuckle at Jamie's expense. It was not often that they got one up on the Bonnie Prince, whose skill with the fiddle awed audiences at the Friday night *cèilidhean* and whose stunning good looks wowed their wives, and they were making the most of the situation.

An impatient "woof" from Fergus reminded them that there was work to be done, and they turned back reluctantly to the sheep.

Jamie began to move in the opposite direction, and his personal flock came with him. Anxious to escape, he thought about darting into a shop, but he didn't think Murray the Meat or Beathag the Bread would welcome the intrusion of a mob of non-buying customers. He headed in the opposite direction, away from the Square, hoping the crowd would get discouraged. Those who had secured autographs turned back in search of other excitement, but the bulk of the group stuck with him, including the music analyst and the female folk song collector, who was now comparing the various versions of "Barbara Allen," and looking up hopefully at Jamie for his input.

Trapped, he glanced wildly around and realized he'd strayed down a side street and was now standing in front of the building housing *The Island Star*. With any luck, Anna Wallace's door would be unlocked and he could slide through it into safety. He blurted, "Grand to meet you all, but I've got to get back to work. See you tonight at the concert," and with a quick twist he slipped through his admirers, up the sidewalk and was through the door of the building before they realized he'd escaped.

He retreated to the back of the room where he could eyeball the crowd through the window without being seen, and to his relief saw that they appeared to be dispersing. He heard footsteps on the stairs and realized that not only was he inside, uninvited, he was standing by Anna's desk and staring down at the papers on it. He stepped away hastily just as she appeared.

Anna had been upstairs, leaning against the bathroom door, engaged in one of her favorite activities, watching her new husband shave. He was stripped to the waist, his jeans were not fully buttoned, and his coffee-colored hair was rumpled from sleep. He was dead sexy, Anna thought.

She'd never seen a man use a straight razor before; her previous live-in lover Gus had been one for a quick scrape with a safety razor. Zachariah Trelawney went at shaving like a surgeon getting ready for an organ transplant. First he prepared a fragrant lather, beating up bits of "Barber's Pride" soap in a mug. Then he spread the lather carefully all over the planes and curves of his lean face. He let it rest for a moment, then took a lethal-looking straight razor, stropped it on a leather belt, and began in a leisurely manner to remove the previous night's crop of whiskers.

Anna watched, and wondered what he was thinking. Looking at his bare chest reflected in the mirror, she knew what she was thinking, and restrained herself from acting upon it. The last time she'd sneaked up behind him and run her hands over his taut bottom, he'd nearly cut his throat. She wouldn't do that again.

Zach was thinking long, dreamy thoughts about archaeology and sex, mostly about sex. He knew his wife was observing him. With any luck she'd stay until he was done, and he could capture her, unbutton her blouse and rub his freshly shaven face over her bare throat, making her squeal.

Perhaps he could even back her up against the door and have his way with her, lifting her up on her tiptoes, bending his knees so they'd fit together. She'd like that. She liked making love in unusual positions, he'd discovered one day when he'd caught her in the back of her office and tipped her over her desk. Her reaction had been most gratifying.

Anna was so engrossed in her own pleasantly lustful thoughts that she'd missed, at first, the jangle of bells that signified that her front door had opened. "Who's that?" she said, and turned reluctantly to head down the stairs, where she discovered Jamie.

"*Feasgar math, a Sheumas,*" she said in surprise. "*Dè nì me dhuit?*" What can I do for you?

"Ah—nothing at all. If you must have the truth, I'm hiding." He waved his hand at the crowd outside.

Puzzled, she looked them over, then got it. "Fans?"

"Aye." Deprived of the pleasure of watching Fergus work the sheep, he'd been contemplating gloomily the possibility that he'd have to make a dash for it through the crowd and up the streets of Ros Mór to the main road home. He wondered if he could outrun them. Probably not, for he had twenty years on most of them.

"Do you want to slip out my back door?" offered Anna.

"Could I? *Tapadh leat,* Anna," he said gratefully, and slid through the door that she opened carefully, first checking for lurking fans.

He sneaked through side streets and alleys, after a glance at his watch showed him it was almost time for the fiddle workshop that he and daughter Eilidh were holding at the Rose Hotel. There was a crowd in front of the Rose, so he went through Sheilah's kitchen door, startling her so much that she nearly dropped the tray of scones she was pulling from the oven.

"Sorry, sorry," he murmured and eeled his way through the kitchen and out into the hall that lead to the Residents' Bar, where the workshop was to be held. On the way he heard music coming from the Public Bar, and could not resist poking his head in.

Two fiddle players were there, sawing away at their instruments and producing a driving, highly rhythmical music that made his feet itch to dance. It was not quite Scottish, to his experienced ear. Curious, he listened until they finished, then said, "Hi. What's that you're playing?"

"Set of reels from Cape Breton. Can't remember the titles."

Of course he knew about Nova Scotia's Cape Breton Island and its rich tradition of fiddle music of Scottish ancestry, and had been curious about it for years. What luck, to find Cape Bretoners at the Festival. "Jamie MacDonald," he said, extending his hand.

"Howie MacDonald," said one, and "Andy MacDonald," said the other.

"Brothers?"

"Nope, cousins, third or fourth; all Cape Breton MacDonalds are related in some degree or other. Have to ask our mothers. I'm from Mabou and Andy's from Judique. So you're a Scottish MacDonald. Maybe you're a cousin too? What do you play?" said Howie, casually assuming that everyone in the vicinity of the Festival was a musician.

"Fiddle."

"Where's your instrument?"

"Damn," said Jamie, realizing an important omission. "I left it at home."

Andy shook his head. "Can't do that, gotta have it with you all the time at these events in case there's a spontaneous outbreak of music. Are you here for the workshop?"

Before he could answer, a bright young face appeared at the door, and a bright young voice said, "Workshop's about to start, but the teacher's not arrived."

"Mary Alice MacDonald, my sister," said Howie. "Say, Mal, we've just met a Scottish cousin and he's interested in our music. Come give him a demonstration."

"'Kay." Obligingly she stepped inside, took her fiddle out of its case and began to play in the same vigorous style. After forty-eight bars, to Jamie's amazement she put her fiddle down and began to dance, upper body relaxed and a bemused look on her face, while below the knees her feet were tapping vigorously, crossing and re-crossing, ankles rolling, while her brother and cousin played accompaniment on their fiddles.

"That's *miorbhuileach,*" said Jamie, when she finished. "What do you call that?"

"Cape Breton step dancing," Mary Alice said, putting her fiddle back in its case. "We all know how to dance, back home. I'm not as good as Natalie MacMaster, who can fiddle and dance at the same time, but I'm working on it." Then she got a closer look at Jamie. "Well! I guess we're not late for the workshop if you're here. Your daughter's been looking all over for you, Mr. MacDonald."

"Damn," muttered Jamie again. The workshop about to start, and he didn't have his fiddle. He'd planned on going home after his trip to Ros Mór to collect his instrument, music and notes, but all his time had been taken up by sheep and fans, and he'd forgotten. What was he going to do now?

Eilidh MacDonald Munro appeared at the door to the Public Bar. "Here you are, *a Bhobain!* I might have known I'd find you knee deep in fiddlers. It's time for the workshop. I've got your fiddle and your stuff—I knew you'd forget something—so come next door and let's get started."

Vastly relieved, Jamie followed her meekly. Behind him, the penny dropped for Howie MacDonald, and he nudged his sister. "Is he who I think he is?" he said.

"Sure is."

"Wow," said Howie respectfully. "He seems like an ordinary guy, not a fiddle god."

"Wait till you hear him play," said Mary Alice.

Jamie had been so interested in talking to and playing with the Cape Bretoners that he'd almost been late to supper at *Taigh a Mhorair*. When he told his story about the sheep and the fans, Darroch said kindly, "Remind me one day to tell you how to make yourself invisible in a crowd."

"I'll just be doing that," said Jamie.

Forty-two

Let us haste to Kelvin Grove, bonnie lassie, o,
Through its mazes let us rove, bonnie lassie, o,
Where the rose in all her pride paints the hollow dingle side,
Where the midnight fairies glide, bonnie lassie, o.

Scots folk song

Jamie was not the only member of *Tradisean* making connections with the visiting musicians. Jean and Darroch had gone to a Cornish Culture workshop Wednesday afternoon, and had been fascinated by the lively dances and the playful dance music of Cornwall. Even Màiri, busy as she was with organizational tasks, had gotten lured into a pianists' jam session in the High School's music lab, and found her creative juices start to flow and a tune take shape in her head. She never wrote music, but this tune was so compelling that she couldn't resist it. She got Eilidh to write it down for her, and was intending to spring it on the rest of *Tradisean* at the Thursday night concert in her solo spot. They'd be awed, she thought smugly.

The week rolled along too fast for all the participants. On Thursday morning, Jean was finishing up the breakfast dishes when she heard the distant sound of singing, and curious, she went to the door to listen. As the singing came closer, she picked up Gailleann, smoothing back the wisps of red-brown hair so like her own that had begun to sprout only last week. She started up the hill to where their lane joined the main road, Rosie trotting beside her.

It was one of those rare golden days of early autumn when the warmth of the morning sun meeting the still-chilly ground created fog, and now as it was burning off the air shimmered and undulated like something out of a fairy tale. Lured by the morning's beauty and filled with the sheer joy of

living, Festival-goers had left their B and Bs and taken to the road, tram-
pling along singly at first, then in couples, then in groups.

All the visitors were confirmed folkies with large song repertoires, and
as they walked they vied with each other to start up their favorite tune.
Coming down the hill from Airgead toward Jean was an Irish group, and
they were singing:

In eighteen hundred and forty one,
I put my corduroy britches on.
I put my corduroy britches on
To work upon the railway.
Fillame-orie-orie-ay, fillame-orie-orie-ay,
Fillame-orie-orie-ay,
To work upon the railway.

Coming up the hill from Ros Mór was a Scottish contingent singing:

Oh, ye'll tak' the high road
And I'll tak' the low road
And I'll be in Scotland afore ye,
But me and my true love will never meet again
On the bonnie, bonnie banks of Loch Lomond.

The two groups met at Jean's crossroads and roared out their songs at
each other. It should have been a cacophony, but somehow the two songs
blended into a glorious wall of sound echoing up to the lovely clear blue sky.

Jean laughed and sang first one, then the other, while Rosie danced
excitedly around her and the baby snoozed peacefully in her arms. All
this needs, she thought, is for a Cornish group to come along singing
"Camborne Hill," and a mob of Welsh belting out the "Cwm Rhondda."

Roaring their tunes, the singers watched the tall woman in the simple
green dress, the sun sparking highlights in her whisky-colored hair and
turning her bare throat and arms golden, a child in her arms and another
dancing at her feet. For a rare moment she glowed in the sunlight, in the
middle of waves of song, and the singers thought, sentimentally, that she
seemed the very spirit of Eilean Dubh, more so than if she'd been a statue in
the Ros Mór square.

Then someone recognized her, and the members of the group elbowed
each other and one brave soul shouted, "Give us a song, bonnie Jean!"

Oh, dear, she hadn't expected that, but how could she refuse? She cast about in her memory for a tune, and came up with:

How blythe was I ilk morn to see
My lad come o'er the hill,
He leaped the burn and ran to me.
I met him wi' good will.
Oh, the broom, the bonnie, bonnie, broom,
The broom o' the Cowdenknowes;
Fain would I be in my ain countrie,
Herding my faither's yowes.

She sang all the verses, her voice rippling out over Eilean Dubh's fair green pastures, as fair as those in the song, and the crowd joined in on the chorus.

She'd delighted them, and when she finished there were excited calls for another. She'd forgotten how greedy music lovers could be, and wondered what it would take to satisfy them, and how long her children would put up with an impromptu concert. The baby was quiet, but she could tell Rosie was getting restless and excited by the crowd. Any minute now she would turn to her latest passion—panties—and would start pushing up her mother's skirt to investigate what pair Jean was wearing today. Or she'd flop down on the grass and edge up her own skirt to slyly display her own current favorite, a jazzy yellow number imprinted with lurid pink roses, hot from the Co-Op.

Which would be more embarrassing, Jean wondered: her daughter's exhibitionism, or having to cope with the tantrum that would follow repressing it?

There was a disturbance in the ether, and Bonnie Prince Jamie materialized beside her, golden hair aglow in the sun, as handsome as a Greek god, his fiddle tucked under his arm. Rosie gave a squeal of delight and rushed him, demanding to be picked up. He shook his head and showed her the fiddle, and she contented herself with seizing a fistful of his trouser leg and leaning against him.

"Where did you come from?" asked Jean.

"I heard your lovely voice ringing out like a bell, *m'eudail,* and it drew me as a bee is drawn to honey. What shall we give them as an encore?"

"How about 'Dumbarton's Drums?'" He nodded, lifted his fiddle and Jean began with the chorus:

Dumbarton's drums they sound so bonnie,
And they remind me o' my Johnnie,
What fond delight doth steal upon me,
When Johnnie kneels and kisses me.

The song ended, and at the last repetition of the chorus, Jamie bent down and brushed his lips against Jean's.

A long drawn out "oooh" of envy from most of the women and some of the men echoed across the crossroads. Jean gasped and sighed, and felt her knees go weak.

Jamie grinned, put his fiddle under his chin again and danced the instrument into a lively Irish jig.

Feet began to move in rhythm, and dancers wafted out of the crowd and met in the center of the road in groups of five couples. This group began "The Haymaker's Jig," with advance and retire, then turning, swinging, lacing the shoe and arching. Another group of two men and four women were dancing "The Fairy Reel," performing diamonds and squares and the monkey's puzzle.

A young redheaded lad, the map of Ireland in his face, noticed Rosie's excitement, and danced over to her. He exchanged a look with Jean, and receiving her nod of approval, took the little girl's hands and chasséed her across the road and back, then around the circle of dancers and returned her to her mother's side, wide-eyed and giggling with excitement.

Jamie brought his impromptu concert to a close with a flourish. The dancers bowed, the others cheered, and the two groups parted and walked on.

The baby stirred in Jean's arms, and began to show familiar signs of wanting his mother's breast, smacking his lips and making rooting motions with his head. Jamie said, "Trade you the fiddle for the bairn." They made the swap and headed back to the cottage, Jamie cuddling the baby and murmuring to him to keep his mind off of lunch, and Jean cradling the precious fiddle in her arms. His creativity stirred by the crowd's joyful exuberance, Jamie felt music rising in his head, a march-like tune that he knew would be called "The Road from Ros Mór to Airgead."

The crowd began to wander off in separate directions. The Scottish voices struck up Robert Burns' stirring song about William Wallace, "Scots, Wha Hae." The Irish, not to be outdone, retaliated with "The Tri-Coloured Ribbon," as they headed off to Ros Mór.

Halfway to *Taigh a Mhorair,* Jean and Jamie heard another burst of singing led by an unmistakable voice. Darroch had walked down to Ros Mór for a loaf of bread, and had been discovered by members of his pod, and others who recognized him as the Magician, the Laird, or the wonderful male lead singer of *Tradisean.* Like the Pied Piper, he'd collected quite a crowd around him as he'd left the village.

He was leading them in *orain luadh,* Hebridean waulking songs, traditional chants sung by groups of women beating wet tweed to shrink it and make it more durable, "waulking" the cloth from hand to hand, thumping it rhythmically against a hard surface. This one was from South Uist, and he'd wowed the concert-goers with it the night before, teaching them the chorus so that the whole auditorium was soon roaring out the Gaelic. He sang:

Bho dhòrn gu dòrn, clò nan gillean.
(From hand to hand, the cloth of the lads.)
And the crowd roared out the chorus:
Iomair o hó, clò nan gillean!
(Waulk, o hó, the cloth of the lads!)
Darroch sang:
Luaidheam gu luath, clò nan gillean.
(Let me waulk quickly, the cloth of the lads.)
And the chorus rang out again.

At his crossroad, Darroch finished off the waulking song and left his followers with another round of cheers and applause ringing in his ears, and came to join his family and Jamie. They walked to *Taigh a Mhorair* for a cup of tea.

Darroch made the tea, and they sat around the kitchen table. Jean settled the baby to nurse. Rosie, at her side, piped up, "Uncle Jamie kissed Mama."

"Did he, indeed," said Darroch, looking from his wife to his best friend, eyebrows raised.

"I've no privacy any more with this little chatterbox around," mourned Jean. "Last week Rosie told Minister Donald that her Mama had beautiful pink panties trimmed with black lace, and she was going to have a pair, too, when she got a little older. And did he want to see the pretty ones she had on today? When she started to lift her skirt, poor Donald didn't know which way to look; he was so embarrassed. Helen saved the day, of course, by changing the subject to something a little more innocuous."

"Hmmmph," said Darroch. "About this kissing . . . "

"It was perfectly innocent," said Jean. "Just the high spirits of the morning."

"I'm not sure it was all that innocent," said Jamie. "Your wife is very kissable, Darroch."

"I know that fine. I'd like to think that her kisses were reserved for me. Most of the time, anyway."

"Most of the time," agreed Jamie. "Except for periods of high spirits."

"Exceptionally high spirits," said Darroch sternly.

"It's a good thing Nick Borth isn't here any more," said Jean. "Imagine what he'd have made of a simple kiss between friends."

Darroch hmmphed again, and thought he understood the character of Othello even better.

Forty-three

In Ros Mór once there lived a lass,
Y-callt the floo'er o' the Mac an Rìgh.
Resolved she her ain life tae lay doon
Tae win peace twixt her father, and his enemie.
She's drappit her needle and braided her hair,
And kiltit her white gown aboun her knee,
And gaen tae the dreid forest, where nane ither dare,
Frae to charm the MacQuirter, her clan's enemie.

"Gae oop! Gae awt! Thou'rt a witch; death to thee,
Sae dree ye your weird, tae be droukit in the sea!
There'll ne'er be peace twixt your clan and mine,
For I am your father's sworn enemie."
Oop crepit young MacQuirter, in her ear whispered he,
"But tak my hand, come along, come wi' me.
I'll tak ye safe home through yon forest dreid,
Though you are my father's ain enemie."

He's ta'en the lass by her snow white hand,
And through the dreid forest to her hame led her he.
Gained her father's consent, and they twa were wed,
Nae mair MacQuirter was Mac an Rìgh's enemie.

Eilean Dubh ballad,
translated by Darroch Mac an Rìgh into thirteenth century-style Scots

*J*ean and Darroch's tales and legends workshop met for several afternoons, and by the last meeting, on Thursday, everyone in the workshop had obtained a copy of Jean's new book, and had read it cover to cover. Now they clamored to hear Darroch tell an Eilean Dubh story in person. "One that's not in the book," said a participant.

"*Ceart math*," said Darroch. "Settle yourselves down comfortably, for this is a long one. It begins with an old ballad, and Jean and I will sing it." She tuned her guitar, and they began the legend of Fiona the Peacemaker.

How Clan Mac an Righ and Clan MacQuirter Were United

The Legend of Fiona the Peacemaker
As told by Darroch Mac an Righ

Once there was on Eilean Dubh a young girl named Fiona, the seventeen-year-old second daughter of the chief, Alasdair Darroch Mac an Rìgh. She was as empty-headed a lass as could be found in all of Eilean Dubh. She cared for nothing but music, dancing, storytelling and flirting, and could not fathom why all the young men of her clan did not feel the same way.

Instead of paying attention to her and her court of giggling maidens, they talked, practiced and thought of nothing but the art of war and their unending feud with Clan MacQuirter, whose land adjoined that of the Mac an Rìghs. Oh, the young men were attentive enough at nights around the communal fire, but let one stalwart youth approach another and the talk quickly turned to fletching arrows, tomorrow's wrestling competition, and what they would do to a MacQuirter should they ever catch one.

It was the same even if the youths had pretty maidens nestled as close to them as they dared, given the eagle eyes of their mothers. The young women had to pretend interest, and that was so boring. After all, they didn't spend their time with their swains talking about washing clothes and cooking, which were their daily tasks.

Fiona, the Mac an Rìgh chief's middle daughter, decided to do something about the situation, and her wild imagination led her to an even wilder idea. She would go herself, under a flag of truce, and negotiate a cease-fire with the MacQuirters. The idea appealed to her immensely. Not only would it be an amazing adventure, it would ensure her a role in clan history as Fiona the Peacemaker. She would be famous forever as the valiant (and beautiful) lass who'd risked her life for a grand cause.

The adventure had to be carried out with the utmost secrecy, for if her father the chief got wind of it, he'd lock her in her room on bread and water until she was a doddering old woman in her thirties, or until he could find a man brave enough to take on her management.

She knew whom he'd choose, too. Not one of the handsome young fellows, but someone of mature years. A widower, like as not, with children her own age, or older. She'd be saddled not only with an old man, but with a passel of ornery brats as well.

She wouldn't mind having one of the lads for a husband, as long as he was bold, spirited and lusty, and could promise her a good time in and out of bed. When they thought the young lasses weren't listening, the married women in her clan whispered about what it was like to be bedded by their men, and it sounded quite *miorbhuileach* to Fiona. So much so that she'd tried a shenanigan or two with a couple of the bolder lads, and had very much enjoyed their stolen kisses and fondling hands.

She'd never let anyone make love to her, though, no mattered how hot she and the lad got. She'd no intention of being trapped into marriage with some gormless young lout, handsome though he might be, and skilled with mouth and hands.

Fiona was led astray by her popularity with the young men and the knowledge of her own desirability, both as a beauty and as the chief's daughter. She knew she had only to tell a wistful suitor to jump, and he'd say, "How high?"

So her inflated ego led her into a very dangerous conclusion. Inflamed by legends of great deeds, all done by men and recited around the fire by the storytellers—the *seanachaidhean*—she decided on a course of action. When she'd interceded with the MacQuirter chief (who by most accounts was a hairy, yellow-bearded barbarian), and made peace, the young men would no longer talk about battle, but about music and dancing and love.

She rather thought she'd wear a white flowing dress on her adventure, and her beautiful black hair loose on her shoulders, with perhaps a bit or two of heather braided into it when she approached the MacQuirter chief. She'd fall to her knees before him, spread her arms wide, and present such an appealing picture that the MacQuirters one and all would be hers to command.

Foolhardy as she was, she was not foolhardy enough to undertake her mission at night. The woods that divided Mac an Rìgh and MacQuirter lands were so thick in places that a man had to go through them sideways, like an eel through rocks in the sea, and they were interlaced with horrible bogs that would suck down an unwary traveler. She'd need the light of day to make the trip safely.

Afternoon was best for her purpose. It was summer, and everyone rose at daybreak, and broke their fast at mid-morning with an enormous meal of venison, roast pig, thick hearty soups and stews. And mugs of ale to wash it all down with, which left the clansfolk fat and stupefied by food, and ready for the traditional two hour nap over midday when the sun was at its hottest.

On the day that began her great adventure, Fiona ate heartily, knowing that she had a long walk ahead of her, but she drank sparingly of the ale, limiting herself to two mugs so that she could keep her wits about her.

When the great hall was filled with snoring bodies, Fiona crept from her place at the chief's table and up the stairs to the room shared with her sisters.

She pulled her finest gown from her storage chest, then stopped and looked at it in dismay. There was a huge grease spot at stomach level on the gown's front, a souvenir of an evening feast several weeks ago. Feckless as ever, she'd forgotten to rub wood ashes on the spot and put it to soak in the burn.

She couldn't fling herself down in front of the MacQuirter with a great grease spot on her belly. She'd look like a kitchen wench instead of a chief's daughter, and would be lucky to escape a cuff round the ears, and to be laughed back into the kitchen and ordered to scour the pots.

After a few moments thought, she came to the obvious conclusion. She'd borrow her older sister Mairead's best white linen dress. Mairead was such a fanatic for cleanliness that no grease ever dripped from her chin, and no bit of meat would have the effrontery to drop into her lap.

Surely Mairead would not mind her dress being used in the noble cause of peace. Fiona pushed out of her mind the thought of her sister's notorious temper, and donned the dress. Mairead was a good three inches shorter than Fiona, and less generously endowed in bosom and hips, and the dress, loosely cut as it was, hugged Fiona tightly in crucial places, and showed off her pretty ankles in a brazen way. Still, it would have to do.

Fiona pulled from the chest her oldest cloak, of an unattractive brown that had faded to mud color, and wrapped it around herself to conceal the white dress, hoping that no one would see her and ask why she was such a fool as to wear a wool cloak on the hottest day of the summer.

Ready at last, she crept down the great wooden stairs and threaded her way cautiously through her slumbering clansfolk. Young Seumas woke from his slumbers, and stared at her dumbly. Fiona put her fingers to her lips and smiled in a conspiratorial way. He smiled back, puzzled, and fell asleep again.

The guard at the door, though half awake, was inclined to stop her, until she drew herself up regally and waved at him to open the door.

Who was he to disobey a command from the chief's second daughter? He pulled the door open, and she passed through.

Outside, she glanced around cautiously, then headed for the path that led to the tiny seaside settlement called Airgead. It was a well-traveled path by both Mac an Rìghs and MacQuirters, who'd go along it to meet and barter and trade during the few times when they weren't at war.

It led through the dark thick woods. She had forgotten just how alarming the forest could be, even from a path in broad daylight. Creaks, groans, whimpers issued weirdly from the trees around her, and even though she knew the creaks were tree limbs swaying in the breeze, the moans were gusts of wind, and the whimpers were from small forest animals disturbed by her passing, still she began to be frightened, and remember the *seanachaidhean's* tales of spirits and beasties that lurked just outside their settlement.

Most particularly she remembered the legend of the Great Gray Man that stalked travelers on dark nights. It took little imagination to conjure up one lurching after her.

It had been a bright sunny day when she'd started out, and rays of sunlight had occasionally penetrated the thick canopy of branches overhead. Now, she realized, it was growing dark, and clouds were beginning to cover the sun.

Please don't let it start to rain, Fiona prayed, and as if on cue drops began to patter on the overhanging leaves.

Please don't let it become a downpour, she prayed, and as if to mock her, rain began to lash down through the branches. She hugged her cloak closer and began to run, pursued in her imagination by the Great Gray Man so close behind her that she could feel its cold breath on her spine. Or perhaps it was the rain, slicing through the trees and down her neck.

She rushed headlong down the path, snapping branches, and, whimpering loudly with fear, she burst into a clearing that marked the beginning of MacQuirter land, and directly into the path of two very surprised MacQuirter clansmen, who'd been set to guard their border.

They'd been telling stories, each man trying to frighten the other, and the first had just finished a tale about a wicked forest fairy who seduced mortals into her clutches and away from their souls, when Fiona tripped over a root and fell at their feet.

Fiona's sudden arrival frightened them almost as much as it frightened her, and their dirks were in their hands in the short space of time it took them to drop the wineskins with which they'd been enlivening their boring duty.

In an instant they were on her. One yanked her head up by her hair, and the other aimed his dirk at her exposed throat.

Fiona shrieked.

"Kill it! Kill it before it seduces our souls!" shouted one of the guards.

Fiona thrust her hand up to fend off the dagger just in time, and gasped, "I come in peace!"

"Why do you hesitate, *a Fhionnlagh*?" shouted the first man, who was almost as broad as he was tall, with fearsome bristling black eyebrows. "Has it stolen your soul already?"

"Ach, it's naught but a wee lassie, *a Mhurchadh*, ye great puling bairn," said Fionnlagh, an immensely tall man with wide shoulders. "Look, she's smiling, aren't you, lass?"

Fiona managed a tremulous smile.

"Wicked fairies can smile, ye gowk! Kill it!" and Murchadh raised his dirk and aimed it at Fiona's breast.

Fionnlagh said, "I'll not have the death of a young lass on my soul. Besides, she might be someone important to be coming so boldly through the woods like that. Maybe the chief has sent someone to spy on us, to make sure we're doing our duty as guards."

"Kill her, then, and she'll not be able to tell tales on us."

"She's very bonnie," said Fionnlagh, who'd pulled Fiona's cloak open and was appreciating the curves of her body clothed in the tight dress.

"Aye, so she is. Let's take our pleasure of her first, then kill her."

"Please don't," begged Fiona, now truly terrified. This peacemaking business was not going at all as she'd planned.

Fionnlagh said, not unkindly, "One chance, lass. Who are you and why are you in our woods? You're not a MacQuirter. Make your story a good one, or you'll have to die."

Fiona drew herself up, hid her trembling hands in the fold of her cloak, and said with as much dignity as she could muster, "I come to the MacQuirter chief to seek peace between our clans."

Both men gawked at her. Murchadh growled, "Peace? Who wants peace? How is a man to prove his bravery if he's not tested by facing death in battle?"

"Hush yer whist, *a Mhurchadh,* for God's sake; you chatter like an old woman. Who are you, lass?"

Fiona drew herself up proudly. "I am the second eldest daughter of Alasdair *Mór* Mac an Rìgh, the great chief of Ros Mór and all the lands surrounding it."

The two men stared at her appraisingly. Then Murchadh growled, "She is a spy, just as I told you. Let's rape her and kill her, and take her head to the MacQuirter for a reward."

"Ach, ye great daftie, she's worth more to us alive than dead. Their chief will pay handsomely to get her back untouched, for I'll wager she's a virgin. Only a virgin could be silly enough to march onto our lands in search of peace. Come along, lass." To his companion Fionnlagh said, "Lead the way, *a Mhurchadh,* and I'll guard her from the rear in case she tries to slip away. We'll take her, head and body joined, to the MacQuirter."

Conscious that she was in trouble far beyond her imagination, Fiona stumbled along between the two hulking clansmen. She needed to relieve herself, her cloak was sopping wet with rain, and she was terribly afraid that she'd torn her sister's dress when she'd stumbled over the root and fallen. The idea of Mairead's wrath made the idea of being murdered by the MacQuirters almost palatable.

After a long, miserable walk, they came to a large clearing surrounded by small wooden shacks, and in the center a taller building, like the Mac an Rìgh chieftain's great hall. "My father's house is bigger," she muttered under her breath, but not loudly enough for her captors to hear.

They entered the hall, and a stunned silence fell when the assembled crowd turned and spotted the two guards and their prisoner.

"*A Ruairidh Mhór!*" shouted Murchadh, eager to get his announcement in before Fionnlagh spoke. "We have brought you a prize. We've captured a Mac an Rìgh spy!"

At the end of the great hall was a dais, and on it was a long wooden table at which sat a handful of people resplendent in fur-trimmed robes. One of them rose, pushed back his mane of yellow hair with a giant paw, and thundered, "Bring your captive forward."

Murchadh grabbed Fiona roughly by one arm, and Fionnlagh took the other, whispering in her ear, "Courage, lass. Hold your head high."

Fiona stumbled forward between the two men.

The loudest voice she'd ever heard bellowed, "This is your captive? All hail my brave guards, who've subdued a ferocious slip of a boy."

"It's a lass," mumbled Murchadh.

The voice of Ruairidh *Mór* erupted again. "A lass? My stalwart warriors have conquered a wee lassie? How did you dare accomplish such a feat?"

The great hall erupted in laughter.

Fiona was very conscious that she did not look her best. Her hair was tangled with leaves and twigs, her face, hands and cloak were covered with dirt, and the white dress on which she'd staked so much was ripped in several places. Mairead would burn the dress, then kill her. Slowly.

"Come forward, lass, and speak to us." The huge chieftain's voice rumbled like a slide of rocks down a hill.

Fiona stepped forward, trembling, and when she dared look up she gasped. Ruairidh *Mór* was a giant of a man, and on the dais he towered like a mighty oak. His shoulders were broad, his belly magnificent, and his legs were like two ancient pine trees, gnarled and bristly. His hair was bright yellow and fell in magnificent abundance over his massive shoulders, framing a face crowded with strong features and finished off with a rippling yellow beard. Icy blue eyes glared at Fiona, but his voice was surprisingly kind. "Who are you, lass, and where do you come from?"

"She's a witch from the forest," offered Murchadh, "and she tried to steal our souls. I wanted to kill her, but Fionnlagh said no."

Unease spread through the crowd. A woman shouted, "A witch!" and the crowd hastily stepped back.

"I am not a witch," said Fiona indignantly. "I am the second eldest daughter of the chief of Clan Mac an Rìgh, and I come in peace." She added the last part hastily, as the faces in the crowd turned threatening while they contemplated the idea of a Mac an Rìgh on MacQuirter land.

Ruairidh *Mór* drew himself up, offended. "Why does the Mac an Rìgh send his daughter—his second eldest daughter, at that—to sue for peace? Has he no stalwart sons fit for the task?"

"My father doesn't know I'm here," mumbled Fiona. "I came on my own."

Ruairidh *Mór* stared at her, dumbfounded. What was he to do with her? The chief's son, well, that was simple enough: test him in various feats of strength against MacQuirter men, then send him home defeated, his tail between his legs.

But a lass! What was he to do, set her to a trial of butter-churning against a MacQuirter woman? He sighed deeply. There was no help for it. Honor—his and the Mac an Rìgh's—demanded the ultimate sacrifice. And soon, for his clansfolk were growing restless, and murmurs of "Kill the witch!" were increasing in volume.

Twice widowed, pushing fifty, with five sons (three living) and four pert daughters, the MacQuirter figured that he'd done his duty to the clan. He deserved an entire bed to himself, and the freedom to bathe or not, as he chose, and to eat and drink whatever he pleased without a woman constantly nagging him about his girth. But he would have to make the ultimate sacrifice. Luckily, the lass was a pretty armful.

"In the name of peace between our two great clans, I, Ruairidh *Mór*, will honor the Mac an Rìgh by taking his second eldest daughter to wife," he announced.

Fiona stared at him in horror. Her situation had definitely gone from bad to worse. She blurted, "But I don't want to marry you!"

The crowd erupted with anger. "She has insulted the MacQuirter! Kill her!"

Ruairidh *Mór* frowned menacingly to conceal the fact that he was thinking hard. She didn't want to marry him, which was *miorbhuileach*, but she had to marry someone, or be sent home dishonored, which would lead to a tedious and bloody confrontation with the Mac an Rìghs.

He glanced around the room. His eldest son was already wed, and his youngest had disappeared, having anticipated his father's next move and decided to play least in sight.

"Then you shall marry my second son, Hugh *Dubh*," he announced.

A furious shriek erupted from the crowd, and the woman who'd first cried "witch," Elspeth, a buxom beauty with flashing eyes, heaving breasts and a mop of hair the color of straw, shouldered her way to the center of the room.

"Hugh *Dubh* is promised to me!" she shouted. "And he's taken my virginity as proof of his love. Even now I may be quickening with his child. He shall not marry that wicked witch, who comes flouncing onto our land pretending to sue for peace. And any man who wants peace is a great woman of a man, anyway."

Hugh *Dubh* blushed, watching his would-be fiancée reveal the formerly private details of their liaison, which he'd carefully kept secret from his father and hers. Now he looked up at Ruairidh *Mór* apologetically and shrugged his shoulders, hoping that combined filial wrath would not fall upon his hapless head.

Fiona made a desperate attempt to seize control of the situation. "I don't want to marry anyone! I've, uh, taken a vow to remain a virgin all my life, and, uh, spend my days in prayer for peace and prosperity."

"A likely story, ye brazen hussy," shouted Elspeth, and women's heads nodded in agreement.

Thoroughly flummoxed, the MacQuirter turned to his elderly, somewhat addled, advisor, Seumas Peadair *as sine*. "What am I to do?"

"You took your time in asking," grumbled the old man. "The solution is simple enough: put her to the test and let the sea decide whether or not she is a witch."

Ruairidh *Mór* shuddered. Chain this beautiful young lass to the horrible *Creag a' Bhàis*, the Rock of Death, where she could contemplate her sins while the tide rose slowly up to cover her head, and she drowned? Not even a witch could turn the tide, and the girl would die, slowly and dreadfully.

He sighed deeply, and looked at Fiona in pity. "So be it. The test it is. Murchadh and Fionnlagh, as the lass's captors, I charge you to take her to *Creag a' Bhàis.*" As the two hulking men moved forward, Murchadh eagerly and Fionnlagh with reluctance, the MacQuirter added, "Chain her loosely, so that she does not suffer, and take yourselves away, so that she may have the solitude to prepare herself for death. When the sun begins to set, we shall all come to the Rock to see if she has been spared."

"Now just a minute," began Fiona, but was whisked away by her captors for her date with the Rock of Death. The MacQuirter silently watched her leave. He scanned the crowd, and when he caught sight of his youngest son skulking near the doorway, he jerked his head at that youth to indicate that he wanted a conference, and with no delay.

Dragged between her two guards, Fiona stumbled along a steep and rocky path towards the roaring sea. At last the trio reached their goal, a large jagged rock erupting from the sea on the pebbled shore. *Creag a' Bhàis* was flat on the side facing the water, and to each of its halves, top and bottom, iron rings had been attached. Fiona was shoved up against the rock facing the sea, and her hands were seized and tied with rope to the upper rings.

"Now her feet," growled Murchadh.

"No! You heard the MacQuirter. She is to be made comfortable in her last hours. She's but a wee lass; there's no need to tie her feet."

"Very well," growled Murchadh, and approached the helpless Fiona, his hands grasping the bottom of his ragged kilt.

"What are you about, man?" snapped Fionnlagh.

"I'm going to take my pleasure of her."

"You can't do that. She's a maiden."

"Aye, well, she should know a man before she dies," Murchadh snarled, raising his kilt purposefully.

Fionnlagh drew his dirk, and stepped in front of the girl. "Over my dead body will you rape her. She deserves to die a virgin."

"I don't want to die at all," cried Fiona. "Can't you just take me to the path into the forest and let me go, and pretend I'd escaped?"

"Lass, if I could I would, but the MacQuirter has ordered you to the test by the sea, and I'll not go against his orders. I'm sorry it's come to this, and I humbly beg your forgiveness." He nudged his companion roughly. "Go on, beg her pardon."

"I'll beg her pardon after I've had my way with her," said Murchadh, advancing toward Fiona and her defender.

Recovering her spirit—she was, after all a Mac an Rìgh, and the second eldest daughter of a great chief—Fiona shouted, "Touch me and I'll curse you to all eternity! Your man's parts will wither and fall off, your hair will turn gray, you'll become as weak as the wee-est bairn in your clan, you'll . . . " Unable to think of anything more dire, she drew herself up and glared defiantly.

"Witch," snarled Murchadh, but took a step backward. Perhaps enjoying her wasn't worth the risk, after all. But he would humiliate her in her death. He shouldered his way past a startled Fionnlagh, whipped out his dirk, seized the front of Mairead's poor dress, and sliced it all the way to the hem. The wind flicked it open, and for a moment both men were treated to a view of Fiona's fine young breasts, belly and legs. Then the wind blew her clothes about her, and Fionnlagh seized his companion by the shoulders and marched him away, shouting over his shoulder, "God save you, lass!"

Left all alone, Fiona saw the sun beginning its slow descent, and felt the water lapping at her knees. At last her gallant, befuddled spirit faltered, and she began to weep. Tears rolled from her eyes, fat and salty, as she wept for her parents, her brothers and sisters at home whom she'd never seen again, and even for the wreck of Mairead's best dress, now hanging in shreds around her.

Fiona wept, great scalding tears that burned her cheeks, and choking sobs that shook her body. Later she'd stop weeping, make her peace with the One Who Listens and prepare for death, but now she was weeping like the frightened seventeen-year-old girl that she was.

Around the corner of *Creag a' Bhàis* appeared a head, its most prominent feature a sharply pointed nose that seemed designed to peer around corners. The head was crowned with a mop of hair that couldn't make up its mind whether to be red or yellow. Cool blue eyes surveyed the scene, then widened as the wind whipped Fiona's dress away and exposed her luscious curves and her skin glowing golden in the sunset.

The eyes stared, the body hardened, then their owner abruptly withdrew so that he could get himself under control. Lust was not part of the bargain he had made with the MacQuirter; rescue was.

A glance showed him that the maiden was discreetly covered again, and he sprang forward into Fiona's view.

She gasped. She was going to be raped, and this time there was no kindly Fionnlagh to save her. She opened her mouth, ready to give voice to a wail of despair.

She was stopped before she began by a hand clamped fiercely over her mouth. "Hush yer whist, or we'll have the whole clan down our throats. If you can be silent, I'll have both hands to free you. Understand?"

Fiona nodded, and the hand was removed. Silently she watched the young man pick fiercely at the rope tying her hands to the iron rings, cursing and mumbling in frustration under his breath. At last, desperate, he drew his dirk and sawed through the ropes, and they dropped into the water, out of his reach. "Come away, there's no time to lose," he hissed. "The sea will have us both if we don't hurry."

And indeed, the sea was lapping at their thighs, trying to suck them into its embrace.

He seized her hand and started forward, Fiona stumbling on the rocks as she tried to keep up, her stiff cold limbs refusing to cooperate and her wet cloak dragging her down. But he was relentless; he dragged her on until she nearly fell. Conscious of the need to hurry—the sun was sinking fast and that was the signal for the clan to gather on the shore and keen the departed soul to its eternal rest—he wrapped an arm around her waist to hurry her on.

Fiona yanked her cloak around her body, picked up her feet with determination, and plunged bravely forward to the shore, where he yanked her into a run towards the dark forest.

When they reached the shelter of the trees, he stopped and looked keenly around. Finding the path he sought, he pulled her forward again and they plunged into the forest. To Fiona it was all one mass of twisted branches and out-thrust roots, but he seemed to know where he was going.

Raghnall, the chief's youngest son, was what the other young men called a *fear sona*, a head-in-the-clouds layabout. Men his own age gathered together to tell lies, sharpen their knives, and amuse themselves with contests of wrestling that left them filthy and disheveled, to their womenfolk's' loudly voiced dismay.

That was not for Raghnall. He spent his free time in the woods, learning the nearly invisible paths that cut through it, learning what was edible and what was not, finding trees to strip for basket-weaving bark, clay deposits for pottery making, and setting snares for rabbits. Since he always returned from his expeditions with booty of some kind, he got away with his unexplained absences. The lads who scoffed at his endeavors received cuffings from their mothers and sisters, who demanded to know why they were not as resourceful and useful as young Raghnall.

This did not make him overly popular with his compatriots, but no one challenged him any more after an episode several years ago when he'd been goaded into a wrestling contest, and had soundly thrashed his two challengers because he was lithe, quick and intuitively understood balance and momentum.

Since then Raghnall and the others had operated in an uneasy state of truce, and he was being whispered about as a successor to Seumas Peadair *as sine*, the cranky old wise man.

Now he faced his greatest challenge, that of getting this foolish young lass safely back to her clan.

The sun was setting as they slipped into the woods, and Raghnall's keen ears caught the sound of many voices. Clan MacQuirter was coming to the Rock of Death to see if the witch had escaped, or if an innocent maiden had met a watery end.

A chill ran down his spine. He had a head start of only minutes, and the young girl with him was frightened, exhausted and cold, her wet shoes squeaking and sloshing with every step. He'd not make good time with her.

A cry rose from the shore, first of awe, then swiftly changing to anger. Raghnall felt a wave of despair. It had been too much to hope that his clan would think that Fiona was indeed a witch, and had escaped by magic. The ropes that had bound the girl must have drifted back with the tide. One glance at the cut strands would establish beyond doubt that the Mac an Rìgh witch had had help in making her escape.

And, he realized, as his spirits sank into his sopping wet boots, it would not take too much imagination for his kinfolk to figure out who had helped her. Once they began to take attendance, he would be conspicuous by his absence.

They would be furious that he had helped the witch to escape, and his father would not dare defend him. He was an outcast from his clan.

It frightened him terribly and for a moment he thought of turning around, pushing Fiona ahead of him and shouting that he'd captured the runaway witch.

He relinquished the idea without a second thought. The girl was now under his protection, and it was his duty as a MacQuirter and to his chief to get her home safely. Honor demanded no less.

"Not a word," he hissed in Fiona's ear. "Hold firmly to my hand and be silent."

She obeyed, stifling her groans and cries of pain as branches slapped her in the face, twigs scratched her arms, and rocks dug into the soft leather of her shoes. She wanted very much to tell him that she had enough sense to be quiet, and actually had her mouth open to do so, when the noises from the shore rose to howls and the crackling and snapping of tree limbs indicated that they were being pursued into the woods by the furious MacQuirters.

Fiona had never been so frightened in her life. The hair on the back of her head rose on end and a gurgle of terror escaped her throat.

A frantic jerk on her hand stifled the gurgle, and she followed as quietly as she could, hearing his muttered curses when she stumbled on a loose rock or caromed off of a tree.

Raghnall knew it was a race against time. If he could get to one of his secret clearings before it got dark, they could spend the night there safely. The MacQuirters would not dare follow them into the forest once the light was gone.

The sky was purpling as the sun slipped below the horizon. The angry shouts behind them rose to a crescendo, then subsided to a muttering, and finally died away altogether. Desperate to reach his goal, he dragged Fiona on, with little care now for the noise either of them made. Just as the last flicker of twilight began to fade, they stumbled into his bolthole. He had just enough light left to locate the pile of brush that served him as a bed before they were plunged into darkness.

He had several of these refuges scattered throughout the forest, as he was always conscious that sudden fierce storms might strand him overnight. Each was stocked with a brush bed, a skin bag full of water and another holding dried meat, a torch dipped in pitch, and stones and twigs for fire making.

He'd stayed overnight in each one, once because he'd been stranded by bad weather, and twice just to prove he could do it. Each overnight absence had added to his knowledge as a woodsman. And, he realized unhappily, this absence would confirm what his clan must suspect by now: that he had rescued the witch. Any hope that he'd had of returning to his family was dashed forever. He could only hope that the clan would not take out their anger on his father.

The darkness in the forest was absolute. Fiona had never experienced such darkness before; at home there had always been a fire burning all night in their village. She stood stock still, afraid to move in any direction for fear of stepping in a hole or falling off a cliff.

Raghnall took both her hands and coaxed her down gently into the pile of brush. "It's all right; it's safe," he said.

At those reassuring words Fiona's knees buckled, and she collapsed in a heap on the scratchy, pine-scented brush.

Raghnall allowed himself a few moments to catch his breath. Then he felt around for the tree against which the brush was piled, and for the ropes that hung down from it. He pulled one, and down came his bag of dried meat. He touched it carefully, and was relieved to find that no marauding animal had gnawed its way through the bag. A pull on the second rope brought down the water bag.

"I'll spread out my cloak, lass, so we can both sit upon it." And keep away from the spiders and the mice nesting in the brush, he was about to say, but thought better of it.

He opened the water bag, and conveyed it through the darkness to Fiona's hands.

She'd never tasted anything so *miorbhuileach* as the brackish, skin-tasting water, or the tough sliver of dried meat that he offered her next. "Chew on it a while to soften it up," he advised.

They dined in exhausted silence. Presently the moon rose, and shone so brightly through the trees that they could see each other's faces. The moonlight was a great relief to them both, for he'd not dared to make a fire so close to the MacQuirter village.

Fiona studied her rescuer shyly. She could only make out a mop of hair and reassuringly broad shoulders. "Thank you for rescuing me," she said.

"Think nothing of it," he said, not allowing the bitter regret he felt show in his voice. In the space of a few short hours his entire life had been destroyed, all to save this girl. Ah, well, he thought, you wished for adventure, and now you've got it.

He contemplated the painful possibility that he would never again see his father the Chief, his dear mother, his two aggravating brothers, his three bossy sisters. Gone was his future as the successor to Seumas Peadair *as sine*, and advisor to his brother when he became chief. Gone was the pretty gaggle of yellow-haired MacQuirter lasses, three of whom he'd been contemplating as bride possibilities, some time in the future.

Life now held nothing for him but the wandering path of the outcast.

Just then the moon came out from behind a cloud, and illuminated Fiona's mass of black hair, turning it to liquid silver. Raghnall blinked. Perhaps things weren't so bad after all. He said, "We need to sleep now; we'll have to rise early and make our way off MacQuirter land. If you need to relieve yourself, go to the edge of the clearing."

Fiona did as he suggested, and felt much better. She had time at last to contemplate her ruined clothes, and realized suddenly that a great deal of her was on display. We've got to sleep, he'd said, and she was quite aware that he meant for them to sleep together on the brush pile, rolled into his cloak. Common sense demanded no less.

And self-preservation demanded that as much as possible of her should be covered, to keep her rescuer from temptation. She'd been close to rape today, and half naked in front of three men, and her maidenly modesty had received a severe wake-up call. Men were interested in her body, and it behooved her to keep herself covered.

She yanked up the hem of her dress and tore off a long strip, then wrapped the pieces of the ruined dress around her and tied it shut with the makeshift sash. She pulled the old brown cloak close.

The two of them arranged themselves as comfortably as they could on the brush, Fiona preserving a safe distance between her body and his. But he reached out a long arm and dragged her to him, and wrapped the wool cloak over her so tightly that she could not wiggle away.

She decided that she did not want to wiggle away. His body was warm and reassuring against hers, and one of his bare legs was thrown over one of hers, and the combination of warmth and bare skin was so exquisite that she nearly swooned. Instead, she fell asleep.

Fiona slept soundly, but Raghnall could not allow himself that luxury. He knew his kinsmen and he knew it was unlikely that they'd venture into the nighttime forest in search of the witch and the traitor. But there was one or two young men who might, with pitch torches, tackle the wilderness for the glory of the capture. To be taken would mean death for the pair of them, a painful, messy death. It might even mean the overthrow of his father the Chief by his rival, his cousin Dòmhnall MacQuirter, who would argue, with justice, that a man whose son had turned traitor was not trust-worthy to lead the clan.

He slept fitfully and woke often, disturbed by any crackle of brush under the feet of a passing fox or weasel. The third time he woke the moon was disappearing into the trees and a chill wind had begun to blow. He snuggled closer to the girl, pulling his cloak up around their shoulders. She muttered something and wiggled, raising havoc in his body. Damn, she was a tempting armful. He realized that she was trying to turn over, and loosened his hold, and was rewarded by the touch of her soft cheek against his chin, then her breath on his throat. When she nestled her hand in his chest curls he nearly fainted with pleasure. Fiona was too exhausted to be entirely aware of what was going on between them, but she was young and healthy enough to be aroused by his closeness, even in her sleep.

The fourth time Raghnall woke up, the sky was ablaze with stars. He stared up at them, then suddenly became aware of a presence, very close to them. Old Seumas Peadair's stories of forest willies and boggles came to frightening life in his mind, and he went cold with terror.

Then he heard something snuffling, and felt the lightest of touches on his back. He lay absolutely still. The snuffling intensified, and something pawed at his hip.

He relaxed. On his nights alone in the forest he'd experienced the curi-osity of wild animals, felt their warm moist breath on his face, been poked in the back by large investigating noses. Once something had taken an exploratory nibble on his right arm, prompting him into a yelp of indigna-tion, and a rise to a sitting posture. The terrified animal had backed away, and after a tense moment while he wondered if it had felt threatened enough to go on the attack, it had suddenly snorted in defiance, then turned and crashed off through the trees, not even taking care to be quiet.

This visitor was a wolf, he reckoned, and a big one, judging by the weight of the paw draped over his hip. If he lay still it would lose interest and slink away.

Fiona stirred in his arms and opened her eyes, and found herself staring by the light of the stars into the deeply shadowed eye sockets of a large hulking shape with its jaw wide open (it was panting with nervousness), that seemed about to chomp down on her rescuer's shoulder.

What came out of her mouth was not a scream; she hadn't breath for one. It was a half a shout of defiance, half a chortle of terror. Raghnall stiffened in shock and the wolf leaped in the air in surprise, then jumped away. It went down on its front paws like a playful dog, yelped defiantly, then slunk away into the forest.

Raghnall stared at Fiona, who was raised on her elbows, head high, black hair billowing around her shoulders like an animal's mane. "You're a brave lassie," he said, grinning, "to frighten off that old wolf."

"I thought it was going to eat you, and I had to save your life, as you saved mine."

"My thanks to you, my brave rescuer. Now come down under the covers before you take a chill."

She snuggled down, and once again one of her hands tangled in his chest hair. His hand went to her shoulder, which he was pleased to discover was bare. In fact, quite a bit of her was bare, as the sash had come undone with her movements.

He whispered, "What's your name, lassie?"

"Fiona Mac an Rìgh, second eldest daughter of the chief of the Mac an Rìghs. What's yours?"

"Raghnall MacQuirter, third son of the chief of the MacQuirters."

"Thank you for saving my life, Raghnall."

"It was my duty, and my father's command."

"Oh. Your father is quite . . . umm . . . "

"Fearsome," finished Raghnall with a sigh.

"I was going to say majestic, and handsome. But I didn't want to marry him."

"Nay, he's too old for you."

"How old are you?" she said.

"Seventeen years."

"Oh. I'm seventeen too. Why are you not married?"

He shrugged. "Never yet met a lass I wanted to marry. Why aren't you?"

"Never met the right lad."

Abruptly the clouds passed, and all the stars in the world came out at once, and the sky was so bright that they could see each other's face.

"You're a bonnie lass. What color are your eyes?"

"Green as the blanket of clover that covers the hills in summer. Yours?"

"Blue, like the sky on a summer day. What color is your hair?"

"Golden-red like the sky at sunset, and it's the same color on my chest, where your little hand is playing."

Fiona gasped, and would have snatched her hand away, but he seized it and held it to his chest. "Leave it there; I like it. Do you like this?" He caressed her bare shoulder, pushing the torn remnants of her dress down to her elbow. From there it was a short trip to her breast, and he slipped his hand around it. "And do you like this?" he whispered, as his thumb fondled her nipple.

This is what men enjoyed, Fiona thought, remembering the hopeful caresses of her suitors, and how reluctant she'd been to turn away, as she knew she must. But she'd enjoyed those caresses too, and she was enjoying his warm hand even more than any suitor she'd ever had. "I like it," she said, and pushed herself against him boldly.

They nestled together, and their lips met. Both found the kiss delightful, and it grew deeper and deeper until teeth and tongues became involved. Stars and danger and the hard young body pressed against hers swept away any caution that Fiona might have felt, and replaced it with a firm determination to explore more of him. She yanked at the bottom of his shirt and pulled it upwards.

Dizzy with the possibilities that the night had brought him, Raghnall sat up and pulled his shirt over his head. He unfastened his belt and kicked his great kilt off. Then he turned to the girl. He found the torn edges of Mairead's poor dress and pulled them away, then pulled her chemise over her head until she was as exposed as he was. He pressed his pelvis against hers and moved slowly back and forth, relishing the sensation of naked body against naked body.

Fiona was now fully aware of what was about to happen, and she welcomed it eagerly. Raghnall was brave and strong, and her rescuer, and she'd never met a man like him before. "I'm a virgin," she whispered.

"So am I," he said. "Shall we learn the way of love together?"

"Aye." She'd almost been dead twice, and she might yet be dead before she got through this adventure, and she didn't want to die before she became a woman. He was going to make her a woman now, and she could hardly wait. At last she'd know what all the married women of her clan had whispered about. She lifted her hips invitingly, and purred her consent.

He moved on top of her, and found, awkwardly, the place where they should be joined, and entered her. "Oh, my," Fiona squeaked, as he slid deeper. "Ouch!" she wailed, as he thrust through the barrier that separated girl from woman.

"Am I hurting you?"

"Aye, a wee bit."

"I am sorry," and he was, but he couldn't stop, for the sensation was so delightful that he had to explore it more fully. He began to move with long deep strokes that made her gasp, until finally she could stand it no longer and gave way to a long satisfied wail that made the forest animals shiver and huddle deep into their burrows, terrified at the wild creature that had been unleashed into their midst.

They fell asleep, and woke several hours later, and he loved her again until both of them were drowsy with contentment.

Raghnall woke to a glorious sunrise, and found the impudent young hussy draped over him, nibbling at his nipple and rotating her hips against him invitingly. Then she used her fingers to guide him inside, tightening her sore muscles around him until he groaned and began to thrust upwards, helpless against her invitation. Dear God, maybe she is a witch after all, he thought.

At last Fiona rolled off of him and sat up, combing her long black hair with her fingers into a braid. She grinned down at her lover. "Good morning to you, m'eudail."

"And to you. We should be off. We must reach your father's lands before we are caught by my people."

Fiona pouted. "Can we not stay here in the forest and make love and live with the animals and the trees forever?"

It was a tempting thought, but highly impractical. "We'll run out of food, and we can't live on love alone. Come along now, have a bit of meat and some water, and we'll be on our way."

Fiona sighed, and cast around in the folds of his great kilt for her torn chemise. She put it on back to front, and put the wreckage of Mairead's dress over it, and ripped loose another piece of fabric to tie around her for a sash. "I'm ready," she announced.

Now began the greatest challenge yet of Raghnall's young life. He would have to track from one hidey-hole to the next, making sure the lassie did not fall and injure herself, and keep an ear cocked the whole time for the sounds of pursuit. It would take one more night, he estimated, to get Fiona to her home and family.

And then he would die. He had no illusions about what would happen to him, a stranger in Mac an Rìgh territory, and the seducer of the chief's second eldest daughter. Oh, Fiona would weep and plead for him, but like as not the fierce Mac an Rìgh chief would condemn him without a thought, and without giving him time to explain what had happened, and how he had saved his daughter's life.

His charge from his father had been simple enough. Free the lass and get rid of the ropes that had bound her, and everyone would think that she was indeed a witch, and that an evil spirit had helped her escape. Seumas Peadair *as sine* would prose on about the clan's near escape from doom by witchcraft, and use it as an excuse to remind the MacQuirters about their duty to their chief. People would make up stories about Fiona's appearance, her dazzling beauty and her Evil Eye. Fionnlagh and Murchadh would bask in the glory of having captured the witch, and Elspeth would use her new notoriety as the first one to recognize the witch to force Hugh *Dubh* into marrying her at last.

And Raghnall would slip back into the settlement, his absence unnoticed in all the stramash, and his father would owe him a favor that would come in handy the next time he was in trouble.

But the scheme, so simple, so beautiful, had gone terribly wrong just because he had not buried the ropes in the forest. He'd cast them into the sea, and the wretched tide had brought them back for his clan to find, and realize his treachery. He had gotten rattled, and it was likely that it would cost him his life.

Raghnall brooded as he led the way through the forest to his next bolthole, while Fiona chirped and chattered beside him, skipping when the path permitted, stumbling when the way got difficult, and righting herself each time with a giggle. He hushed her every now and then, half-heartedly, knowing that he was too far away now from his own land to fear capture by the MacQuirters.

She's a talker, he thought, and wondered how her future husband would cope with it. But she was good company, exclaiming with pleasure over the wild beauty they were encountering, murmuring over the pretty patches of wildflowers they came across, and picking them until her arms were full, Raghnall steering her away from the ones that stung.

When they encountered a mountain spring and stopped to drink and rest, she wove the flowers into garlands and draped them over his shoulders and in his hair, ignoring his frown and mutters about how nonsensical she was. "I'm going to sleep a bit," he growled, and stretched out on the grass under a tree. Fiona curled up beside him obediently. He woke to find her hands busy about his person, and he pushed aside his doubts and worries, and made love to her until she screamed with delight.

They reached his final shelter on MacQuirter land by sunset and stopped for the night, feasting on berries they'd picked nearby. Their love-making that night had a tinge of desperation on Raghnall's part. He was going to his death, he knew, but at least he wouldn't die without knowing the pleasures of a woman's body.

They were up at daybreak and pushed on to the edge of the forest. Recognizing the dwellings and neatly fenced gardens of her clan's settlement, Fiona tripped merrily ahead of him, then stopped when she realized he wasn't following.

"Come on!" she commanded. "We're home."

He skulked about the edge of the forest, considering the merits of disappearing into it and taking his chances with the wild beasts and the combined anger of two clans pursuing him. Better to die a brave man than a fugitive hunted down like a timid rabbit, he decided, and stepped forward to take her hand.

They marched forward together into the heart of the Mac an Rìgh settlement, to the stunned silence of all who saw them. Some shrank back, and made the sign against evil, which puzzled Fiona until a wee lass piped up, "We thought you were dead! Are you a spirit?"

Fiona drew herself up proudly and announced, "I've had a grand adventure. And this is Raghnall, the third son of the chief of the MacQuirters, who rescued me from death and who has brought me safely home."

"A MacQuirter!" muttered the crowd fearfully.

Mairead, Fiona's sister, stepped out of the great hall, and stopped in shock. "My dress!" she shouted. "Mother, she's back, and she's ruined my dress!"

The Mac an Rìgh and his wife appeared next, and Fiona was clasped tenderly to the maternal bosom. "My dearest child, we thought you were dead," murmured her mother, then turned to Mairead and snapped, "Hush yer whist, you silly wean, and never mind about the dress. Your sister has returned, and we should all rejoice."

The Mac an Rìgh chief's ice-blue eyes fell next upon Raghnall, and he frowned menacingly. "Who might you be?"

"The greetings of the chief of the MacQuirters to you, *a Mhic an Rìgh*, and here is your daughter, safely home," said Raghnall, and prepared himself for death.

The chief growled, "Where have you been, lass, and what have you been up to? Your mother's been worried sick."

Fiona had been thinking, too, and it had dawned on her that certain things were best left unspoken, like the Rock of Death, her near escape from rape, and Elspeth's shrill cries of "witch." And especially the incidents with her lover in the dark forest the last two nights, and once in the morning and once in the afternoon.

She said, "I went to the MacQuirter chief to sue for peace between our clans," she announced. "He listened with respect, and honored me with a feast, then sent his third eldest son to escort me home. Only we got lost and had to hide from wild animals, so our journey home was full of danger. And hard on my clothes," she added, catching her sister Mairead's evil eye.

It was on the tip of Raghnall's tongue to blurt out indignantly that they hadn't gotten lost, for that was an insult to his woodsman's skills, but he suddenly realized what Fiona had done. If the Mac an Rìgh bought the story, he might be home free.

The Mac an Rìgh studied Raghnall for the longest three minutes of his young life. Cold eyes roamed over him from his fiery red-gold hair down to his worn leather boots. Raghnall's first impulse was to quail, his second was to dart for the safety of the forest, but his third was the one that prevailed. He was the chief's son, he told himself, and his honor demanded courage. He straightened himself up proudly.

At last the tall chief snorted, and beckoned Raghnall close to him. He bent and whispered in the younger man's ear, "Have you had her?"

Raghnall went pale with fright, sure that his moment of doom had arrived. "Aye, sir," he answered bravely.

The Mac an Rìgh said, "You'd best marry her, then." He raised his voice and bellowed, "In recognition of the service done to our clan by the third son of the MacQuirter chief, I bestow upon him the honor of my daughter's hand in marriage." He gave Fiona a fierce sideways look. "Any objections, lass?"

"Oh, no, Father," she twittered. "For I love him for . . . um . . . his bravery."

Her father leaned close and hissed in her ear, "Marriage is for life. If you don't want him, I'll send him back into the forest. Or kill him."

"No!" she shrieked. "I want him!"

The Mac an Rìgh grinned. "So be it, then. The wedding will be held two nights from now. And, Isabel," he said to his wife, "can you no get the child a decent dress to be married in? She looks a fright in those rags. What are you thinking, to let her go about like that?"

The marriage took place, and Fiona triumphantly paraded her new husband around the campfire circle to the envy of the unmarried women, who muttered crossly about the fact that Fiona had disobeyed all the rules of proper behavior and had still ended up with a man, a handsome one at that, and a chief's son.

The Mac an Rìgh was all for sending a marriage announcement straightaway to his opposite number in the MacQuirter camp, reasoning that the other chief would want to know of the respect shown him by the acceptance of his son in marriage. Both Fiona and Raghnall realized that this would give the game away, and probably enrage the MacQuirters so much that they might attack the people who had married the chief's son to a witch.

Raghnall stalled, and circulated stories about how thick the forest was, how difficult the path, and how fierce the wild animals, until there was no one among the Mac an Rìghs brave enough to volunteer to carry such a message. Fortunately, an early winter set in with an enormous snowfall, and talk of making contact with the MacQuirters was set aside until springtime. By then, Raghnall thought, Fiona would certainly have presented him with a child, and the joyful news of the first Mac an Rìgh-MacQuirter heir would go a long ways toward reconciling his own clan to his marriage.

As it turned out, the subterfuge was unnecessary. The Mac an Rìgh maidens, after brooding all winter on the unfair way that Fiona had acquired a husband, decided to take matters into their own hands. Hiding their work carefully from their mothers, they all began making themselves flowing, snug-fitting white dresses, and plotting to invade MacQuirter land as soon the snow melted. This they did, and the stunned MacQuirter border guards were treated to wave after wave of white-clad damsels, blushing and fluttering and demanding to be taken to Ruairidh *Mór* so that they might sue for peace between their clans.

The MacQuirter women were none too pleased by this turn of events, as the most eligible men were being snapped up by the invaders. They retaliated in kind, and soon the forest path grew so congested with palely-clad women flowing back and forth that it began to assume the status of a well-trodden road, with passing places and rest areas stocked with skins filled with water and dried meat.

When Fiona and Raghnall's son, named Alasdair Ruairidh for his two grandfathers, was born in May, it was almost an anticlimax, for by then the two clans had been well and truly united by many marriages. No one could foretell, of course, that young Alasdair would grow up to be chief of the united clans, and rule long and well, assisted by his wise man, his father Raghnall.

And that is the legend of Feckless Fiona, the Peacemaker.

At the end of the story, when the workshop participants were dispersing, a tall, astonishingly handsome man with cinnamon-colored hair came up to Darroch, extending his hand. *"Feasgar math,"* he said. "My name is Angus MacQuirter."

"Is it just!" exclaimed Darroch. "You'll be of Eilean Dubh, then."

"Oui, my papa emigrated from here forty years ago and settled in Québec, and married my *Maman.* So I am half Scottish, half French." He turned to the pretty woman standing by him. "This is my wife, Dorcas, who is all American."

"Are you here looking for relatives?"

"I won't mind if I find some, but we came here so that I could do research. We stumbled on the Folk Festival by accident."

"What sort of research?"

"I'm a writer, and my next book is going to be set on Eilean Dubh."

"How interesting," said Jean, coming up to join them. "What is your book going to be about?"

"It's a romance, a love story about an American woman who comes to this Island and falls in love with the Laird." He grinned. "It's an unbelievable idea, *n'est-ce pas?"*

Darroch gave Jean a sideways glance. "Aye, that's pretty unbelievable."

Jean agreed, "Never happen in a million years."

"Oui, but readers like that sort of thing," said Angus.

"I know I do," said Darroch. "Come along with me and I'll make a couple of phone calls and round you up a dozen or so cousins."

With a smile over his shoulder at Jean, he led the MacQuirters away.

Forty-four

See the smoking bowl before us!
Mark our jovial ragged ring!
Round and round take up the chorus,
And in raptures let us sing.

Robert Burns

*N*ow there was one last event, the Grand Closing Concert on Thursday night, and the Festival would be over. Jean congratulated herself that she'd managed quite well with all her responsibilities to both family and Festival. Before the week began, she'd washed every bit of clothing the four of them owned, so they'd all have plenty of changes. She and Darroch had cleaned the cottage from top to bottom, and she'd made and frozen main dishes for every meal they might eat at home during the week. And she'd expressed and frozen breast milk for the times she might have to leave the bairn with a baby sitter.

The First Daughter filled that role. Sally attached herself like a limpet to her mother, sister and baby brother, ready to step in at any time child care was needed. It had been needed quite a bit during the week, and she'd found herself on occasion with two babies and Rosie to look after, if Ian's Catrìona had been needed away from home. Caring for the children had given her plenty of information on what to expect if she and Ian *Mór* decided to try for an offspring, and she rather thought she could handle the situation when it arose.

The Island was awash with children. In a totally unprecedented development, Màiri had decided to close the Playschool for the week. She'd never done that before, not even during the week of the sit-in. All the women connected with it, including herself, Jean, Barabal, Ian's Catrìona and the rest of the teachers, had responsibilities with the Festival, ranging from pod leader to workshop presenter to catering corps, and they could not be spared from these duties. Nor could the children be left at home alone, so they were organized in a floating battalion under Helen's leadership, and ferried to the High School gymnasium each day, where they were cared for by the students, and to everyone's surprise, Lady Margaret, who pitched in as storyteller and cuddler.

Festival visitors were attracted by the cheerful chatter, the laughter and the occasional wail when a child tripped or missed its mother, and they'd pause by the gymnasium door, and enjoy the sight of children, high school students and an elegant old lady playing games, listening to stories, and settling down for naps. What a pleasant sight, the visitors thought, and wondered if life was always this happy on Eilean Dubh.

On the evening of the Grand Concert, Sally sat in the wings with Ruth and the two Mac an Rìgh children, and prepared to watch her mother and Darroch dazzle the crowd once more.

All the other performers had played, and *Tradisean* took the stage led by Jean, resplendent in her flowing turquoise dress and tartan jacket, hand in hand with Darroch, tall and distinguished in his kilt. Màiri and Jamie followed them, with Màiri taking her place at the piano, and Jamie stepping forward with his fiddle, ready to begin their last set of the amazing week. The spotlights shone brilliantly on the Folk Festival's Fab Four.

They played their most popular tunes, finishing with "Eilean Dubh:"

A maiden fair as the Island sky, beneath the oak tree softly sleeping.
I'll wake her with a tender kiss.
Our hearts will rise, and rise forever.

And as their encore, the tune most associated with *Tradisean*, the poignant "Emigrant's Lament:"

Away, away, o'er the sunset sea, going home to the beloved Island.

Sally watched and sighed, and felt a wave of love for her family, for Eilean Dubh and for her life there wash over her. It was followed by a queer little flutter just below her heart, and she knew, suddenly, in the way that women know, that she was pregnant. No bigger than a peanut inside her, a new little *Eilean Dubhannach* was making its presence known. She smiled, and thought of her mother's joy when she heard the news, the delighted shock that Ian *Mór* would experience when he learned he was to be a father, and the fun she'd have in telling all of them.

Tradisean took their final, triumphant bow, the crowd erupted in cheers, and on cue the rest of the Festival performers filed on stage behind them, each Celtic nation ready to sing their own beloved anthems in their own beloved languages. Darroch had planned this part very carefully, and had worked hard to learn each one so that he could join them in song. Jean didn't have his amazing actor's memory, and had managed only to learn the words of the Welsh anthem, from a tape supplied her by Blodwen the Welsh Wizard, Darroch's accountant.

The Bretons began.

Ni, Breizhiz a galon, karomp hon gwir Vro!
Brudet eo an Arvor dre ar bed tro-do.

Zach Trelawney and the Cornish were next, to the same tune:

Bro goth agan tasow, dha fleghes a'th kar!
Gwlas ker an howlsedhes, pan vro yw dha bar?

Then the Irish, raising their voices in "The Soldiers' Song:"

Sinne Fianna Fáil a tá féi gheall ag Éirinn . . .

The Manx sang:

O Halloo nyn ghooie,
O Chliegeen ny's bwaaie . . .

And then the Welsh, with Jean joining in, thanks to Blodwen:

Mae hen wlad fy nhadau yn annwyl i mi,
Gwlad beirdd a chantorion, enwogion o fri . . .

Jean might not be able to sing all the anthems, but she'd studied the English translations carefully, and knew that each nationality was singing of its love for its homeland, its language and its people, and of their determination to protect all three. Damned fine sentiments, she thought, and resolved anew to help Darroch and Màiri in their struggle to protect their Island and their Gaelic language against all comers.

The Scots were last, and Darroch led the crowd in "Flower of Scotland." It was not a traditional song, having been written by Roy Williamson of the Corries musical group in the 1960s, but it had attained the status of

Scotland's unofficial national anthem. Everyone in the audience joined in and the beautiful song soared to the auditorium ceiling and out the windows to the sky, proclaiming its message of Scotland united against any aggressor.

O Flower of Scotland,
When will we see
Your like again,
That fought and died for,
Your wee bit hill and glen . . .

At the end the audience burst into shouts and applause, and everyone bowed. Lady Margaret came on stage leading Russ by the hand, and he got to take a bow, too as Festival co-organizer.

"I've never been on this side of the footlights before," he said to Jean, over the noise of cheering.

"Do you like it?"

"It's kind of overwhelming, but yeah, I do."

"You deserve it, Russ. You've done a brilliant job with the Festival."

He grinned sheepishly. "Thanks. Just wanted to do my part to help out the Island." He leaned closer, and whispered in her ear over the applause, "We haven't told you, but Ruth and I will be staying here a while longer. Rod and Lucy are happy in Milwaukee. She's started back at the University and they've got Andrew Russell settled in a great nursery school, so they don't want to leave. They asked if we'd mind leaving our arrangement the way it is, and we said sure."

He looked over his shoulder at Ruth, standing with Sally at the edge of the stage, and gave her a private smile. "Ruth likes it on Eilean Dubh."

"What about her daughters?"

"The three oldest are happy with their jobs and their schools in Milwaukee, and they're all living together in Ruth's house, looking after each other, with Rod and Lucy next door to lend a hand. And Jen's going to come to Eilean Dubh for her junior year of high school. It's a study abroad thing."

"How *miorbhuileach!*"

"Yeah, Ruth's happy."

"Are you happy, Russ?"

He gave her a long thoughtful look. "It's pretty weird, me being a dynamic go-getter kind of guy, ending up on this quiet little Island. But you know, the place has not turned out to be so quiet after all." He waved his hand at the crowd, still cheering noisily. "In fact, I'd say it's downright Excitement City, Arizona. I might even have to go back to Milwaukee for a little peace and quiet one day.

"But that's not going to happen for a long time, because, yeah, I am happy here. Give me a kiss, honey." He bent and touched his mouth to hers.

Darroch, on her other side, said, "There you go again, Jean, kissing strange men."

"Oh, Russ is not so strange. Not anymore," she said, smiling.

Russ said, "You know it's all down to you, Jean. You got us into this Eilean Dubh stuff, Sally, Ruth, Rod, Lucy, me, and now Jen. How did it happen?"

She shook her head, lost in all the memories. "All I can think of to say is the line from that Grateful Dead song. Know the one I mean?"

Russ grinned, and eyes locked, they said in unison, "'What a long, strange trip it's been.'"

Forty-five

Sweet's the lav'rock's note, and lang, lilting wildly up the glen;
But aye to me he sings ae sang, "Will ye no come back again?"
Will ye no come back again? Will ye no come back again?
Better lo'ed ye canna be. Will ye no come back again?

Scots folk song

The Festival was over, the visitors had gone home, leaving on the Cal-Mac ferry on Friday to a rousing send-off complete with Island musicians playing "Will Ye No Come Back Again?" and a mass of *Eilean Dubhannaich* waving their good-byes.

Then the Islanders scattered to clean up the remnants of the Festival, and by Sunday, everyone was ready to go to kirk, rest and reflect, as was proper on the Sabbath.

On Monday they picked up the reins of their lives again, and made a *miorbhuileach* discovery: the Island was awash in cash. Shopkeepers, B and B owners, hoteliers, and restaurateurs had all discovered to their joy that the greatest goal of holiday-makers was to spend money.

And eat. Besides their raids on the Co-Op, they'd discovered the little old ladies in black and the other food vendors on the Square. Beathag the Bread had done a brisk business in brioche, bridies and brownies (supplied frozen, baked in advance by Sheilah Morrison from her special recipe). Beathag's opposite number in Airgead had reported similar success with her specialty, lemon tarts.

The visitors had spent freely for goods to take home as remembrances of their holiday. Deirdre's souvenir shop's entire supply of tee shirts with silly sayings on them was sold out. The ladies' clothing shop had been ransacked for quaint, old-fashioned items like aprons and headscarves, which it had in plenty. Even the ironmonger in Airgead had gotten visitors' business; a small army of them had brought their bicycles and soon were happily careening up and down the Island hills, whooping with pleasure. Punctures, damaged chains, uncomfortable seats brought them into the ironmonger's for assistance, and his teenaged daughter, with a smile and a wink, sold all of them the bike stickers she'd persuaded her father to have made by Anna Wallace's printing shop. They read "I've been to Eilean Dubh," with the Festival logo, and they flew out of the shop. "Next year we'll have a tee shirt with that motto," announced the daughter, and her father agreed meekly.

Jean's pet project, the Crafts Fair, had also been a stunning success. The seniors had raked in the money, and the visitors had gone home laden with doilies, wee houses, mugs, stained glass window ornaments, sachets filled with genuine Eilean Dubh lavender, and jars of jams and jellies made by a variety of *Eilean Dubhannaich.* Deirdre had been impressed by the sales, and had offered to stock on a regular basis what the seniors produced. They'd had a meeting at the Residence, and all had agreed to contribute a portion of their earnings for the purchase of their own bus to take them shopping and on excursions.

The Islanders counted their pennies, and gave thanks for the Festivalgoers, whose exuberant generosity meant that the coming winter would not be a hard one. Better than that, for they were rolling in money, drowning in cash, and they could afford improvements to their crofts, their wardrobes and their furnishings, and maybe have the odd pound or two left over for a splurge, like a weekend holiday in Inverness, or even Edinburgh. All the Islanders agreed that life on Eilean Dubh was good, and in case that sounded like gushing, or tempted Fate to retaliation, they added, at least for now.

Minister Donald was very concerned about his congregation's new affluence. They'd been led astray once before by Nick Borth's siren call of big bucks, and luckily that had been shown up for the empty, dangerous promise that it was. Now wealth was a reality, and they were exposed to all the temptations that money could procure for them. On his honeymoon one afternoon, waiting for Helen to dress for an excursion, he'd snapped on the satellite television set, and in twenty minutes of watching he'd been appalled by the vulgarity and violence that the world outside Eilean Dubh offered at the click of a remote.

No one on the Island could afford satellite television or any other temptations of the outside world, until now. Would they be led astray by another devil's song, and succumb to the crass lures of modern life? Foul language, Sabbath-breaking, cruelty? Unprincipled, unrestrained sex? Worried, he began to prepare a sermon.

Then Helen came in to report the results of the Ladies' Guild's hastily got-up appeal for the victims of a weather disaster in Southeast Asia, enthusing over how generous the *Eilean Dubhannaich* had been with their newly-acquired funds.

Donald thought about that for a long time. Then he thought about the delegation that had appeared at his door several days ago, and had presented him with a check for the repair of the Manse's roof, which had been leaking for an age with no hope of money for its repair. All the *Eilean Dubhannaich* knew that the Minister had not profited from the Folk Festival. How could he? He had nothing to sell, nothing to trade for gold. It seemed only right to them that they share their largesse; it was the unwritten motto of their lives, to look after their community. What better way to do it than by taking care of that troublesome roof for the man they admired and respected?

Humbled, Donald scrapped his scolding sermon and prepared one instead on the blessedness of generosity. He delivered it to a kirk full of people happily smoothing the sleeves of their warm new coats, wiggling their toes in their stout new shoes, secure in the knowledge that their bills were paid, their larders well stocked, and they'd a bit tucked away for emergencies. For a fishing and crofting community that existed always on the knife-edge of financial disaster, security was a completely new sensation.

Perhaps his people had their heads screwed on so firmly that not even wealth would turn them. Perhaps he'd been worrying for no reason. He'd keep his fingers crossed, and give them his whole-hearted blessing.

Don't borrow trouble, he thought. Better the devil you know than the one you don't know. Nick Borth had been the devil they didn't know, and penury was the devil they all knew, and life had taught them ways of dealing with both.

Forty-six

To have created the pleasure
of the single malt Scotch is a magnificent achievement.
How odd, then, to keep it almost a secret,
which the Scots have done for decades.

Michael Jackson

There was one more result from the Folk Festival, one that only a few people would know about for some time, and it involved Kenneth Morrison, a large, bear-like, brown-bearded, semi-recluse of a man. He was the one who'd done the grand work of collecting and writing down of Eilean Dubh's remarkable body of folk song. His contribution was widely recognized on the Island, and at Màiri's request, he conducted a workshop on the songs for the Folk Festival.

A kindred spirit attended the workshop. His name was Frank Logan, he came from Speyside in Scotland, and he was as much of a folk music fanatic as Kenneth himself. He fell madly in love with Eilean Dubh's music, and shortly thereafter with the Island itself. He and Kenneth hit it off at once, so much so that two meetings of the workshop were not enough for the pair of them to exchange all their musical questions and anecdotes. So Kenneth invited Frank home for supper before the Wednesday night concert, and they talked until they were hoarse, liking each other more every minute.

After the meal, Kenneth brought out a whisky, a special malt called A Drop of Eilean Dubh.

He distilled it himself, in an ancient, much patched, pot still that had been handed down in his family for generations, from barley that he grew on the rich black soil of his croft. All by himself he malted the barley, dried and fermented the malt, distilled the mash and re-distilled the spirit. This he cut with water from the icy cold burn that flowed through his croft's peat bogs, and put the result to mature into an oaken sherry cask that had washed up on the shores of the Island many years ago.

The whisky was very, very good and very, very illegal, and because it was illegal, it was very, very secret.

Everyone on Eilean Dubh knew about it, of course. No one told Constable MacRath, who knew about it too. No one would tell the excisemen, should they ever show up, which they never did because there'd been no report of illegal distilling on the Island for decades.

Every year at Hogmanay, Kenneth opened a cask that he'd laid down ten years previously, and produced two hundred and twelve bottles, that number because that was all the bottles he owned. He gave two to the Laird as a token of respect and duty, and two bottles appeared mysteriously on Constable MacRath's doorstep on Hogmanay Eve, just in time for toasting in the New Year. Two he gave to Sheilah and Gordon Morrison, Gordon being his cousin, and Sheilah being his best customer for the produce from his vegetable garden and his orchard, and for the trout that frequented his burn.

Six he kept for himself.

The rest he sold at the very reasonable price of £20 a bottle to the *Eilean Dubhannaich* lucky enough to be his customers, a dearly-held right passed down from generation to generation. Every year buyers were reminded to save and return their bottles, and if one was broken, which did not happen often, it was expected to be replaced, and was.

The money Kenneth earned from these sales augmented his meager earnings and was almost as welcome to his pocket as his whisky was to his customers.

No one not of the Island had ever been offered A Drop of Eilean Dubh. Frank sensed the importance of the gesture, and noticed that the bottle was unlabeled. He was instantly aware that it was home distilled, and he expected a coarse, unsophisticated *uisge beatha*. Nevertheless, as a polite guest, he treated the whisky with respect. He held up his glass and admired the color, a deep glowing golden amber. Next he swirled the whisky around, and brought the glass close so that he could inhale the nose.

He froze in shock. Iodine, of course, and heather honey. But there was something more. He swirled the glass again, and inhaled deeply. Smoke, grass, lavender. Something else—flowering currant?

Trembling, he brought the glass to his lips and took a sip.

A wave of flavor engulfed his taste buds, and he could hardly breathe for sheer pleasure. Wordless, he held out his hand for the small water pitcher, and added precisely ten drops to his glass. Then he swirled and tasted again, and tried desperately to sort out the palate of the finest whisky he'd ever drunk. There was oiliness and seaweed and spice, a big full body, and a long orangey finish with a note of something he couldn't identify, and had tasted only in a dream.

Frank Logan was a whisky man and the son of a whisky man and by pure dumb luck he'd stumbled upon a miracle.

"Kenneth, my friend," he said. "We have to talk."

"*Ceart math,* but not now. We'll be late for the concert."

"But the whisky . . . "

"You like it? Oh, that's grand. I distill it myself, you know, but I must ask you to keep that to yourself, for I haven't a license. It's, um, a hobby."

"You distill it yourself?"

"Aye. Come along now, we'll miss the opening act."

"But I want to know more . . . "

"Ach, there'll be time for that. Come over for supper tomorrow."

And Frank had to be content until the next day, when he visited Kenneth again and was given a tour of the tiny home distillery housed in Kenneth's sprawling two-hundred-year-old barn, with its three-foot-thick lime-washed stone walls and dirt floor.

"Kenneth," Frank said, "My father is a whisky man, and I'd like him to share a dram with you. Will you trust me to tell him about it?"

Kenneth scratched his head, and pondered. At last he said, "Aye, that'd be grand. A whisky man can be trusted not to grass to the excisemen."

Frank went home on the ferry, and went straight to his father, who was Francis Charles Edward Logan, the owner of one of Speyside's most distinguished distilleries, Glen Logan, and producer of one of Scotland's most honored whiskies, The Pride of the Glen.

On the Monday after the Folk Festival, Frank, his father Francis, and four men in black suits so identical that the men inside them all looked alike, though they differed in height and girth, arrived via Murdoch the Chopper's helicopter, and climbed into Murdoch the Taxi's waiting minibus. It took them deep into the glen by *Loch nan Iasg* where Kenneth's small croft lay nestled in fields of barley.

Kenneth was taken aback by his visitors; he'd expected Frank and his father, but not the suits. He invited them all in, saying, "I would have borrowed chairs, had I known so many would be coming," as Frank and his father took the rocker and the easy chair, and the suits perched themselves uneasily on the piano bench and the window seats.

"Ach, never mind that," said Francis. "It's the whisky that matters."

"Right," said Kenneth, and poured all of them a dram.

They inhaled, and swirled, and sipped. Francis gave a long sigh of appreciation, and the suits looked first at the miracle in their glasses, and then at each other.

"I'd like fine to see your distillery," said Francis.

"It's not much, but come along, then," and Kenneth led them to the barn. They inspected it with minute care, the suits taking careful notes, and when they were led to the small attached shed that was Kenneth's aging room, they stared in awe at the ten casks inside it. "The whisky in each cask is a year older than the one next to it," said Kenneth.

"So your oldest whisky is ten years old?"

"Aye, for I've only the ten casks that washed ashore from a shipwreck back in my great-great-great-grandfather's time."

"The whisky we were tasting is only ten years old?"

"Ach, no," said Kenneth, embarrassed. "I've run out of last year's ten-year-old, and I'm in the silent season now and won't be bottling this year's ten-year-old until November. What I gave you was a wee bittie from a four-year-old cask that I tapped off as a sample just to see how it's maturing."

Frank, Francis, and the suits stared at him. A four-year-old whisky, and it tasted like heaven itself? What would the oldest taste like? The suits nudged each other, and mumbled words like "micro-climate" and "heathery-character peats" and "oloroso casks." Francis took Kenneth's arm, and like his son before him, said, "We have to talk."

Inside the house, Francis said, "My friend, I want to buy you."

"What?"

"Your knowledge, your barley, your water, even your casks and your barn. Glen Logan distillery is at your feet. Name your price."

"I don't know what to say," said Kenneth, bewildered.

Francis leaned closer, and the suits leaned closer too. "It's been my dream all my life to produce the world's greatest whisky, and you're the laddie who's going to help me do it. Come in with me, and in ten years the world of whisky drinkers will hail you as a god. We'll build a distillery here on Eilean Dubh, and you'll the Chief Distiller. We'll call your whisky—"

"A Drop of Eilean Dubh," said Kenneth firmly. "For that's its name."

"We've a deal, then?"

As Kenneth hesitated, Francis said, "We'll commission all the crofters in this glen to plant barley, for there must be something special in the soil here. Do the locals want jobs? We'll need carpenters and construction workers when we're building, and others we'll train to work in the distillery and in our office. It'll take money, but I'm prepared to spend what is needed to get this whisky to market. What do you say, lad?"

"I'll just talk it over with the Laird," said Kenneth.

At *Taigh a Mhorair*, Darroch and Kenneth conferred for a half an hour. Then Frank and Francis were invited in to join the discussion, and hammer out the details of the deal. The suits milled about outside around the minibus, smoking cigarettes and scuffing their feet in the dirt. Jean felt sorry for them and took them out mugs of tea, and received their mumbled thanks.

A Drop of Eilean Dubh thus became a reality, and construction work on the distillery would begin next spring, with many fine jobs now and to come for the *Eilean Dubhannaich.*

Darroch had no way of predicting the future, and no idea how A Drop would change his own life. Both Frank and Francis were mightily impressed by him, and in ten years when the whisky was debuted, they would tap him to become its spokesperson and its symbol.

Clad in a midnight-blue velvet jacket, a shirt frothing in expensive lace at collar and cuffs, and a beautiful new kilt in his Mac an Rìgh tartan, his hair (now silver-tipped) tied back with a ribbon, Darroch would appear in all Glen Logan's advertising campaigns. His elegant silhouette in miniature would appear on A Drop's labels against a background of his tartan.

Magazine ads would show him lounging in an elegant armchair in an elegant library, holding a glass of whisky and looking at it thoughtfully.

Television campaigns would feature him in the same armchair and library, pouring himself a dram from a bottle of A Drop, swirling the glass, inhaling and at last taking a sip, while his voiceover proclaimed the whisky's slogan, "A Drop of Eilean Dubh. A gentleman's whisky."

Francis had wanted the slogan to be "The Laird's whisky," but Darroch put his foot down about that, so they went with "gentleman" instead.

But that was all in a future that not even Jamie could foresee.

Forty-seven

Oh, Eilean Dubh, where my heart does dwell,
I will sing the song of you forever.

Eilean Dubh folk song

In *Taigh a Mhorair,* the Monday after the Festival, the Mac an Rìghs and Jamie MacDonald gathered for a cup of tea, a wee dram, and a welcome opportunity to rest sore feet and fingers and tired voices, all worn to the nub by four days of picking and singing.

"I haven't seen my wife since the Festival ended," mourned Jamie. "She's been closeted with yon Russ up there in his office counting their money, piling up the stacks of golden coins and cackling like a pair of old misers out of a Dickens novel. I only hope they won't grow so attached to the gelt that they decide to scarper with it. I can see them now, scooping pound notes into filthy old suitcases and sneaking off the Island at the midnight hour, rubbing their hands together in glee."

"They'd need a rowboat if they're leaving in the dead of night," observed Darroch. "There'll be neither ferry nor helicopter."

"Rowing away, singing sea shanties, and when they reach the mainland, off they'll go to some wee town like Kirkcudbright or John o' Groats, and spend the rest of their lives hidden away in a crumbling old housie, surrounded by moldering piles of money which they count now and then, chortling and giggling insanely, and only emerging to creep out to the local for bottles of beer and packages of crisps to gobble while they watch old American shows on the telly."

"That's quite a picture," said Jean, amused.

"Aye, well, the imagination runs rampant when you've not had a cuddle in weeks. Darroch, could I just borrow your wee wifey?"

"Depends on what you want to do with her," said Darroch, mildly alarmed.

"Nothing naughty, never fear. I only want a female presence in the house, bustling around in the kitchen making my favorite meals, brushing her lovely long hair before bedtime, flipping a feather duster around over the furniture . . . "

"I've never seen Màiri with a feather duster," said Jean.

"I'm embroidering the tale a wee bittie. There's a certain sensual appeal about a woman with a feather duster, and this is only imagination, remember?"

"I think you need a cold shower," said Darroch.

"I think you're right," said Jamie, sighing.

At last Màiri and Russ emerged from his office and joined the group at *Taigh a Mhorair*. They'd paid all the bills, dispensed all the money, and they announced, in triumph, they'd made enough to build the Playschool addition. Màiri said, "The pot was sweetened by Cal-Mac. They've donated ten percent of what they made on the charters to our fund, and they're eager to do a repeat next year. You must write their chairman a letter of thanks, Darroch."

"Aye, I know," he grumbled. "You don't have to tell me my duty, *a Mhàiri*. I ken it right enough."

She ploughed on, ignoring him. "And then we'll have to start planning for next year. Deciding what project we want to raise money for, analyzing what worked and what didn't, lining up performers . . . Oh, you'll have to write letters of thanks to all of them for this year, Darroch, and we'll send out the invitations in those letters, so they can put it on their calendars."

Darroch groaned, and Jamie said, "Give over, woman, can you not let it be for a while? Can you not rest on your laurels for a day or two?"

"It's best to plan these things well in advance. We'd scarcely had enough time to plan for this year, with only six months to put everything in place," she said stubbornly.

"That's my girl," said Russ fondly. "Got a great head for business."

"She's *my* girl," said Jamie, giving Russ a "hands-off" look, "and I'll be requiring her services for a time before turning her over to you and your wicked plots again."

"Oh, sure," said Russ, abashed. "Didn't mean to poach on your territory, *a charaid*."

"My goodness," exclaimed Jean. "Miracles never cease. We've got Russ speaking the Gaelic."

"Just picked up a word or two here and there," he mumbled. "Seemed appropriate."

"Damned right it's appropriate. Good man, Russ," Darroch said. He got up and fetched the whisky and a supply of glasses, and poured everyone a dram. "I'd like to propose a toast." He lifted a glass. "To the Celtic Folk Festival, and to all those who sailed in her, and especially to the crew that's seated in friendship around this table."

Everyone raised their glasses and drank the toast.

"I'd like to propose a toast, too," said Russ. He stood, and looked at them all: his dear friends Darroch and Jean, with Rosie on her father's lap and Gailleann in his mother's arms, Jamie and Màiri MacDonald, and his own wife, Ruth. "I didn't know what to expect when I had to come here because of my heart attack. I thought I'd be bored, maybe lonely. I never expected to find the kind of friendship you all have given me so wholeheartedly, and I certainly never expected the challenges we've all met, and handled so well. This is a very special place, and the *Eilean Dubhannaich* are very special people, and the love we share for our Island"—he said the phrase boldly, now—"is the kind of glue that the world needs to hold itself together."

He took a deep breath. "I've been listening to all the slogans the Celtic folks that came here have for their countries. *Alba gu bràth*—Scotland forever—*Cymru am byth*—Wales forever, and several others that I can't even begin to pronounce. And I'd like to propose a new slogan, and it's my toast: Eilean Dubh forever."

He took a deep breath, and ventured the unfamiliar Gaelic: "*Eilean Dubh gu bràth!*"

Touched, they all looked at him, some with tears in their eyes, and raised their glasses again.

In unison they said, "*Eilean Dubh gu bràth!*"

Eilean Dubh forever!

Epilogue

Adieu, O daisy of delight;
Adieu, most pleasant and perfite;
Adieu, and have gude nicht:
Adieu, thou lustiest on live;
Adieu, sweet thing superlative;
Adieu, my lamp of licht!

Alexander Montgomerie

*J*amie had not been near the archaeological dig for some time, not since he'd frightened Nick Borth away from Eilean Dubh. Had he had his druthers, as Jean Mac an Rìgh would say, he would never have ventured near it again. But the site lay half way between Ros Mór and Airgead, and he could not go on forever concocting excuses as to why he never went to the northern town. Besides, the Airgead ironmonger was the only one on the Island, and he needed nails and lumber to repair the lambing pen before the weather made that task impossible, leaving his ewes with no place to drop their lambs but the snowy field.

So today he'd taken his courage in both hands, and headed for Airgead in his old rattletrap truck, knowing that he'd have to drive past the dig. But the archaeological crew would be there to drive off any boggles or willies that had survived the dig so far, and he thought he could risk it.

He tried very hard to drive on by the site, even averting his gaze to the ocean on the other side, nearly running off the road in the process. But something made him stop in the scenic outlook, and park the truck. Something else made him get out of the truck, cross the road, and approach the fence surrounding the dig. Zach Trelawney had torn down Nick Borth's high wooden fence, and replaced it with chain link, knowing that the Islanders, with their unrivaled curiosity, would want to see what was going on. He was perfectly happy for them to see, but he had no intention of letting them approach his precious dig too closely. They had stopped frequently to stare, at first, until the novelty of gazing on a barren mound of dirt marked off by a string and stick grid had worn off, and they'd gone about their business as usual, grumbling, "Not much to it."

Jamie went to the fence, leaned his elbows on the top rail, and stared at the place that had frightened him silly, twice. It was deserted. It was a student worker's twenty-first birthday, and Zach and her mates had taken her into Ros Mór to MacShennach's for a celebratory pizza, which had stretched into a hilarious event three beers long. When the party had started to get rowdy, Zach gave them the rest of the afternoon off; after all, they'd been working hard the last several weeks. Besides, he didn't want his precious dig manhandled by drunken university students. And as a bonus, he might be able to corner wife Anna in her newspaper office, and lure her upstairs for an afternoon cuddle.

All alone, Jamie leaned against the fence and stared at the wildflower patch. Some archaeological process was about to happen there, he thought; it had been divided into a stringed grid like the rest of the site. Perhaps they were going to start excavating.

The thought gave him only a momentary shiver, he was happy to discover. He was getting no weird vibrations, no psychic input, no eerie music. Perhaps whatever had been there had left with the advent of the archaeological team.

Or perhaps not. The air over the wildflower patch began suddenly to shimmer and undulate, as though the ground below was rippled by an earthquake. Jamie clutched the top rail of the fence, and cursed the need for nails that had brought him once again face to face with his nemesis.

The misty wisps began to arise once more from the wildflowers, and once more they formed into a circle. In its center rose the familiar tall figure. It put the flute to its lips, and the tune that had haunted Jamie's dreams began again. The wisps formed into a procession and began to trudge mournfully around the circle's boundary. No dancing this time, just a slow, ceremonial march, transparent heads bowed, rent garments trailing behind them like smoke.

Oddly, the sight and sound inspired no terror in Jamie, as it had before. Instead he found himself in the grip of sadness so intense that he sagged against the fence and would have collapsed to the ground, had he not been clinging with both clenched hands to the top rail.

The music flooded him with pain, each keening note of the flute like the weeping of a tormented soul. Mourning eight thousand years old surrounded him, made him part of the circle as surely as if he'd been standing in its center, engulfed him in the burial rites of a people long gone and far beyond earthly woes.

Tears rolled down his cheeks, and his chest was clenched with sobs that never reached his throat. Motionless, soundless, he wept with the misty wisps.

The tall figure stopped playing. It took the flute from its mouth and bowed, put the flute on the ground in the center of the circle, and sank to its knees. The misty wisps sank to their knees. The scene began to dissolve slowly, until nothing was left but the memory of the haunted tune.

Jamie stood for a long while clutching the fence and staring at the wildflowers waving in the breeze, while the sadness drained out of him. At last, empty of emotion, he stepped back from the fence and bowed respectfully to the wildflower patch. Then he crossed the road to his truck and drove home, nails forgotten, need for a whisky intense.

Several weeks later Zach Trelawney announced with trembling voice the startling significant, highly important discovery of a body, shriveled and leathery-brown, that had lain eight thousand years in the bog beneath the wildflower patch. In the body's crossed arms lay a wooden flute, all organic matter miraculously preserved by the peaty waters of the bog.

Zach had discovered the body himself, guided to the exact place by some faint whisper in his ear one morning before waking. He'd repressed the memory of that whisper, denied its existence, assuring himself that it was science and his archaeological training that had led to the discovery.

The body was female, and they were calling her "Eilean Dubh Woman."

Jamie MacDonald was not in the least surprised by the discovery. What needed to be found, had been found, and all would be well beneath the wildflower patch.

The world was full of stories, and each had to be told in its own time and its own place.

Acknowledgements

*T*hanks to my family, Michael, Anita and Aaran, John and Carla, for love, support, and book-selling, and especially to my dear husband Mike, who is always there with a meal, a martini, a suggestion, and a great sense of humor. You've made it all happen, Mikie!

The Devil and the Dark Island is dedicated to Sherry Wohlers Ladig with good reason. A fine composer and musician, she's been there on the Dark Island with me since her first reading of the manuscript of *Westering Home*. Sometimes she's been ahead of me, as was the case with *The Devil*, when she composed "chunes" for scenes while they were still just ideas in my head!

I am delighted to welcome to the family of Eilean Dubh contributors our friend Don Ladig. Don is a musician, garden designer and artist, husband to the esteemed Sherry, and a really Fun Scot. Don's pen-and-ink drawings decorate the beginning page of each fairy tale.

The *Eilean Dubhannaich* would never have gotten this far without Judith Palmateer of Beaver's Pond Press, and her never-failing encouragement and help. Thank you, Judith.

Thanks to Jaana Bykonich of Mori Studio for designing this book with such instinctive understanding of what I wanted. And thanks to The Boss, Milt Adams of BPP, for assembling such a wonderful team!

Thanks to Catherine Friend, who possesses all the traits of a good editor: perspicacity, patience, and the willingness to get swept into the story.

Thanks to Carla and John for another distinctive book cover.

Thanks to Lara Friedman-Shedlov, a wonderful Scottish country dance teacher, for "The De'il's Awa' wi' the Islander." Composer Sherry dedicates the music for this dance to Lara for "all her tireless and talented work in Scottish dancing."

And thanks to another grand SCD teacher Bonny McIntyre, for her help with "Donald and Helen and Rosie's Wedding," which was devised at Joy Gullickson's graduation party June 11, 2005. Congratulations, Joy!

Mòran taing to folksinger Donnie MacDonald from the Isle of Lewis for vetting the Gaelic in this book. Any mistakes are entirely my own.

Thanks to Gibson Batch, the poet of the Twin Cities Branch/RSCDS, for allowing me to quote from his book *Eternal Man: a Journey Through the Minds of Men.*

Thanks to Paul Fackler and Amy Shaw for their comments on Cape Breton music, and to Mark Plenke for the information on headlines, and to Veronica Windsor-Gifford for her help with Irish dances.

To the memory of Twm Siôn, the world's best kitty, and to Teddycat and MacDougall, who are following in his pawprints. Please support your local feline rescue organizations!

scottishislandnovels.com

Notes on Scottish References in the text

Notes on Scottish references in the text:

"Flower of Scotland" is Scotland's unofficial national anthem, heard wherever Scots gather. It was written in the 1960s by Roy Williamson of The Corries musical group.

The Great Gray Man is a being similar to the Yeti and Bigfoot, a hugely tall figure covered with hair that pursues travelers in the passes of Ben MacDhui in Aberdeenshire. Its Gaelic name is *Am Fear Liath Mór*, and this story has been dramatized in John Drewry's wonderful Scottish country dance, "Ferla Mór."

"I Belong to Glasgow" was written in the 1920s by the music hall entertainer, Will Fyfe (1885-1947). "The Northern Lights of Aberdeen" is a traditional song that refers to the aurora borealis frequently seen in northern Scotland. Aberdeen is known as the "Granite City" because so many of its buildings are built of that material. "Ye Canna Shove Yer Granny Off a Bus" was written by beloved Scottish entertainer Andy Stewart (1933-1994).

The Royal Scottish Country Dance Society is headquartered in Edinburgh, and has 165 branches all over the world. If you learn to dance with one branch, you can dance with any branch anywhere in the world. The languages may be different, but the steps, formations and dances are the same, and it's great, intelligent fun. Check rscds.org for the branch nearest you. If Russ can learn to dance, so can you!

Regarding the music in the text of *Westering Home, The White Rose of Scotland,* and *The Devil and the Dark Island:* this music is meant to be played. If you encounter any difficulties in reading the notation, e-mail me at:

scottishisland@visi.com

Gaelic–English Glossary

A Bhobain, a Dhadaidh: oh Daddy.

A Dhia!: oh God! *A Dhia beannaich mi!* goodness gracious me!

A Mhic an Rìgh: respectful form of address to the Laird.

as sine: the elder; *as òige:* the younger.

bàta: boat.

B. P.: In archaeology, Before the Present, with the present being defined as 1950.

cailleach: witch, crone.

ceart math: okay.

cèilidh: a social evening of music, dance and storytelling.

a charaid, mo charaid: oh friend, my friend. Plural: *mo chàiradean.*

ciamar a tha: how are you?

Co-Op nan Figheadairean: the Knitters' Co-operative.

dè nì mi dhuit?: what can I do for you?

diabhol: devil.

Eilean Dubh gu bràth: Eilean Dubh forever.

Eilean Dubhannach: inhabitant of Eilean Dubh. Plural: *Eilean Dubhannaich.* Feminine: *bana-Eilean Dhuibh.*

fàilte gu Eilean Dubh: Welcome to Eilean Dubh.

fear sona: easy-going one.

feasgar math: good evening. *Oidhche mhath:* good night.

gabh mo leisguil: excuse me.

is mise Anna: my name is Anna.

madainn mhath: good morning.

miorbhuileach: marvelous.

misneach: courage.

mo leadaidh: my lady.

mór: big.

samhradh air leth teth: very hot summer, a scorcher.

Sasannachan: English people.

'se gille a th'ann: it's a boy.

seanachaidhean: storytellers.

seiseanan: music jam sessions.

selkies: seals that can assume human form when they shed their skins. If a selkie's skin is hidden from it, it cannot return to the sea.

Sìne: Jean. Pronounced "sheenuh." When aspirated (an h is added after the s) it becomes *Shìne;* pronounced "heenuh."

slàinte mhath: good health.

smoor the fire: to cover it with peats keep it alive all night, a tradition associated with Brighid, the Celtic goddess who is the keeper of the home's hearth.

stramash: disorderly commotion (Scots).

tapadh leat, tapadh leibh: thank you. Second phrase is plural, formal or respectful.

thà gu dearbh: yes indeed.

uisge beatha: whisky.

Terms of Endearment

a ghaoil: dear.

m'aingeal: my angel.

mo chridhe: my heart.

m'eudail: my darling.

mo fhlùr: my flower.

mo ghràdh: my love.

mo luaidh: my loved one, my dear.

Places

a' chreag: a cliff.

àite laighe: helicopter pad (literally, a resting place).

Beanntan MhicChriathar: the MacChriathar Hills.

Beinn Mhic an Rìgh: Mac an Rìgh's Mountain.

Caisteal Mhic an Rìgh: Mac an Rìgh's Castle.

Cladh a' Chnuic: Cemetery Hill.

Creag a' Bhàis: Rock of Death.

an Eaglais Easbuigeach: the Episcopal Church.

an Eaglais Chaitliceach: the Catholic Church.

an Eaglais Shaor: the Free Kirk.

Gàradh Anna: Anna's garden.

Loch nan Iasg: Lake of Fishes.

Na Mara: the sea.

Rudha na h Airgid: Airgead Point.

Stàitean Aonaichte: United States.

Taigh a Mhorair: the Laird's house.

Taigh Rois: the Rosses' house.

A note on the Gaelic: in certain circumstances some initial consonants aspirate, that is, are followed by an 'h'. One instance is after the word *a*, the usual form of address which precedes names and titles, and means 'oh.' For example: A *Dharroch*—oh, Darroch.

I hope you enjoyed reading The Devil and the Dark Island. *If you did, please tell your friends and your local librarian about my Scottish Island Novels, which are listed below. And send me your comments via my web site. I love to hear from readers.*
thanks,
    Audrey McClellan
    www.scottishislandnovels.com

The Scottish / American Series

Westering Home (2003)

Jean Abbott leaves her unfaithful husband in Milwaukee and heads for tiny Scottish island, Eilean Dubh, where she finds music, laughter, and love with actor/reluctant laird, Darroch Mac an Rìgh.

The White Rose of Scotland (2004)

Will Jean ever agree to marry Darroch? She might, now that she has exciting news to share with him. Darroch, Jean, and friends Bonnie Prince Jamie MacDonald and feisty wife Màiri become folk music stars, while the younger generation of Islanders tries to sort out sex and love.

The Devil and the Dark Island (2006)

When a smooth-talking money man arrives on Eilean Dubh planning to develop its unspoiled coastline, can the Islanders resist the lure of big bucks tourism? What is mysterious Cornishman Zachariah Trelawney searching for, and why is wildflower preservation nut/newspaper editor Anna Wallace helping him?

The Canadian / American Series

Magic Carpet Ride (2005)

Cape Breton Island in spring is beautiful, and so is *Québecois* writer Angus MacLachlan MacQuirter. And he's funny and sweet—both Scottish and French, the answer to a maiden's prayer. But Dorcas Carrothers has had two previous lovers, Poor Old George and Horrible Harry, and they've left her love-wary and guy-shy. Can Angus break down her resistance? He certainly is going to have a lot of fun trying. A funny, sexy romp set in Cape Breton Island, Nova Scotia, and in Minneapolis, Minnesota.

Down by the Salley Gardens (in progress)

Cranky poet Edward Jones from *Magic Carpet Ride* meets plain, unlovable Wylie Kennerly, who's won ninety-two million dollars in the lottery. She's not telling anybody about her win, but someone finds out, with dangerous results. Angus, Dorcas, Scotty, Judith and the other Mad Scots show up to make life lively.

The Woman Who Loved Newfoundland (in progress)

Cleo English lost her husband to leukemia two years ago and still hasn't gotten over it, so she comes to her childhood fantasy island, New-Fun-Land, to recover. Gruff but charming (when he wants to be) B and B owner Max Avalon tries to help her, but has his own problems with ornery staff and demanding guests.

The Scottish Island Novels are published by Beaver's Pond Press of Edina, Minnesota.

www.beaverspondpress.com

To order, visit www.BookHouseFulfillment.com or call 1-800-901-3480.